TRACKS OF THE PURPLE CAMEL

TRACKS
— OF THE —
PURPLE
CAMEL

Peter G Williams

Magnum Press

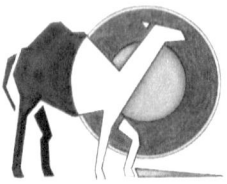

This edition published in Australia in 2018 by Magnum Press, PO Box 1477, West
Leederville, Western Australia 6901
Facebook: *Friends of Billy Peters* Peter G Williams
Order this book from Amazon.com

Tracks of the Purple Camel
ISBN-13: 978-0-9871485-1-3

Fiction

Managing Editor: Christine Nagel, Christine Nagel Literary Services
Original cover artwork: Steve Clarke (RIP 2017)
Cover design: Leon Mackie
Prior works: Book one of the Bill Peters series: *Tracks to Exile*

Dedicated with love to my parents
Mabel Grace and Don Williams
(RIP)

1

TAINTED LOVE

The star-splashed beauty of the darkening Sydney sky belied the events unfolding on the grassed expanse of the Concord sporting oval below. From gates-open at five o' clock the stadium had filled with a mass of vivacious concertgoers and the annual forty-eight-hour Mega Bash buzzed into homogeneous existence. It was just on six-thirty, and as a popular Sydney pub band fired up on the main stage with booming 'One! two! two!' and solo guitar riffs, Dan Dever and Annie Jackson crept into their two-man tent.

They had zipped their sleeping bags together and, with rising excitement and anticipation, slipped now into the satiny cool of the lining. Their friends called cheeky farewells as Dan and Annie were left alone in the small wagon-circle of territory in the designated tent land.

The close-knit peer group of Mascot teenagers had claimed the spot earlier and marked it off with a barrier of tents, collapsible chairs and eskies full of booze and food. Annie and Dan had drawn the first guard duty to protect the group's possessions and that precious territory.

Annie Jackson was nineteen years old, a native of Mascot in Sydney, New South Wales—the airport suburb. She was an artistic girl and had left the frustrating drudge of compulsory education as soon as she was sixteen. She had found work in the local supermarket, and social succour in like-minded youth who explored their self-expression in parties and piercings. Annie was 'a good kid,' her tearful father would later tell the world's media, standing against the backdrop of the family's modest three-bed, one-bath fibro cottage in the old Sydney suburb. Annie's matronly little mum, red eyed and devastated, clinging to her husband's portly frame, desperately unbelieving of the evil that had visited their contented existence.

Dan Dever was Annie's boyfriend; had been since they fell into that acne-patterned blush of puppy love at fourteen at Mascot High. With the blessing of both families the two kids had grown their relationship into 'a lovely couple' destined for marriage, for kids, a mortgage down the track; a mirroring of their working-class parents' predictable path through suburban life. Dan had one year left to go of his automotive mechanical apprenticeship. He had done well, particularly in the practical work experience. Not so good in the bookwork at the tech college, but his natural affinity to grease and for tools, and his ability to deconstruct and reconstruct anything that stood still had ensured his success. Dan was looking forward to a long career in the trade.

Both Annie and Dan had dabbled with the illicit chemical escapism on offer to their demographic in the tiki-tack Sydney suburbs. They indulged in the rush of speed, or, when they could afford as a special treat, in the eccies, the love drug, their favourite.

Now with the familiarity of their five years together, almost like an old married couple, the two youngsters began the dance of physical love with the well-practised prompts of touch and kiss that each knew from experience would arouse the other. Buttons unbuttoned, and zips unzipped. A twirl of tongue against tongue, a caress down sensitive back and a light squeeze and parting of buttock. A soft-suck of a tender nipple as fingers lightly teased the fairy floss of pubic hair along the labial lip, and Annie's soft palm encircling tumescence to rigid hardness. And then with gentle ceremony the two soul mates slipped into each other's mouth the purple ecstasy tablets. The pills slowly dissolved and pulsed into their stomachs and seeped into their bloodstreams. Dan, with a sigh at the never-ending fascination of the sensation, placed his hardness into her yielding softness and entered his life's love. Now, with deliberate control, both stilled the instinct to push and pull. They waited locked together for the drug's effect to accentuate, to exaggerate, to intensify the act.

Within ten minutes the sleeping bag began to surge, to jump, to cruelly mislead. Annie and Dan convulsed not with the sensual-sexual pump of life but with the fatal seizures of an excruciating death. And as they died plugged together, terrified eye to mortified eye trapped in the shit-soiled bag, the touch of the other became not that welcome confirmation of a mortal love, but the most intense agonising aggravation that either could imagine. First the smaller Annie, and then Dan, died.

2

ONLY WOMEN BLEED

Three months before the two soul mates perished in Sydney, Australia, Bob Marley's guttural reggae soared incongruously through the pristine sterility of a laboratory in Amsterdam, Holland. Nodding in dreadlocked accentuated rhythm, Adolphinious Schmidt, Rastafarian lab technician of West Indian origin and now Dutch residency, hauled back on his limp stogie of loose leafed New Guinea gold cannabis heads. Vini, as his Dutch friends called him, sighed deeply as the herb's seeds popped and crackled. He gasped and held the smoke deep in his stained and long-abused lungs, and the THC passed into his living lung tissue, and then by blood to brain and nerve, and he finally began to relax.

'Fuck mon!' Vini breathed out loud to no one and slumped back into the cushioned black vinyl of the chair. The heavy white smoke he exhaled clouded in an unlikely halo above his head before dissipating into the exhaust vent of the air conditioning system of the illicit underground lab.

Vini had arrived as usual at midnight to take over from Amir, the late shift caretaker, previously of Ankara, Turkey. Amir was now also a citizen of Holland along with a cultural polyglot of the developing world's pleasure seekers, cast-offs, leftovers, refugees or simply travellers and adventurers who called Amsterdam home.

Vini called home a small third floor attic apartment on the Rue Van Goosen, on the south bank of the deep black-water canal, a lazy twenty-minute cycle from the lab.

The lab was clandestine. Its product was the cult drug ecstasy, known by police forces and chemists as MDMA. The tiny lab was hidden in a long-forgotten cellar and converted WW2 bomb shelter under the concrete floor of a deserted old wooden warehouse. The warehouse hulked musky dark in the old port precinct and its isolation allowed the production of the drug 24/7.

Vini's was a watching brief only. A caretaker. The production was totally sterilised and automated. All Vini had to do was react to any of the pre-set alarms from the spotless mechanics of the tiny conveyors by turning the plant off and waiting till morning. The whole operation was contained behind a glass barrier. The pharmaceutical tablet pressing and packaging plant had, in an earlier life, mixed, shaped, pressed, dried and finally packaged legal analgesic products that had calmed the nerves and soothed the sores of society's hurt or ill. The process was failsafe, foolproof, Vini-proof. The plant whirred away all night until the powdered product in the stainless-steel vats at the start of the line was virtually exhausted. The dimple-packed finished tablets were spilt by conveyor at the other end of the process into a locked glass chute that dropped the tablets through a wall, the other side of which Vini had never been and had no desire to see. Vini was not told by Amir and still did not know who owned or operated the plant. He had been warned by his Turkish friend of the price of 'fuckeen up' and understood that this was deadly serious business. Amir paid him well; cash in fresh Euros, a reward far beyond his caretaker role.

Vini should have been happy with his life; had been happy, was happy, but for the 'fucken skinheads, mon!' Three nights earlier he had been cycling happily to work on his squeaky old bike, weaving along the access road, down into the dark and always forbidding wharf precinct. They had been parked up, hitting up with speed in an old panel van. Four white supremacists sharing one dirty needle, each dressed in tribal uniform of shaved head, black T-shirt with braces, blue jeans with cuffs turned up, high-laced black paratrooper boots. Their pale white skins were marked with crude racist and swastika tattoos.

This feral fringe group had an outlook on life as far removed from the relaxed Rastafarian, who now cycled past in front of them in the darkness of the cold night, as could be imagined. To the skinheads, Vini was a vision of a despised sub-being, black skinned and a Rasta! To Vini the sight of the darkened van suddenly spilling the shouting skinheads into his path was his ultimate nightmare.

That first night they roughed him up. Mugged him. Ripped his tea-cosy from his head spilling out the metre-long dreadies by which they swung him around and around in a game of sadistic maypole, and stole his stash and his cash. They found his identification cards and laughed out loud that this cowering, begging Rasta was an Adolf by name but not by nature. Vini played along. He gave them all he had and they appeared happy with the haul of the finest blended cannabis available in the drug cafes of the city. They also found and took his folded Euros and then finally let Vini cycle on with a slap and a kick or two to hasten him along. The trouble was they were back the next night and again this night, and played out the same scenario, stealing his dope and warning him that he must bring more each night or they would 'Fucken kill you, Adolf Rasta man'.

Now, safe in the lab as the drug kicked in, Vini sighed again and wondered what he could do. If he told Amir it could be the end of the job. He couldn't afford to take that chance. There was no other way to get to the warehouse except along the dark road that skirted the narrow isthmus down into the wharf area. The skinheads knew that. Worse, they had his ID cards and knew where he lived. The deal was, not quite by the mutual agreement of both parties, that each night that they might bother to be there he must pay a toll to pass, to breathe, to be.

Gunther, the alpha male of the skinhead gang, had explained the rules to Vini this night. The toll was to be a deal bag of cannabis and twenty Euros. If he failed to pay the toll, if he didn't come, or if he reported the matter, the gang would come and visit him at his home.

Vini was terrified. Along with the increasing drug-induced psychosis that his extended daily use of the herb had caused over the years, he also had a horror of physical pain. As he closed his eyes and leaned back into the seat his befuddled mind began an unusual task of analysing his situation, and the process of determining a course of action to extricate himself from his dilemma. And as he sat and listened to the rhythmical clicking and purring of the ecstasy plant an idea began to evolve in his brain that would forever change his life.

The only answer to ridding himself of the unwanted attentions of the skinhead gang was to rid the world of the skinhead gang. This was a decision not within the strictures or preachings of his religion, but he was sure that he could find a justification in those teachings if he searched.

That night he nervously unscrewed the glass plating of the exit chute where it abutted the wall at the end of the conveyor just before the shrink-wrapped blister packs spilt out of sight. He took one packet only of the Es, ten tablets, each of three hundred milligrams, of which roughly two hundred milligrams were MDMA; the other one hundred milligrams was pharmaceutical filler, an inert clinical chalk. Each tablet was hexagonal, purple-tinged and Vini noted that each was stamped with the silhouette of a single-humped camel. Over his employment he had seen that the stamped impression on the pills changed from time to time to suit whatever customer or trend requirements there were at the points of sale. Such points he suspected were in the nightclubs of the western world, markets as far flung as the UK, the USA, Asia, South Africa, and maybe even Australia.

Vini clumsily refitted the screws to fix the glass plating, and quickly hid the pack of tablets deep in the waxed follicle jungle of his dreadlocks. He slept little that day. At eleven-thirty that night he met again his nemeses at the dark roadblock. When Gunther held out his hand to Vini, who had obligingly pushed his cycle up to the passenger window of the van, Vini handed him the pack with a 'Check dis out, mon,' in his deep lilt.

'Vat de fucks is dis, asshole?' Gunther enquired pleasantly, but was then excited when his victim explained that he was willing to pay the toll each night in this new currency, 'if dat's okay, mon?'

So it was agreed, Vini would supply the drug. The skinheads were happy but warned that the quantity of the toll would rise each week with the same promises of pain and suffering if the non-negotiable toll was not paid. Vini this night avoided the physical discomfort of slap and kick. His tormentors were happy with him, it appeared. Vini supplied the skinheads with ecstasy for one week before hatching his big finale.

The old warehouse had rats and lots of them. Big, aggressive, fearless needle-toothed, pink-snouted *ratus ratus* that had roamed through stinking, busy generations the wharf areas and the vessels that traded at the port. Through those filthy centuries, with interbreeding and crossbreeding, the current vermin of the wharf precinct were hardy and fearsome survivors.

'It ees de caretaker's job,' Amir had told him those many months past at his induction, 'to spread de rat poiseen over de floor from time to time.'

And, dressed in a WW2 gas mask, full-length clinical gown and heavy orange rubber-gloved protection, Amir had shown Vini how to spread strychnine in spots along the concrete floor near the ancient warehouse walls. Amir had soberly and carefully insisted that Vini take extreme OHS precautions when handling the strychnine.

Now, Vini brought the tin of poison from the steel locker on the ground floor dressed in his PPE. Looking like a huge black octopus, he carefully prised open the lid and scooped several spoonfuls of the crystalline compound into a plastic bag. The alien apparition then shuffled down the dark stairwell and into the lab, the plastic bag held carefully out in front and holding enough strychnine to poison a small town.

It was near his shift's finish and Vini had already opened the glass covers at each end of the plant, at the vat, and at the wall. He now lifted the stainless steel hinged lid of the vat and saw a small pyramid of E powder left, about two kilos. Into that he carefully poured the rat poison and watched as the mixing process in the vat folded and combined the clear strychnine crystals into the purple mixture. Vini nervously followed that entire batch through the automated plant, watching as the deadly mix was dried and pressed and packaged into the camel-stamped purple tablets. Finally, he took two of the packets from the conveyor; twenty tablets. Despite his usual fog of cannabis-affected thought he carefully secured the glass plating of the processing plant back into place. Vini hid the booty of the two blister packs in a small leather pouch and secreted that pouch again into the waxy depths of his dreadlocks, finally covering his head with the Rasta hat.

Meanwhile, from that tainted two-kilogram mix a further five thousand or so of the deadly camel tabs clinically flipped in their ten-piece blister packs off the conveyor into the hidden room through the lab wall. What Vini didn't consider or foresee was that the following morning the entire night's production of some one hundred thousand tabs, clean and poisoned alike, would be packed by Amir into two pale yellow pigskin briefcases. The entire night's production of the ninety-nine thousand, nine hundred and eighty tablets were then uplifted at a desolate rendezvous on the city outskirts. A covert transaction from the manufacturer's representative to the purchaser's representative.

Later that night, Ali Khan, a twenty-eight-year-old Pakistani merchant seaman, walked the two suitcases unchallenged up the steel grated gangway onto the Panamanian flagged *MV Bogota*. There he was met by his captain and relieved of his contraband. Khan's ship, due to sail at midnight, was an eighty-thousand-tonne timber trader bound from Amsterdam to Jakarta. From Jakarta the drugs would be dispersed to the markets of the region.

Death was on its way to the nightclubs of the world.

3

SAVE THE LAST DANCE

Vini slept very well that day after his weary cycle home and dragging himself up the old wooden spiral staircase into his apartment. Before he clambered into the dank bedding he made sure the eccies were safe in his small leather pouch and tucked them under the stained mattress of his bed.

That night, under a clear black sky, Vini met his problem again at the dark rendezvous. Almost cheerily, he presented Gunther with the two blister packs and the skinhead greedily took them and growled a 'Fuck off, Adolf' in gracious thanks. An hour later the gang of four was clumping heavy-booted down a dark stairway into the heavy rock cacophony of their local music grotto. The trade was brisk and seventeen of the tablets were sold within minutes. The buyers were keen. The previous night the uncontaminated pills had been sampled and enjoyed by the frightening looking skins and white powdered Goths who head-banged to the primitive beats in bar.

Gunther this night chose speed over ecstasy and swapped his tab for a foil of that white powder. He took his hit into the stinking toilets to heat it with water in a blackened teaspoon and then inject into his abused veins. Oblivious to the piss stench of the cubicle as the high potency amphetamine smashed his nervous system, Gunther crouched, smiling twitchily, his head resting on a scummy toilet seat. He missed the early action out on the grotto dance floor.

Twenty assorted skinheads and Goths sloshed the camel-stamped tabs into their stomachs almost simultaneously.

Strychnine acts as quickly in humans as it does in rats, usually within ten minutes. Vini's little concoctions averaged one hundred and fifty milligrams of strychnine per tab, usually enough to only sicken and distress a healthy human adult. But this strychnine was entirely different from the shop-bought variety. The same flawed genius chemist who had cooked the MDMA for his criminal masters had toyed with the basic organic chemical recipe of the strychnine in moments of boredom over lonely nights at the lab. With a morbid experiment in his casual destruction of the warehouse rat pack, he had synthesised that tin of rat poison into ten times its usual purity—this was a deadly mix.

A cruel irony of a strychnine death is that noise and touch exacerbates the convulsions. Although not entirely unusual at this time of night in this club, it was generally recalled afterward by some of the surviving patrons under sober and sobering police questioning, that twenty persons fell to the floor in apparent agony within minutes of each other. Each afflicted person was noted to have frothed bubbling white messes of saliva emitted from the mouth and nose. Most had gyrated crablike across the dance floor in painful, intense muscular convulsion. And within fifteen minutes of the macabre mass dance of death on the filthy concrete floor, and just before the arrival of the first urgently called ambulance, each died.

The problem for Vini was that Gunther had not died. But worse, each of the persons that Gunther knew that he had provided a camel tab to had died. Although he was not the sharpest knife in the drawer, as he knelt beside his writhing companions on the grotto floor and cried in speed-sharpened sympathy for their agony, Gunther managed to put one and one together and came up with Rasta.

The following night, one happy Rasta, having read about the massacre at the nightclub under the headlines 'Local skinhead gang wiped out!' was whistling a jolly Caribbean tune and cycling to work. As Vini approached the usual meeting place he automatically tensed but then saw that there was no van waiting and relaxed with a hearty, self-conscious laugh. His humour was cut short, however, as a darkened van coughed into life and pulled out from an alley opposite its usual park and into his path. Vini screamed in terror as the heavy vehicle bunted him down and under the front bumper. Trapped and hurt in a mangled mess of his bike against the roughness of the cold bitumen, Vini shat his pants in steaming humiliation. He screamed for his mamma in primal shock as Gunther alighted from the driver's seat and Vini at ground level watched the paratrooper boots crunch slowly around to the front. Vini looked up past the heavy black steel bumper into the face of murderous rage. Gunther carried a baseball bat and had company: two other large skinheads. Vini begged for mercy in his desperate lilt, pleaded, screamed, 'Help me, mon!'

Gunther coldly reached down and pulled him from under the van with a vicious grip deep into the heavy towropes of Vini's dreadlocks. Vini knew that at least one of his legs was smashed at the knee, the pain bone-grating and unbearable as heavy tears poured from his eyes and he chanted 'no mon, no mon, no mon.' Gunther did not speak. Once he had a free hit at the gyrating form on the road he worked up and down the screaming victim in a terrible revenge. An aluminium baseball bat swung strong and wide has a crushing, breaking effect on the human body. As Vini's skeleton was deconstructed into a bone chip red-yellow marrow jelly, the crushing of his flesh and tearing-bruising of organs compounded the dreadful pain that racked and twisted him on that lonely road. Mercifully his body closed down, its receptors recognising the shocking life-threatening damage, and Vini's lights went out.

Panting, Gunther stopped and flipped the bat into the van. His two companions stood guard. Spectators. This was Gunther's work. He reached into the van and returned then to the prone form of the barely alive West Indian. Gunther knelt as if to comfort Vini. Knelt by his head. Vini's bloodied dreadlocks spread from his battered head like a stranded starfish under the weak light of the moon. Vini stirred. Awoke. Aware of a cold stinging wetness on his head through his hair he warily opened his eyes to the satanic grin of his tormentor above him. And then Vini realised Gunther was soaking his dreadlocks in lighter fluid. He had poured the entire contents of a half-litre flask of the icy petroleum based conflagrant into his hair, across his face and chest. Through smashed lips and broken teeth Vini screamed.

As 'Mamma!' echoed back off the warehouse walls, Gunther stood, stepped back and flicked the match.

4

DAYDREAM BELIEVER

'Birds at two o'clock!' The call from the deckie in the bow drifted up to the flying bridge. Bill Peters, charter fishing boat skipper, twisted quickly around from looking aft to scan the fifteen degrees to the starboard of the Shark Cat's twin bow peaks. Bill's deckie was one slim, black and beautiful twenty-year-old Aboriginal maiden, Ms Bonnie Anu of Broome.

'Good girl,' he murmured under his breath. Spinning the chrome wheel, he gunned the powerful fuel-injected Volvo 450 cubic inch engine of the sleek thirty-metre white fibreglass craft towards the flurry of gulls swirling, diving, smashing the glassy calm of the tropical turquoise waters of the Indian Ocean.

The charter fishing vessel *FV Freedom* was thirty kilometres off the Western Australian coastline. The continent, a distant murky red pancake on the shimmering eastern horizon, was haloed above by strata of brown-grey-white smoke from a huge wildfire in the unseen south. The land was suffering from the harsh ravages of a particularly persistent and cruelly dry El Nino weather pattern. But out this far from the landmass with a slight on-shore breeze, the sky was that incredible deep blue typical of that place and that time of year. Not a single fluff of white cloud above, just the hot yellow sun baking the land in the distance and radiating its intense heat down onto the vessel cutting across the placid sea below.

Bill could hear the patter of hisses as ice-cold cans of beer popped open and the chilled contents flowed, fuelling the interaction back on the main deck. His guests were relaxing under the cool protection of the white canvas shade as Bonnie, her tiny fluoro pink splash of bikini intense against the oiled ebony of her skin, charmed the men with her exotic looks and friendly humour.

They had speared away from the Port of Broome's jarrah wharf three hours earlier at nine that morning. The charter party was a group of eight oilmen, executives one and all, valued employees of one of the world's major exploration and petroleum supply companies. They were a pleasant, polite mix; a combination of the entrepreneurial local West Australians and slow-drawling Texans, ambassadors of their employer. The men were in town for business and now had time for pleasure as the corporation rewarded them at the conclusion of their annual conference. This year dozens of them and their spouses were ensconced at Broome's famous Cable Club Beach Resort in tropical luxury.

And as the powerful vessel had cut twin wakes through the soft morning waters away from Broome, a friendly pod of bottle-nosed dolphins delighted the visitors by escorting them a way off shore. The sleek grey creatures played, cheekily surfing the bow waves in breathtaking athleticism. Torpedo heads twisted, turning uncomfortably intelligent eyes up to scan the besotted hard men of the corporate world, who were suddenly like a bunch of excited children watching the dolphins at play.

The guests were happy. Bill had stopped one hour out over the old wreck of the coastal trader *Honest Venture*, a 10,000-tonne steel-plated product of the city of Birmingham docks in the 1920s. The rusty old coal burner had injudiciously been caught out at sea by a cyclone that smashed the northwest coast of Australia in October 1956. But with that death, both of the ship and of the poor souls who had served her, came life. The hulk had settled onto the sandy bottom at one-hundred-and-twenty metres, and the creatures of the warm salty soup of the sea recognised opportunity and progressively gave her new life as a reef.

'Fucken amazing,' Bill sometimes thought to self. As he did every time the Shark Cat arrived on autopilot at the X that marked the GPS longitude-latitude co-ordinates of the spot. And then, as icing on the hunter's cake, when sitting above the unseen reef he could view a green red electronic real-time movie show of his prey below on the boat's fish finder screen.

Bonnie had seated her guests and served coffee and was busy now presenting to sighs of male appreciation platters of the most succulent fruit from the town's local tropical market gardens. The musty sexy-scented nectar of the mango, fat purple sugar explosions of globe grapes, and the contrast of the icy half-moon slices of the green–yellow honeydew melons all grown from the fertile red soils of Broome. The men snacked heartily.

While they ate, Bonnie set up the rods: light lead sinkers smoothly oval to avoid snagging, with two hooks set a half-metre apart and the same distance off the sinker for the bottom feeding fish at the wreck. She baited up the hooks with generous hunks of squid. With breakfast finished the men had eagerly lowered their lines in competition to win the prize pool for first fish caught. In a line–ball decision, a tall Texan scooped the pool, his flapping, scaly victim hoisted from the water just before the others. Typically, in these rich waters, when each man's line hit the bottom, each hook was rapidly savaged by a greedy reef fish. In quick succession all the participants were rewarded, and each man whooped and yelled with delight at the ease of the hunt.

Bill joined his guests then as the *Freedom* floated gently over the wreck and he and Bonnie were kept busy removing the struggling catches, rebaiting ravaged hooks and photographing the happy and triumphant fishermen. All variety of the local bounty of the sea were rudely hauled to the surface. But Bill kept only the best of the eating fish, mainly the beautiful fat-filleted coral trout, throwing back the not so tasty mess of lesser species. His guests laughed at Bonnie's colloquial and broad Aussie accented description of the lesser species.

'That bony one we call neighbour fish, eh, cause that's who you give it to. That funny big-mouth slimy one with the googly eyes we call your mother-in-law fish,' she giggled.

With the boat's chiller filling nicely they stayed at the site for an hour and in that time had enough el-primo fish for the resort chef's requirements for a convention treat.

Now they smoothly cruised another sixty kilometres to the south at twenty kilometres west off the coast. Another one hour burst south and then into shore would put the Shark Cat into the tiny deep-water shelter of the Beauty Bay resort. Bill's thoughts about that place were gently interrupted as Bonnie arrived sinuously up onto the fly-deck ladder with an offering of a very long black coffee in his stainless-steel pint mug, and a skipper-sized platter of the tropical fruits.

'I know who you're missing, eh?' she teased, having seen his thousand-yard stare toward the coast.

'Nah, Bon—just wondering what Gypsy and Tommy are up to,' he replied, and took a long swig at the coffee.

'You sweet on that girl,' Bonnie said, and Bill, to his surprise, found that he may have blushed under his tan, recalling that Bonnie and Gypsy had been friends and no doubt confidants.

Gypsy was, to date, his great, unrequited tropical love. She was a rare combination of beauty, powerful intellect, and presence—almost a spiritual beauty. Gypsy was by trade a masseuse; she had manipulated the wealthy tourist trade from a tent on Cable Beach. But she had moved from Broome six months before with her man Tommy. The two, both of whom became Bill's friends, had bought and now operated Beauty Bay, a tiny niche tourism resort 150 kilometres south of Broome. The bay was probably Australia's most isolated tourist destination catering to those who Bill jokingly referred to as Gypsy's ferals.

Her description differed. 'The resort,' she had explained to Bill those six months ago as he lay in Broome Hospital, 'caters for the seekers of the answers. Answers to their being, their own humanity, their spirituality.'

'The askers of the "why" questions,' Bill had teased.

'Bill, Beauty Bay is lovely. Breathtakingly beautiful,' she had gushed, excited, green eyes sparkling. 'Our guests will stay in gorgeous little huts or bures dotted around the bay's hillside of tropical bush. There is a raised wooden walkway above the bush. It's all built around a small half-moon bay with native trees and plants that grow down nearly right into the sea. There is no television, no wi-fi, no refrigeration or even air conditioning.' Gypsy informed him, as he nodded and lay back, still a little foggy from the operation. 'Just lovely peace and quiet.'

He learnt from her that late tropical afternoon that she was to treat the converted and convertible to the healing arts of massage and meditation in a 'holistic eco holiday experience'.

Tommy was to run the practical business side of the operation she told him. 'Bill, the more adventurous can go offshore fishing in Tommy's boat. Then there is estuary fishing, only a short four-wheel drive up the beach at Rowe Creek,' she had said.

Bill already knew from his own experience fishing with Tommy that the explosive silver flash of the fighting barramundi in a shallow tidal riverbed did surely provide one of the world's great fishing moments.

'We've also adopted a camel breeding operation,' Gypsy had continued, 'so we'll be doing the sunset thing.'

Bill had seen on red sunset evenings in Broome the cameleers lead a long towline of the exotic huffing creatures along Cable Beach for the romantic tourist rides out at the sunset and back in the moonlight.

The trouble was, Bill had learnt from his occasional phone call through to his friends, there was trouble in paradise. The target market had proved a small and not a typically wealthy group. A cold commercial fact was that the less spiritual, less holistic tourist sought comfort and amenities closer to home than the extremely remote Beauty Bay. They needed television and internet access to distract the packs of obese, demanding, processed-sugar-fuelled offspring. They definitely wanted air-con to cool down sweaty-hot and tired bodies; needed fridges to chill huge supplies of alcoholic relief and saturated fat foods; and didn't give a flying fuck about seeking the inner being while on Mr and Mrs Citizen's short annual escape from the grind of suburbia.

Gypsy reported that things were tight in Beauty Bay. They had borrowed heavily to take up the lease on the resort and in Bill's phone calls to her she spoke of how Tommy was uncharacteristically tense as they faced losing it all.

Bill was worried for her. She had been his saviour when he had escaped to Broome on the run from the police in NSW in a previous life. At that time he was still recovering from the violent loss of two people he had loved that had occurred only months before in New Zealand. That was another story and they had died not at his hand, rather as a terrible unseeable consequence of his and others' acts and omissions. When he had run to Broome Bill had shared his loss with Gypsy, told her of the police undercover operation in New Zealand that he had been the integral part of. Gypsy had listened, and she had cared and she had helped to heal him. His attraction to her was an intense but ultimately frustrating connection. He knew that the emotion he felt for her as a physical being, and indeed as a spiritual, intelligent woman, could only be described as love. And as she had cared for him, nurtured him, healed him emotionally over that lovely summer, he was gently told, and ultimately accepted, that she was, in all aspects of the word, loyal to her man at sea, the gentle Tommy. And so although Bill still struggled to understand even now how to value this love of an unattainable but much desired woman, he actually strangely enjoyed the knowledge that his was a friendship and would never be more. It was perhaps an appreciation that his affection was uncomplicated in that sense. He could and did feel the emotion, and Gypsy recognised this, but his commitment would never be tested by that depth of a relationship, the grind of day to day living.

Gypsy loved Tommy. And Tommy had saved Bill's life as he sank, speared like a snapper, below the waters off Joys Creek. All that was in the past now. Here he was now, twenty-eight years old, no ties, and the freehold owner of a seven hundred-thousand-dollar charter boat. Plus he was living in the most wonderful place imaginable.

Gypsy was in trouble but would not accept his help, wouldn't take his money. He had even moved out of their house in Broome's old Chinatown so that they could rent it out. His entire world materially was now the *FV Freedom*, which he parked on a mooring in the quiet Roebuck Bay, a short paddle and wade to and back from the bay's namesake pub in Broome town. He was worried for Gypsy and for Tommy and knew that he must try to find a way to help them out. But for now thoughts of his friends faded, tucked away for later as he aimed the big Shark Cat's bows at the circling, diving flock of gulls. As the vessel surged forward at the charge he sounded her air-horns, incongruously blasting the first few bars of the politically incorrect southern Confederate army's rebel yell to the absolute yippee-yahooed enjoyment of the Texans on the lower deck.

5

SIX MONTHS IN A LEAKY BOAT

At twenty knots they closed quickly on the birds. This was ideal for the day and the client's enjoyment, Bill thought to self, and he thanked Bonnie for her vigilance as she clambered up onto the fly bridge from the lower deck to the wolf whistles of the oilmen below. They good-naturedly admired her boyish hips but unmistakably feminine curve of buttocks, her pink bikini a fluoro-flash atop her sinuous legs as she climbed the inset ladder.

Bonnie delivered an ice-cold home-brewed ginger beer and Bill thankfully gulped it down in a sugary rush.

'Hopefully, mate, we might get us some mahi mahi,' he said, referring to the mad athletes of these waters also known as dolphin fish. Despite the name, these long, big-headed, brightly coloured fish were no relation to the intelligent, big-brained aquatic mammals. These cold-blooded vertebrates swam furiously in rapacious packs just below the surface and were among the finest fighting and eating fish of the local waters.

Usually birds feeding on a spot on the pulsing canvas of the ocean meant that small fish were on the surface in a frenzied school. It also followed that beneath the small, frightened school was the cause of that panic: bigger, hungrier predators, and then under them bigger and hungrier again. Such aquatic interaction was a fisherman's paradise, the possibility of plunder through layers of ravenous excited prey.

'Set them up for the mahi mahi, gorgeous,' Bill asked Bonnie, and she spun away, all cheeky plump-lipped sensuality. Again to the whistled appreciation of the guests below, she slid smoothly down the ladder handrails without stepping once upon the steps and got busy setting up two trolling rigs. She expertly removed the sinker and hook leaders and replacing them with steel traces and brightly attractive plastic lures as Bill aimed the *Freedom* right through the school and bought her down to a gentle trolling speed.

Excited at the prospects, the eight guests set up under Bonnie's direction. Two men quickly were selected by the group based on executive seniority to have the first tries with a rod. The pair strapped themselves into the fishing chairs set either side at the stern and released the catches on the smooth mechanics of the heavy game reels. The teasing lures skipped along the surface, roiled from the props, and the plaited nylon line hissed out from the spinning reels without the restriction of drags. Bonnie told each how far to go out and then each man clicked the reel control and set the drags and then settled back for the strike.

Bam! One and then almost immediately the other. Bam! Two! Both game fishing rods bent near double and the heavy-duty reels whirred out line against the friction of the drag.

'Strike!' yelled both men. Bill stood high on the fly-deck to look back down at fish and fishermen to co-ordinate the retrieval. The guests were uniformly ecstatic with the excitement of the two big fish hooked. The six not involved in the exhausting fight against the shivering muscularity of the catch teased and tormented their friends in good-natured if not impatient expectation of their own turn at the rods. Slowly, inexorably, the prizes were bought in to the water-splashed transom at the stern where Bonnie stood with a long gaff, while Bill operated the controls minutely back and forward to assist the fishermen. Two of the prized mahi mahi arrived at the boat. Bill checked and nodded his assent to Bonnie that they could be taken. Bonnie expertly swung the vicious steel hook into the gills of the first fish with the crimson lifeblood spurting and staining the sea and further exciting the mad splash of fish and raucous screech of the sea birds over the patch of activity. Safely held, she lifted the flapping metre-long fish on board to be released from hook, knocked senseless with the wooden cosh and flipped into the dark finality of the chiller, and then repeated the crude welcome with the second fish.

As the men took their impatient turns at the rods each troll brought a new surprise. More mahi mahi. The torpedo-shaped shimmering power of the yellow fin tuna; the violent smash and grab of the huge silvery Spanish mackerel; and the violent head shaking of tiger and bronze whaler shark, as each took the lures and fuelled the excitement of the day for all those on board the *Freedom*.

Finally after ninety action-packed minutes of the troll and of the catch and mostly release, the birds' squawking cacophony quietened, the bubbling of fin and fish on the subsurface ceased, and the *Freedom* sat quiet on the waters. The baitfish school had dived and gone with the feathered predators above denied, and the gilled predators below in pursuit. Bill's guests gushed and raved, reliving their triumphs and backslapping each other in the recognition that this day would be remembered.

Now Bonnie fed the men as they floated peacefully on placid waters popping beers and enjoying the day. Bonnie soon had bloody rib eye steaks sizzling on the gas barbecue fitted off the rear rail, the meat sealed in tangy garlic perfection. Bill had found from his relatively short experience as a charter skipper that men enjoyed a steak on board while fishing, more so than the apparently logical meal of the fish that they had just hauled out of the sea. It was one of those strange but true facts that he had decided not to over-analyse.

After the adrenaline-fuelled excitement of the day so far, the guests found that they were ravenous and set upon the fare spread across the broad central deck table.

Later Bonnie and Bill cleared away the detritus of the meal while the oil men relaxed into more serious beer consumption and increasingly tall tales. Bill climbed back up onto the fly bridge and fired the big engine back into purring life. Meanwhile, Bonnie began the expert cleaning, dressing and packing of the fish taken for food as Bill prepared to turn toward home port.

And then Bill saw it. Three hundred metres to the east. Something big and black floating and surrounded by the circling threat of fins, two, no, three sharks. With a call to Bonnie, Bill cruised warily over to the floater.

'Too big to be a person,' he muttered fervently under his breath, as the oilmen craned out over the side to see what had attracted the sharks. Then Bill smelt it. 'Fuck me,' he grunted. An all-pervading sickly stench, as bad as a kangaroo smashed and rotting in the sun on the hot desert highway. He was reminded of road kill that travellers in the north-west of Western Australia might happen upon periodically, driving into a musty almost visible vapour cloud invariably filling any approaching car with the foul, retching sweetness of decay.

With the early afternoon sea breeze just ruffling the waters Bill took the *Freedom* around the windward side of the thing and approached cautiously. A big Texan leaning over the bow rail of the starboard hull saw it first.

'I think it's a big ole hoss,' he shouted back.

Bill eased the *Freedom* into neutral and clambered down from the fly-deck to join the enthralled throng on the bow.

Bill leaned over the bow rail and peered down.

'You're right and you're wrong,' he told the tall man. 'It's a horse designed by a committee, it's a fucken camel!'

And it was: a big floating stinking mass of camel.

'Look,' Bill pointed, 'the entire hump's gone. Must have been the tasty bit. Old Noah's chewed it right off.'

On cue, one of the sharks rolled in for a lazy gulping attack under the bulk of the poor beast, which floated on its side, just breaking the surface.

'A big old bull,' Bill commented and pointed at the sad bag of the creature's lost potential floating jauntily between the camel's hindquarters. 'Must have got the ship of the desert thingy fucked up,' Bill muttered as he made his way back up the steel ladder to the bridge.

As Bonnie entertained, fed and watered the happy guests, Bill spun the chromed wheel to port and gunned the powerful Volvo engines to aim the *Freedom* back towards Broome.

6

BAD MEDICINE

Rastafarian Vini Schmidt died of his dreadful injuries in May. By early September the purple camel tabs were making their way across the Nullarbor Plain of the Australian island continent at a cruise controlled 119 kph. The illicit cargo headed south and then east on Highway 1. This elongated asphalt vein connected west to east and skirted the aptly named Great Australian Bight, the Bight being a geological feature that looked as if some extra-terrestrial monster in ages past had indeed taken a bite from the underbelly of Australia.

The driver of the nondescript white Holden Commodore hire car was a male, third generation Vietnamese Australian. Van Nguyen, now thirty, was a mid-level member of the Spider triad gang of Cabramatta, a troubled suburb in Sydney's west.

This was the first time that the Spiders had dipped a toe into the upper end of the trendy cult drug market. Es were all the rage with the affluent young nightclubbers of the nation. It had been deemed by the gang bosses that they may as well supply a demand and therefore would experiment with a shipment of the happy-touchy-touchy party drug. As he journeyed Van sang melodically to the taped disco ditties of his grandparents' homeland and cautiously drove at the legal speed limit toward Sydney town.

Van arrived back into Cabramatta on Friday night, the sedan now red, dusty and smeared with insect and moth guts. The trip of some five thousand tedious kilometres had been taken by car to avoid the improved abilities of the nation's law enforcement agencies in the detection of drugs moving across the wide red land by air or sea.

In fact part of the reason for his trip was that the gang's heroin-importing business in the air and sea divisions had been severely dented over recent times, with the combined expertise of the various states' police and the new federal Border Force working closely together and with international counterparts to foil such traffic. The increased sophistication of the forensic intelligence gathering and drug import detection capabilities, indicated that maybe, just maybe, the good guys were creeping on top of the bad guys. One practical consequence, however, was a much-diminished supply, particularly of heroin, to the streets.

An obvious side effect of that damaged supply was also a corresponding detriment to the cash flow of the Spiders and related gangs. They were not happy arachnids. Furthermore, as traditional product became scarce, the gang's disloyal and fickle customer base wandered off to sample new sensations. Some were to be lost forever from what the Spiders had naively assumed was to be a lifetime relationship between supplier and user, client and customer, dealer and addict. Hence the gang's first incursion into ecstasy. And the timing of the arrival of some one hundred thousand tablets, purely by coincidence, was perfect. It was the September school and university holidays and the city's youth were partying hard as usual before the last third of the school year began and the dark clouds of impending examinations became academic reality.

The beaches, pubs and nightclubs of Sydney town were cooking. And coming up that very break was the annual two-day weekend concert in Sydney, the Mega Bash party. Here, dozens of local and internationally favoured musical groups followed each other on to stage from Friday night through to Sunday. Tens of thousands of happy and generally chemically affected young adults pulsed and surged on the grass of the huge sporting ovals in an orgy of dance and celebration.

A market! That was what the inscrutable gang bosses saw, a business opportunity. One hundred thousand tabs of E at thirty dollars a tab wholesale, or fifty dollars retail, equals close to five million dollars, cash, non-taxable. Outlay $750,000.00 US! The dealer teams were ready. Low level contractors properly briefed and fitted with body corsets cunningly fashioned into trendy clothing so that any one of the young men or women could carry into the park hundreds of units of product to work the crowd through the two days.

Van, somewhat road-weary, dropped the booty off to Spider HQ, a nondescript factory unit in Cabramatta in the commercial area near the railway station. His masters were happy. The coming weekend was looking prosperous and Van was given it off by his satisfied bosses. And as a special reward, just before he headed home, he was presented with one pack of ten camels to try or trade at his leisure. Van was a contented drug courier. Still glowing from the rare praise of the boss he stopped on his way to his apartment on Park Road, Cabramatta and bought takeaway seafood char kway teow from the Long Hung Beijing Barbecue joint. While he waited for his food he flirted crudely with the young almond-eyed Chinese waitress. Her father glowered murderously at him from the kitchen. Dad cursed under his breath in Mandarin with colourful descriptions of his opinion of the Vietnamese, while chopping up the seafood with exaggerated blows of the heavy black-steel cleaver.

Van breathed in the garlic soy sauce scents from the hot brown paper bag on the passenger's seat and made a stop at the Stardust Hotel drive-through. There an armed security guard sat on watch as staff served through the protective steel mesh barrier. As a treat to himself, Van ordered the Johnnie Walker Black, the 1.5 litre, and paid the young Chinese attendant in crisp fifties.

He left the dusty hire car in the common security parking alongside his apartment block with a nod at the elderly guard who whirred the electronic gate shut and bowed his head in fearful deference to this dangerous man.

Van Nguyen was glad to be home. Back in to the cool comfort of his modern apartment he placed his meal into the buzz of the microwave to warm. He took the time to flick on a Vietnamese music DVD of the latest hits from Ho Chi Min City while he took a long, hot cleansing bath in his bubbling Jacuzzi. Clean and dried, Van dressed in a pair of black silk kung-fu pants and his brand new T-shirt. He sat then at the small dining table in the kitchenette, alone in his bachelor pad, and enjoyed the succulent delights of his flat noodle, brown-sauced feast. He skilfully plucked from the mass with smooth wooden chopsticks the generous portions of prawns, scallops, mussels and hunks of sweet fish with lip-smacking, teeth-sucking delight. Appetite sated, Van poured into his thick-glass tumbler a malty splash of the Scotch nectar. On the rocks—untainted by water or other foul mixers. He sloshed the liquid heat into and around his mouth and the honeyed fluid pulsed down his throat.

'Ayyyy yaaaaaa,' he breathed and relaxed before the exotic contortions of the popular songstress on the DVD. Van casually lifted the ten tabs of ecstasy, still amazed at the gift from the boss. Van was only a rare casual user of the products that fuelled the gang's coffers. He had heard of ecstasy. The gang had sought expert description of its chemical make-up, its use and its effects on the human body and mind. Knowledge was power to the gang and product knowledge was encouraged. Van knew that with the gang now handling this new product he had been given the opportunity to try it and would be expected to report on his experience. And so he popped a tab from the blister pack. '*Dong goi chuyen nghiep,*' Van thought to self in his parent's native tongue, appreciating the professional appearance of the packaging of the pills. He held the small round tab up in front of his eyes and admired the art displayed with the stamping of the single-humped camel on each face. And then Van Nguyen popped the tablet into his mouth and swished it down into his stomach with a chaser of fine malt whisky. He sat back and waited for the drug's hit. He had been told that typically the MDMA was felt within fifteen to thirty minutes.

Within ten minutes the young man was dead. An impartial observer, a figurative fly upon the same wall where many thousands of such flies would soon sit chewing their cud so to speak, would have witnessed Van's handsome Asian features change from contented expectation to grotesque realisation in a frame-by-frame tragicomedy of the puppet theatre of death. It was 'Thunderbirds are go!' stuff as he tried to stand, tried to walk, to get to the door, the phone, but his writhing body failed him. His lonely passing was excruciating and messy. Van adopted the classic sawhorse position on the floor as his well-developed trunk and back muscles contracted and broke his spine. He flushed from all orifices and convulsed on the carpeted floor as Vini Schmidt's synthetic Dutch rat poison stole his precious life force. His gangster spirit left his being to the shrill farewell of a Vietnamese songstress from the CD. Van died alone with a strychnine rictus grin on his face.

7

GAMES WITHOUT FRONTIERS

'PADDLES UUUUUUP! GO!' came the bellowed command. In Bill's boat twenty varnished wooden T-bar paddles flashed in near unison. Outward and downward they arced, smashing as one into the warm waters of the Indian Ocean. Four identical dragon boats abreast, twenty paddlers in each boat, ten pairs side by side, eighty paddlers on the water. The four sweeps crouched low at the stern of the boats trailing long steering oars, barking the race calls over the bent backs of their straining crews. Four little drummers chosen for their size and balance sat facing precariously backward from the high seat at the bow, booming time for the straining paddlers on goatskin drums.

In lane two, running off and along the beach off Roebuck Bay, the Mangrove Muddies dragon boat team powered the slim aluminium vessel forward from the start line and into the five-hundred-metre race distance. Through the start sequence the practiced team of ten men and ten women hammered and splashed with flashing synchronisation as the shallow draft craft picked up speed, got up onto the surface of the glassy waters and planed. After the insane flurry of the start, the crews perceptibly changed gears and the sweeps began to chant 'long-and-strong!' providing the timing and the paddlers leaned into the work of the ancient Chinese sport.

In the old pearling port of Broome it was Shinju Matsuri Festival time. This was an annual celebration of the lives and memorial of the deaths of young men from that land of the rising sun, and others, who had searched for the wild south sea pearl in the early development of the area.

'Power on three...two...one...POWER!' roared the Muddies grizzled old sweep, George Patrick, an obese fifty-year-old detective senior sergeant based at the local police station. 'Doc,' as he was known to the locals (who had quickly recognised the possibility of a nickname from his initials of GP), had recruited his crew by summons. Actual police summonses that he had personally typed and served on his chosen twenty several weeks before the festival. Doc Patrick took himself seriously when it came to competitive sport. He had played Aussie Rules football at a senior club level in the WAFL in the Perth competition as a much younger man. Now that age, alcohol and circumstance had slowed him down in his middle age, Doc had found no more satisfyingly competitive sport then the gut wrenching explosive aggression of a dragon boat race.

Bill Peters had first met Detective Senior Sergeant Doc Patrick months before, when his life on the run from the law came to an end in Broome Hospital with a visit by his old boss, the New Zealand Police Commissioner.

Accompanying the commissioner had been Kingi Potiki, retired detective superintendent, NZ Police. In a past life, Kingi and Bill's fathers had been virtual blood-brothers. That bond and one other almost equally dear to Bill's heart had been fatally broken as a loose consequence of Bill's own actions as an undercover agent in New Zealand. Before he had left Broome back then, Kingi had sat with Doc Patrick in the small police station and briefed him fully on the sad events that had led the young Bill Peters to the tiny northwest Australian coastal town. As the meeting had drawn to a close Doc Patrick had undertaken on a sombre handshake to 'look after your boy'. Over the months since Doc had kept his word and had even reported back periodically to an e-mail address in New Zealand.

Doc had also done his best to involve himself in Bill's life in the town. At Doc's persistent instigation Bill now trained the Broome Police Boys Club kids in self-defence classes, drawing on his past skills as an exponent and teacher of tae kwon do. Three nights a week, dressed in the heavy white linen, sweating like a pig in the tropical humidity with his hard-earned black belt around his waist, Bill had attempted to drill the formalised patterns of the ancient art into the gaggle of easily distracted youngsters. The local kids were a colourful, vivacious mix of Aboriginal, Anglo, and Asian youth.

'Like herding fucken cats, mate,' Doc would mutter sympathetically under his breath as he helped supervised the noisy classes.

Doc would also come fishing on the *Freedom* whenever he was able, and Bill had found a shallow masculine friendship of sorts developing, allowing for the difference in their ages, backgrounds, lifestyles and dreams. Although he tolerated the sober Doc, Bill was increasingly uneasy when Doc had bonded with his old friend, whisky. To his increasing discomfort, Bill had also realised that he had apparently become Doc's new best, and only, 'maaate'. That relationship was not reciprocated or encouraged by Bill, but had been hard for him to avoid in the tiny town. Once, sometimes twice, a week now Doc would arrive uninvited at the *Freedom* at night to pursue his fascination with the malted liquor. Typically, after Doc's long-winded and increasingly single-malt-affected tirades on the ills of the world, a certain ugly red-necked misogyny would come oozing out of the older man's core. 'Still,' Bill thought, 'at least he is someone to talk with.'

On one recent night Doc had arrived at the *Freedom* completely sober and full of good fellowship and intentions. Bill found him a beer, somewhat surprised at the lack of a whisky bottle in the fat man's mitt— like Bonnie without Clyde.

'Maaate, look, I am forever getting inquiries, from all over the world actually, for me to track down someone's son or daughter thought to be in the town,' said Doc. 'Bill, it's not my job. No concern really of the police that their kids are rooting their way round Orstralia. I don't give a flying fuck, maaate. So I was thinking today, there's a fucken job opportunity for someone to take on this type of shit and make some money looking for little Sumi or little Lars at seventy-five bucks an hour plus mileage!'

'Riiiight?' Bill queried.

Doc's face flushed with the heat of the late afternoon and the alcohol's effects. 'Right, maaate. Broome needs a private investigator, and by sunset tomorrow we will have one—you.'

'Okay, Doc,' Bill laughed, 'that sounds okay. So what's all this stuff?'

Bill pointed at the pile of official looking documents that Doc had plopped down on the table.

'Maaate, this is the PI application to be processed by your local police—me. Sign these, there and there, son, and I need to snap a photo, and tomorrow I will be dropping off your PI licence.'

Bill thought about it, saw and heard no immediately obvious evil and signed.

'Okay, maate, it's now awe-fishal. You're it. Magnum PI!' grinned Doc, and he reached to clink his beer against Bill's.

And so it proved. To be honest, Bill was happy to fill in the occasional quiet days at seventy-five dollars an hour searching the local caravan parks and back-packer hostels for a son or daughter missing in paradise. He did that work, periodically reporting back to concerned parents in Oslo or Tokyo, or even Sydney or Auckland. He had laughed when Bonnie teased him that his PI chariot was a rusty old khaki jeep that would hardly chase down a local kid on a ten-speed—a far call from Tom Sellick's red Ferrari.

8

IT'S A LONG WAY THERE

'OK MUDDIES! I need all you've got! POWER FOR TWENTY ON THREE—TWO—POWER!' And the boat's bow lifted again with the extra spurt of concentrated muscular effort to plane again. Twenty paddlers straining in perfect time and wonderful style to respond to the sweep's mid-race call to accelerate, to surge forward from the desperate fleet, to crush with exquisite pressure the will of the crews on either side. But the boat next to them on the bay side jumped when they jumped, that crew kicked when they kicked, for they were the terrorist crew, the tourist aliens from Perth.

In the previous weeks Doc had learnt that the mighty Cockburn Blades dragon boat club team from the distant metropolis of Perth was on its way to his patch to plunder the trophies from the Shinju this September. He got angry. Then he got ready. From the populace of the small town, Doc selected his crew. He chose twenty of the town's fittest and most athletic youth. He convinced them that it was definitely in their own interests and the interests of their town, indeed of the Kimberley region's civic pride, that they join the team. Doc trained his shanghaied crew hard. Each Tuesday and Thursday and then, as the race grew closer, each Sunday morning, he would pick up the twenty, including the amused Bill and the happily enthusiastic Bonnie Anu, and deliver them to the bay. Then would follow two-hour training sessions on the warm calm waters, the twenty victims becoming increasingly boat fit and expert in the styles and rhythms of the ancient Chinese sport.

The crew was a multicultural microcosm of the town's unique population. Bonnie was Aboriginal Australian as were three wiry male rowers. Five of the crew were out of the various ethnic bloodlines of China and of Japan decades past. Three Malay and two Indonesian crew members spoke of earlier immigration waves by forefathers who came to fish or trade and stayed to populate and contribute to the rich racial tapestry of the town. The other six were of the varied Anglo, Saxon, Celt and Aryan tribal mix that provided the paler pastels to the kaleidoscope. Others like Bill were rank newcomers, barely out of the terrorist/tourist category.

Doc had selected his bloodlines well and as race day grew closer his intensive training had produced a well-oiled machine, as truly competitive dragon boat crews must be. In this sport, Bill soon learnt, the teamwork and exact co-ordination of the twenty individuals was the key to the success of the whole. No one paddler, no matter how powerful, how macho, or singularly aggressive, could win the race on his own. If the twenty wooden paddles did not hit the water at the same moment and sweep in unison under the surface in beautiful rhythm, then the race was inevitably lost to the other crew who had perfected team timing.

The Perth team had arrived at the town on the Thursday before the Sunday race. The thirty assorted paddlers and officials were to be accommodated at the sprawling Roebuck Inn. Doc now involved his team in his dishonest endeavours. Each team member in the conspiracy was tasked to locate and provide a shadow. That is, each had to find and convince a person of as poor physical shape and capability as possible to pretend to be a paddler in the Mangrove Muddies. Bonnie convinced her dad.

Mozzie Anu was eighty-two. The old stallion had conceived Bonnie when he was sixty-two and his child bride Millie Anu a mere forty-eight. The couple had earlier conceived and reared one set of male twins who were now close to forty. The boys worked Mozzie's cattle fattening station on the outskirts of Broome while Mozzie retired to the township to sun himself and fish daily for his dinner from the port wharf.

Bonnie was a mistake, not of parental love or intention, but of nature. Somehow the old man's powder had not been as dry as Millie had presumed, and when the town discovered that she was pregnant again, rumour and innuendo spread unfairly with jokes about milkmen and delivery boys until the baby girl was born. The beautiful little girl was the spitting feminine image of earlier photos of Mozzie, who strutted and swaggered about the shopping precincts with the precious bundle in his arms, making proud comments about virility and boasting loudly about having oiled the seized cogs of Millie's biological clock. With his long life experience as an Aboriginal struggling to rise and survive in the conqueror's enforced society, Mozzie Anu had developed one aspect of his character to the nth degree, and that was a keen sense of humour. So when his precious gift Bonnie put Doc's deal to him he laughed raucously and agreed.

Bill thought long and hard about his shadow as the others drew upon friend and family to recruit the town's infirm, old or just plain unhealthy. Bill finally plucked up the courage and went in search of his old friend Mavis. He had met Mavis the year before when on the run from the authorities and working for board and food with Gypsy in her massage tent on Cable Beach. Mavis had been his first massage victim as he had struggled through a training session under the supervision of the beautiful Gypsy. Mavis, however, and much to Bill's surprise, had apparently enjoyed his ministrations. She had then single-handedly created a market for his gradually more skilful manipulative endeavours until he had attracted a steady clientele of the elderly female population of the town, much to Gypsy's delight, and his initial confusion.

Mavis was one of the classic Grey Nomads, Australia's unique retired population who had made brave mid-to-late-lifestyle decisions to escape grey lives in grey cities. They sold up fixed assets, bought caravans or motor homes and then travelled the tropical climes on a never-ending circumnavigation of their nation and of their fading lives. Mavis was now in her eighties. Bill wasn't sure if she was in town. He knew that she was due to appear at some time soon, all going well with her old bus and her own health, and so he went to look for her.

He soon found her at the town's nude beach off the main family area at Cable Beach. Bill wasn't brave enough to visit his old mate in all her wrinkled glory on the beach itself, although he could spot her familiar sun-faded rainbow beach umbrella and a pair of stick legs protruding seaward some one hundred metres away along the white sands.

He decided to wait for her, enjoying the vista of the varied hues and physical packaging of the numerous young women, typically in a minute tease of bikini as they made their smoothly feminine way to and from the famous waters up and down the cliff stairs. He marvelled, as always, at that essential difference between his hard masculine lines and the glorious sensual curvaceousness of that other sex.

'Shit, it's been a long time,' he breathed to himself as a realisation struck him that he hadn't tasted the beauty of the female form since the previous year, since the two Swiss backpackers, and for one mad moment he missed them.

But he had been too busy, really, buying and outfitting the boat. Then there was the advertising, promotion and the actual day-to-day operation of the charter fishing business. But also there was his strength of emotion that he had devoted to Gypsy, although she had left town, and him, with her man Tommy six months before. He knew of course that his was a hopelessly one-sided attraction but he had focused his energy on that woman to the almost automatic exclusion of any other. And because of that he had either missed or misread the subtle invitations from others from whom otherwise he may have sought comfort, companionship, and/or relief of spirit and body.

With the passing of time and the inevitable dimming of the pain and memories of the past events in New Zealand, Sydney, Kalgoorlie and Perth, he had found lately that his masculine instinct was no longer to be denied. As his increasingly painful early morning erections were turgid testament to. As he sat on the beach he laughed quietly as he recalled his conversation of the previous night on the back deck of the *Freedom*. Doc had arrived after six with his usual minimum daily allowance of one bottle of single malt. Bill had sighed when he heard the police four-wheel drive squeak to a stop on the heavy jarrah planks of the Broome port wharf.

'Gidday, maaate,' the already slightly sozzled Doc had sourly breathed as he stepped down onto the Shark Cat's transom. Bill had found a glass and some ice for Doc, and got himself a can of lager. As usual, Doc ran through the national news stories for him; a paraphrasing of the newsworthy comings and goings of the politicians to the south, a critique of the activity of the federal boys and girls in cold Canberra over east.

Doc spoke with his usual foggy passion about the major crime stories from the nation's big cities. He spoke also of the progress, slow and dying—'Thank fuck, maaate, eh!'—of the now huge El Nino-inspired wild bushfire that from time to time had looked like racing north.

'Spose to be a fucken southern oscillation, that El Nino cunt,' Doc slurred, still in his khaki uniform, now sweat stained at the armpits. The fabric strained across a hairy ginger gut, rolls of which were visible through the undone top five buttons, as he plotted the course of the big fire clumsily on some paper for a less-than-fascinated Bill at the table.

The country had been in a drought crisis for ten hot years now. The wildfires were simply a consequence of a landscape heavy in fuels from previous good years when rain had fallen in the semi-desert. On Doc's mud map of a very unusually shaped Australia, the fire blotted more and more virgin bush on its smoky crawl from its core north of Lake Waukarlycarly near Telfer. Weeks before on an eerily powerful electrically charged evening, a massive sheet of awesome white lightning had hit the dry spinifex lands and ignited the fiery beast into being.

Bill was vaguely interested in the fire and its meandering slowly closer to the coast. But then as always, once he had the other's attention, Doc wandered into the initially sly and then increasingly strident commentary on the evils of, and his barely concealed hatred of, women, as a sex, as a class, as a 'Fucken alien species, maate'.

Bill sighed. 'Here we go again,' he murmured as the now slurring older man retold stories of the tragic misuse and cruel abuse by his 'two-bitch-slut-cunt ex wives'.

Bill had noted however that at the very least this man was not an obvious racist. At least he had not seen any indication of that. No; to be fair to the man, Doc just hated women: black women, white, yellow, red, pink or brindle coloured women. But he wasn't a racist. It was then Bill's game of distraction began. Doc, suddenly drunkenly aware that he was losing his audience, threw a searching question at his young friend.

'Anyway, what the fuck are youse doin for a fuck, maate? If you doan mind me aksing?'

Bill smirked at the use of *aksing*, a word that was typically part of Doc's tortured vocab.

'Ah, me, Doc? Mate, nothing doing in that-them hindquarters, sadly.'

'Doan be fecken saaad, maaate,' Doc insisted, querulous now.

'Keep well away from them, maaate—in my pinion…Take it from me, maaate. Ya never trust something that bleeds once a month and don't die.'

Bill squirmed at that disgraceful pearl of wisdom. 'Ah, Doc, don't say that.' The problem for Bill was that he adored women. Loved every little thing about the fascinating creatures, ached, ached to hold a woman right now away from this smelly, sweaty, fat, bald, pathetic prick of a thing. But Doc continued, sly grin on unshaven dial.

'Maaate…now, Bill…Ya gotta agree—if they didn't fuck, y'd throw rocks at the cunts! Well that's what I reckon anyway.'

Bill sighed again, 'Come on, Doc, give it away.'

But he could see the pattern that he had become accustomed to developing again: uninvited, unwelcome, half-pissed arrival…the world according to Doc, update on the news…rude invader rapidly getting more pissed as one bottled contents ingested…spray on women in general seeking some mutual agreement…inevitable semi-consciousness approaching as alcohol numbs…slurred goodbye… stagger back to police car…weaving disappearance off the wharf… gone.

But Doc wasn't quite to the leaving stage just yet, as he offered his bent intimate opinions and suggestions to the nice young Kiwi bloke that he had promised that scary Maori copper Kingi Potiki he would 'look after'.

'Na, maate…jus do what I do…crank the fucken maggot!'

Bill coughed back up a fine spray as the lager went down the wrong hole as he attempted to laugh, or possibly to cry at the unwanted sudden vision of Doc 'cranking a maggot'. Doc leaned across the deck table to bash the younger man on his bent back as his breath finally resumed normal operation.

'What, Doc?' he gasped. 'You reckon it's best just to visit with Mrs Palmer and her five lovely daughters?' Bill perhaps in hindsight foolishly challenged.

Doc looked at him with the beginnings of a smile. 'Yeah, maate, yeah maaate, yeah maaate, haha, stroke the joke.'

Apparently it was on—Bill's turn—but he didn't want to play this silly game with an old perve such as the local senior sergeant of police was indeed.

'C'mon…play the blue veined flute, eh, Bill….eh….eh…blue veined flute c'mon...c'mon,. Doc leered snorting with laughter. 'C'mon...c'mon,' he urged as Bill shook his head sadly, knowing that Doc was always looking to compete in just about everything, even a battle to win a wanking words competition.

But Bill refused to play and instead he picked up the remote off the table to turn the stereo up so that the Waif's beautiful song about war brides leaving Fremantle on a train to travel across to Sydney and on to America dominated the immediate space.

'Ah, shiiiiit,' Detective Senior Sergeant George Patrick groaned and rose to leave, the tired and emotional officer of the law not a Waifs fan apparently. He clumped sulkily off the *Freedom*, tripping over the bulwark of the wharf, nearly falling into shark infested waters, but catching himself in time to stagger across to the driver's door of the police vehicle.

'See ya, maaate,' he called sadly back to Bill before kicking the throaty Toyota diesel into smoky life and reversing in a half circle transmission whine back to face the shore.

Bill skolled the last of his warming beer and watched from the rear deck, shaking his head again, as the white and blue four-wheel drive wove away down the wide-planked wharf and onto the smooth seal of the port road back to town. He saw the brake lights before he heard the sudden screech of an emergency stop. Bill winced, and then laughed as the tinny whistle of the vehicle's public-address system kicked back through the tropical warmth of the night air.

'Masturbator, sir! You're a freakin masturbator!' came booming over the water and then Doc disappeared stage left with a triumphant 'toot toot' of the horn.

But thinking about it now at the beach Bill decided that masturbation was indeed a poor substitute for the real thing. 'Me want woman!' he had sighed to the moonlit night. And then Mavis entered his vision.

'Young Billy, my boy! How are you, love?' his old friend gushed, and he rose to hug her frail wiry body and kiss that sun browned wrinkled cheek. Then the two mates sat at the beach kiosk and Bill put the scenario dreamt up by Doc to Mavis and she laughed and agreed immediately.

9

BRILLIANT DISGUISE

One week out and the shadow Muddies were bought down to Town Beach by the actual team.

'What a fine collection of wasted, damaged, and worn humanity,' Doc commented quietly to Bill.

They stood thigh deep in the warm sea holding the floating dragon boat steady against the gentle tidal surge. As the shadows gathered on the shore Bill noted that the team had chosen their shadows well. From the simply old, such as Mozzie Anu and Mavis, there were also two amputees and one wheelchair-bound senior. Perhaps the masterstroke though, was Doc's recruiting of four of the town's complement of hopeless alcoholics picked up out of the local parks. Doc had taken them before the JP's court and each was sentenced to his custody by the town's barber, who was also the Justice of the Peace presiding. One week of public works for persistent public drunkenness, was the sentence. The balance of the shadow crew was a collection of the morbidly obese, the totally unco-ordinated and the frail. The group, however, had common qualities: a slight fear of Doc, a proud and strong civic pride, and an evil sense of humour. As Doc explained his cunning plan to the actual team and to the shadows that morning there was a general eruption of delight at the warped genius of the man. The trap was set.

The confident, some would say, arrogant Cockburnians had arrived in town on Thursday night. Doc and his shadow team, dressed gaudily in their Broome Luggers sponsor's team shirts, met the trim and slim aquatic athletes off the plane. The shadow Muddies warmly greeted the visitors and limped and shuffled them across to the buses, where the Perth group was subtly split up into smaller groupings and helped onto two buses. This was Doc's phase one divide and conquer strategy. On the buses the first cans of ice-cold beer were popped and forced on each of the paddlers who happily gulped down the chilled contents. With friendly insistence and assistance, the drinking continued unabated as the buses made long work of a very short journey from the airport on the town's southern boundary, only a few short kilometres as the crow flies to the pub. The four old fringe dwelling alcoholics were in their version of heaven, cackling gleefully at the fantastic circumstances whereby they were serving their time. Finally they arrived at the Roebuck Bay pub where the shadows continued to perform their hydrating random strangers task admirably late into the night.

On Friday morning after a late awakening and groggy with hangovers, the Cockburn team was advised by Doc that there was to be a compulsory civic reception that afternoon and no refusal would be accepted. The buses with the annoyingly friendly Mangrove Muddies riding shotgun arrived at midday. The jaded tourists were herded on board and welcomed with a pint cup of a refreshing, but secretly dangerously alcoholic concoction. It was local rotgut white rum disguised in the sweet orange mush of chilled mango juice which they all drank on the way to the reception. The Broome mayor and his councillors were in on the joke. The civic reception, fuelled by large amounts of ice-cold beer and gallons of the deadly mango punch, dragged on for several hours. Finally after midnight, those Cockburnians who could walk were helped off the busses back at the Roey and cruelly diverted like chemically concussed sheep into the sorting yard of the garden bar. Meanwhile, Bill Peters on coach's orders was in bed on the Shark Cat at nine and fast asleep within minutes, dreaming the dreams of the innocent. Bonnie Anu and eighteen other young Broome residents were similarly tucked up early and away with the fairies for a good night's sleep.

On Saturday morning the Cockburn paddlers rose late. From the sweaty feral stench of the bus's seats or floors; from the various bush beds under fragrant frangipani trees, mosquito and bull-ant bitten, cramped, dehydrated and exhausted, hardly-tuned ex-athletes struggled red-eyed to their rooms for showers and to crash moaning on their beds. At midday the Muddies were banging happily on their doors.

'Rise and shine, boys and girls!' Mozzie, Mavis and the other shadows cajoled their shattered victims. 'Come on, dears, training in thirty minutes.'

Down at the water and despite their obvious alcoholic distress, it was soon apparent to Doc as he swept his boat hysterically crewed by the shadows in a comic unco-ordinated tangle, that the Cockburn crew was still a dangerous foe. It was obvious to Doc that partying was part of the culture of the Perth based dragon boaters. Although down on petrol, it was clear to Doc, and also to the actual Mangrove Muddies hiding back off the beach in the mangroves spying on the training, that the Cockburn paddlers were still strong. In fact they were clearly enjoying the blow out. The problem was that with physical exertion in the tropical heat they got thirsty again.

The other problem was that Doc had organised that the Cockburn team march in the Shinju Matsuri parade through Broome at seven o'clock that night. After training they met in the bar and drank until the parade arrived. On the roadway a conga line of locals gathered in a variety of local esoteric sporting, business, or other macro-interest groups. The locals cheekily called for the *terrorists* to join them. Excited at the welcome and with an enthusiastic slightly high-kneed gait, the blue and yellow uniformed visiting mob were herded together by Doc and marched out of the bar and onto the road. To the slow-step provided by dragon boat drums strapped to local drummers, the parade headed for the town oval via Chinatown. With the knowledge and collusion of the entire community the team was then enveloped and overwhelmed by the locals for Doc's phase two. They were divided and conquered all night the locals forcing fatty, clogging food and strong liquor down the relatively foreign throats until the early hours.

Sunday morning. Shattered terrorist paddlers were scattered far and wide over the Broome township and surrounds. As they awoke, the heat of the rising tropical sun started rivulets of mango-tangy sweat as fatigued, dehydrated bodies and cell-reduced brains tried to rouse. The big race was at ten o'clock. When the Cockburn coach counted bodies at the back-packers he found only five damaged paddlers who had somehow got away and staggered back to the rooms on autopilot.

Worried but not yet flustered, the coach urgently rang for his new good mate Doc on a mobile number that Doc had been available on 24/7 since their arrival in town.

No answer.

He tried the police station. Not there. Don't know how to get in touch.

He rang the bus company. No answer.

He rang hotel reception. No answer.

He ran downstairs and found that the reception door was locked with blinds drawn, and the only staff he could locate was the yardman who knew 'nuffin'.

Anxious, the coach gathered up his five sad and sorry paddlers and rang Broome Taxis.

'You are from where? The Roey? Ah, the Perth team! Sorry, all our cabs are busy.'

'What the fuck! That's got to be bullshit!'

'Sorry mate try at ten-oh-one.'

'The race is at ten! Fuck! Fuck! Fuck!'

The coach herded the five and they walked.

'It's only a couple of k anyway to the bay,' he reassured them as they trudged off in an involuntary zigzag, heads so sore that most physically held them with their own hands as if to hold them together. On the way almost magically the team assembled; out of bushes, running down roads, joining on the end of the sad procession. By the time they arrived at the beach the Cockburnians had a team. Not the team selected, but basically a group that could compete and should still 'kick the arse' of the Muddies that they had seen at practice the day before.

'But wait just one fucking minute!' The coach swore.

Maybe not the young, muscular, fit and smiling team they now saw sitting waiting in the shallows in their boat. And there on the bank waiting and waving in welcome, each armed with blue and yellow cheerleader pom-poms and forming an almost, sort of, human tunnel to the Cockburn boat, stood the tragic mob of hospitable shadows that they thought they were racing.

'Shit! We've been had!'

On the water one hundred desperate metres out from the finish buoys the Muddies reacted in beautiful unison to Doc's call with even bigger, even longer bites of the water. The sleek boat jumped forward from the line of surging bows with the grinning dragonhead inching out from the fleet. At this the three other sweeps reacted and responded with screamed variations of the demand from the gasping crews for 'POWAAAAAAAAAAAAR!' and the fight was on.

'HOOOOOME YOU BASTARDS on THREE, TWO, ONE... HOOOME!' screamed Doc, and grunted in time with the rate set by the strokes in seat one. 'HOME! HOME! HOME! HOME!' The young drummer smashed the goatskins in a frantic beat. Over that final gut-busting thirty, twenty, ten metres of heart-pounding effort the Muddies fought the good fight. As a unit, the team withstood the immense pressure from the crews on either side. Finally the dragonhead crossed through the buoys a short surging half neck in front to the hysterical cheers of the proud supporters on the beach.

'First Place in the Shinju Matsuri Dragon Classic, the Mangrove Muddies!' echoed the PA, and the locals on the beach rejoiced, laughing, clapping and chanting, 'Muddees! Muddeeess! Muddeeess!'

'You know, it's amazing what a small town can do if you all pull together,' proudly exclaimed the mayor.

In the winning boat two exhausted paddling partners in seat seven, Bill Peters and Bonnie Anu back-slapped and hugged everyone they could reach. The vessel turned smoothly beach-ward with its race momentum as a smug Doc manoeuvred the long craft back into the shallow waters with an expert twist of the long sweep oar. As the bow crunched on the sand of the beach the boat lurched from side to side as if the dragon was belly laughing, and the twenty bandits rolled out of her to rejoice in the salty waters in a convoluted mess of slippery limbs. Bill found himself wrapped around the sensuous bikinied beauty of Bonnie Anu in the warm salty waters.

And he was suddenly intently aware of how damned good she felt.

10

PURPLE RAIN

On the other side of the continent at the Concord Oval, Dan and Annie had still not been discovered. This colosseum was usually the home to the various football codes of the city where the modern mortal gods of sport battled each other. The great Australian game of Aussie rules football, more native to the State of Victoria, had crept across the border to challenge the more traditional NSW codes of rugby league and rugby union. This night, however, it was society's gods and goddesses of the arts, the princes and princesses of excess, of music, rhythm, and dance who took centre stage. They played to the masses from the temporary meccano construction set sitting slap bang in the midfield. And all around that stage pressed tight against each other and against crowd control barricades were the city's young and some not so young lovers of music and a good time. By eight-thirty there were tens of thousands in the arena. Although the young Mascot couple were later confirmed by the science of forensic pathology as probably the first victims to die that night from the poison curse of the purple camel, the two young lovers were soon joined by many more.

Rico Florenza died at twenty-four years of age. He was a promising young professional rugby league player for the Blacktown Lightning. Rico had gone to the concert at Concord on Friday night in the company of three teammates, Bill Wright, Sione Smith and Phil Charles. In the early hours of Saturday a devastated Phillip John Charles sat in the police command bus parked outside the oval in a stationary convoy of police and emergency service vehicles. The white-liveried bus was a purpose-built mobile crime scene control vehicle. Phil and his official interviewer sat in a soundproof bay while he sadly, haltingly, told of the events of the prior eight hours that had changed his future forever and taken the lives of his three closest buddies.

'I bought them...it was me,' Phil said to the sombre uniformed inquiry officer across from him at the small fold-out table. The constable checked that the unit's digital video recorder was glowing green for go. A force of habit to ensure the interview was being captured.

'Just tell me what happened, Phil.'

'I fucking bought em. Me! Shit!' And he sobbed and sank his head onto the table.

'Okay, mate, just take your time, son. Another coffee?'

Phil straightened, determined now to get this over and done with. 'No thanks. Okay, I bought four tabs of E—the boys all gave me their fifty, and I went to the shitters and made the buy.'

'By the shitters you mean...?'

'Yeah, I mean the portaloos near the main gate.'

'Who did you buy them off?' the officer asked.

'Listen, if I knew the prick I would give him straight up to you...but I had never seen him before. Viet bloke, normal, you know, short, black hair, trendy rap type clothes, nothing about him any different from any other Viet.

'I knew where he was selling. Some chick told us to just go talk to the Viet near the shitters. He was there, I said how much, he said fifty a tab, I said give us four. He said give me two hundred and I did, and he gives me four tabs.'

'What did the tablets look like, Phil?' The officer looked up from his notes.

'Coloured purple with a stamped camel design.'

'Good, Phil, what time did you do the buy?'

'It was quite late. We got there late, had a few drinks after work at the Workingman's Club, we all met up there. We caught a cab about nine-thirty-ish.'

The constable made notes on an A4 lined pad in clear deliberate view of the CCTV lens.

'Yeah, we went by the mosh pit first then Sione was talking to this chick he knew who was on eccies. She said they were top gear and told us where to buy some. So I volunteered. Fuck! I volunteered! And anyway I bought them.'

'Go on, son,' the middle aged officer urged.

'So I came back and the boys had stayed near the mosh pit watching the chicks dance, then the Graceful Fred started their set on the main stage. I gave the boys each a tab and we all swallowed them. Then we sort of just began to mix and talk to the chicks near the mosh pit.' Phil went quiet, stared the thousand-yarder as his memory cruelly recovered the images.

'What happened then, son?'

'Shit, it was only, say, fifteen to twenty minutes later—that was all. Then I saw the boys were in the shit.'

'How do you mean?'

'Mate, I was getting the good buzz, my pill was good stuff; it was strong E. But the boys within about five minutes of each other just fucken fell over in the mosh pit—you know—just sort of rolled around. I thought they were just pullin the piss for the chicks; everyone just ignored them at first. They just rolled round on the grass. Then the Freds began to play Dead Fred, you know, their big hit. And then fucken hundreds of cunts came racing into the pit! They just fucken ran over the top of the boys! Mashed them! There was fuck all I could do! I was screaming, yelling at the cunts to get off the boys, but no one could even hear me...'

Much later, following the clinical inspection of the boys' damaged bodies, the forensic pathologist recorded that multiple contusions and fractures of the three strongly built young men were in fact suffered after their deaths. Death was found to have been by strychnine poisoning believed to have been a component of the three purple camel tablets swallowed by Florenza, Wright and Smith. The last souls to leave the oval.

11

CRUEL SUMMER

Good morning, ladies and gentlemen. Welcome to this In Depth News exclusive. By ten pm last evening, Friday the thirteenth of September, seventy-one patrons of the event known as the Concord Mega Bash had died or were dying as the result of a mass poisoning. Another twenty-six persons are currently in the intensive care wards of the Sydney's major hospitals being treated for poisoning. Sydney's medical facilities are stretched.

In Depth News has been advised that it is suspected that the poison was an ingredient in the illicit cult party drug known on the streets as ecstasy.

In Depth's investigation at this early time has revealed that the police, the event organisers, medical staff, and security staff were not immediately aware of the enormity of the problem last evening. By nine o'clock there were in excess of forty-five thousand persons within the venue.

We are told that the poison is strychnine—rat poison!

Early investigation has revealed that in most cases friends tragically attempted to protect the victims from the authorities by carrying or dragging them away from medical help into dark secluded areas of the venue. At nine forty-five the main act, No-Root-No-Ride, a heavy metal group from Texas, USA, began their set on the main stage. We have spoken exclusively to the band's road manager. He has told our reporter on the scene that the group members were supplied ecstasy tablets purchased from inside the venue.

Evidence, including CCTV footage taken by the organisers, shows the group on stage and playing the opening number of their set. The footage, which we cannot release at this stage on the request of the New South Wales Police and the coroner, clearly shows that as the band began to play the second number, first the drummer Bobby-Ralph Cleaver, then the lead singer Jeremiah Tuska begin to show signs that they were in serious distress. With the band members falling to the stage, the event organiser immediately called for medical assistance to the main stage.

Medical assistance did not arrive on the stage until fifteen minutes after the call to the medical centre. Our investigation suggests that the reasons for this delay were twofold. First was simply the difficulty of access through the crowd around the stage. And then the fact that from nine-thirty there were sudden and increasing calls for emergency aid from frantic friends and relatives of victims from all over the venue.

With the death on stage in front of some forty-five thousand patrons of the major international act NRNR, the organisers advised the audience that concert was cancelled and appealed for calm. However, it appears that the vast majority of the crowd had no understanding of what was happening and they erupted into unrest. With a massive riot brewing the police officer in charge of the event organised that the next scheduled band play a set on the secondary stage. This action allowed time for police reinforcements to be called and to arrive at Concord.

Witnesses from the event have told In Depth News that it took about an hour for the audience to finally understand what had happened. They found out not from the increasing police presence, not from the organiser, but from the vibe, the buzz, the grapevine that ran through the massive swell of humanity, that people had died, were dying.

Eventually, the police were able to get people out of the venue.

Seventy-one of our fellow citizens are gone. All died the same terrible death. Human bodies dot the oval like a battlefield.

The NSW Police are now tasked to seize and freeze the biggest crime scene that any police officer could have ever have imagined in his worst law enforcement nightmare. The investigation of this nation's worst mass murder has begun and In Depth News will keep you updated with every development as the police investigation begins.

The shot faded, Clapton's *Tears in Heaven* softly flooded out into TV-land as the In Depth News promo imposed itself across images of the bodies lying on the oval. Then the vision switched to a light beer commercial.

12

BLACK PEARL

A few hours earlier in Broome, young Bill Peters, champion Shinju Matsuri dragon boater, was also experiencing a muscular and ultimately involuntary convulsion. In truth, Bill's little convulsion was more a contraction of about the only muscle in his alcohol-infused body that wasn't aching from the dragon boat racing earlier that day.

At this midnight hour he was on the darkened third floor bedroom balcony of the Roebuck Inn. He and Bonnie Anu stood on that balcony, hidden by the fragrant lushness of a big frangipani tree.

Bill's exquisite convulsion was forced by the peaking of the intolerable sensations of the erogenous zones of his striving muscularity. A small but powerful mass of muscle fibres within him squeezed hard. The contraction with the force of the young and long-frustrated, shot the potent soup of spermatozoa's slippery sugars and proteins out of his rigid member into the satiny vise of the woman who held him there almost unbearably hot and tight. Bonnie Anu moaned in her own release as she felt it pour from him into her; that primal hot infusion.

Bonnie leaned forward weakly; sweating and panting on her elbows on the wooden balustrade of the tiny balcony, with Bill still joined from behind, between. His big hands held her slim ebony hips. Their athletic bodies conjoined sweat-wet in the yellow moonlight, swaying weakly now with the final rhythms of the waltz of lust and sexual pump.

Bill finally retracted from her, turned her by the hips to face him, held her enveloped, kissed her soft and long.

Down at ground level, backed into a dark corner of the bar under the fragrant spread of the frangipani tree, Doc Patrick grinned an evil dingo-grin. He had witnessed the connection through the incomplete camouflage of the garden bar's tree canopy with a voyeur's envious fascination. And even as there was an angry primal stirring from his own yeasty crotch, he blessed the sensual endeavour with a muttered and slurred, 'Ya fucken dirty slut-bitch!'

Wordless, Bill slickly lifted Bonnie, smiling and dreamy, and carried his lover gently into the room they had commandeered. They lay together on the cool sheets of the double bed under the warm lazy swirl of the ceiling fan. In his loving embrace she fell into her dreams and he shook his head with wonder at the turn of events that had rewarded him so wonderfully this night.

Bill laughed quietly in his recollection of the triumph of the dragon boat ambush that Doc had so masterfully put together earlier that day. The Cockburn paddlers had taken the loss reasonably well with an ironic appreciation of the huge and co-ordinated community effort. They recognised that it was a conspiracy that Doc and the entire town of Broome had planned and executed to set them up for the fall. In truth there was fuck all they could do about it anyway. They were forced to accept the loss gracefully even as they were warmly welcomed back to the shore by the entire town.

To defuse any passionate complaint or indignant protest, Doc had the boat met at the beach initially by the infamous shadows. They had quietly sympathised, hugged, teased and comforted the shattered southern egos with warm humour, until the Town Beach was soon one big happy Broome party again. From the beach the entire town had flowed back up to the big garden bar at the Roey where massive amounts of food and huge amounts of the mango punch and cold ales were waiting. Once the local band, the Pigrum Brothers, hit the raised stage the party really began.

Bill had found himself deliberately keeping close to Bonnie in the garden bar. That morning wrestling in the tide each had realised what he supposed later should always have been an inevitable attraction between two young, healthy adults with similar interests and outlooks.

Now, as he lay in bed next to Bonnie, and particularly when moaning on top of her later in the night, he had again thought of Gypsy with an inexplicable stab of guilt. It was of course his confusion about his feelings toward the unattainable Gypsy that he now realised might have distracted him about Bonnie. This young Aboriginal woman had a natural and exotic sexy beauty, but she was a friend of Gypsy's. So in his initial dealings with Bonnie he related to her from that base. But also, Bill thought, when he employed her he had automatically assumed a boss-employee-type role that should necessarily force limits and inhibitions, real and perceived.

'Really,' he thought, as he lay beside her and she snuffled warmly against his side, he was curious now as to why had he been so bloody slow, and he moved to kiss her forehead in the dark.

It had all really started thanks to the Pigrum Brothers' thumping melodic rhythms in combination with the close company of the dragon boaters and their admiring public. Bill had been standing companionably close to Bonnie in the mass of partygoers in the bar. Bonnie had stood in front of him, both facing the band. They had been squashed warmly together which had resulted in Bonnie's taut sarong-covered buttocks rotating in tantalising circles against him. At first he tried to maintain a centimetre or so polite gap between their bodies. But with the mangorum imbibed by Bonnie and by him, the music, the crush and, he later discovered, Bonnie's cheeky deliberate intent, he was soon enjoying the almost constant just-a-fraction-too-much-friction. As he hardened under the cover of the night and his cheap cotton board shorts, any doubts about the inevitability of the moment disappeared when long, sensuous fingers reached back, found, traced and then held his pulsing rigid outline. And then Bonnie turned her face back in the darkness and kissed him.

It was he who had desperately but gently pulled her away under cover of the frangipanis into the darkest corner to explore the moment. But it was she who had taken his hand and led him from kiss to kiss into the dark back entrance of the hotel stairs and finally up onto the balcony of the third floor bedroom. With sarong, shorts and shirts near torn away they were soon naked, and at first he had tried to taste and tease her on the room's wide bed. But it was then, when later he looked back in analysis of their relationship, that he first discovered her quirk for sexual adventure. For Bonnie led him outside onto the balcony, turned teasingly away from him as she bent over and then guided his heated impatience into that most heavenly consummation. They were in public view on that skinny balcony only ten metres above friend and foe below, including Bonnie's immediate family, her Uncle Rock and her two very big brothers. She, by her later admission, and then he, found that an extra thrill in the circumstance, of danger, of the risk of public discovery added to their intense excitement. But as he thought back she awoke from her post-orgasmic nap and rolled herself cat-lightly over onto him. Without speech she reached a soft hand back, holding, reviving and guiding him again, and he sighed into her soft, full-lipped kiss and wondered where this little chapter in his life would take him.

13

FIELDS OF FIRE

Seventy-one bodies were medically examined where they lay on the grounds of Concord Oval. Having died on Friday night through Saturday, they were formally medically declared as deceased, forensically identified by precise official number, toe-tagged, photographed, videotaped, and GPS-plotted to an exact location on the killing field. That massive task took time and finally by five o'clock on the Sunday afternoon they had all been removed one by one in a sad procession from the arena. The forensic processes involved were based upon well researched and logically prepared and presented police operational plans. Plans developed over decades from other previously experienced, subsequently imagined, and then well-rehearsed mass trauma and death scenarios. Plans for tragedies such as Jumbo jets smashing down from the skies; packed Sydney Harbour ferries rolling over or the like; and, more recently, for potential internationally motivated terrorist attacks.

In the cool light of day early on the Saturday morning the written word of those coldly precise protocols gave the crime-scene police and the scientists evidentially correct guidelines to follow. Numbered bullet points instructed the officers what to do from the handling of the bodies to the collection of the real evidence. Lists required the capture and protections of each evidential aspect that included recommended recording medias relevant to the subsequent reconstruction of the scene, and of the scenes within that larger scene. There were orders as to basic communication, staffing and logistical requirements. There was advice, suggestions and listings of the legal requirements necessary to identify and to protect the evidential chain that may lead an investigator from that clue of lost humanity back to the cause of each death. Such calm control of such a scene was known by experience of this and of other nations' law enforcement services to be totally necessary. This was particularly so at such a large and a terrible scene where emotion and confusion could otherwise interfere with or destroy vital clues and evidence. If the forensic investigators minutely controlled such a massive crime scene then, after the forensic dust had settled, the police might find they had in fact already discovered such evidence necessary to present to the inevitable court proceedings. Legal proceedings that could include criminal, coronial or even civil hearings.

At the very least every individual personal tragedy had to be relived at the Coroner's Court, as modern society by law values each human life and properly requires to know where, when, how and most importantly, why each sad human shape had had its mysterious spark snuffed out at the Concord Oval.

And so progressively through the late afternoon and into the night of that Saturday and into Sunday, truck by refrigerated truckload of bulging body bags were transported to the city's big teaching hospital, the Royal Sydney Hospital.

The state's contracted Forensic Pathology Unit, the FPU, was based at the RSH. Its facilities include the nation's largest morgue that could store up to one hundred bodies racked in the big steel fridges. The busy public hospital's morgue was based in brightly lit, white tiled clinical rooms in the cold bowels of the massive building; symbolically underground of the healing floors. As well as the huge fridges, the icy chill of which stalled the disintegration and decomposition of the human cells, the FPU comprised two large marbled rooms. Each of those cold wards allowed for the display of twenty bodies at any one time, laid in rows of ten down each side. Each corpse was rolled from trolley to the stainless steel table in turn. There the pathologists clinically dissected the dearly departed in specified order to provide a scientific explanation as to why that human being was no more. This was the teaching place where nervous student doctors saw their first dead, and who then could practice on the uncomplaining fibre of those who lay in the macabre rows.

This was the place where Detective Superintendent Fredrick Hall was early on Monday morning overseeing the work of the police forensic and evidence teams. A thirty-year veteran of the NSW Police Service, Fred, as he was called by his boss the commissioner, had joined the police as a recruit straight out of the Australian Army. He had served his nation as an intel officer in Bosnia and Iraq where he had worked three rotations always at or near the bloody coalface. Now aged fifty-nine, Fred was due to retire in twelve months.

Detective Superintendent Hall was a well-respected investigator administrator and personnel manager. His reputation and success as a criminal investigator related in the main to his precise and impeccable attention to the minutiae of any criminal case that he was assigned to. 'F–all gets by F Hall,' his detectives at City Central would boast with humorous respect for their boss.

Early on the cool Sydney Saturday morning, Fred had been woken at home by the electronic klaxon of the bedside phone. It was a call from the Boss herself, and the commissioner quietly alerted Fred to the immensity of the human tragedy at Concord the night before.

'It's yours, mate. I have appointed you to lead the Combined Task Force. You are in charge, but you will be assisted by the feds and customs because of the drug angle. Use whatever men and resources you need. Fred, this is a big one. We need a result,' the clearly worried Commissioner pleaded with her top investigator.

Fred quickly gathered his senses having woken foggy from the romantic red-wine lubricated dinner the night before. He had been snuggled close to his wife Di, who now breathed softly beside him in the warm bed. Di rolled away from him and his conversation, muffling her head with the pillow with a resigned moan; used as she was to her weekends being intruded upon by the demands of her man's job.

The Boss continued: 'It's because of the scale of it, Fred. The CTF will be multi-organisational, feds and customs. But you're OIC, mate. The feds will work with you. That's because of course it's possibly a terrorist action. At the moment anything's possible. No one has claimed responsibility yet. I need you downtown ASAP. A meeting at my office at nine.'

And with that Fred Hall, although reluctant to leave his snug marital bed, but with an excitement that every experienced copper has when the big jobs come, gently pecked Di on her warm cheek and rolled from the bed to shower.

By eight-forty, Detective Superintendent Hall looking all business in a crisp white shirt, dark blue silk tie, black suit, and smelling sweetly of the expensive French aftershave his wife insisted on spoiling him with, strode out of the lift on the top floor of Sydney Central. He was waved through into the commissioner's office by the Boss's superbly efficient PA Ms Gladys Wright, a fifty-something widow of immaculate manners and plastically coiffed presentation.

Even as he greeted NSW Police Commissioner Margaret Gibson with a firm handshake, as always Fred's gaze was irresistibly drawn to the view from the office over to the beautiful harbour. An ever-stunning visual feast. The view was of the contrasting panorama of the structural steel majesty of the suspension bridge that so distinguished and identified the location, against the graceful swooping lines of the opera house to the east.

Fred was first in, and Gladys soon had his usual long black filtered coffee before him on the polished deep red-grained lustre of the jarrah conference table. Meanwhile his employer and friend of three decades Margaret Gibson passed him the first situation report, known in police-speak as a sit-rep. While he read, she sipped from her mug of sweet milky tea in companionable silence.

Just before nine Gladys announced the arrival of the other meeting participants, among them a weary Inspector Denton of the Concord Station, he having worked sleepless through the night. Fred shook hands with Commander Bob Hopkins of the Australian Federal Police. Bob was a slightly built, bespectacled officer and a respected professional crime fighter who had worked with the state police on other major operations in the past in his role as the senior NSW federal policeman. Also present at the request of Bob Hopkins when the team was being put together was Customs Senior Agent Sally Ryan, an officer of Her Majesty's Australian Customs Service. Her speciality was the analysis and co-ordination nationally of intelligence concerning the importation into Australia of illicit drugs.

Fred had read that the initial pathology of the first half dozen bodies from the morgue had confirmed that the mass deaths had been caused by a new synthetic version of the naturally derived poison, strychnine.

The early interview results from friends and family of the deceased were pointing towards a common factor. All the victims were known to have ingested the party drug ecstasy immediately before their passing. It did appear likely that the poison was possibly carried in the drug.

Others present around the table were a mix of senior NSW police, some in uniform, some not, and a few of the senior forensic scientists from the government CSIRO labs, some of whom had already assisted at the crime scene, and who would have a vital ongoing role in the events.

'Welcome folks,' Commissioner Gibson bought the gathering to order after Gladys had catered to the caffeine requirements of each of the group of twenty or so now seated around the oval table.

The Commissioner Gibson made introductions as she identified and in précis professionally qualified each man and woman present. Now Gladys sat beside the boss, notebook in hand, her old-fashioned shorthand busily but unnecessarily supporting the digital recording of the meeting.

'Okay, I declare this meeting open. I ask Inspector Denton to brief the meeting on the situation that occurred at the Concord Oval last night,' said Commissioner Gibson.

She nodded at Inspector Denton who was too tired to be overawed by the highly ranked company he was amongst. Denton referred to his notebook, more as a comfort cushion in this esteemed company than as a memory guide, as the events of the night were burned into his memory forever. He presented to the group his sit-rep in typical police verbal shorthand.

'I was O/C Event at Concord, known as the Mega Bash party, with an expectation of fifty-five thousand to attend, and some forty thousand pre-sales. My team was on site at 1400 hours yesterday, Friday, in preparation for gates open at 1700 hours. Police scene command base was situated behind the main stage, near the main gate. The crowd built steadily from 1700 hours with the warm-up bands starting on the main stage at 1800. I had a team of fifty uniformed, some twenty plain-clothes inquiry officers, and advice that Sydney Drug Squad would also be covert in the venue over the weekend. We had Canine, Tactical Response and Armed Offenders Squad on stand-by if required.'

Denton looked up and was reassured by a friendly nod from Fred Hall to continue, which he did, basically echoing what the In Depth

News coverage and preliminary police sitreps had already informed each person present. Ten minutes later the inspector concluded his presentation.

The commissioner spoke: 'Thank you, Inspector. Unless anyone has more to ask of you immediately, I suggest that you may want to get away to hit the computer for your initial reporting,' and she scanned the meeting with a questioning look.

'Just a quick one, Inspector,' said Fred Hall. 'Any seizures from the search of the crowd as they left the venue?' The inspector looked up through dark-ringed eyes.

'No, sir. The word got pretty quickly around, I think, that we were searching at the exit choke point. I do know that a lot of stuff was found just dropped on the ground or in the bins further back inside.'

Fred Hall spoke, marking his ground as the operational commander, much like the alpha wolf. 'Thank you very much, Inspector Denton. By all accounts including your own very professional report to us today, your actions reflect well on yourself and the service, well done.'

'Thank you, sir,' said the younger man, and he stood dressed still in his crumpled dirt and sweat stained blues from the previous night's endeavours.

With a respectful nod to the gathering he was off into the lift and down several levels to the seventh floor, the assigned operational area known as the War Room at Sydney HQ.

These were to be the new operation's offices. They were always kept empty, always ready between operations for this very scenario. Here, Denton would record his and others' actions at his level of command into the virginal database of the forensic criminal investigation operation. This was a database that was destined to grow by many gigabytes in the months to come.

Meanwhile, in the commissioner's boardroom, the first meeting of Operation Concord continued, run now by Fred Hall. The crime scene commanders, then the police forensic and CSIRO scientific input was presented throughout the morning and into the afternoon of that first day. The evidence so far collected in minute detail was calmly presented by still and by digital video footage showing the terrible, but professionally fascinating scenes displayed by the overhead projector. When Gladys had electronically whirred shut the curtains the picture-postcard view of the beautiful harbour was swapped for the digital panorama of mass death and destruction on the screen and that was just as fascinating to the crime professionals within.

Late in the day when each report had been presented they knew what they had. Seventy-one citizens were dead. Cause, strychnine poisoning. Source, purple camel-embossed ecstasy tablets containing a mixture of MDMA and the deadly white chemically concentrated rat poison. What they really had in forensic effect was a mass murder beyond anyone in that room's previous experience or imagination.

'But, people...and it's a big but...' said Fred Hall at five that afternoon, 'is last night the last of it?' His was a rhetorical question and there was reflective hush around the table.

'Because now we know. We know from interviews of survivors, from analysis of the camel tablets found discarded inside Concord, that not all of those tablets were tainted. Some, lots of them in fact, are pure MDMA. Is this thing over? Or are we going to have more deaths? Is this incident a deliberate criminal act? Is this an act of extremist religious terrorism—or is it just a terrible accident? The answers to these questions, my friends, are our professional task and our sombre responsibility to discover. We meet tomorrow. Sunday morning at 0730 hours. Level 7 as a command group to plan and to manage the ongoing operation. Right?'

Fred rose to close the meeting just as the boardroom door opened. An impressive head entered despite the Do Not Disturb sign. All of the senior command and specialist section heads turned to see Gladys's 'do' precede her face by some centimetres, having held its impressive form all day. Fred knew that this immaculately professional woman would only interrupt with good cause and gestured for her to come hither. The commissioner's PA made her way by force of habit to her boss who listened to a whispered communication and then waved her over properly to Fred Hall, as the others around the table shuffled together papers and notes and tidied up ready to leave.

'People.' Fred spoke as Gladys backed away from their brief conversation. 'I have just received advice of another incident where it appears the same batch of ecstasy tablets may be the cause of deaths. Another five deaths, early hours of this morning at a nightclub in Oxford Street.' He looked at Gladys who nodded her unnecessary confirmation as the messenger. 'Local Paddington detectives are still at the scene; the lines of communication have only just come together as the local boys treated it as an overdose situation initially. Roger, I need you and a team straight down there to tie it all together,' Fred barked at one of his command team detective inspectors, who nodded and made to leave the meeting.

'Okay, the rest of you tomorrow as planned, please, and tonight…' he paused and looked across at the Sydney Police Command's Public Relations OC Al Musta, 'tonight, Al, we need you to get the message out loud and clear to the public of this city, to Australia and to the world. Use all available media—you ride the purple camel at your own peril.'

14

FLESH FOR FANTASY

It was to have been a celebration of the beautiful people of Sydney's chic salons. A gathering of the artistically inclined dressers of the public hair, the fancy fondlers of the follicles of the city's A-listers, with many a fringe and pseudo A-lister and yes, many more B- and C-plusses among them. It was the annual Sydney Hairdressers Ball, held on Black Friday the thirteenth of September when the best of the best celebrated their own self-promoted, indulgent, but generally limited celebrity with the traditional party and awards ceremony at the Golden Fish nightclub.

The Golden Fish sat bright and gaudy in Oxford Street in the trendy inner-city suburb of Paddington. These guys and girls knew how to party. The profession they had chosen, while not quiet the oldest, attracted more than its fair share of the narcissistic, the self-centred, flashy seekers of the sensual experience. Among them were those who sought to heighten the mortally restricted capabilities of escapism with a chemical friend.

By the time Lewie Hong, an outrageously camp Vietnamese-bred hanger-on of the sub-culture that was the industry, had arrived at the nightclub at one o' clock on the Saturday morning the joint was jumping. The intense techno-throb of the music pounded the senses in time with the synchronised light show, and the dance floor appeared to be a heaving homogenous mass. It was a huge near-naked hermaphrodite body topped by a moving sea of beautiful heads and perfect hair.

Lewie was an affectionately accepted member of the extended family. He was the drug dealer to the stars. The candy man to the needy of the latest, and the consistently purest of the party feel-good drugs that this self-anointed social elite chose to indulge in. And they indulged at a significantly higher ratio then other target customer groups of the Spider Gang. Incongruously perhaps to some, Lewie was also a Spider soldier.

Lewie kissy-kissed his way through the throng of sweaty sexuality on the dance floor to a curtained corner booth. His special friend Neville, a late-middle-aged Caucasian bloke, awkwardly escorted him. A chartered public accountant in his former life, the older man had only recently come bursting out of the closet. He had, somewhat to his own surprise and certainly to his adult children's supreme horror, found himself a young Asian lover. Neville now pretended that he protected Lewie, albeit self-consciously with a clumsy paternalistic affection and a desperate love. Lewie sat prettily now in the darkened booth and began to ply his sinister trade. Cash money for small hexagonal tablets in surreptitious under-the-table swaps.

The terrible truth, though, was that Lewie had picked up his trade supplies early on the Friday night from the gang house at Cabramatta as his balding lover Neville had waited nervously outside in the radical yellow Saab. This was the car that Lewie had suggested strongly that Neville simply *must* buy as proof of his devotion. He had sulked and withdrawn certain special favours until, against all his conservative and mathematical instincts, Neville bought the car.

The news of the unfolding tragedy at Concord Oval was unknown to Lewie and to Neville. They had spent the entire afternoon and early evening up to that point doing the business in the trendy love nest Neville had bought in both of their names, as further proof of his love for the younger man. They had only risen to shower, powder and perfume very late that Friday night to then head down to the ball to do the other business—the business that kept Lewie in gold chain bling and expensive French perfume.

As the party pumped so did Lewie's sales. But by one-thirty, within half an hour of his opening for business, the first of his glamorous customers in the nightclub began to dance the fatal fandango as the strychnine hit and the dying began. So even as seventy-one bodies were being counted at the Concord Oval through those early hours, five more tortured, but beautifully coiffed souls clicked through the turnstiles and added to the deadly total of the camel's curse.

As ambulances and night shift police cars wailed and screamed in light-flashing convoys to the Golden Fish, finally another terrible crime scene was established, controlled and subsequently forensically processed. Much later the investigators would agree that only one obvious good had come out of the night. That was that the task force now had a target: a name—the dealer. Any number of the shocked survivors at the nightclub had given up Lewie to the investigating police. The all-points-bulletin went out across police radios, text messages to mobiles and at shift briefings all over Sydney, and even via Interpol to the shocked forensic world: 'Find Lewie Hong'.

15

EYE OF THE TIGER

At seven-thirty-one on Sunday morning, Superintendent Fred Hall waited for silence in the massive open plan room that took up almost an entire floor on Level 7 of Sydney Central Police Headquarters.

This room was to be the operational home of the team assigned to the Concord Task Force (already being referred to colloquially as the CTF), for as long as it took to solve the crime. Each of the assembled police investigators, blue-uniformed and plain-clothed men and woman of various ages and years of forensic investigative experience, chatted amiably in keen anticipation of the briefing. Those chosen to do the job had been handpicked by the senior officers, themselves handpicked by Fred Hall for their varied expert skills. Here were the human elements of the jigsaw of investigative expertise that needed to come together in such a complex investigation.

Fred Hall called his troops to order and welcomed and introduced the various guests from outside the NSW force who were to work in close co-operation as a multi-faceted and agency combined task force. The AFP Commander Bob Hopkins; an ASIO special agent with an observer's role; Sally Ryan from Her Majesty's Customs; and the CSIRO scientists.

A briefing paper marked 'Strictly Confidential' was distributed to each person in the room and Fred Hall allowed a ten-minute study time. Each folder included a photograph of the suspect Lewie Hong.

As the occupants of the briefing room raised heads back up from the starkness of the facts recorded in the black computer type, Fred rose.

'Team, following this initial meeting of the entire task force you will break into your various command groups as detailed on page one of the briefing notes. At that time please move quickly and quietly to the briefing rooms nominated. At this point you are all aware in broad terms of the events at Concord Oval and at the Golden Fish nightclub Friday night into Saturday morning last. By the completion of your command team briefings each of you will know as much as I and your commanders do at this time.'

He paused and looked out into the room at the concentration of total focus that radiated back from those present.

'Before we break for the team briefings I would like you to know exactly what has happened to our fellow citizens. Those seventy-six human beings. People who died a terrible and painful death. People, please listen now to our good friend from the CSIRO Professor Phil Brayne of the Forensic Pathology Unit.'

Fred Hall held out a welcoming arm, as a small bird-like man in a white coat that matched his shock of silvery white unbrushed hair stood. He nodded to an assistant who worked the controls of the overhead projector. Another nod at a waiting senior officer near the door and the lights in the briefing room clicked off. With a buzz and bright beam of coloured light a digital display of a single camel-embossed purple pill appeared on the white drop-down screen.

The wonderfully named Professor Brayne began, 'Ladies and gentlemen, you are tasked to find out how a pill sold as the illicit street drug ecstasy has killed so many people. It is my task now to simply describe to you a brief origin and description of what these purple camel-embossed pills actually contain. That is a mixture of MDMA and strychnine.'

He paused as the chemical formulae of the drug and the poison flicked onto the screen. 'Okay, let's start with the cult drug MDMA, ecstasy, adam, XTC, E, eccies, candy, disco biscuits, love doves, mitsubishis or any one of the ever-changing multitude of other trendy names that the purchasing public give to the drug. The cute little names used by the dealers and the users in the nightclubs are somewhat understandable when confronted with the scientific description which is methylenedioxymethamphetamine. Just a wee bit harder to pronounce, particularly at the usual point of sale, a noisy nightclub or public toilet. Imagine if you will such a conversation,' and the tiny professor spoke in a tough guy Aussie accent to the supressed amusement of the gathering: 'Hey, mate...Would you like some, methyl...some methylenediox...oh fuck! Want some eccies?'

Despite the solemn purpose of the meeting the group laughed at the eccentric scientist's atrocious acting.

'Now where did it come from? Well, without talking about *zee war!* let's blame the Germans. German chemists first manufactured the drug in 1912 as they searched for useful concoctions in the legitimate field of medical research. But in this case they failed. The drug has no such use. The Americans looked again at the drug in the 1950s as that nation's military chemists researched more sinister applications for use in chemical warfare. They experimented with its effects on human guinea pigs, intended to chemically extract secrets from enemy soldiers, or to immobilise those opposing forces with a surreptitious supply to those armies.

'The Americans again experimented with MDMA in the 60s in an attempt to resolve the confrontation between Mars and Venus. It was trialled in counselling of couples, as the drug has a perceived property of making persons feel in tune with each other, at least momentarily. When in the 1980s research on poor old laboratory rats suggested that the drug may damage the brain by bleaching the grey matter, its use with humans was banned in the biggest of the legal and illicit drug markets, the USA.'

The professor took a quick drink of water and then continued. 'It was also last century in the 80s that the house music scene evolved in America, on the holiday island of Ibiza, and then into the clubs of the UK. The feel-good effects of the drug led to a resurgence of its use by the affluent sensation-seeking youth of the western world. This demographic just wanted to dance all night, and love everyone in the vicinity for a few hours of escapism from the grind.

'As with any other of the illicit drugs, where there was demand the entrepreneurial criminal underworld saw only opportunity. It was not long before the purchasing public was being cheated with doctored, adulterated and sometimes totally fraudulent mixtures flooding the market. Unsuspecting and naive users were often supplied tablets of varying concoctions of amphetamines, ketamines, heroin, and in some famous cases fish tank cleaners and dog worming tablets, being sold at huge mark up on the veterinary supply prices.' He paused again— another sip. 'So that, ladies and gentlemen, is a quick history lesson on MDMA.'

The professor nodded at his assistant working the mouse on the laptop and some examples of the white crystalline poison appeared on the screen.

'Now, strychnine is an ancient and deadly biologically derived poison processed from the plant *strychos nux vomica* and other related plants. At point of legitimate sale to those involved in the eradication of rats and other nasty vermin or creatures unfortunate enough to be a nuisance to modern man, the poison is colourless and crystalline but is marked by having an extremely bitter taste. In humans the fatal dose has been found to vary depending upon the victim. But research and history has roughly concluded that as small a dose as five to ten milligrams has caused the typically pain-racked convulsive death in man, woman or child.'

The professor paused. 'So far we have found from the tainted tablets seized that they average one hundred to one hundred and fifty milligrams of strychnine. One hundred and fifty milligrams in each professionally mixed, compressed and packaged camel-stamped three-hundred milligram pill. But we have also discovered something dreadfully different with these pills. These pills contain a highly concentrated form of strychnine that the scientific world has not seen before. Ladies and gentlemen, we estimate this synthetic variation is ten times more powerful than usual.'

The investigators looked up at Brayne almost as one.

'From the science of poison researchers' recorded data, where a human being has deliberately or inadvertently fallen victim to the effects of the rat poison, it has been discovered that from ingestion the crystals work within five to thirty minutes. As with the old *ratus ratus*, the human victim's death experience involves muscular convulsions of terrifying, even backbreaking force as the muscles spasm in intense bursts of fatal energy. The victims remain horribly conscious during these painful periods of hyper-flexia,' the scientist paused as if for effect.

'Then there is an added attraction to any morbid witness. It is that of the typical and horrifying smile of death labelled by the ancients *risus sardonicus*, as the muscles of the face pull the face involuntarily into the lie of a smile. Death can be slow as the muscular tensions prevent the lungs from drawing precious air and the exhausted victim fades from respiratory failure.'

The professor sat down, the lights came on and the sombre officers filed silently out to the various briefing teams.

16

SUSPICION TORMENTS MY HEART

And then they found Van.

They found him on the Wednesday following the concert weekend. In all the distracting excitement of the mass of death and destruction and the resultant media blitz, the Spiders had suddenly realised that no one had seen their courier for near on a week after he had arrived tired but triumphant back at the gang's HQ.

When the seventy-one bodies had been taken from the oval the gang did not connect at that time that the cause was their supply of purple camels. The fatal pills were, after all, only about five thousand in number amongst one hundred thousand. Huge amounts of the untainted tablets had been moved to the customers through the usual networks with generally glowing reports on the purity and lovey-dovey effects of the product. It was not until the massacre at the Hairdressers Ball at the Golden Fish nightclub in trendy Oxford Street that the penny had dropped with a clunk! That was because Lewie Hong had reported in a tearful, panicked description the events in the darkened hall of pleasure and pain.

Growing suspicion and concern arose in the Spider Gangs higher echelon meetings. They tucked Lewie and his friend Neville safely away, and then they tried to contact Van. But he was not answering either his mobile or the landline at his apartment. The coded messages left for him in increasingly strident demands on message banks went unanswered.

And so late that Wednesday afternoon two senior soldiers drove to the apartment block intending find their man, even if that meant entering Van's apartment by force or persuasive coercion.

As the gang arrived however, Senior Constable Reg Knight and his offsider Constable Thao Lee had just pulled up at the security gate of Van's apartment block in the Cabramatta Station East incident patrol car. The two glowering Spiders saw that the hated blue gang had beaten them to it. The Spider driver cruised past and stopped against the curb adjacent to the bustling currents of ethnicity on the broad pavements, and watched proceedings.

The reason that the two day-shift coppers were there was that a hire car was overdue. Van had given a false name; confirmed to the rental company with an expertly forged NSW driver's licence, when the vehicle was hired out of Broome, Western Australia. But when the car was not delivered back to the rental agency in Parramatta on the Saturday morning as contracted, the usual alerts went out. Not only to the police but also to the Sydney tow truck companies, taxi companies and private security patrols with the usual spotter's cash reward of one hundred dollars folding.

A towie from Cabramatta Towing and Smash Repairs had spotted the dusty rental parked in the apartment block car park from his list of cashies stuck to his driving wheel, and he called in the find to the hire company. Normally, once the car was confirmed as the missing vehicle, the towies would simply hook it up and return it to the hire agency. But when the towie tried to convince the apartment security guard that it was in his interest to open the gate, the old man had refused. He was unwilling to face the wrath of the sinister gangster he had seen park the car the previous week. So the police were called and Reg and Thao attended. They soon calmed the old guard down enough to give them the apartment number of the car's driver. Then it was just a case of knocking on Van's door, and when there was no response from inside, Reg had the building caretaker unlock the Yale with the master key.

Senior Constable Reg Knight was a twenty-five-year veteran of inner city suburban street policing and he knew well the smell of death. So when the door swung open two inches and then caught on the heavy link chain, Reg's somewhat bulbous, vein-cracked proboscis sucked onto the olfactory sensors of his instrument that sweet stink of decomposition.

A less experienced officer might have then forced the issue, kicked the door open to gain entry and track that dreadful scent to the source. But Reg knew that this man was a Spider—he called for the detectives.

At this early stage there was no connection made to the spate of deaths throughout the city, and the detective on duty at the local station was routinely assigned by his detective sergeant to sort out what the uniformed officers had called in. In this suburb drug related death caused by accidental overdose, and other random violent sudden death among known gang members was not an especially rare occurrence. So Detective Kelvin Ray had no other expectation except that Van Nguyen, a known Spider Gang member, was apparently dead in his locked apartment, a fact which in itself suggested a self-induced drug death.

'Reg, Thao,' the middle aged, red-headed Detective Ray greeted the uniformed officers at the apartment door. Reg filled him in: 'The tenant is an adult male of Vietnamese origin, one of the Spider boys. Mr Van Nguyen. Do you know him?'

'Na,' Reynolds replied, slipping into a white cloth overall taken from his silver aluminium evidence case, and handing one to each of the two patrol officers.

'I've had a few dealings,' Reg told the detective as he searched for the packets of surgical gloves. 'Years ago, though. Van's about twenty-eight now. I arrested him for standover extortion on a restaurant, about eight years back. He got off when the victim suddenly went quiet,' Reg commented cynically.

'Okay, what else do we know about him?' the detective asked, as the two others ripped open the glove packets and a fine talc powder clouded onto the worn hallway carpet.

'The super tells me that he lives alone,' the matronly Constable Thao reported, holding up her black leather-bound notebook. 'He's lived here, no problems, for two years. Keeps to himself. The old security guard tells me that he arrived back home one week back, parked the rental and has not been seen since. But the car was the rental car out of WA that the towie spotted.'

'What's happening with that?' the detective queried. 'We need the towie to stand by till we release it.'

Thao responded that the tow truck driver had been told and was waiting.

'Good work.' Ray praised the officer and then gestured her back away from the door as he selected a set of bolt cutters from his case. 'Okay, folks, let's see what's inside,' and with that Ray snipped effortlessly through the chrome links of the security chain and carefully pushed the door open.

And there he was, mid-room, obviously and grotesquely dead. Van had opened the bathroom window the night of his death to clear the steam from the spa. And through that space over the following week a steady stream of the great Australian bio-matter recyclers had flown in on busily buzzing gossamer wings, tracking along scent trails that had wafted outside from the increasingly attractive stink of the dead man inside. Van had proved a generous and uncomplaining host as the tiny black creatures laid their clusters of white eggs onto his moist spots and within hours the babies started moving and grooving through generational changes. Now Van was a roiling landscape of industriously wriggling maggots.

'Jesus!' the hardened officers of the law muttered in chorus. Thao handed a jar of Tiger Balm from the evidence case to the men, and each smeared a smudge under their nostrils to at least attempt to disguise the chewable thickness of the air.

Ray took charge.

'Okay, folks, if you both stay there I'll do a quick recce for anything obvious.'

Ray tracked deliberately and minutely around the wall of the room. His careful path avoided contaminating the scene of what was either a simple death or, perhaps. a murder. He stepped slowly around the perimeter of the living room toward the kitchenette and was then close to the body.

'Yeah, I reckon he's dead, no obvious pulse, although he is obviously pulsing,' Ray joked back to his companions as the terrible destruction of the body came into closer, smellier focus. The stain of the body fluids spread out from the mass in an outline of the body. Ray stood still and scanned the room from that focal point. Floor level first...all clear. Then mid-level; and then he saw them. A blister pack of tablets. He focused on the pack. One tablet missing from the silver foil on the pine-grain table next to the spilt whisky tumbler.

'Hello, hello, hello!' he joked silently to himself, 'what's this then.'

Because the remaining purple tablets had a camel imprint stamped into each of them! With rising professional excitement, he reached for his mobile with rubber-fingered care.

The Cabramatta detectives' office along with all the Sydney suburban and regional offices, had been briefed by senior CTF officers about the suspicion that the deaths in the city over the past weekend were as a result of tainted party drugs.

Detective Kelvin Ray had immediately recognised the probability that the camel-embossed tablets on the table of Van Ngyuen's apartment may well be part of that shipment. Phone in hand, he voiced his opinion to the other officers as he stood against the wall, arms crossed.

'Righto. One: the deceased is a criminal, a Spider soldier. Two: he was alone with his door locked. Three: he is dead. And four: these tablets, the packet anyway, indicates that he took one. You know what, lady and gent? I think I had better call in the Concord Task Force.' And with that he carefully retraced his path out of the apartment back to the corridor.

When the call came in to the Task Force HQ at Sydney Central, Superintendent Fred Hall spoke to the Cabramatta detective himself. He realised quickly that he was dealing with a competent investigator as Kelvin Ray calmly and logically detailed the facts and his suspicions.

'Okay, Kelvin,' Hall said, a tingle of excitement stirring as the old copper's instinct for the value of a fresh clue kicked in. 'You stay there. We are on the way down. You know what to do, freeze everything, the car too,' he instructed.

From his smoke-glass panelled office Fred Hall strode into the crowded Concord Task Force main office where investigators, analysts, intelligence and forensic personnel worked the phones and the various computer databases in a murmur of efficient industry.

'Attention, people!' Fred announced, and the room fell quiet immediately, faces turned toward the boss. 'We may have something. I want Detective Inspector Lopez and his team, plus Team 1 Forensic on their way to Cabramatta. We have the sudden death of a Vietnamese Spider Gang member in his own apartment.'

The teams began to gather their tools even as the boss briefed them, excitement building in the task force office.

'The local man Detective Kelvin Ray is at the scene; he's frozen it. He's found some purple tablets, embossed with a camel design.

It appears that the tablets relate to the death of the subject. Once you get there, DI Lopez, assess the situation and call me.'

The squat, muscular detective inspector nodded back at his boss.

'No worries, sir.'

With a hand gesture and rise of eyebrow at his team of three detectives, and then at the Forensic Team 1, led by Detective Sergeant Adam Hill, the immaculately suited forty-year-old and his group eagerly left the task force office, impatiently rode the lift down the seven floors into the basement of Sydney Central and into the task force cars.

As the unmarked Holden Commodore sedan and the white transit van squealed out from the concrete exit ramp onto Phillips Street, DI Lopez logged in with CTF HQ.

'Red Team Leader 1 and Foxtrot 1—10/2.'

The radio operator next to Superintendent Fred Hall's office logged the call and confirmed, 'Copy, Red Team Leader 1, out.'

17

CRAZY LITTLE THING
CALLED LOVE

After that first night of passionate exploration Bill fell into an easy relationship with Bonnie as they explored the possibilities and the potential. From their working relationship and with the casual boundaries of a friendship already nurtured over the past several months, Bill found that that the journey into the stronger emotional and passionate bind was an almost seamless development. A *relationship*. It was not that at this stage he envisaged a future with Bonnie—it was too early for that—but *damn*, he was enjoying the present with her.

The young Aboriginal girl with her strong cultural ties to her clan and to her land became the teacher. He delighted in learning from her the oral history of her family, her clan, and her descriptions and explanations of the dreaming of her tribe. He learned about her people in that paradise of Broome, and their 'country'; the waters, and the interactions at both the physical and spirit world levels between the people and the plants and creatures. He had read of the song-lines and of the spiritual relationship between the ancient traditional owner peoples and their perception of their world, so different from the material superficiality of the paler invaders. And Bill felt a special privilege to learn that from her and from the family Anu as they warily welcomed the 'wadjela fella, Bill of Bonnie girl'.

Mixed blood and race relationships in isolated multi-cultural Broome were not rare, but Bill was new. The town had only known him for eight months and all had heard the rumours and stories of his past. Like most parents, Mozzie and Annie Anu cherished all their issue. But Bonnie was especially close to their hearts. She was also very much protected by her big, hard cowboy twin brothers, Elvis and Snowflake, and by their similarly aged Uncle Rock, who was always to be found in their company. Of the three, Snowflake was the biggest and meanest. Shit, he had to be with that name lovingly assigned to him by Annie at his birth when she saw a close-up photo of a snowflake in a *Woman's Day* and fell in love with its intricate design.

Bill did all he could to have Bonnie's family accept him. Accept that he obviously very much enjoyed the company of their daughter, and sister, and niece. When Bonnie invited him he attended the Anu family home for meals with Mozzie and Annie, Uncle Rock and the twins. He did all the right things, bringing flowers for Annie, fresh caught fish and a few cold beers and tobacco for Mozzie and the boys. He tried always to engage the trio of the younger silent, suspicious men in friendly conversation.

Bonnie didn't care about the cold judgmental scrutiny of her brothers or her uncle. They were much older then she and she loved them dearly, but even the twins were more like uncles, having been already adults as she grew up. Bonnie just enjoyed life as it arrived in front of her and she meant to enjoy her man, Bill. And she did enjoy him. She loved his physicality, his touch, his experience as a lover, honed to a fine degree (unbeknown to her) in a previous life, by two voracious Swiss backpackers. Bonnie loved sex. She adored every aspect of the sensual tension between a man and a woman. She had enjoyed and engaged carefully but carefree with targeted male tourists from countries far away, who in Dutch, Swedish and American accents had gasped at her hunger and heat in their sweaty engagements at the backpacker hostels.

Bill met and enjoyed her passion, for he had long sought, long needed such release. He spoiled her with slow sensual massages on his double bed on the *Freedom*, teasing and torturing her with targeted 'accidental' oily caresses until she could take it no longer and fought him for her satisfaction. He found, though, that her brazenness in public view sometimes terrified even him; although he usually submitted even to the riskiest possibilities as the sexual excitement overcame sensible inhibition.

Through the week after Shinju, Bill's and the town's attention was inevitably drawn in morbid fascination to the terrible events in Sydney. It was near impossible not to at least know that the poisonings had occurred. Every form of media was saturated with the drama of the dead. The scene had been photographed in terrible colour and splashed onto plasma screens, across the state's daily newspaper, and was talked about relentlessly on the AM and FM talk-backs. But perhaps sadly, as with most incidents in modern life, Concord and the Golden Fish had happened so far away and were so alien, that although Bill and the Broome locals identified the dead as Australians, the poor souls were in reality unknowns. They may as well have been Eskimos, so distant was the connection between the big east coast city and its shenanigans and the lazy northwest coast tropical surrounds of their existence. The townspeople did try to follow the events, and the tragedy was the topic of conversation over coffees or around the water cooler or pool table for a few days before more immediate local events took over. Bill took time when working on the boat, hosing off the blood and guts of a day's fishing, to think about it and wonder at the motivation of anyone to cause such chaos. But somewhat numbed, like most of his fellow citizens, by constant over-exposure of the visions of death and destruction beamed from around a troubled world that syndrome lessened his direct concern at such events, even in a peaceful nation. And of course Bill's attention to the poisonings was further distracted by his growing realisation that for the first time in a long time he was actually happy—happy for a reason; and her name was Bonnie.

One week after the race Bill was on his best behaviour at an Anu family dinner. Mozzie and Annie had been effusive in their appreciation of the gifts he had brought to the table: thick white aquatic steaks carved from the sumptuous coral trout he had harvested that afternoon especially for the meal. A stop at the tourist showcase Willy Creek pearl farm just out of the town had delivered to him kilos of the rich, slippery pearl meat that Annie had accepted with gusto and a big hug of thanks. She had turned it into a delicious, marinated spicy dish that the family now feasted on over the big hardwood dinner table. Bonnie sat opposite Bill, her glossy black curls accentuated with a purple and yellow frangipani bloom tucked over her left ear, her ebony skin and naked shoulders glowing with beautiful good health and fragrant oils.

Snowflake Anu sat glowering to his right and the sombre Elvis and Rock Anu to his left.

The conversation was driven by Mozzie, who cackled heartily at his own jokes as they recalled the evil genius of Doc Patrick and the dragon boats. Bill was laughing a belly deep reaction to Mozzie's own mirth when something touched his belly under the tablecloth. Bill started with shock as he realised that the treasured daughter's skilful bare feet were at his crotch, and were intent on raising mischief. He had laughed before when Bonnie had demonstrated an unusual skill with the almost finger-like dexterity of her toes. She had entertained him by picking up pens and drawing crude pictures, lifting full cups of water to her own mouth when seated, flicking through pages of books, and throwing all means of objects at him across the cabin of the *Freedom* with her wonderful toes. Now those toes had a death grip on his awakening penis through the micro thin silky barrier of his shorts. He cursed himself too, for as was his fashion in tropical climes, he had gone commando for the family dinner—no jocks—oh shit!

Bonnie had him: a brother either side, an uncle almost opposite, her father three feet away demanding his attention with a long previously told and re-told story of the dragon boat race, Annie fussing over him with questions about 'more of this, son—more of that, son'. Damn Bonnie and her fucking wonderful toes now slowly pulling and stroking, and prodding, and rotating him to an inevitable orgasm all the time sweetly, innocently, tortuously slipping her beautiful gorgeous magic pink tongue tip between those plump luscious cushions of her lips with a teasing grin. And as Mozzie reached the summit of an oft-told joke he was rewarded by the nice young fella of Bonnie's responding with a shouted paroxysm of glee, followed by the wadjela softly banging his head on the table and moaning in apparent laughter as young Bonnie near wet herself giggling on the other side of the table.

Meanwhile Snowflake, Elvis and Uncle Rock stared at the wadjela and li'l sis Bonnie with curious shakes of their heads.

18

DANCING IN THE DARK

In most intense police criminal investigations there is a breakthrough moment. Sometimes that clue, that name, that moment leads to a forensic snowball of momentum in the inquiry. The clue rolls through the mass of disjointed information and takes form, gathering in the related flakes of data to point a way forward—a direction.

When Van was found he was wearing a brand new, although now somewhat soiled, T-shirt with the logo of *Beauty Bay* proud upon it. The logo alone was strangely alien to him, to his culture and sub-culture, to his nature—and so such a breakthrough moment occurred. Then when the hire car was proved to have been rented in Broome, Western Australia near where a place called Beauty Bay existed, and had been driven back to NSW, connective data surfaced in an emerging chain of links, and a direction for the investigation evolved.

The homicide scene search at Van's apartment had been completed. The dusty hire car had been forensically inspected in a well-lit police garage; only the fingerprints of Van found, dusted and lifted. The pathologist had carried out the dissection of Van and minutely documented the destructive tracks of the purple camel located in body fluids: collected, isolated and chemically identified.

It was now five days after the massacre at Concord Oval, two days after the homicide scene was finally released for cleaning at the Golden Fish. All of the bodies had undergone forensic pathological examination.

Seventy-six bodies were released to grieving families for burial.

One gutted Spider soldier remained under lock and key in a dark fridge at the Royal Sydney morgue with no one wanting to claim him, apparently.

Late on the Friday afternoon back at the Operation HQ, the Concord Task Force met in the main office: some eighty crime-fighting professionals in sombre mood, determined to persist in this huge tragedy that excited their professional interest with its magnitude, the enormity of the death toll. Some of those present there were vaguely, almost guiltily, satisfied that they could be a part of this investigation, could assist in the solving of a famous crime. Each man and woman, whether detective, forensic scientist, photographer, or analyst, hoped to contribute in some way to the success of the investigation. They wanted to be there at the conclusion, the scalp, the kill.

'Okay, ladies and gents, your attention, please,' announced Detective Chief Inspector Bob McKenzie. He was Hall's 2IC and was the officer in charge of the homicide operations command centre. Bob McKenzie was a short, stocky, dark-haired fiftyish senior detective, affectionately renowned even by his friends as a pedantic anal-retentive. With his obsessive attention to every minor detail, this ex-Major Fraud Squad man was a perfect choice. Perfect to ensure that the precise, dry operational routine, the faultless logistical management, and the overseeing of the collation of the mountains of evidence and documents created by such a major police operation occurred without error.

McKenzie's announcement, made precisely on the second of the minute of the hour that the meeting had been scheduled for, cut through the subdued chatter. Each member of the homicide team straightened and turned to face their leader, Detective Superintendent Fred Hall.

As if for dramatic effect, Fred had dressed for this occasion in his full NSW senior officer's dress uniform with lashings of thick gold braid. 'Thank you, people,' Hall announced, shades perhaps of his military influence in his command of tone and inflection. 'Thank you all for your attendance and for your work to date.'

Hall turned to the Australian Federal Police Commander and the Customs and ASIO agents who had worked with him over the five days since Concord, since the first meeting at the NSW Commissioner's Office.

'Again welcome to our friends from the AFP, Australian Customs and ASIO. And thank you also to our scientific and medical friends.' Fred nodded at the head table of learned looking forensic specialists invited to this significant briefing. 'Let me recap the current sit-rep. In précis: Five days ago, on Friday night at the Mega Bash concert at Concord Oval seventy-one people died. The same night, early morning Saturday at the Golden Fish nightclub during the Sydney Industry Hairdressers Ball, Oxford Street, Paddington, a further five persons died.

'Following crime scene investigation at both scenes and post mortem investigation of each deceased, it has been established that in each case the cause of death was poisoning. The poison has been identified as strychnine, a common rat poison, but this batch is a much more powerful synthetic version. In each case the post mortem testing has also confirmed the presence in each deceased of MDMA, an ingredient of the street drug we all know as ecstasy.'

Hall paused. Everyone in the room knew what had occurred to date, the reason they had toiled with only snatches of sleep for the last five days. But each also appreciated the formal etiquette of the briefing as the stenographers recorded the address word for word in shorthand while the electronic tapes stored it as digital history.

'People, you are each a vital team member in the most significant mass murder investigation that this nation has experienced. Each of those people at Concord and at Oxford Street is a victim of murder. It is black and white. The crime is murder and we must work to identify the motive for these acts of murder.' He paused again and looked slowly, deliberately around the room, and each man and woman there felt that he looked them directly in the eye. 'You and I will find the person or persons responsible for this act. By your professional and dedicated work that person or persons will be brought to account before the justice system of this nation.'

The commander fell silent, and then, unusually for such occasions, someone started to clap at the back of the room and then they all joined in. The superintendent held his palms up as if in surrender, and there was an almost embarrassed silence before he brought them back to the matter at hand.

'We have a development. On Wednesday, officers from the Cabramatta Police Station attended at an apartment in Cabramatta. The tenant, one Van Nguyen, a known Spider Triad gang member, was found deceased inside the locked apartment. Beside Mr Nguyen was a packet of tablets since proved to consist of a mixture of strychnine and MDMA.'

Hall stopped and nodded at McKenzie who started a digital projector connected to his laptop computer. The death scene at Van's apartment appeared on the white backdrop behind Hall.

'Here is the deceased as found in-situ.' Fred Hall stroked the red laser beam from the electronic pointer gently across Van's ruined face. 'And here next to him on the table are the tabs that scientifically we now know killed him.' Hall paused. 'Is he another victim?' he put to the room. 'Yes, of course he is a victim, but we also believe that Mr Van Nguyen may lead us to the source of the camel tabs.'

McKenzie clicked his mouse to change the shot to a close up of nine remaining camel-embossed purple tablets. Each man and woman in uniform and in plain clothes waited silently for Hall's next announcement.

'What I am about to tell you all must not leave this room. You have all signed the operation's confidentiality agreement and I expect you all, without exception, to maintain operational secrecy. You have been hand-picked for your integrity as well as your skills, and I know and trust each of you.

'Inquiries have revealed that our suspect travelled by Virgin from Mascot to Perth three weeks ago. Two hours later he left Perth and flew to Broome on Qantas and stayed three days at a three-star motel in the town, by himself. He then uplifted a Hertz hire car previously booked as part of his entire trip through Cabramatta Lucky 888 Holiday Club. He then drove to a small resort called Beauty Bay, one hundred and fifty kilometres south of Broome off the coastal highway. He stayed there for one week after booking in on arrival in the name of Francis Wong. On the twelfth, Van drove from the resort direct through to Cabramatta.

'We do not believe that he made any other significant stop, although we are waiting for the electronic tracking statement from the bank to show the trail of his credit card. Clearly, at a drive close on five thousand kilometres, he must have stopped for sleep, for gas and food, and so on. We do know that he arrived back at his apartment on the fifteenth. Ladies and gents, Van Nguyen is a senior soldier of the Cabramatta chapter of the triad gang known as the Spiders.'

Hall stopped and nodded to the officer manning the desk by the lights and the room was illuminated once more. Fred Hall continued.

'As you are all aware, we are currently looking to locate one Lewie Hong. Mr Hong has been named as the dealer of the tablets that killed the five people at the Golden Fish nightclub. We have not yet found any trace of Mr Hong, but we can confirm that Lewie Hong is also a soldier of the Cabramatta chapter of the Spider Gang.

'Shortly I will hand you back to Detective Chief Inspector McKenzie. You will be assigned into squads, briefed and tasked to execute search warrants in the early hours of tomorrow morning at every known dwelling, private, and/or business premises of the Cabramatta Spider Triad, and at all known associates. Armed Offenders, TRG, local area uniform back-up, Traffic and Dogs are ready to go. Each squad OC will be given written operational orders with all relevant information on their specific targets, specific risks, et cetera.'

Hall paused again, looked out over his troops, then nodded to McKenzie. Once more the mouse clicked and the image on the screen shocked as the split digital picture showed both the massacre at Concord, with dozens of sadly twisted bodies dotted across the landscape, and the tragic beauty of the immaculately coiffed few at the Golden Fish nightclub in terrible living colour.

'People, in conclusion, we have a very hard and, I would suggest, a very long road to follow. The tracks may lead us to Broome, may lead us to Beauty Bay, will lead us overseas. But we start here in Cabramatta. We started at Concord and at Oxford Street. We will meticulously investigate, we will record and we will analyse. We all, each of us here, have a part to play. We must all play that part for this team to succeed. Because, comrades, this is nothing more or less than bloody murder!'

19

HUNGRY LIKE THE WOLF

The problem, among myriad others, for Fred Hall and his homicide team, was that the Spiders had held their briefing forty-eight hours before the police.

Lewie Hong and his friend Neville were still tucked away in a gang safe-house. Lewie was an inconsolable ball of effeminate misery while the suspicion that his dealing in drugs had also been dealing in death was investigated by the gang's commanders. Now that the sad story of Van was known, the five criminal pragmatists that made up the triad's senior management team met. They gathered in a dusty factory where during the day the wives and daughters of the city's recently arrived Asian immigrants worked off the grossly inflated Spider assisted fares, noisily churning out cheap piece-rate clothing over long working days. These five very old men had survived the hard streets of Saigon before it became Ho Chi Min City. They were the ones who had come to the new land decades back as criminal entrepreneurs and had set up the structure for their web of deceit and tax free profits from the dirty and dangerous games they, and now their sons and grandsons, played.

They knew now that they had a problem, and the talk was not of the innocent dead of Concord or of the Hairdressers Ball victims. No, theirs was a more selfish interest. They still had ninety-five thousand units of product left. But what to do? The irrefutable evidence was that their goods were tainted. A friendly chemist, the grandson of a senior Spider, had analysed and confirmed the chilling suspicion that they were literally dealing death.

There was no choice really. The Vietnamese grandfathers drew the meeting to a close with consensus reached. They would take the financial loss, temporarily anyway. The remaining product would be hidden, safe from the reach of the opposition, the round-eyes in blue. The eldest spoke in the language of his birthplace.

'Tonight our sons will spread the word, clean the houses, clean the factories, clean the cars, say nothing, do nothing—just wait, for they will come. Now go.'

Later, in the early hours, a hole was dug into the hard red soil of French's Forest on the north shore of the city. Two muscular young Spider soldiers in dark clothing buried two black briefcases vacuum wrapped in plastic. The remote but exact location was confirmed forever by a handheld GPS. The merchant wholesalers intended a return to sender of the goods under a warranty of threat.

The Sydney Spider Triad spring clean was completed twenty-four hours before heavy black-soled paramilitary boots splintered suburban front doors, long before purpose-built TRG four-wheel drives bull-barred down factory gates. And before hundreds of police entered to search, to seize, to interview, to analyse.

By Monday, Fred Hall and his team knew that they had nothing; not a skerrick of evidence to link the Cabramatta Spider Triad to the camels. Nothing except a frigid carcass under lock and key in the mortuary, and a soiled Beauty Bay T-shirt secured in the homicide evidence safe at Sydney Central. But the Concord Task Force also knew from detailed interviews of the shocked survivors of the Hairdressers Ball that an effeminate Vietnamese drug dealer, one Lewie Hong and his elderly Caucasian companion, needed to be found and interviewed ASAP.

20

WASTED DAYS
AND WASTED NIGHTS

One week after the death of Van Nguyen, Superintendent Fred Hall and a select need-to-know few had met and carefully briefed two of the state's elite undercover officers: Agent Desire Kettle and Agent Mal Weggers. The officers, both in their late thirties, had worked in association with the NSW Drug Squad for the previous twelve months on drug operations in the western suburbs. Now, as Mr and Mrs Barnes, they were on their way out of Mascot Airport into Perth and then on to Broome, Western Australia. Their primary brief was simple. Find, record and digitally photograph the guest register before, at, and after the dates that Van Nguyen was at the resort. Around that task the extended brief was to book into the Beauty Bay Resort, stay for as long as it was possible without arousing suspicion, observe, inquire, and report back by satellite phone each evening.

The Task Force had discussed crashing into the resort with a search group and tearing it to pieces. But Fred Hall wanted to know what they were up against. The old soldier was a believer in the recce before the battle. In any event, all they had was the suspected courier wearing a resort T-shirt. Their man had been in Perth, Broome and then through every town and city between Broome and Cabramatta on his journey. There was no evidence that the drugs had come from Beauty Bay. There was no evidence as yet that provided enough to even prepare a search warrant that would satisfy a judge. No, they needed more; and the task that these two agents embarked on was one of many varied mini-operations within the operation.

Hall and his command officers, his intelligence and analyst officers, had already briefed other agents and investigative teams on their tasks. Already other teams of men and women were on their way to Western Australia to retrace the known tracks of Van Nguyen. The Beauty Bay operation was only one piece of what was hoped would form the jigsaw of evidence in this case.

A week later the two agents returned to Operation HQ in Sydney. They brought back digital images of the resort's guest register, photographed entry-by-entry, page-by-page, in a covert midnight raid. The register, including an entry for Mr Francis Wong, would provide interesting but not especially valuable fodder for the police and ASIO intelligence analysts.

Apart from the agents' lovely suntans, their braided hair, their relaxed and invigorated bodies and expanded spirituality, thanks to their new friend Gypsy's gentle ministrations, in evidential effect they brought back zilch. The operational commanders knew that the agents had done what had been asked of them. Fred Hall put it best as the senior group analysed the result of the covert insertion.

'We need someone in close and dirty.'

21

DIED IN YOUR ARMS TONIGHT

Even while the undercover Mr and Mrs Barnes of the NSW Police were luxuriating under the warm, healing hands of Gypsy Lawson in the scented gloom of the healing dome at Beauty Bay, the Spider Gang, courtesy of the same two strongly built second tier lieutenants, had been tying up some loose ends.

Lewie Hong and his friend Neville had run for their lives from the Golden Fish that fateful night as Lewie's precious clientele had fallen dying in front of him. Neville, terrified and devastated, sobbing in disbelief at the dramatic turn in the otherwise mathematical certainty of his professional and personal life (pre-Lewie at least), was pulled along in a gasping, flustered escape. Lewie had naturally sought refuge in the care and custody of his crime family. Cunning as a perfumed sewer rat, Lewie had avoided the immediate convenience of the yellow Saab parked in the nearby secure underground car park. He chose instead to flee the dreadful scene of the crime on foot. Even as he and Neville had rushed awkwardly down the clanging fire escape steps into the dark and dirty alley at the back of the nightclub, Lewie immediately realised that his beautiful carefree life was over. He put one and one together and came up with two. The dear friends who had taken his drugs had died before his eyes. It must be his product, the ecstasy! 'The fucking purple fucking camels!' he lisped. Lewie knew also that others in that place that night would have no hesitation in connecting him to those deaths. The police would be after him: a mass murderer.

So he ran, and he took Neville with him. Whatever happened, Lewie knew he had to be in control of the older man; as he had always been in their short erotic partnership.

Cursing under his breath in English and in Vietnamese, Lewie flagged down a taxi two blocks away from the Golden Fish on a crowded inner-city street. 'Anyway,' he muttered, 'the wise old men will know what to do, my dear uncles, my family.'

Of course the sinister old men knew what to do. After a quick mobile phone discussion that night soon after the desperate pair had arrived on the back doorstep of a restaurant owned by the gang, Lewie and Neville were hidden in the musty boot of the restaurant's old Toyota Camry. They were driven away from Cabramatta to safety. Away past the screaming police sirens to a distant western suburb on the fringe of the sprawling metropolis of Sydney. There, with Neville increasingly distressed, they emerged bedraggled from the car boot into the darkened garage of a small suburban house. Led by a silent young lieutenant, and with Neville held in Lewie's protective embrace, the two were tucked away into the safe house under inscrutable, watchful eyes.

But the old men had coldly, logically agreed. Four days after the last hairdresser fell frothing to the waxed dance floor of the Golden Fish, Lewie Hong and Neville Smith also gasped their last. Laid together, face down on the double bed, two hefty bodyguards straddled and controlled them easily. Strong plastic bags taped around their necks quickly muffled Lewie and Neville's hysterical cries. Terrified eyes on each other's face, they rapidly breathed in that last tiny bubble of atmosphere as their assailants sat chatting like two cowboys on bucking bulls.

Just before midnight the Camry rolled quietly into the stockfeed factory owned by a kinsman of the Asian clan. A massive roller door squealed up only as far as the small sedan needed to creep inside, lights off. In the blackness, silent men humped two shapes to a steel behemoth of a machine built to masticate any edible protein left on slaughter-house-stripped meat carcasses. The black plastic was cut from Lewie's and Neville's cooling corpses, and their two naked bodies, in a final obscene indignity, were fed onto the rollers of a cold steel conveyor. At the push of a big green button, Lewie Hong and Neville Smith made their last short journey together into the crushing, tearing cogs of the machine that transformed them within minutes into pig food pellets.

22

ALL I NEED IS A MIRACLE

Three weeks after the fatal camel weekend, Federal Police Commander Bob Hopkins made a suggestion late one night in Fred Hall's operational office.

'We need to get someone into Beauty Bay,' Bob said. 'Someone who can get close to the owners, Gypsy and Tommy Lawson. Someone who will be part of the furniture. Better maybe that he or she works there,' he mused. 'Someone who can stay for as long as we need, until we either have something, and can crash the place, or until we know we have nothing and can concentrate elsewhere.'

Fred Hall was in shirtsleeves and slumped over mountains of paper; Sally Martin from Customs hugged a large polystyrene cup of very strong black coffee; and McKenzie the martinet sat quietly.

'Okay, Bob, I know you too well. What have you got for us?' Fred Hall inquired.

Hopkins grinned. 'I can call in a favour. I know a man who may be able to help us in Broome.'

Fred Hall sat upright.

'His name is George Patrick, a serving WA Senior Sergeant at the Broome Station. George, or Doc as the locals know him, is a thirty-year man in the WA force. He is up in Broome thanks to me. I used him as an undercover agent to crack a Mafia cell in Melbourne eighteen years ago. His reward was to change his identity and move him around WA from country town to country town as a copper. He has been in Broome now for ten years, and two marriages.' Hopkins took a sip from his foam cup of skinny latte.

'How can we use him, Bob?' Fred was definitely more awake now than a few moments earlier.

'That I don't know. I simply seek the authority of the meeting to inquire.'

'Authority granted,' announced Fred Hall. 'Let's call it a night, people. Please advise me as soon as possible as to how you go, Bob. And thanks, mate.'

Meanwhile, twenty kilometres away, the Spider elders met again. This was the first chance they had had since the police raids to meet, as they had every Saturday evening for decades, at the Saigon Seafood Palace in Chinatown, central Sydney.

Each large black German-built sedan had been followed by the Task Force surveillance teams, known in the force as 'the dogs', from the suburban mansions to the restaurant. Each emptying of Spiders onto the sidewalk and each entry into the red and gold decor of the eatery was filmed and photographed.

But no police agent could possibly enter that place with or behind the Spiders without immediate detection and real danger. And so frustrated, the police watched the curtains being drawn and simply waited.

As the hullabaloo of the younger family members increased across five large tables the five old men gathered. They sat together in a quiet function room in the centre of the restaurant. Li Bo Van, the restaurant owner and a long-term Spider soldier, ceremoniously opened a Johnny Walker blue label and placed it in the middle of the dining table where the five leaders sat. Before each of the elders he respectfully placed a heavy crystal shot-glass, and offered ice and iced water, before scuttling out of the room and pulling shut the sliding door.

'We have satisfaction, my friends.' The leader was close to eighty now, his longevity due to the cunning and ruthlessness that had placed him at the peak of the Sydney branch of the triad. 'The bad is to be replaced by the good.'

There was a grunt of understanding from his four younger companions, average age seventy-five.

'Our connections in Holland have dealt with the manufacturer.

It was an accident, but the man who was to blame has been dealt with also.'

Another nod from the group. They were not a bunch for wasted chit-chat this powerfully evil little cadre.

'But we need to return the bad and exchange it for the good. The delivery will be eight weeks from now. We will send the grandchildren.'

With glasses filled with fine liquor, the five symbolically clinked the five glasses together in the centre of the table in agreement.

23

GOOD GIRLS DON'T

'Bonnie's a bad girl...ahhhh...Bonnie's a very...very...very bad girl...' Bill moaned as quietly as he could, seated high up on the fly-deck of the *Freedom*. They floated on placid azure waters thirty kilometres up the coast north of Broome. A muffled giggle arose from deck level as Bonnie continued with her wicked ways. Her hot, gorgeous mouth teased his ambushed tumescence as below on the main deck Mozzie, Annie, Elvis, Uncle Rock, and Snowflake relaxed. Meanwhile Bill distractedly cruised the big charter boat closer into the mangrove coast on this fun family day out.

Bill had invited the Anu clan out for a fishing and crabbing treat the very night that Bonnie had mischievously spilt the gravy at the family dinner. And now here she was again, up to her evil tricks and risking an embarrassing and surely dangerous discovery.

Bill not so much feared punishment from her lovely parents, but he certainly did from her heavily-built siblings on the lower deck. He had tried to push her away as she had surprised him with a sinuous crawl below his vision. But this girl was not to be denied her fun and he was finally forced to surrender as his damn body failed him again and rose to the occasion. It was hard, and so was trying to stay focused as currents of wonderful sensation swept up from the suction of her marvellous mouth through the core of his being, as he brought the vessel in close to a sandy beach through shallow aquatic weed gardens.

His intention was to gently slide the *Freedom* softly into the beach so that the Anu clan could access the exposed mangroves and find the hidey-holes of the fearsome looking but succulent mangrove crabs. As he delayed his approach slightly, with the *Freedom* down to a knot or so forward, and feeling intently another inevitable arrival, he only vaguely registered the young dugong floating fatly past the bow. The dugong was close, but so was he. And as his body finally and totally surrendered to her amazing torture Bill was a horrified witness to the ancient Aboriginal warrior Mozzie Anu taking what was his.

Mozzie had seen the dugong too. He loved dugong, but sadly not for their big sad eyes, or lovely personality. His people had traditionally feasted on the sweet, fat meat of the gentle sea cows for many a generation. He did not mean to miss this opportunity. He took the razor sharp fishing gaff, positioned his gnarly old body off the port bow, and as the *Freedom* drifted above the peaceful mammal he launched his black-wrapped pack of sinew and muscle off the boat and down onto its back, and gaffed a big bloody hole into the neck of a very surprised and soon dying young male dugong.

Bill's reaction would have been comical if it had not been so painful, and so publicly embarrassing. He shouted 'Noooooooo!' and jumped to his feet, right at the moment of his exquisite ejaculation, his body's procreative liquor arcing above the dark gloss of Bonnie's curls. She, unaware of the excitement below, instinctively held on to the two well-rounded friends that she had been squeezing and teasing, as her man finally gave her what she had so assiduously worked for. Bonnie simply failed to release and this brought Bill back to earth painfully quickly.

Luckily, Elvis, Rock, and Snowflake were all focused in whooping delight at Mozzie's heroics and missed the over exposure above them. But Millie Anu saw all and cackled in hysterical delight at the erotic floorshow on the top deck. As Bonnie's head and lovely smiling face appeared over the transom she joined with her mother in the laughing. This increased as Millie gave her maternal approval of the events with a 'Too lovely, girl!' a cheeky thumbs up, an exaggerated wink, and a humorous over estimation of size with her hands, as if boasting about a fish caught.

Meanwhile, Bill lurched, deep breathing and crotch clutching back in his helmsman's chair, furiously tucking bruised bits back into his shorts.

Now the three younger men had dived into the shallow waters to help Mozzie, and they pulled and pushed the desperately flopping beast onto the beach and stood about it. In their ancient dialect they discussed Mozzie's killing technique as the old man smashed the cruel fang of the gaff down into its skull. And Bill, recovering logical thought, muttered 'What a fucking mess' as he kissed the Shark Cat's twin bows softly onto the gentle slope of the beach.

24

HOLDING OUT FOR A HERO

Even as the rich red blood of the marine mammal glooped from its rudely dissected belly into the white soak pad of the beach sand, AFP Commander Bob Hopkins sat in the air-conditioned comfort of the Broome Police Station across the messy desk of his old agent George Patrick.

Doc was embarrassed. Surprised by the sudden appearance on his official doorstep of the immaculately-suited Bob Hopkins, he was suddenly aware of how he must present to his old mentor from those days of their mutually earned professional glory so long ago. Doc stank and he knew it. An hour ago, he had dragged on the same sweat-soiled khaki uniform that he had dragged off at midnight the previous evening after another lonely, whisky-fuelled night in his one-room flat at the back of the police station. A lukewarm shower and overkill from the Old Spice into the hairy caverns of his armpits had only briefly disguised the ammoniac reek of the unwashed clothing. Doc was sure that Bob Hopkins could smell him over the desk. Hopkins, though, was sensitive to his old charge's embarrassment. He knew also of Doc's decline into the grip of alcohol over the eighteen years since the two had worked to bust the crime family and its drug operation in Melbourne. Bob had periodically tracked the progress of his agent's career in the WA Police through contacts in the higher echelons of the state force and had been saddened to hear of Doc's trials and tribulations.

But here and now Bob needed official help from Senior Sergeant George Patrick, officer in charge of the Broome Station. After the initial shock of his appearance at the station, Bob and Doc had sat across the desk over a jug of iced water and had discussed the terrible events in the east. Doc had religiously followed the media reports and the interstate police alerts of the events with his usual keen forensic interest. Obviously with such a huge death toll and in an international climate that feared and expected terrorist revenge for real and/or perceived slights, the events in Sydney still dominated all national and even international media as the world's citizens followed the investigation with morbid interest.

Bob brought Doc up to speed on the huge multi-functional resources poured into certainly the biggest homicide/suspected terrorist investigation in modern Australian history. And then he told him about the Beauty Bay T-shirt tag of identity on the body of the dead drug courier.

'Beauty Bay...' Doc muttered. 'Yeah that's a bit south, but yeah, I know the couple who run it. Tommy Lawson and his missus, a woman called Gypsy. Gypsy Lawson. Both long-term Broome locals. He was a pearl farm leaseholder, pretty good bloke, quiet, honest, hardworking. She's a looker, a masseuse, used to run a massage tent for tourists off the resort down at Cable Beach. Nothing untoward about them as far as I know. She was pretty popular around town.'

'Good,' Bob commented. 'George, there is nothing at all to implicate these people or the resort, except that T-shirt on Van. But we think we should take a look at them, get a feel for what is happening down there.'

Doc nodded in deep contemplation, suddenly excited to be doing 'real police work' again with his old boss. Doc was eager, maybe desperate, to help the big Concord operation.

'What can I do for you, sir?' Doc asked.

'We need to get someone into the resort, someone who can get close to the couple, without suspicion. We need an agent in close and dirty,' Bob said, using Fred's words.

Doc considered that for a moment and then spoke: 'Bob, I think I may have just the man for you.'

25
I SEE RED

Thirty or so kilometres to the north of the Broome police station, Bill Peters stood shaking his head on the tiny mangrove-fringed beach. The Cat sat gently at anchor, her twin bows still slushing the sandy bottom, and with the hook off the stern to hold her blunt end into the deeper waters. The tide was on its way back in. The waters in this region rose and fell with such spectacular movement that Bill had asked the family Anu to be back at the boat as soon as they could after he sounded the boat's air-horn. The tidal movement wasn't why he was contemplative though. It was the deceased dugong lying on the beach.

After its brutal end Mozzie and his three sons had blessed the totem spirit of the beast with a sombre ceremony. They sang its story in the nasal music of their ancient tongue. Mozzie lit a small grass fire and waved smoke from a torch of twisted grasses over the animal as the four men and Millie sang-chanted-danced to honour the beast and to thank its departing spirit for the gift of its flesh. Bill watched in fascination, standing respectfully back from the ceremony with Bonnie by his side. She smiled when Mozzie included her wadjela in the ceremony by branding his forehead with a splash of the salty blood of the beast. The men then gutted the dugong, discarding the stomach, lungs and bowels, but keeping the treasured heart and liver for feasting back in Broome.

Which was why Bill was shaking his head. How the hell could he take a freaking dead dugong back to Broome? He didn't know too much about the animals, but he did know that they were a protected species. What Mozzie and the family had quite innocently kept from him was their enshrined right to take the beast. The white man's own law said that the traditional owners could take the traditional food source. But there was a rider, a statutory condition. The kill was supposed to be by traditional means. It might be that a leap with a modern, razor sharp, stainless steel gaff from a seven hundred thousand dollar Shark Cat could be seen in the black and white logic of a courtroom to have been not *that* traditional. Bill just instinctively felt that it was wrong, killing a dugong. He was sure of it.

But now he saw that the Anu mob had arrived back at the boat with the rising cushion of the sea visibly lifting the *Freedom*. The family was happy. Bonnie had stayed with Bill and had fallen asleep in the shade of a trunk-pregnant boab tree just up past the mangroves. Bill had stayed with the boat just in case the tide fooled them all, as was wont to happen in these climes.

Mozzie, Millie, Elvis, Rock and Snowflake had gone hunting the big mangrove mud crabs. Big, fat-fleshed, armour-coated crustaceans that hid in shallow holes among the mangrove roots, safe from all except the cunning intelligence of man. They came back with a half dozen, the massive crushing claws trussed with twine.

'We back, Billy! Wake up, Bonnie girl,' Mozzie called happily as the boys gathered up the hulk of the dugong and carried it into the waist-high waters to dump it with a moist splat onto the back decking of the *Freedom*. Bonnie woke, stretching like a sinuous ebony cat and then joined the family to raucously huff and puff over helping Mozzie and Millie up the fixed steel ladder at the stern of the vessel and back on board.

Bill knew that somehow he had to get the dugong off the boat before he cruised into the very public view of the Broome wharf. But, hey, he had a couple of hours to decide that matter perhaps by sober and convincing argument to the Anu mob. So he allowed, or really just accepted, that the beast was aboard as he pulled the stern anchor onto the back deck. He gave a thumbs up to Bonnie to gun the main engines and she reversed the big vessel off the beach, spun her smoothly around and pointed the twin hulls south toward the home port.

26
HOT IN THE CITY

'Tell me about this Bill Peters, George,' said Bob Hopkins, and so Doc told him the story so far.

'He was basically on the run, Bob. He is that ex-New Zealand copper, the undercover agent from two or three years back. Do you remember? The thing with Commissioner Italiano and his wife in New South Wales?'

Bob Hopkins did recall those events and he grew more intensely interested.

In his position as an Australian Federal Police commander Bob Hopkins had a clear recollection of the prior story of Bill Peters. He had, in his professional capacity, researched the man's past at the time that Peters was a wanted desperado, accused—falsely it was later established—of suspected rape, possession of drugs and a heinous assault on a senior NSW police officer. From that research Bob Hopkins knew also about the events in New Zealand two years earlier and the aftermath when Peters was forced to disappear into the heartland of the Australian continent, running from NSW through Victoria to Kalgoorlie in the west. He had known that Peters was finally found in Broome, but by that time the deceit and corruption of the serving NSW police commissioner had been found out, and Bill Peters was exonerated, compensated in fact.

'So this is that man,' Bob breathed, and felt that tingle of excitement as pieces of a puzzle of possibilities came together to show a way forward. 'Will he help us?' he shot at Doc, who was watching the expert analyst's face, the forensic thinker who he had known from those years before, shuffle mentally through the process: a concept—an argument—the pros the cons—a solution.

'I don't know, Bob, but I do know that he is close to Gypsy. He worked with her in the tent, had a thing for massaging little old ladies, from memory. But I reckon that we could use that relationship as a lever.'

'Can I meet him?' Bob asked quietly.

'Yes, of course. I know he is out on his boat today. I saw him take a local family out early this morning. The Anu mob. Very long-term locals, originals, in fact. Bill is trotting out the daughter, Bonnie.' Doc paused. 'Give us a minute, I'll give the *Freedom* a call on the radio,' and he moved across to the two way base set on a bench in the office.

'FV *Freedom*, FV *Freedom*, this is Broome Police, over.' No immediate response. 'FV *Freedom*, FV *Freedom*, this is Broome Police, over.'

This time a short wait, then a click and, 'Broome Police this is the *Freedom*. How goes it, Doc?' tinnily transmitted back through the stereo speakers into the room, and Bob Hopkins heard the voice of the man who he now eagerly sought to meet.

'Roger, *Freedom*, it goes well. ETA please *Freedom* back at Broome wharf?' Doc asked.

'Roger, Doc. Thirty repeat three-zero minutes, twenty repeat two-zero ks north tracking back south now, over,' Bill responded.

Back at the wheel of the vessel Bill tried hard to keep the stress out of his voice and decided that the fucking dugong was going over the side as soon as Doc got off the blower.

'Roger that, Bill. I will meet you at the wharf. See you round like a rissole. Over and out.'

'Shit!' Bill cursed, and Bonnie looked over from her bed on the curved white imitation leather lounge on the fly-deck where she and Bill had reclined, trusting the auto-pilot as the rest of the Anu mob enjoyed a beer below on the aft deck.

'What's up, una?' she asked sleepily.

'Bonnie girl, that was Doc. He must know about the dugong. He's going to meet us at the wharf. We have to chuck it over the side.'

'Shit, una. The boys won't let you,' she warned, sitting up, serious now. 'And dad will be shattered, una!'

They looked at each other, thinking.

'Hey, why don't we drop them off on the little boat off Cable before we get near the port, then Doc won't see nuthin,' she suggested.

Bill thought about it. He was in the Anu good books with the entire family now. Even Snowflake had patted him on the back when they returned from the crab hunt. And he wanted to be in the good books as this thing with Bonnie was nice. He wasn't sure that he loved her. He wasn't sure that was in him anymore. He had loved and lost Mere Lopes four years ago. That had hurt beyond belief. He had loved, and did love Gypsy; but that was a love that could never be more than his infatuation. Sometimes he thought in many moments of quiet reflection, that his emotion for Gypsy might be a love of a perfect idea. Perhaps it was just the fascination of a concept of the perfect woman. But in whatever way his damaged psyche was now capable, he had to admit that he did in fact, 'kinda' love Bonnie, his spirited funny Aboriginal princess. He loved being with her. Loved her humour. Loved the energetic physical connection between them. And so he agreed with her that they would at least try to sneak the Anu mob and their dead dugong ashore onto Cable Beach.

27
HEART OF GLASS

The police cruiser was on the tarsealed car park on top of the ancient coastal sand dune where the Broome Surf Club now sat with panoramic views out to the Indian Ocean, and north and south along the popular beach. Doc was alone, as he had arranged to pick up Bill and deliver him to Bob Hopkins, who was settling into his room at the Mangrove Hotel back in the town.

Doc had his police-issue high-powered binoculars resting on a small tripod on the doorsill. He saw the *Freedom* punching her twin hulls against the gentle swell. She tracked toward the port on a parallel line along the world-famous expanse of Cable Beach. On this hot school-holiday afternoon, with the temperature in the high thirties, the white sand was packed with locals and the tourists that the locals affectionately referred to as terrorists. Tanned bodies and multi-coloured beach umbrellas, and the gentle inner break completed the postcard vista of action and colour.

Through the powerful optics of the lens Doc could now pick out Bill seated at the wheel of the *Freedom* up on the fly-deck. After some initial confusion he grunted in disgust as he realised that what he had at first thought was a shadow across the skipper's lap was in fact the naked back and buttocks of little Miss Anu. He gave another grunt at the further realisation that the bare back of the first mate was bucking on the captain's lap in a much more vigorous fashion than the seas were causing the *Freedom* to ride.

'Oh, you dirty little fucken bitch,' Doc exhaled. But he kept the eyeglass on the action until Bonnie finally disconnected and silkily slid from her skipper's affections and lay back onto the sofa, legs akimbo. And all the time the fat, flushed man kept one hand holding the binoculars steady on the sill while the other squeezed and rolled and pulled at his sweaty genitals via the pant leg of his khaki shorts. Finally, with a gasp like a huge beached blowfish, and moaning in a depraved chant, 'Ya dirty fucker...ahh, ya bitch...ya dirty fucking bitch!' Doc soaked into his grimy Y-fronts.

Even as he recovered his senses, looking quickly and guiltily about his parked vehicle to ensure no one had witnessed his official discharge, Doc saw the *Freedom* slow and pull a sharp left towards the beach. At fifty metres back off the slight swell of Cable Beach she sat in neutral, and Doc focused intently now on the bustle of activity on the back deck. With the Cat shunting her stern to the beach, Bill was now clearly in view and was apparently loading the Anu mob into the vessel's tender that had been skipping in the bigger boat's twin wake. Confused, Doc was too far away for a clear view or understanding of what was developing, so he called in his cavalry. With his policeman's curiosity piqued he simply wanted to know what this mob was up to. What the fuck was that big black object they were awkwardly loading into the tinny? Doc grabbed his mobile and rang the beach chair and umbrella hire operator on the beach, where he was seated in front of his tent almost directly in line with the *Freedom's* tender. Doc noted that the bigger vessel was now underway again.

'Mohamed...Doc here, maaate. Look, I need to know what the Anu mob are up to, maaate. Yeah I know...Yeah, that's them just come off the *Freedom*. Yes, maaate, have a look and let me know, right? Yeah, something big and black, mate, from the *Freedom* to the tinny. Call me back, right? Ta, maaate, I owe ya a beer.'

As the *Freedom* with only Bill and Bonnie aboard slid smoothly away from the drop-off and headed south along the beach front towards the small Broome Port, Snowflake Anu steered the smaller boat and its happy, cackling crew directly towards dry land.

Millie had had the idea as to how to get a dugong from the boat to the Anu family ute that was parked in the car park back from the crowded beach. She had found one of the old hire wetsuits in the main cabin.

'Hey, dad! Hey, boys! What say we put that fella in here, eh?' and they all saw the logic and at the same time the hilarity of dressing the dugong in one of the wadjela's wetsuits. So without Bill seeing or even wanting to know, that's what they did.

The dugong was a smallish but plump young male of some sixty kilos. The one-piece wetsuit and the attached rubber bonnet fitted quite well, and the dugong's small side flukes tucked nicely into the sleeves. With some little effort the brothers tucked the flexible tail down one leg and tied some twine halfway down both legs to make him secure. Snowflake tried to park the small tinny close to the boat ramp at the northern end of the beach. There, the small concrete ramp separated the main beach from the nudist beach to the north. The hull slid up nicely onto the sand and Elvis leapt from the boat and took the line forward to tie her off for Bill's later collection.

There was a fair bit of casual spectator attention given to the noisy Aboriginal family who unfolded themselves from the boat onto the beach. Millie and Mozzie in particular had hit the generous supply of cold beers on the two-hour trip back and Millie's glass-shattering cackle rang out to draw further attention to the activity at the boat ramp.

Mohamed was one such observer to wander over to watch the popular local family carry their catch of mud crabs from the small boat. But it was when Snowflake and Rock lifted an apparently lifeless scuba diver from the bottom of the boat that a large and growing crowd of curious tourists gathered to chatter and point. The two big black men dressed only in black footy shorts, tribal scarring patterning their wiry frames, staggered under the weight of their rubber-wrapped load. The two empty legs of the suit flapped with their motion as they held him like an unconscious drunken mate and hurried him across the expanse of the beach toward their rusted old ute. By now roughly one hundred scantily clad beachgoers encircled the strange procession from boat to ute.

'What you got there, you Anu mob?' Mohamed called across to the boys, and then the inevitable happened.

Just as Snowflake called back in jest to the chair-man, 'Diver bloke got chewed by shark!' the twine on one leg gave way and three pints of pale diluted dugong blood, followed by the slosh-splat of the fleshy liver slid and splattered messily out onto the sand. A French tourist screamed, and then that was it. The seas parted. The crowd simply peeled away from the 'shark victim' and screaming people ran to warn swimmers and beach-based families of the fatal shark attack. From a seagull-eye view it was like a pebble splashing into a still pool. There followed a rippling chaos-effect of the mass evacuation of Cable Beach radiating progressively out from the black bullseye that was the Anu mob. In the chaos, the family made it to the ute and plopped the body into the steel tray. Mohamed saw the dugong then, its whiskered countenance and big black empty eyes smiling dully out of the wetsuit. Mohamed laughed and slapped his thigh in delight as he reached for his mobile phone.

28
TELL ME LIES

'Fuck! He's there, waiting for us! Good thing we ditched Dougie-de-deceased-dugong without attracting any attention,' Bill commented down to Bonnie. Dressed now in tiny frayed cut-off denim shorts and a tastefully tattered red, black and yellow T-shirt, she stood on the lower deck with a noose of blue nylon mooring rope at the ready as Bill steered the *Freedom* smoothly through the pale turquoise waters of the Broome port. He spun her gently around and kissed the starboard bow up against the old tractor tyre buffers near the open water end of the wharf's dogleg. This gentle bump allowed Bonnie to reach out with the lasso and tie the *Freedom* onto a bollard near the rusted steel stairway.

Doc Patrick stood beside the red-dusted police Land Cruiser on the end of the wharf and greeted them with an exaggerated Benny Hill salute. Bill flipped a friendly bird back as he held the vessel against the tension of the bow rope. Bonnie, lithely bare-foot, skipped along the boat's length and made the mooring connection from the boat's stern to wharf and Bill turned the key to still the purr of the engine.

'Gidday, maaate,' boomed from the heavens and Bill looked up the two metres to respond to the flushed freckled face that peered down at them from the heavy planked top deck of the wharf.

'Hi, Doc, what's up, mate?' Bill queried as casually as possible in his dead-dugong-deception-driven state.

'Hey, it's me whose aksing the questions, Mr Peters,' Doc shot back, suddenly serious, all official like, and for a moment Bill wondered.

'I am investigating the suspicious disappearance of the Anu mob, seen leaving Broome Port on the *Freedom* this morning and now, on your return, no bloody where to be seen! That's what's up, you two fuckin suspects.'

Bill and Bonnie laughed.

'You silly old bugger, Doc,' Bonnie giggled. 'The family took the tinny to Cable to drop their crabs off in the ute.'

'A likely story, a likely story, Miss Anu,' and Doc smiled as Bill followed Bonnie up the ladder to the wharf deck. 'But seriously, Bill, I need to sit with you on another matter, can you spare me some time?'

'What, right now, Doc?'

'Yeah, maaate. Look, I need you to come with me and meet someone from Sydney. Someone pretty important, maaate.'

Bill, eager to please, now that it appeared Doc knew nothing about a cruelly slaughtered protected aquatic icon, agreed to go with him. He pecked Bonnie on the cheek and whispered, 'I'm going to pay you back later for what you did today, my girl. I'll cop-u-later, missy,' in her ear.

Bill handed her the keys to his old jeep that sat rusting near the services building. He had inherited the trusty old US WWII vehicle from Gypsy and Tommy months before when they had left the town. Bonnie fired her up and coughed smokily away while Bill joined Doc in the air-con-cooled cab of the Toyota.

Doc sat, suddenly contemplative. He stared out to the port over the small fleet of commercial and pleasure craft as they rocked softly on heavy cyclone moorings. The bulky strength of the moorings always spoke to Bill of the potential of the cyclonic winds of destruction that occasionally swung down from the north.

'Bill,' he spoke, and Bill tensed, realising now that Doc had crossed from his usual alki-comical-casual-Broome persona into his WA Police official persona. 'I need your help. I am going to take you to a very old friend of mine, a bloke called Bob Hopkins. Bob is an Australian Federal Police commander. He would be about the AFP's third ranking officer in the nation.' Doc turned to look meaningfully at the younger man.

Bill nodded, somewhat intrigued now. Where was all this leading?

'Maaate, years ago when I was a sober young fella, eighteen years in fact, I worked undercover in Victoria under Bob Hopkins. We worked on a Calabrian Mafia cell moving drugs into the state. Bob was in charge.

All went well. A big success. After it was over I was moved back into the WA force and shifted around the country towns. Always one step ahead of the Mafia contract that was put on my head.'

Bill felt a comment was needed. 'Shit!' was the best he could muster, still wondering where the fuck this little talk was headed.

'Maate, I didn't respond as well to coming out of undercover as I have seen you do. Bill, you know I am a drunk. A fucken lonely old feral bull.' Doc went quiet, and Bill stayed silent for several long moments.

'Whisky, whisky, my old friend,' Doc incongruously sang quietly. 'Booze, mate. That was my answer. My answer to the expectation that one day a nice Italian gentleman would fulfil the contract. That's why I drink and that's how I fucked up me life.'

Bill was starting to wonder if he was expected to be an unwilling partner in a counselling session with Doc.

'Bill, there is something that Bob Hopkins is going to aks you to do. All I want to say is please listen to him.

Maaate, this is big, and you and I can play a part.'

'What the fuck is it, Doc?' Bill was tiring of Doc's mysterious bumbling around the issue. By this stage all he wanted to do was meet with this man Hopkins and find out what the hell was going on.

'No, mate, Bob will tell ya. But Bill, this is very fuckin important to *me*. This is something I need to do with ya. I will take you there now but I want you to know that you have to, you must do, what Bob wants you to, okay?'

Bill shifted to twist in his seat to look at Doc.

'Doc, what is it you need me to do?'

'I can't tell ya, maaate. Bob will tell ya. I'll take ya to Bob.'

And so, finally, with a very confused passenger, Doc steered the big four-wheel drive in a tight circle and back along the creaking jarrah planks of the wharf up along Port Road and into Broome township without any further discussion.

Bill could feel a palpable anxiety emanating from Doc as he parked the Land Cruiser in the car park of the majestic old Mangrove Hotel off Carnarvon Street. Doc stopped him with a hand on his forearm as Bill reached to open the passenger door.

'Maaate, I don't want to do this. But this is such a big thing. Look, it's so important to me, as a police officer, as a man, as a friend of Bob Hopkins that I have ta.'

A pregnant pause with Bill now totally confused.

'Bill!' and Doc leant across suddenly professionally aggressive. 'Bill, if you don't agree to co-operate with Bob, I will personally fuck you!' he said and a particularly nasty vision leapt into Bill's conscious thought. 'I will fuck your life! Put you in prison. Chase you out of Broome. I know you took a dugong, Bill! I have it! My men seized it from the Anu mob and they have made statements that your boat was used to hunt it.'

Bill cringed. 'Oh fuck!'

Doc continued on an angry roll. 'It's a major federal and state crime mate. You *will be* arrested! So will your fucken girlfriend, and the entire fucken Anu mob. Your boat and everything on board will be seized under warrant. You stand to lose everything, maaate, including your freedom. The last bloke that took a dugong is doin ten years hard,' Doc growled.

Bill held his breath, hoping for a 'but'.

'But, Bill, look, just do what Bob aks and nuthin will happen bout the dugong. That I promise ya.'

'Okay, Doc, let's just go and see the man,' Bill answered calmly, belying the sudden rush of emotion and foreboding that Doc's words had effected deep within.

29

BAD

On a much smaller wharf than Broome Port and on the other side of the continent, that same Sunday afternoon the Spider grandfathers met again. The fleet of sleek black Mercedes was parked in an unlikely collection at the shore car park, each with a young male Vietnamese driver inside, seated and waiting. The five old snakeheads of the Spider Triad sat on canvas camp chairs on the small wooden jetty and fished for herring.

From a variety of vantage points surrounding the bay the NSW Police surveillance dogs cursed in frustration as they captured a digital still and video history of the meeting, but missed the vital audio evidence of the discussion that was taking place. The old men faced out to the deep blue waters of the mighty Sydney Harbour, avoiding even the remotest possibility that their faces could be filmed for later translation by a Vietnamese lip reader. Each also wore the traditional cone-shaped hats of the Vietnamese peasant farmer, which shaded their faces and provided an extra layer of camouflage with a strip of black cloth from the nose down.

The eldest spoke softly: 'It is time. We are agreed; it is time for the grandchildren. The new generation. Our sons have met and the five issue have been chosen. They need to be at that place in six weeks. Each will leave separately. Each will travel first to a different location at a different time. The sons made this plan, and it is good. Soon we can step back and leave it all to them. We can while away our autumns at teahouses, meet as we do today for fishing or cards, and talk about our past and our great-grandchildren. And wait for our winters.'

The other men grunted in agreement and drew on fragrant Asian cheroots, enjoying the beauty of the Sydney summer day. A fleet of racing yachts with technicoloured spinnakers fat with the onshore breeze battled for line honours over a twisting course a kilometre off the bay.

'In four weeks they leave to reach that place. Each will arrive into Broome from a different airport. They travel as tourists. They are the unknowns to the round eyes. Your grandson Pham, the teacher, your grandson Thu, the chemist, your grandson Li, the market gardener, your grandson Tao, the soldier, and my granddaughter Li Li, the lawyer. They are the unknowns. They will succeed.'

30

BLINDED BY THE LIGHT

Bob Hopkins answered the door and welcomed Doc Patrick and Bill Peters into the suite. Bob was an expert reader of men, a learned student of the science of body language, a great personnel manager. He knew immediately as he shook Bill Peters' hand that he was mightily upset about something. Bill was stressed, anxious, but hiding it well against all except an observer with the experience of the AFP commander. Bob cast a quick, querying look at Doc, immediately suspecting that his old and damaged protégé may have overstepped his mark, gone against his strict orders and revealed to the young man the purpose of the meeting. Doc blanched under the questioning stare but made the introduction.

'Bill, this is the man who needs to talk with you. This is Bob Hopkins.'

Bob took Bill's hand in a firm and friendly shake, taking hold of his forearm in that additional power-play contact used to accentuate the greeting.

'I am very glad to meet you, Bill, and thank you for coming with George to talk with me. I appreciate this very much.'

Bob was eager to relax the man before him and steered him over to the comfortable rattan easy-chair setting. Doc followed in anticipation of participation in the briefing.

'Look, George, I trust you don't mind, but would you be so kind as to leave Mr Peters and myself together for this initial meeting? Thanks, George,' Bob said.

Without waiting for Doc's agreement, Bob physically steered Doc back towards the door.

'Listen, would you wait for us, in the bar maybe, have a drink, use my tab and relax a while.'

Doc looked devastated as Bob stepped briefly outside with him, lowering his voice.

'Thanks, George. I will call you as soon as we have an indication that he will help us or not.' Doc nodded sadly. 'It has to be this way, mate,' Bob offered, and Doc was pleasantly surprised that Bob had called him mate; he had never done that before. 'George, now what have you said to him?' Bob asked gently just outside the door. 'I need to know what you said to get him up here'

Doc answered, 'Nothin boss, just aksed him to come and see someone important, and he agreed, nothin else was said really, he's a bit of a mate, see?' and Bob patted his shoulder

'Go and have a well-earned beer on me, my friend. I will call you back up here as soon as I know either way.'

And then he made an offer that he regretted as soon as it was said.

'Doc, I will want you to help me run this man if he agrees to help us. Okay?' Doc's response was a wide halitosis grin, tobacco stained teeth revealed in all their gory glory as he turned and hurried off to the bar to celebrate this turn of events.

Bob returned from his ushering out of Doc.

'Bill, I don't know what Doc has said to you, but please be assured that I mean you no harm.'

Bill nodded and took the chilled Crown lager offered to him by the slightly built man, still immaculately dressed in his pinstriped suit. Bill felt very much underdone in comparison, dressed as he was in his faded board shorts and salt-crusted floral T-shirt.

'Bill, I am a commander in the Australian Federal Police based in Sydney. That is how I know your man George Patrick there.'

'Yes, sir.'

'Please call me Bob, son,'

'Ahh, okay Bob. Yeah, Doc told me about the UC op in Victoria on the way up here.'

'Did he now...did he now?' Bob queried. 'Well, Bill, let me just say that I do know you.'

Bill looked closer at the other now; as if to try to recognise a man he was damn sure that he had never met in the past.

'No, son,' Bob chuckled, 'not personally, but from your infamous adventures some years ago in NSW.'

Bill nodded. Of course a senior commander in the feds would have followed that story.

'But that is not why I am here today talking with you. Although let me say that from the literature available on those adventures of yours, I was most impressed.'

'Thank you—I think,' Bill responded, starting to relax in the company of this impressive man.

'Yes, very impressed. The commissioner's wife, eh?'

Bill groaned, but then joined in the laugher as he discovered a little-known secret: Bob Hopkins was a snorter! One of those rare beasts who involuntarily snorted like a pig when they laughed.

'Anyway, on to the business of the hour. I am involved in the Concord Task Force homicide investigation. That is why I need to talk with you, Bill Peters.'

'Okay, Bob, but I am struggling here. Why me?' And Bill *was* struggling to understand how in any possible way he could be connected to the terrible mass murder case that he had followed only vaguely since it had happened weeks before.

'I need to start from the start,' Bob announced as he picked up the remote control to the CD player. At his digital command the plasma TV screen kicked into electronic life. The scenes from the news and forensic police coverage taken at Concord played.

'Let's just watch this and then I will put to you what I need. Then if you don't want to help us, you walk straight out of here. And further, you have it on my personal guarantee that whatever George Patrick has threatened you with, will not happen.'

Bill looked at the other man in surprise; this man had a skill of empathy and perception.

And so they watched the CD, and although Bob Hopkins had seen the vision a hundred times already his attention remained as fixed and as professionally fascinated as at his first viewing.

Bill knew that he was watching footage that was operational in-house forensic evidence. He saw not only an extended version of the

In Depth News coverage that he and all of Australia, and indeed most of the civilised world had assiduously watched soon after the terrible event, but he was also witness now to the close-up horror of the crime scene at Concord and at the Golden Fish. He watched as crime scene investigators solemnly but clinically removed from Concord Oval the dozens of bodies, including those of Annie and Dan Dever. He watched the frighteningly grotesque displays of the autopsies at RSH. Saw the unreal visual overkill of platoons of bodies laid in precise rows. He watched the forensic dissections that showed the fatal damage that the purple camels had caused.

Bob Hopkins also watched Bill closely, measuring the effect that the vision was having. Then as the footage neared its end there was the inescapably emotional vision of the many funerals, the distraught families, devastated mothers and fathers, sobbing siblings, but in particular the heart rending scenes of the little children of the dead.

Bob paused the playback and spoke to the clearly moved young man.

'Bill, with all due respect to you, I now must follow protocol. I need you to sign a Commonwealth confidentiality agreement that what I show you and discuss with you now will not be disclosed by you to any other person or agency. This is a strict legal agreement with severe penalty provisions. Let me repeat that if you want to, you can walk out this door now. But, Bill, I would ask you to stay, and hear and see what I have and what I need.'

Bill thought about what he had just seen. He understood that this man would not have travelled across the wide red continent on a whim. So even though he still had no idea what Bob Hopkins could possibly want from him, he decided that if simply walked away he would never know and would always wonder.

'Okay, Bob, I am happy to sign the agreement and to abide by it.'

And so that was done. A legal document that in forceful plain English warned him of the consequences of divulging secret information was duly signed by citizen William Peters and witnessed on behalf of the Commonwealth of Australia by AFP Commander Bob Hopkins.

'Thank you, Bill,' Bob said as he handed to Bill a second cold beer, and then they sat and Bob restarted the paused CD. The scene was a small trendy apartment. On a table was a blister pack of nine tablets. One tablet from the pack of ten was missing. The camera zoomed in on a tablet and Bill saw a purple single hump camel clearly embossed in fine detail. The camera drew back to a wide shot and swung down. There on the carpeted floor was a mess, a human form crawling with fat white maggots. And there on the corpse, body-juice stained but discernible, was a T-shirt. The camera zoomed again and Bill started in disbelief as he read the distinct black-lettered logo.

I was healed by Gypsy at Beauty Bay—WA

31

BORDERLINE

Bob Hopkins paused the CD on the logo, which leapt accusingly out of the technology with its damning, incongruous and clearly false boast. 'Gypsy?' Bill breathed in disbelief.

'I know that Gypsy and Beauty Bay are known to you, Bill. Let me explain the big picture here. The cause of death of some seventy-six innocent citizens in Sydney, at the Concord Oval and the next night at the nightclub, has been proved scientifically to have been from poisoning. Terrible, messy, painful deaths, Bill. Deaths that no human being should ever suffer. And the poison, we now know, was in ecstasy tablets that were sold to the unsuspecting victims at the venues. In those tablets was strychnine—rat poison.'

Bob paused. Bill knew basically all that he had just been told from the media releases following the events anyway, but Bob's cool professional delivery still had a salutary effect that made him consider how those poor souls had died.

'Now, this man you have just seen wearing the T-shirt. He was a senior man in a criminal gang based in Cabramatta, Sydney. It's an organised crime gang that happens to be based on ethnic origins, Vietnamese, and it is known as the Spider Triad. Its main business is to import and sell illegal drugs. We believe that that young man, whose name was Van Nguyen, may have been the courier who brought the poisoned ecstasy into Sydney.'

Bill was shocked. The drugs came from Beauty Bay, he supposed. 'No!' he muttered.

'Wait, Bill. We don't know where Van may have picked up the deadly haul. We can trace his travel. We know that he flew to Perth. Flew to Broome within a few hours of arriving, didn't leave Perth airport to do that. We know that he stayed in Broome for three nights, hired a car and drove to Beauty Bay where he stayed for five nights. We know that he then drove, by himself we believe, the five thousand kilometres from Beauty Bay to Cabramatta. Clearly Van could have picked up the drugs anywhere along that route.'

Bill started to relax. It was way too loose! They had no hard evidence that the gangster had picked up his drugs at Beauty Bay.

'You are right, Bill,' Bob Hopkins commented, seeing the emotions pass over the younger man's face. 'We have no proof that Beauty Bay and your friend Gypsy and her man Tommy are in any way involved in this. But, and I am sure with your past you will appreciate this, we need desperately to know.'

'Look, Bob, I appreciate that of course, but where do I fit in? What do you think I can do to help you?'

'Let's cut straight to the chase. We need you to go inside Beauty Bay. We need to know if there is anything at that place that may connect it to the events of a month ago in Sydney. To put it bluntly, Bill, I am asking you to go undercover again.'

Bill physically winced at the thought.

Bob continued quickly, 'Look at it this way. We know Van was at Beauty Bay. He stayed five nights. Why? Why would he come all the way over to Broome, Western Australia, and then stay five nights at the most isolated of places. We don't think that he picked up the drugs in Broome. We don't know if he picked up the drugs on that long road trip back to NSW. And of course we have no evidence that he picked up the drugs at Beauty Bay. But put yourself in my shoes for a minute. If you had that scenario before you, where would you be looking the most closely at, based on Van's movements?'

Bob halted his staccato analysis suddenly as Bill sat in deep thought before his muttered agreement.

'Yeah, Beauty Bay.'

Bob Hopkins stood to remove his jacket, slipped off his monogrammed silk tie as the younger man stared out at Roebuck Bay. The tide was receding with the extraordinary rapidity of that place revealing convoluted mud flat beyond the mangroves. Bob stayed silent, wanting Bill to absorb all the information that had been pushed at him, needing him to contemplate what he had just seen and heard. Five minutes passed and Bob took the opportunity once again to refresh both his and Bill's Crownie.

'Right, Bob. Tell me exactly what you need from me,' Bill finally asked.

'I need you to go into Beauty Bay and simply observe and report. We need you to stay there for as long as it takes for you to be convinced or otherwise, that any person at that place had any involvement in the events at Sydney.'

Bill nodded almost imperceptibly. Now Bob delivered the angle that he had thought about and planned for the appropriate time in the interview as most good detectives did. The crunch! The kill!

'I want you to look at it this way—you know Gypsy and Tommy. They are currently under strong suspicion of involvement in this nation's biggest mass murder.'

The commander was unashamedly exaggerating the quality of his bait in order to catch his fish.

'You going undercover at Beauty Bay may well be the ultimate way that you can help and protect your friends. This is different to what you did in New Zealand with the TK Gang,' he said.

Bill saw that this man had done his homework.

'With them you were clearly acting against their criminality. With Beauty Bay you may well be acting in the interests of Gypsy's and Tommy's innocence, protecting them.'

Bill sat, taking the occasional contemplative sip from his drink. He ran Bob's persuasive argument again and again through his head. He thought past what the man was saying. He knew that if he didn't go undercover for the police he had no way of helping Gypsy. He knew that the alternative was probably the huge disruption of a mass arrival of a police task force to search, to tear apart, and to frighten the crap out of his friends. But to go undercover at the Bay! To be once again a Judas! To spy on his only real friends. How could he justify it, how could he qualify that? But finally of course he knew that he had to.

'Okay, Bob, count me in.'

Bob Hopkins simply reached across the gap between the chairs and shook his new agent's hand.

32

BRASS IN POCKET

Phone calls needed to be made. Bob Hopkins called the hotel bar to have the barman ask the local police senior sergeant to report back to the room. The barman sighed in relief as he passed the request on to the increasingly annoying alcohol-fuelled and animated Doc. The bar staff had been driven to distraction by him. Doc had insisted on enlightening them to the progress and nature of the big El Nino-inspired wildfire still one hundred kilometres to the southeast of the town, as they attempted to serve the increasing numbers of thirsty house guests arriving into the restaurant for dinner after a long hot day of doing touristy things.

While he waited, Bill called Bonnie from the room's phone. She was expecting him at the Anu home to feast on the usual gastronomic delights prepared by Millie. She was also waiting patiently in expectation that he would be honouring his whispered threat of feasting on her own succulent delights. Bonnie was by nature an understanding and casually relaxed girlfriend, so she simply accepted what he told her. That he needed to spend some time with Doc's 'important mate, on a matter involving the *Freedom* and a new tourist venture.'

'Okay, una, this time I will forgive you, Billy. But that's one you owe me, and I always get back what you owe me.'

'Thanks, girl, and hey, I just want to say,' he whispered into the mouthpiece as Bob Hopkins strode to the door to open it for the returning Doc, 'I think I am falling in deep like with you.'

'I like you too, my deadly wadjela boy, and, hey, by the way, you better be free tomorrow for lunch. Mum and dad and the boys are putting on a big feed for the tribe. You are just about part of the tribe now, Billy,' she laughed. 'Dad said to make sure you are here to taste the dugong and the crabs, eh?'

'I wouldn't miss it for anything girl…hey wait on! Did you say the dugong?' Bill asked, suddenly aware that Doc's recent threats against him involved the alleged official seizure of the aquatic sea-cow as a police exhibit.

Bonnie mistook his surprised query for apprehension at being invited to eat the beast. 'Yes, my little white meat. Mum's preparing the dugong right now. You gunna get to taste some native meats.'

So the real briefing began and finally, in the early hours of the morning all was agreed to and all was clear. Bill would go undercover. He was to call Gypsy at a civilised hour during the day. He would take up her many prior invitations to join them at the resort. He would offer his services to work with his friends during the wet season that was almost upon them. The timing of this was coincidentally apt, as Bill was soon to lift the *Freedom* onto the hard and store her away during the cyclone months.

Bob discussed payment for Bill's services, insisting that the operation must pay him and that this would be done in accordance with the hourly rates that he would have charged under his new state private investigator's licence. But Bill argued against payment.

'Bob, there is no way that I am going to be paid for this; I am doing this for Gypsy, not for money.'

Bill's attitude was that he was not working as such for Bob Hopkins, either as a PI under his state licence, or as a contractor to the Australian Government or even as a fucking deputy dog. He was doing this dirty stinking job for love. But he saw that Bob would not take no for an answer and accepted the inevitable. Finally it was agreed that Bill would be paid, but that the money would go directly into Doc's local Boys Town youth programs via the Broome Shire Council.

Doc contributed little to the detailed discussions that took place over the succulent room service meals. They ate heartily of the thick, rich fillets of the fighting barramundi that had been caught that morning in a tidal creek a few kilometres from the hotel. Doc was struggling to appear sober in front of Bob Hopkins and so he was avoiding talking, which would surely reveal by slur and verbal trip that he had taken Bob's 'have a few on my bar tab' a little too enthusiastically.

Bob moved away from where Doc was seated watching the latest news of the bushfire on the TV and gestured for Bill to join him. He gave Bill a satellite phone, advised him that the technology would allow calls to him directly from the bay to the CTF headquarters in Sydney Central.

'Bill, when you need to talk to me just press the button with the number one on it. It is a dedicated and direct link. Everything we say will be recorded digitally. It's all automatic. I want you to call me to report each night if possible.

'Press button number two and it will link you directly to George. That will also be pre-programmed by tomorrow and will connect you to George via a sat-phone that I will provide to him. I don't want you to report to George,' Bob insisted quietly.

'I only want you to call George if you have an emergency. If you need urgent local assistance.' Bill nodded, taking the small black phone.

'Bill, if you need me just call me any time, twenty-four-seven. At all times the call will be recorded. Keep the phone with you and safe. I will be returning to Sydney early tomorrow, but I will come straight back as soon as you need me back. Thank you again, Bill, and keep safe.'

Bob shook Bill's hand to seal the arrangements.

After the meal and with no more liquor ingested, Doc found that he was sobering up slightly. Doc was feeling extremely proud now to be once again involved in such an important operation; although Bob had made it crystal clear to him that he was to be on the periphery only and must not act without his specific approval or direction.

Bill could see that the senior man was cautious and perhaps worried that he even needed Doc's involvement in this operation within an operation. But Doc had been the conduit, the connection, and Bob had decided to include him, hoping to carefully manage him from a distance despite his concerns. And then there was the tyranny of distance. Neither Bob nor his men could stay in Broome, or even in WA indefinitely to await developments. What Bill was doing could take weeks, after all. He needed to have an emergency contingency. He needed a rapid response available should any one of numerous possibilities or probabilities occur that might, for example, threaten his agent's health, his safety or his life. Taking everything into careful account, Bob was prepared to risk Doc taking on that role. He was prepared to trust him until he betrayed that trust.

So, in the early hours with the briefing over, Bob Hopkins thanked Bill on behalf of 'the people of Australia' for what he was about to do. And although being thanked on behalf of an entire nation seemed a somewhat grandiose expression of gratitude, Bill saw that it was sincere and took Bob's hand in respect for the man.

Bob kept Doc behind and Bill suspected that Bob needed to get very direct with the local man. Bill was happy to leave the hotel room and make his way back to the port and to his floating home by cab.

Twenty minutes later, as he climbed the ladder onto the rear deck of the *Freedom*, he could only shake his head in wonderment at the turn of events that had so rocked his new life in paradise.

33

ENDLESS SUMMER NIGHTS

Bill could hear from some distance away that the Anu place was rock-and-rolling as he treadled along Herbert Street on his rusty bicycle after a leisurely ride down the nine kilometres from the port on the warm tropical day. As he got closer he saw his old jeep parked on the broad expanse of red pindan that pretended to be a front lawn. Behind it was the huge tin roofed colonial bungalow, typical of the strongly built dwellings that comprise the older Chinatown suburbs of Broome near to the Town Beach.

Mozzie Anu had bought the family base decades before when housing was dirt cheap during one of the busts of the boom and bust cycles that told the story of the region and of the town. His money had been carefully collected with the raising of prime cattle on his forefathers' Kimberley cattle station. Subsequently, with the advent of the live cattle trade from the Port of Broome, the poor beasts were loaded onto smelly coastal traders for the sea trip to the hungry mouths of Indonesia. Mozzie had seen an opportunity. He built a feed-lot on his land to hold, grain-feed and further fatten other more remote stations' cattle in a final value-added plumping up before the beasts' first and final sea voyage.

His Broome house was set on half an acre of prime Broome land. With the coming of tourism in the town the land values had soared as city dwellers from Perth and from the greater Australian metropolises sought to secure their own slice of tropical heaven. Mozzie could and often did humorously boast to anyone prepared to listen to his long and fascinating dialogues, mainly about him, that he was a local Broome BAM, or a 'bloody Aboriginal millionaire!'

Following his meeting with Bob, Bill had arrived back at the boat just after two am and had slept fitfully until about eight. Then, sick of trying to deal with the mish-mash of thoughts battering his consciousness, he rose and made the phone call to Gypsy. Unsuspecting of his ulterior motives, she was typically warm and enthusiastic that he, her *special friend*, wanted to come to the bay and spend time with her and Tommy.

'Billy, I could think of nothing lovelier! To see you again. The phone calls have not been enough, my friend. I think I need to see you again, you who appreciates me so much, and makes me feel that I am special.

Yes, come, please. And stay with us for as long as you like. Forever would be acceptable, my friend.'

'Thanks, gorgeous one,' he responded, an incredible feeling of guilt of his deception enveloping him. But then he replayed the mantra he had created in the time since he had awoken: 'I am doing this to protect you, Gypsy, to protect you,' and knew that this was true.

Now he needed to tell Bonnie. Tell his lover that he was going to leave her. Stay for an unknown period of time with a woman that Bonnie knew he had a great deal of affection for. But Bonnie also knew that Gypsy was Tommy's woman, so she should not misunderstand, Bill hoped. But what if Bonnie wanted to go with him? He would have to say no. The thought of telling her some version of him doing this as a PI occurred but was discarded as foolish immediately. Bonnie was Gypsy's friend; too risky. But how would she react to his story of a visit for an indeterminate period? Only one way to find out.

With the hubbub of raucous, happy talk amidst melodic acoustic guitar-backed country and western singing emanating from behind the big house, he leaned his bike against his jeep and walked around the side of the dwelling to find her.

Although the diverse fleet of cars, vans, utes and two old red-dusted buses parked along the road at the front of the house should have warned him, Bill still got a gentle visual shock as he came around the corner of the building and discovered that the extended family of the Anu mob numbered around one hundred! That five score and more were a happy and colourful collection of Broome's Aboriginal, Asian and 'white mate' population. When he poked his head shyly around the edge of the bungalow, Bonnie was first to spot him. With a whoop of delight she ran on bare feet from a big marquee set square in the yard to launch herself at her man. Bill caught her as she wrapped her strong, wiry legs around his waist.

'Where you been, una?' she laughed and they kissed as Millie and the other older aunties of the family group cackled and teased the favourite daughter and her embarrassed young wadjela, who was politely attempting to unwind her from him.

Cheekily she resisted, squeezing his middle in an Anu leg lock, ankles crossed behind him. But more immediately concerning for Bill as the entire gathering turned to see what all the fuss was about, was the shameless, deliberate gyration of her groin against his as she pretended that all she was up to was a mock wrestle. Finally, among much laughter and a chorus from the various aunties of 'shame girl—let that boy free!' and 'sham-it little sister un-leg that wadjela' and other cackles of delighted advice, Millie saved Bill with a hefty smack to her naughty daughter's firm buttocks.

Giggling and rubbing the spot her mother's hand had surely marked, Bonnie fell off her man and took his hand.

Bonnie then led him around the party proudly making introductions to the guests, most of whom he had met before in the small town over the last several months. But he politely shook each hand and kissed all of the women on sun-warm cheeks. He was pleasantly surprised when Mozzie Anu took him in a warm, sinewy bear hug near the huge cast iron cooking pot that sat on a trestle holding it above an aromatic campfire in the middle of the garden.

'Welcome, son, welcome. Everyone, this is Bonnie's man, Billy,' Mozzie announced loudly, 'and he's a bloody good bloke—for a wadjela!'

The gathering laughed at the old man's typical humour and shouted 'giddays!' to Bill.

Mozzie proudly showed him the contents of the big pot. He had Elvis and Rock lift the heavy lid by inserting a length of steel rod through the handle. Inside Bill could see a colourful mess of solid fatty-pale meat chunks mixed with the pungency of green vegetables, peppers and tubers. Despite knowing that this must be Dougie-de-dugong, his salivary glands kicked into action. With a little trepidation, Bill took the offered spoonful from the old man and tried to forget the sad eyed flesh-donor who had so significantly contributed to the taste sensation. His mouth was filled with a gastronomic explosion of taste and he chewed and swallowed the tender treat with the required murmurs of appreciation.

Mozzie, satisfied, nodded to the boys and the lid went back on. But Bill was confused.

'Hey, Mozzie,' he queried quietly into the old man's sun dried ear. 'Did Doc give that fella back to you?'

Mozzie shook his old head with a puzzled look. Bill took the query no further, realising immediately that Doc had lied to him. The police had not seized the dugong from the family at all. Bill marked that one down in the grey matter for future reference. Then Snowflake appeared from his right and pressed into his free hand a cold can of beer, and all three of the younger Anu men actually cracked a smile and patted their sister's choice on the shoulder, a fact not missed by his Aboriginal miss.

'See, boy! They like you, but they are not in deep like, like me,' she teased and laughed, and the two of them merged into the spirit and body of the party as it kicked along.

With the steady intake by the huge family group of a huge amount of cold beer, or for the ladies the deadly mango punch that Bill had not seen since the Shinju dragon boat race, the mood over the long warm afternoon mellowed. Bill found himself relaxing again and forgetting about Bob Hopkins, about Doc, and about other people's problems. Through the gradually darkening hours that followed he sat under the shade of the tropical palm and mango trees in the yard, usually with Bonnie on his knee, and drank his share of the icy beer. Later he ate much more than his share of the myriad exotic foods that the woman folk had prepared and then proudly presented under the marquee. Large patterned ceramic and china platters held the best of the local seafood prepared to the recipes of the varying ethnicities of the partygoers. The very tasty dugong stew that he had so hesitantly sampled was delicious and he went back for seconds. The big red-boiled mud crabs' rich white flesh smattered in a variety of light sauces; platters of steamed local deep-water banana prawns and their cousins the tiger prawns bought in by the trawlers from the Arafura Sea to the north east. Oysters and local mussels; and the special treat of the finely marinated, succulent meat of the local *pinctada maximus* oyster, that had enriched the town's population with its pearls for long decades. Then for the carnivores among them, platters of blood-juicy beef ribs from the Brahman-cross house herd Mozzie kept to feed his family, mottled with fat, grown from the lush green pastures of the family station; pink fleshed lamb chops for the town's later arrivals to the rich red lands; and for the original inhabitants, kangaroo steaks, and one dish that Bill decided was just a bit too local, an ember-baked goanna, which some of the old dark-hued aunties oohed and ahhed over.

The juices of the diverse proteins were soaked up off the platters with the doughy damper pulled from black pig-iron pans buried in the embers of the fire. Finally, the heavy meal was finished off with an array of local fruits.

Bill sampled the gorgeous musky orange flesh of mangoes, sugar-bananas, grapes, and the sweet delight of the variety of melons on display in the reds, greens and apricot colours of their crisp sugary flesh.

The day crept inevitably into night as the party buzzed and rolled on, noisy, happy, sated people of good will and in good spirit, and Bill decided that it was time to tell Bonnie that he was going away to Beauty Bay for a while. He whispered into her ear, breathing in the sex-musty fragrance of the fresh frangipani flower so seductively tucked there as she chatted gregariously to some female cousins.

'It's time I paid you back, girl, paid you back for what we both missed out on last night.' She giggled her assent.

'Where, una?' She was a little excited that he was the instigator this time, not her.

'On the oval, girl, Town Beach,' and she stood and took his hand and they slipped away in the dark, unnoticed in the happy confusion of the party.

As they passed the fruit table, Bill, unseen by her, picked up an over-ripe half peeled mango and hid it in his other hand. He walked her down the short distance from the house to the grassy oval at the Town Beach above a small stretch of sand off Roebuck Bay. As they walked onto the lush reticulated carpet of tropical grasses Bill picked her up like a newlywed bride heading to the marital bed for the first time.

As he carried her easily into the middle of the oval he casually checked about at that midnight hour for any possibility of an audience and found no one. The moon was huge in the sky above as he lay her down and lay beside her and kissed his woman as she writhed in her usual passion, exuberantly rejoicing in their physicality together and in her hunger for his maleness. He teased her as usual, at times pinning her hands down in a sensuous struggle as she tried to pull his clothes from his body, and he slowly undid and removed her garments and her fragrantly oiled blackness gleamed below him in the moonlight. And when she tired and lay still in her anticipation he reached for and found the mango behind him and to her initial surprise and then increasing moans of enjoyment, he caressed her body in a soft fruity circular massage, and then leant to taste it, licking its musk from her skin. She tried to fight him now, her hunger desperate, as with one hand he easily held her two slim arms together above her head, and with his legs and feet he pushed and pulled hers apart and held them wide. Then with his right hand and the nub of soft mango flesh he found her wet softness and cruelly caressed her in a slow, teasing, fruity rotation until she gasped her release and cried his name out to the panoramic sprinkle of the Milky Way above them. He lent to kiss her then, surprised to taste on her cheek a salty tear. Worried that he had unwittingly hurt her, he whispered, 'Bonnie girl, are you okay? Did I hurt you? Jeez, sorry babe.'

'Course not, una, course not, don't fuss. Just fucken love ya, that's all,' and he was relieved and kissed her again.

Then with an overpowering emotion straight from his heart he held her head, his big hands softly holding her face either side sliding under black glossy curls and turned her eyes to his and spoke.

'Bonnie, I need you to know that I love you,' and she cried again, sobbed. And they held each other, arms and legs entwined for what seemed like hours until she disentangled and rose in a crouch. She turned then, the other way, and her soft mouth began a gentle insistent suction as he lay enjoying the deep emotion of the moment and the stars above. And when he was ready she mounted him and lay on him, mouth to mouth. They moved in rhythm with each other almost unconsciously. As the moment approached and the two athletic young bodies rejoiced in those overpowering mini-surges toward the avalanche of the climax of their coupling there was a pop! pop! pop! about them. The oval's reticulation system burst into a minefield of sprinkler heads poking up from the grass like a platoon of opportunistic voyeurs. Drenched, the laughing lovers stayed enjoined in a spray of body-warm bore water.

34

DO YOU REALLY
WANT TO HURT ME?

'When the going gets tough?' The question stood out in stark black marker on the main whiteboard in the Concord Task Force's briefing room. Six long weeks had passed since the weekend slaughter. It was Monday morning, and the entire Task Force met as a matter of strict operational routine. Only those out of town on urgent inquiries were excused. Each team leader in turn and then each of the varied professions and experts in the forensic disciplines addressed the gathering that had now swelled in operational participants to over one hundred and twenty. As always, Fred Hall led the briefing. He paraphrased again the well-known sit-reps that always started with the events of Concord Oval and the Golden Fish. This was the weekly reminder—the reason that each man and woman was present and was working sixteen-hour days, seven days a week, each fiercely determined to crack the case.

The going *was* tough and the troops were frustrated; the detectives, the plainclothes, the forensic staff and scientists all searching assiduously for that breakthrough. But despite the massive effort to date there was no real progress. The entire Task Force now felt the pressure of society's expectation. The media and then the politicians started to ask why they hadn't arrested anyone.

The commissioner fought the initial battles alone, determined to protect her team. But the local state politicians saw only the lack of obvious or reportable progress and their initial 'full and total support' began to wane.

On that Monday at 1010 hours, immediately following the operational briefing, the premier of the State of NSW made his well promoted 'morale raising' visit to the Concord Task Force headquarters. With his entourage of dark-suited security and party-political minders and advisers in tow, along with a carefully selected media mob, the silver-maned State Premier Robert Pigeon swept into the briefing room. The premier was determined that he would be seen on the TV screens of the nation and of the world. Seen to be *doing something* to move this terrible tragedy on to resolution, to metaphorically kick some arse to get some action, that thing they called closure, happening. Accompanied by the reluctant commissioner dressed in all the dark blue and gold braided glory of her office, introductions were made under the hot glare of the mercury lighting of the busy media crews. The premier shook hands with the dark-suited Fred Hall and his immediate command team. The operational troops meanwhile stood at respectful attention until grandly waved down to their seats by Premier Pigeon.

Robert Pigeon stepped forward and spoke to the room, or more accurately to the cameras, in his booming baritone. He was brief. In crafted sound-bites, he thanked the team for their dedication and promised, '...my government's total support, and gratitude for your efforts to date, and, I have no doubt, the successful conclusion of this investigation into our nation's worst civilian tragedy'.

The staged-for-public-consumption event was over within a few minutes. The media pack disseminated, trickled away down the lifts to edit recordings and to record intros and editorial conclusions to the footage to be beamed out on the prime-time evening news to assure the public that Premier Pigeon had taken charge.

Meanwhile, behind the commander's closed office door, Premier Robert 'Call me Bob' Pigeon sat across the desk from Fred Hall, having shooed all of his support crew away to a private viewing of the complicated flow charts of the chronology of the operation to date. They were not to know that all the contentious and need-to-know stuff had been selectively removed from this version of the operation's progress.

'Fred, I won't insult you with pretty words—where are we at?' the premier snapped.

'Well, sir...'

'Call me Bob, Fred.'

'Okay, Bob, we are working on some very strong leads,' Fred Hall replied.

'Between you and me of course, we are certain that the Cabramatta-based crime triad, the Spider Gang is the source of the drugs.'

Pigeon nodded, aware of the inherent secrecy required with this inside information.

'Any progress there?' he asked.

'We have an operation underway as we speak,' Fred offered, knowing that he had to give this man something. 'I cannot say too much. We have an undercover agent going inside working with persons of interest to us. The agent is to be inserted at the place where we think that the tainted drugs may have entered the country. We are working closely with ASIO, AFP, Customs, and with another state's police force. I may have some significant progress to report to you in the next few weeks, sir.'

The premier sat back, contemplative. 'It's all a bit *possibly* and *hopefully*, Fred,' he said.

'Well that's...'

'Fred!' the street fighting political animal interrupted. 'Fred, I will give you a month, four weeks. If nothing happens I will have you replaced.'

Fred Hall accepted the political reality of the words, but he was not the type of man to take a threat from a mere politician without a fight. He leaned forward on the desk.

'Mr Pigeon, let me talk straight.'

And the premier, himself a graduate of the school of political hard knocks, and of the fierce factional battles of the down-and-dirty state Labor and union movement, recognised that here may well be his equal. Or his better...

Fred had remained seated across the metre of desk top but under attack had stiffened and unconsciously inclined toward the other man, who shifted instinctively back into the modest vinyl cushion of the chair. Fred Hall was a survivor too. His battles had been actual life and death struggles in the forests of Bosnia and the deserts of Iraq. He had then returned to a civilised Australian society and in the blue combat fatigues had fought equally determined and ruthless criminal soldiers from society's dangerous gangs and cliques in the dirty underground of Sydney city. No unctuous Pierre Cardin-suited politico was going to scare him. Fred's voice lowered to a growl.

'I do not personally give a flying fuck what you threaten, intend, or ultimately do to me! This group of men and women outside has worked sixteen-hour days for the last six weeks to crack this case. The simple fact is that we now know who is involved. We have targeted and are actively working on this organised criminal gang. Together, as a team, we will win this battle,' Fred barked.

The Premier of New South Wales sat in sober thought as the policeman opposite waited, quiet now, his statement made but hackles still up like an aggressive Rhodesian ridgeback before a lion. Then Pigeon smiled, stood, and reached across for a bemused Fred Hall's hand.

'Thank you, Fred. Forget the time line. You have my full and total support.'

35

BACK TO PARADISE

It took a week to get ready. Bill had to get the *Freedom* out and onto the hard to sit on a steel cradle and then craned onto a massive gooseneck multi-axle low loader. Then there was a very short journey up the bitumen and into the big old unused grain silo sitting in its cyclone-proof hulkiness just above Broome Port, where the shire allowed cyclone-season storage of valuable and fragile vessels each year for a peppercorn rent.

The stronger working ships, such as the steel plate prawn and fishing trawlers, either ran for southern ports pre-cyclone-season, or sometimes braved the storms in the violent convolutions of the deeper seas off the local coast. But experienced skippers never risked the cyclone seas. If caught out in the region with such a threat approaching, they ran instead for moorings in coastal creeks and tiny sheltered harbours. There, thick steel cable secured the vessels to heavy land-based anchorage at either side. But even then, the crews left the ships to their uncertain fate and took shelter on the solid base of land.

Through that week Bill toiled, cleaning and fussing over his pride and joy that was his only significant material asset, as well as his floating home. The *Freedom* was gently lifted, manoeuvred and finally settled on her custom-built padded steel cradle in the cavernous silo in readiness for her seasonal hibernation. Bonnie helped him, and it was Bonnie who solved his nagging guilty need to tell his new love that he was going to Beauty Bay without her.

Bill completed the last acts of protecting the *Freedom* with lovingly applied covers of waxes and grease, topping up of oils, disconnection of batteries and finally covering the mini-ship with the shrouds of a huge white canvas dust-cover. As they finished, Bonnie took his hand and told him that he would have to do without her for a while. Surprised, he turned to her as they walked out of the dark steel cave toward the old jeep.

'Wazzup, sister?' he joked. 'You going away without me, girl...got another bloke eh?'

She took his hand and squeezed, grinning at his exaggerated puppy-dog sadness.

'Silly bugger! Just a few weeks, una. Won't be long, eh. Absence will make your deadly hard grow longer,' she laughed at her own rude adaptation of the cliché.

'Jeez, you bloody cheeky girl,' he smiled back at her, suddenly relieved that he didn't need to struggle with his fraudulent explanation as to why he needed to be at Beauty Bay with Gypsy.

'Where you off to, bubs?' he asked, reaching down to swing her into his arms as he carried her and placed her into the dusty, cracked khaki vinyl of the passenger seat of the old jeep.

'Secret Anu family business, Bill,' she responded.

She smoothed the brightly coloured cotton sarong that wrapped her lower body in a sexy confinement, showing the swell of buttock and hinting at her wiry strength of thigh. He admired the view from where he stood above her as she adjusted her skimpy red bikini top that just caught and held her modest ebony breasts.

'The family's got a ceremony. My cousin Randolph, you know him? Ratbag kid from the Boys Town?'

Bill nodded. Young Randy was one of the fourteen-or-so-year-old vivacious teenagers who sweated and toiled in Bill's tae kwon do class at the shed that was the old Broome gym.

'Nice kid,' Bill commented, firing the reliable old WWII rust bucket into life. Bonnie nodded.

'Yea, una, lovely boy, and now he gets to turn into a man.'

She explained that the extended family was to gather on tribal lands up the coast for a week or so of structured celebration as the people followed centuries-old tradition to introduce young Randy to manhood.

As they headed back into the town toward Herbert Street, Bill casually and as if on sudden impulse, announced that if she was to be away, he might just go down and visit Tommy and Gypsy! He cunningly, or so he thought, said Tommy's name before Gypsy's, as if in order of importance. His subterfuge was as unnecessary as it was clumsy. But Bonnie didn't mind. She knew that Gypsy was Tommy's woman, as sure as she knew that Bill was her man. She knew Bill was sweet on Gypsy, but she was not jealous about her man's affection for another woman, as she also felt a strong affection for her friend. Bonnie didn't stress about mere possibilities. She lived simply, instinctively for the moment, for the real, the actual. Although within her was her ancestrally gifted dreaming, that dreaming was of her perceptions, her beliefs, her spiritual reality, her connection to the land, to the sea, the sky, her people, her world. Bonnie did not try to second guess destiny. She did not seek the answers as to her future that others sought in the strict protocols of the white man's religions, or the vague uncertain promised possibilities that others sought in the fringe quasi-sciences: the mysterious arts of astrology; of the soothsayers, painted-card dealers and the fortune tellers. Her people had, as did all human cultures, the magic men, medicine men, the feather-feet. But these men did not presume to foretell exact events coming in the seeker's future. Their intervention was to seek to clear the song-lines, the channels of communication from the spiritual to the human worlds for the benefit of the living. Although it was true that sometimes they asked those spirits to ensure a future fatal event on those dreadful occasions where the bone was pointed, and a death curse was issued.

Anyway, Bonnie was happy that Bill was meeting again with his friends, his people, his own little white sub-tribe. She had worried that while she was away he might again be the loner that she had watched keep to himself before they had become lovers. As they pulled up at the Anu mansion, Bonnie took his hand and insisted he turn the jeep off.

'Come, una, the mob's out buying supplies. We got an hour or so to say goodbye.'

He followed her into her room for a carefully timed fifty-eight minutes of their usual intense passion, always with the thought of the brothers and uncle Grimm bursting through their little sis's bedroom door to the sight of a whiter-shade-of-pale backside plunging the hot, dark and wondrous depths of planet Bonnie Anu.

36

DEVIL INSIDE

At ten o' clock that night Bill was down at Broome Port wharf. He was thankfully free of an Anu brotherly beating, having been found by Mozzie, Millie, Uncle Rock and the brothers-two to be innocently if somewhat haphazardly dressed and seated at the kitchen table across from the treasured Bonnie.

Millie was rarely fooled, though, and cheekily raised her eyebrows to her daughter and got a nod from the glowing Bonnie.

They had sat together in the early afternoon chatting and laughing at Mozzie's bad jokes as he relived the dugong hunt for the twenty-fifth time since that eventful day. At Millie's invitation, Bill joined the family for a final meal, keeping a safe unbroachable two seat differential between his crotch and Bonnie's naughty feet under the table.

Bill asked Mozzie if he could use the landline phone to call Beauty Bay and offered to pay for the privilege, an offer that Mozzie just snorted at and waved away as if being bothered by a pesky fly. Bill made the call to Gypsy, the raucous family noisy in the background, which then had Gypsy laughing in delighted recollection of her many previous good times with the Anu mob.

Then followed the entire family including, to Bill's surprise, the three large younger males, each taking a turn on the phone to speak to their friend at Beauty Bay. Bill was curious at the connection between Rock, Elvis, Snowflake and his friend Gypsy as the big men laughed into the black mouthpiece. Finally after an hour of phone tag by the family, concluded when Bonnie finished her alternating whisper-shout-giggling chat to Gypsy, Bill took the phone, sure that he had been an integral part of that discussion.

'Hi, it's me, finally,' he announced.

'Well, my friend, it's so good to learn that you have been busy, Billy, very busy Billy,' Gypsy said.

Bill felt incongruously guilty, as if he had somehow cheated on her, on his precious relationship with Gypsy.

'Yeah, well...ahh, I'll explain more about that when I get to the bay,' he offered, unwilling to talk about Bonnie when she was a few feet away and watching him mischievously.

'We certainly will, young man,' Gypsy teased again, but then let it drop and asked him to be at the port wharf at ten that night, where he would meet Tommy and the Beauty Bay supply barge, which was loading as they spoke, with three months' of provisions for the resort.

That night he kissed Bonnie and held her tight as they said their goodbyes on the front verge of her home. He needed the jeep to run himself back to the silo to pack his gear on board the *Freedom*, but he told Bonnie that the vehicle was hers to use while he was away. And finally as they parted he held her head again firm with both his hands, as if it was necessary to hold her to impress upon her his seriousness.

Again he told her, 'Bonnie, I do love you,' and she had a tear again as she replied.

'Billy, you are my man, my una.' She stood then, watching as the jeep grumbled away from her.

Right on ten pm Bill walked the planks of the long wharf toward the barge that bustled with the activity of the provedore's employees loading the bulky, crated stores onto the squat deck of the square-built vessel. The barge sat heavy on the high tide tethered to massive hardwood pylons.

As Bill approached he saw Tommy down on the deck awaiting the next netted sling from the small wharf-fixed gantry crane, while directing the busy gang of port workers on where to stack and tie the supplies for safe sailing.

'Hey, Tommy!' Bill called. Tommy, clad only in tattered blue shorts, grinned and waved.

'Come on down, mate,' Tommy responded, and Bill sought out and located the black rusted steel ladder inset onto the wharf, its lower rungs submerged by the warm curtain of the dark sea.

He climbed down and eased onto the barge and was met with a warm handshake and shoulder pat from Tommy. After stowing his kitbag in the tiny aft wheelhouse, Bill was immediately busy in assisting the skipper with the loading.

At the starboard side, Bill saw crated chickens and pigs, and then a huge lump that he had mistaken for freight covered in a blanket, but which, as his eyes adjusted to the dark, turned out to be a camel, and a very big one. The single humped beast reposed in that iconic leg-tucked configuration in a relaxed but somehow arrogant side-to-side cud chewing contemplation of the far horizon. Then Bill saw that a dark-skinned man lay alongside the beast.

But then he was busy, and it was not until the last box of cartons of long-life milk, the last crate of fresh fruit and veggies, the last can of baked beans, the final stacks of beer and wine and spirits had been sorted and secured that he got a chance to speak to Tommy.

At Tommy's gentle command Bill untied the heavy barge from the wharf stanchion and they began the slow but steady chug at eight knots south along the coastline toward Beauty Bay.

Doc Patrick sat in the Land Cruiser, bloodshot eye glued to the bino's under the dark shadow of the decrepit grain silo. He watched the barge leave and toasted *his* agent with a swig of tepid whisky.

As they left the port and turned awkwardly south, staying a safe ten kilometres off the rugged low coastline, Tommy handed the wheel to Bill and Bill looked ahead to the southern sky. Even at this early hour he could see again the heavy smudge of the big bushfire backlit by a smoky red moon. The conflagration was still some one hundred kilometres away from Broome. It was burning hot and untroubled by man's periodic puny attempts to halt its sometimes crawling, sometimes race-car-fast destruction of the flora and the slower fauna as things jumped, ran, flew, burrowed and slithered to avoid its fiery hunger.

As they began the voyage south Bill slept for several hours at Tommy's firm insistence, gently swaying on the aft deck from a comfortable hammock strung between the wheelhouse and the stern navigation light post.

He awoke rested as the eastern sky lightened. He swung out of the hammock and found Tommy busy at the barbecue that hung off the rear of the barge. Declining any offer of help, Tommy soon brought Bill an enamel plate heavy with a perfect omelette. With a sigh of saliva-induced anticipation he saw packed inside the fluffy, yokey blanket a slurry of purple sliced onion, blood-red cherry tomatoes, green olives and the rich tang of melted feta cheese. Bill was immediately ravenous and ate heartily, washing down the breakfast with hot black coffee.

Tommy also took a meal to the cameleer, who had stayed beside the large beast, alternately offering the regal bull a bucket of water or some hay for the journey. Tommy then fed himself, and finally the two could sit and talk on the remainder of the slow twenty-hour chug down the coast to the bay.

Bill was happy to hear that things had come right at the bay.

'It was a close thing, Bill, we did struggle.' Tommy looked away to the seaward horizon. 'At one time, only a few months back, I thought that we might have done our dough, as they say.'

'Yeah, I remember Gypsy saying things were tight in paradise, mate,' Bill replied, as Tommy took a sip of his milky mug of coffee.

'Well, I guess it was lesson for me, Bill. Basically, all of our pearl farm money went on the freehold. I didn't allow as much as I should have for the first twelve months operating the place. Because we are in such an isolated spot the advertising and promotion is expensive, and as you know, the niche market is somewhat small. The bay's not everyone's cup of tea. We miss out on Mr and Mrs Average and the Average kids cause we don't offer what they want. You know, the instant gratification stuff.'

'Right...' Bill sat quietly finishing the last half-inch of his coffee. He stood to refresh the brew. 'So did you trade out of the tight times, mate?'

'No—we got lucky, extremely lucky.' Tommy went quiet then, sat unusually contemplative.

'Lucky?' Bill prompted, but Tommy just looked across at him and then dropped the gaze.

'Some things are better left unsaid, mate.'

Bill's heart sank at this admission from Tommy, so unlike his usual relaxed openness. Bill simply hoped that Tommy was choosing not to discuss his and Gypsy's intimate financial dealings him, a reluctance that was not really that unexpected. But the purpose of his own subterfuge raised its nagging head and he recognised that he must endeavour to uncover the source of Tommy's resort saving *luck*.

'Who's the big brown furry bloke?' Bill asked, eager to ease the sudden tension, and Tommy responded in kind, nodding toward the camel and the man forward.

'That's Namu. He's a cameleer.'

Bill looked forward at the man who sat leaning comfortably against the side of his charge while eating from the plate Tommy had provided him.

'Namu? What sort of name is that? I mean where's he from?'

'Derby, mate,' Tommy laughed.

Bill was expecting Namu's origins to be several thousand kilometres away, perhaps in the Afghan desert or the broad dead expanses of some exotic Arabian landscape, not Derby, about one hundred or so kilometres north east of Broome.

'Yeah, Derby, Bill. Namu's people way back were in fact from Afghanistan, but he is a true blue, fifth generation Aussie, oi oi oi,' Tommy teased, repeating the sporting chant shouted ad-nauseam by beer-fuelled spectators at the national cricket team's regular victories.

'Are the camels his?' Bill asked.

'Ahh, well mate, let's say Namu looks after them. Namu's an experienced camel man. He used to work with the trekkers on Cable Beach. He's one of the best camel men in the west, probably in the nation.'

Tommy waved to the man they were talking about as Namu laid down his empty plate and waved a thumbs up of appreciation back.

'Mate, basically we lease the camels through Namu,' Tommy continued, and Bill realised that he wasn't going to tell him where the *through Namu* went, so he didn't push it.

'What I understand from Namu, although he doesn't say much, but what I believe they are doing, is a very selective breeding program.'

'Oh yeah?' Bill answered wondering who *they* were but also naturally interested in this camel, regardless of his undercover intelligence gathering for Operation Concord.

'Yeah, mate. What I understand is that they are breeding between the bloodlines of the wild camels of the state. Namu says the local camels are quite a pure bloodline from the camels that were first brought to

Australia from Afghanistan well over one hundred years ago. They were used in those days as the perfect beast of burden to travel through the Aussie terrain by the early explorers and settlers. When they brought the camels in they brought their Afghan cameleers as well,' Tommy explained. 'So anyway, Namu looks after the camel herd at Beauty Bay. He runs the program. The feral Aussie animals are apparently huge in comparison to the race-bred camels of the Arab states. Over there a good racing camel is worth millions. So this little operation at Beauty Bay is all designed, as I understand it, to breed the perfect racing camel to take back over to those places—bit like taking coals to Newcastle, ice to Antarctica, Kiwis to Bondi, that type of thing.'

Bill laughed at Tommy's dig at the infamous preponderance of his Kiwi cousins who dominated that Sydney suburb, but he was also fascinated by this previously unknown history. Tommy pointed forward again to the big bull camel that Namu now ordered up with soft commands to allow the big animal to stretch cramped limbs, and it stood solidly balanced on its huge soft padded feet on the gently surging deck.

'So it works both ways,' Tommy said. 'That one there, I understand, is from the UAE. It arrived via Indonesia as the only return passenger on one of the little traders that take the live cattle over. He's been in quarantine for a few months at the Cocos Islands. Now he's been delivered to Namu and is on the love boat to meet a couple of dozen very expectant brown-eyed beauties at the bay for some big-time holiday romancing.'

Both men laughed at the thought, and settled down for a long peaceful day...while Bill mused about *luck*.

37

HEAVEN IS A PLACE ON EARTH

The sun started to lose its overpowering heat on its track down toward the western horizon. The good barge *Beauty Bay* and its weary crew and passengers turned finally into its namesake port after the long slog south from Broome. With a wheezy blast from the rarely needed foghorn, Tommy aimed the old barge in shore through the protective arms of the twin bluffs and into the calm turquoise waters of the very small bay port. Bill saw for the first time the resort buildings tucked haphazardly into the hilly vegetation just off the tiny strip of beach left exposed at this high tide.

There on the wooden jetty jutting only ten metres out from the southern curve of the bay was Gypsy. All long flowing auburn hair and suntanned physicality in a tiny bikini, as usual, and even from fifty metres exuding an aura of physical beauty and good health.

'There she is, Bill—our girl,' Tommy announced.

Bill glanced quickly at him, curious that he would deliberately share his *possession* of his woman with him.

'And, mate, I forgot to tell you, she has a surprise for you,' Tommy said as he steered the bulky vessel cautiously up along the jetty.

Bill laughed as Gypsy stepped down lightly onto the wide bulwark of the barge and into his arms. Gypsy didn't need to tell him what the surprise was as Bill saw and felt the protrusion of her basketball-sized belly against his.

'Gypsy, you've bred!' he teased as they kissed each other on opposite cheeks still in the warmth of the hug—a specialty of this woman who meant so much him.

'You noticed, Billy?' she laughed and stood back, proudly patting the sun browned silkiness of her pregnancy, and Bill kissed her again and took Tommy's hand in a warm shake of congratulations.

Then they were busy at the unloading and Gypsy left them to supervise the care of the dozen or so resort guests at the bar and the buffet restaurant on the balcony of the main building.

Tommy and Bill laboured with the unloading after Tommy had carefully eased the barge first onto the sloping beach, and Namu had stepped the big bull camel gracefully off the front of the barge and onto terra firma. The cameleer walked the swaying beast away to the north and around a tiny headland still within the bay but out of sight in the next tiny coastal indentation, where the camel grounds and Namu's nomad tent stood.

By nine pm they could relax on the smaller balcony of Gypsy and Tommy's quarters on the first floor above the main guest bar balcony. With the buzz of the guests' conversation rising from below, Gypsy fed the two men with a selection of seafood and vegetables cooked to culinary perfection by the chef.

Happy that her guests were in the good hands of her staff, Gypsy circled catlike into the cushioned embrace of a papa-san chair. She told Bill that she was so happy that he had *finally* come to spend time with them.

Tommy, yawning and exhausted from his last few days' endeavours, excused himself with a kiss to his woman and a casual fist bump to Bill and retired to bed.

Gypsy and Bill spoke then. Not of the past events that had forged their friendship. Not of those days when he had been seeking vengeance from, while running towards, the man who had finally died in the seas not too far from this peaceful bay. Bill had closed off that episode way back then. Now they spoke of the present and of the future. Bill was delighted at her relaxed anticipation of the new arrival.

'Sure to be a wonderful combination of your wonderful, and Tommy's barely adequate genes,' he insisted as she laughed at him. And she teased him about Bonnie but sought also to gently sound out how he really felt about her young friend from Broome.

With the mellowing effects of a fine Margaret River chardonnay from the cellar, Bill's usual masculine shyness when talking about emotions, even to her, relaxed, and he spoke of the joy that the fun of the union between himself and Bonnie had brought to him after the barren years.

'Course she's no Gypsy,' he teased, and she languidly reached out with a muscular calf and pretty foot and kicked him softly on the arm from the cavern of the huge chair. He had come to sit next to her, on the floor and leaning on the outside rim of her cushioned sanctuary.

'But, yeah, girl, I must say that I very much enjoy her, enjoy her company. But having said that, Gypsy, I, ah, wouldn't want to predict the future, if you know what I mean.'

He suddenly realised that he couldn't say to this woman that he loved Bonnie. He didn't even know *why* he couldn't do that. It was as if that would somehow devalue the emotion he still felt for Gypsy. He knew that she wouldn't care if he said he loved Bonnie, and thought that he may explore this curiosity with her as she had a way of seeing things that he didn't. Not just a feminine perspective—it was more than that. She was a wise woman. But then he realised that any further clumsy analysis of his own emotional being was unnecessary because Gypsy, who had become quieter in the papa-san, suddenly began almost imperceptible snoring from her fabric cave.

Bill grinned; time for bed. He rose and pulled mosquito netting over the cavern of the papa-san from a roll at the top. This protected Gypsy from the nasties that flew on tiny wings in these climes to seek and taste the blood of mammals, and to pass tiny viral killers into their prey's bloodstream.

His was a small guest bure, the one closest to the sea on the northern edge of the dwellings. This tiny single-roomed teak and tin cottage with slowly rotating overhead fan was the most private of all the accommodation on the site. With ten long steps he could be in the warm shallow apron of the Indian Ocean that lapped gently up against the sand. He had already enjoyed the outside shower by the boardwalk that led from his bure to the main building through a curtain of scrubby native coastal bush. Before dinner, he had showered sensuously naked but unseen by the occupants of the resort, some of whom he could hear talking from the bar balcony fifty hidden metres away.

Bill slept superbly well over the first week as he settled in. He volunteered for any task, no matter how menial, to pay for his board and keep as he began his casual surveillance of his friends. Although unsettled by Tommy's reticence on the barge voyage about how they had somehow saved the resort from financial meltdown, Bill still felt certain that these good people had no knowledge, no involvement, not even the remotest possibility of being a part of the importation of the deadly drugs that had wreaked such havoc in NSW.

Each evening, when he was certain that no one was stirring, Bill called Bob Hopkins to report the lack of progress. The AFP commander took each call personally and each time they spoke longer as Bob worked assiduously to cement a bond of trust between them on at least a level of professional respect for each other. Bob Hopkins was not disappointed that his agent had seen nothing yet.

'It takes time, Bill, be patient, mate. If it's there, it's in the things that don't appear to mean anything at the moment. If it's there, the puzzle will come together for you if you keep looking for it.'

And Bill felt guilty that he had not passed on the tiny possibility of a teasing clue: Tommy's unexplained mention of 'luck' on the barge. Bill knew that he must at least try to find out what had saved the couple, how much that luck had been worth in filthy lucre to his friends, and where the luck had come from. But he had time, and his world was beautiful, tiny, isolated; and he felt that he was among friends.

38
IN A BIG COUNTRY

Ten years of an El Nino drought in a dry land is a cruel process of nature. Farmers on the marginal lands are forced off as stock, feed and crops dry and then die.

Strong El Nino winds bringing the heat of the baking deserts swept in from the east. The wind blew in relentless cycles to blast the relatively better vegetated coastal strips until the conditions were perfect for fire.

Fire is both the curse and the blessing of the native Australian landscape. In long past times the Aboriginal peoples had well planned slash and burn practices. They had carefully used the purifying, renewing effect of the element under exact conditions where control of the burnings, while always tenuous, was most possible. Much of the bush flora had adapted over many centuries of isolation to need the heat and the smoke of naturally occurring wildfires to activate the germination process, and make possible the next generation of the flora.

But now there was a fire that was beyond the control of man. The once-in-a-century wildfire had burnt the sparse grasslands on the edge of the Great Sandy Desert and had travelled into the bushlands above the line of latitude that crossed the continent above Port Hedland in the west and the longitude boundary from Derby in the north. Initially, the experts and the authorities had only monitored, analysed and guessed at the potential of the fire. Hardened fire-fighters from the state's metropolitan and bush fire brigades spoke of it as 'she' and 'her' as the fire spread from her blackened core and headed towards the western coast.

So far only a few isolated station homesteads had been threatened by her voracious appetite. So far they had been able to avoid loss of property and human life. Thousands of kilometres away to the south in the capital city of Perth, the state's political chiefs and the weather and fire bureaucrats' talk was of the inevitability of the massive wildfire burning herself out, and an acceptance of the 'damn good luck' that nothing of material value was really in her way as she surged now towards the extinguishing waters of the Indian Ocean, pushed forward on the unrelenting easterly winds.

39

CHILDREN OF
THE NIGHT

'Ladies and gentlemen, please return to your seats and fasten your seat belts in preparation for our landing into Broome.'

The cultured politeness of the Virgin Blue purser sparked a mini flurry of activity on the Boeing 727 as those making last minute toilet visits or stretching travel weary legs in the narrow pathways of the jet made their way back to the confines of the aircraft's cushioned seats.

Li Li Phat, the twenty-nine-year-old granddaughter of the patriarch and titular head of the Spider Gang of Cabramatta, NSW, adjusted her seat back into the upright position and stretched in relief that the direct flight from Bali was soon to touch down in Broome. Li Li, or Lily as she was known to her Anglo friends and her colleagues at the commercial conveyancing practice in Sydney, was tired and a little nervous. Never before had she involved herself or been involved in the workings of the organisation that her father, his father, and just about every other adult male family member had been part of for as long as she could remember. Her adoring parents had lovingly plotted her path, both in her personal circumstance, and in her education and career.

Li Li was one of the protected ones. Like others from her peer group she was a grandchild of the founding old men. As with others of her ilk, those who at an early age showed intelligence or talent, she had been deliberately buffered from the day-to-day workings of the gang. For eight years now, she had even lived separately from her family in a trendy harbour-side apartment paid for by her father, but now independently maintained by her generous commercial lawyer's salary. However, despite that deliberate separation, Li Li had always known that if she was ever called upon to support the triad, she would answer the call as a Spider Soldier.

Lily and her generation were the gang sleepers. Members placed deliberately into society's mainstream with native cunning, planning and forethought. Theirs was an age-old tactic that assisted the survival of the gang, of the whole, through the sacrifices of a few. When Lily's grandfather had called upon her she had had no choice. She had not even considered declining, denying or avoiding her legacy. The family needed her and so she would act. So here she was, bracing as the jet kissed the sun-warmed tarmac of Broome airport and the captain moved the big engines into reverse thrust and hit the brakes.

Lily was the first into Broome. The others would arrive over the next five days; each monitored for any obvious reaction from any of the law enforcement agencies in this isolated place, be that from the local police or Australian Customs. Each new arrival would catch the town bus to different hotels. Lily had been booked into the luxurious Cable Beach International Resort. The bus trip was a slow stop-start ten kilometres out of town. In the vivacious, happy bustle of the terminal, as two hundred tourists massed around the small luggage conveyor, Lily saw immediately that she would be invisible in the mob of varied nationalities. She noticed near the arrivals area a slovenly looking local policeman, ginger-haired, fat and sweaty in his country khaki uniform. But he was chatting to the airline staff and took no apparent interest in the mass of people moving to the humidity outside with kids yelling, babies bawling and flustered, red-faced mums and dads escaping the crush.

By lunchtime Lily was in her bungalow room designed like a Bali bure in the lush grounds of the resort. She unpacked and then ordered from room service a platter of locally grown tropical fruits. Now she must wait for her team to gather.

40

A GOOD HEART

Bill had been in Beauty Bay for one week. He had guessed from the phone briefings with Bob Hopkins that the command team of the CTF were growing impatient. Bob had started to gently hint that he needed to get more pro-active; that his relaxed watch was not cutting it with the frustrated crime professionals in Sydney. Although Bob was reluctant to push him, he also needed to impress on his young agent that unless there was some progress, at least some action from him, the pressure was coming on to pull him out and perhaps take more drastic and invasive investigative action.

After the call on the Sunday night Bill knew that he was in trouble. He tried to sleep, went to bed, lay there, but his thoughts raced, tangled and circled and he thrashed about, increasingly sweaty and agitated in his frustration. Finally in the early hours he knew.

'I just need to do the fucking job,' he announced to the lazy rotations of the ceiling fan. Do what they wanted him to do. Look, investigate, drag the red herring out and hopefully away from Beauty Bay and leave his friends alone, safe from the dirty deeds of the Judas that he had become, again! And so he decided that he must, and that he would. He would look, pry, search and ultimately, he was sure, clear his friends of suspicion.

Now as the first rays of the new day's sun peeked through the slat wood blinds of the bure, fatigued as he felt from the sleepless night, Bill began to analyse, plan, visualise how he would approach his task.

Right! Back to the old police training acronym SMEAC. Situation-mission-execution, etc.

'Fuck, still can't remember the last two words of the acronym!'

Still it was just a method to identify and compartmentalise the factors at play here in Beauty Bay. What, when, where and how should he approach this? Right: Situation—they suspected that a quantity of a drug had come into this place and been picked up by the Spider Gang courier. Mission—he was here to look and see if there was any evidence of that. Execution okay, first things first: he needed to physically search the living quarters of his friends, pick his way through their personal possessions, trawl through their grubby undies like a disgraceful pervert in the night. He must search for any real evidence.

'A stash of camel stamped ecstasy tabs, for example,' he muttered in ironic anger at himself for agreeing to do this.

He must search for other proof of wrongdoing: caches of cash, journals of suspect writings, anything that would implicate the two persons he considered to be among his few real friends, in the crime of mass murder. This is what he would do—but how? And then of course he had not even really considered before that seven people lived and worked at the bay. Seven suspects! He had concentrated his thoughts only on Gypsy and Tommy.

'Shit!' He realised out loud. Any one of the staff, any one of them could be it, the dealer, the conduit, the lead to how the drugs came in. That is *if* they came in through Beauty Bay. More fucken likely Van had met someone here, another guest, for the pick-up, he thought. But Bob had told him not to risk a search of the guest register.

'There's no need, Bill. Concentrate on Gypsy, Tommy and the staff, mate.'

Rising now to shower and to join his friends at breakfast he had decided that he must do the dirty stinking job that Bob Hopkins had so adroitly manoeuvred him into agreeing to. He would do it well, cynically investigate his friends. Minutely but carefully search the sanctity of their home. Do the same with Namu and with the four full-time staff. Report to Bob Hopkins, and then get the hell out of Dodge.

By the time Bill had walked from his bure on the dew-wet planks of the walkway and through the bush up to the main block he had his plan. As he did every morning, he met Gypsy and Tommy at the breakfast buffet, the food spread across a wide wooden table on starched white cloths outside the main restaurant. He responded to their typically warm greetings and the invitation to help himself to the banquet of tropical fruits and juices, homemade breads and pungent black coffee.

As Gypsy chatted, they sat together while the staff bustled away in the kitchen and around the al fresco tables. The staff were preparing for the imminent appearance of the in-house guests. Bill took that time to think as he crunched into the seeded toast, enjoying the bush-tucker marmalades created by his hostess, and the wonderful tang of black coffee. He took the time to identify each target. First as a couple, a single investigative target, were his marvellous friends. Again he found it necessary to qualify what he was doing. Remind himself that he was *totally confident* they were not involved and would not be implicated in anything vaguely connected to criminality. He had witnessed up close and personal their holistic, alternative approach to existence over the past two years. He had never even seen, heard or in the slightest way suspected that either of them would seek the chemical nirvana of any drug except maybe at times a puff of organic ganga. But they would never entertain, he was sure, a commercial involvement in the handling of such filthy stuff as the deadly Es.

Okay, so who next? Namu? Right, he would be number one, the first real target. Known facts: An old Aussie-Afghan cameleer. Bill had mentioned Namu to Bob Hopkins in his call the first night after the barge trip to the bay. Bob had come back the next night on the first of the nightly debriefs to advise that there was no negative information on the elderly man at this stage. Bob had checked out how the big bull camel had come a-visiting. Just in case, two CTF officers had already travelled to the Cocos Island Australian Quarantine Facility. There they checked on the beast's movements and documentary bona fides as he had travelled by various ships from his home in the middle-east, down through Indonesia toward his hot dates waiting at Beauty Bay. The reports back were that all appeared to be officially above board. The paperwork was in order and the Arab sheik in the UAE who owned the beast had confirmed to Interpol investigators pretending they were animal control the legitimate purpose of the trip. Still Bill knew that at some opportune time, very soon, he needed to be in Namu's tent.

One down. Who next? Target two. The gardener John, or Salty as he preferred to be called. A fifty-something, Brylcreemed, silver-haired loner. Salty kept to himself, Bill had noted, and Gypsy had confirmed his observation in casual conversation. As told by Gypsy, his was a story of rise and fall. It was a sadly typical tale. Salty had been the lead singer for a local-hero rock band that had dominated the pub scene of Perth for a few short years a long time ago. Sadly they never quite made it either in person or in record sales past the Western Australian borders into the bigger cashed-up populations of the east coast or overseas. The potential and promise of the talented group was smashed by the consequences of almost inevitable addictions of the young men, from the lure of too-young female flesh, to the curse of the bottle and then of the needle, until they self-destructed. Salty John had run from his demons and finally found employment and peace tending the gardens in a little piece of paradise.

Target three. Sally. The English rose: a vivacious young backpacker from the old dart. Clones of Sally could be found all over the land working in bars or displaying gorgeously on beaches as the pretty young tourists worked out visas on their big pre-marriage, pre-career adventures before they returned to a colder reality back in the UK. She had worked for Gypsy now for one year and had six months left on her visa. She was a buxom blonde with an earthy humour and personality. Sally charmed the guests with her broad Geordie accent as she worked at the reception or as waitress and bargirl during meals.

Target four. Bella the cook. A fortyish Spanish spinster. Stocky build, hint of black moustache, bad temper. Bill had already crossed swords with her in his first week. Nothing of any moment really. Just a flash of anger and a Mediterranean curse (he was certain) when he had responded to a typical harmless Sally flirt as she served at the dinner table with the flick of his napkin against Sally's firmly-tanned lower left buttock that was only partially captured by her tiny cut-off denims.

And finally, target five. Chip. Bill laughed quietly again that a young American would inevitably be called something like *Chip*. This slim hipped twentyish waiter was only four months into his employment at the resort and his role was general dogsbody. Chip helped out anywhere Gypsy or Tommy needed him. He worked nights at the bar, flirting in his sweet southern drawl with the female guests of all ages. During the day he helped sometimes in the gardens, toiling in his ripped, slim muscularity, shirtless in the humidity at Salty's laid-back commands, suggestions really. And when required Chip was happy to help Tommy with the fishing cruises and Namu with the camel rides.

'Okay. Done,' Bill concluded, as he swallowed the last of his coffee and heard the first of the guests chattering their happy-holiday way up from the bures toward the main building for brekkie.

He turned then to Tommy as they both rose from the feast to give the staff a free run at the serving.

'Massa Lawson, bwana, my creative juices are a-surging, I feel the need to paint. Permission, sir, to touch up everything and anything that needs touching up around your wonderful abode.'

'Ooohh! Me please, me please,' from the cheeky Sally, who had overheard as she guided the first group of guests to their table at the edge of the balcony.

And with laughter from all who had heard, including Gypsy, Tommy agreed that Bill's idea was good and that he should feel free to paint whatever stayed still long enough, and needed 'a good touch up'.

41
CRUEL TO BE KIND

Opportunity can be a wonderful thing if it is recognised and seized, and it came early in Bill's reluctant master plan. That very morning as he emerged from the storeroom onto the track at the rear of the main building, armed with paint-smeared buckets and tins of whitewash, ladder, brushes and various tradesman-like accessories, he ran into Gypsy. She, in her usual uniform of sarong and bikini top, invited him to start his cosmetic urban renewal program in her and Tommy's quarters.

'I have a busy day, Billy, in the massage dome. Tommy and Chip are taking some guests out fishing on the midday high tide. So you can finally work your alleged magic in my bedroom,' she teased and laughed at his response of a cross-eyed, tongue-out, sleazy idiot grin. 'You're such a fool, my friend,' she diagnosed, and then left him alone to his devious devices.

Bill noisily manoeuvred a converted fridge trolley loaded with stepladder, buckets, brushes and paint-splattered drop sheets up the broad slate stairs from the rear of the lobby. Upstairs, he entered the cool, jasmine-scented precinct of his friends' suite of rooms above the main resort floor. The master bedroom had a view over the broad veranda to the bay, and the bathroom and study–nursery were offset behind.

With the anti-ambush barrier of his trolley and carefully placed bits and pieces effectively blocking the entry, not to mention an ear trained to the stairwell, he quickly set up the room to disguise his intent.

Bill spread drop sheets, opened paint tins, placed brushes at the ready, and daubed a few strokes of the white matte paint over the veranda door beams. Then, nervously, he began his painstaking examination of every inch of the quarters.

He read every document, looked under and into the marital bed, lifted the mattress, peered into drawers, rustled through cupboards, chests of possessions, through the clothing, and inevitably, with an undeniable but extremely guilt-ridden voyeuristic thrill, through Gypsy's fragrant assortment of silky smalls. He searched carefully and honestly, but always with an anxious ear to the doorway. Crouched nervously beside the bed, he read letters exchanged between Gypsy and Tommy. He read her deepest thoughts on scented rice paper, written in the early stages of their relationship. Poetic love notes in her elegant hand when Tommy was offshore at the pearl lease for long weeks. These were her most private of private thoughts. Heartfelt declarations of love for him and of her dreams for their future together. Bill read each letter with a fascinated disgust that he should have to do this. After carefully replacing each item in its original position, he was finished in the bedroom.

Into the study, quickly now, knowing that he was running out of time. Through the cupboards, opening, searching boxes and briefcases, and then drawer by drawer through the large teak desk. He found the dry, mathematical recordings of the business ledgers. He was no numerical scholar but a past life as a wholesale merchant when he was working undercover in New Zealand, allowed him to see that this, on paper, appeared to be a meticulous record of the day-to-day running of the resort. He scanned bank account statements, spread them across the desk and compared them to the hand-written ledgers that comprised the business records of the resort, and he saw that this appeared to be an honest venture. He also saw from the handwriting that the financial dealings at the place were exclusively Tommy's domain. This aspect of the operation was apparently not Gypsy's scene. Eventually satisfied, nerves frayed, he was nearly finished. Every inch of the bedroom, the bathroom and now the study forensically searched, nothing found. Thank God!

Now he tidied up. Quickly replaced, double-checked, smoothed and rearranged. He was rushing now, aware that his lack of painting would arouse suspicion if he was rumbled. But, just as he was leaving the study his last glance back spotted it. An old orange fabric suitcase perched high on top of the tall teak wardrobe in the study. He had searched inside the wardrobe but had not seen the suitcase pushed back against the wall and close to the ceiling. Now, he almost left it. It was just a suitcase, stored up and out of the way, and he was increasingly nervous, expecting Gypsy or even Tommy to be back soon from their tasks. 'Bugger it!' Quickly he pulled the desk chair across the broad stone tiles and up beside the wardrobe. He stepped up onto its wooden seat. Reached, snagged and pulled the dusty suitcase towards him and down onto the floor.

From its weight, it did contain something, not excessively heavy, maybe some unused clothes, baby stuff, even, he hoped. He lugged the case across to the desk and swung it onto the desktop and pulled the heavy black nylon zipper noisily open. Inside, held firm against the bottom of the case by the restraining strap, was a yellowish pigskin briefcase. Bill pulled the case free and set it on the desktop. He almost didn't want to click the twin chrome catches free, didn't want to look inside. But he had to. He twisted the tiny keys in each lock and the small catches clicked. Slowly, he pulled the case open. 'Fuck!' he grunted in disbelief. He had never seen such a stash of cold, hard cash. A colourful mixture of used bank notes stacked perfectly by denominations and by country of origin. US greenbacks occupied half the case in bundles secured by elastic bands. Yankee dollars, a mix of one hundreds, fifties and twenties. Aussie dollars in familiar green hundreds and orange fifties took up the rest of the space. Bill's heart sank while he felt the surge of excitement of a significant find. Evidence, surely. But of what? Was this cash the *luck* Tommy had referred to on the barge? But even in the confusion of conflicting emotions, Bill instinctively knew that such impressive amounts of cash in used notes and not deposited in a good old bank typically related to dirty dealings.

42

CRUMBLIN' DOWN

One hundred thousand or so US! Eighty thousand or so Aussie! As he painted, Bill repeated his quick count of Tommy's stash to himself, still unbelieving. He had replaced it, put the briefcase back into the old suitcase and stashed it back in its hidey-hole. Now he quickly spread the drop sheets and began his honest endeavour. To disguise the lost two hours or so that the search had taken he smeared the glutinous cover of whitewash over sun- and weather-tarnished beams and the limestone blocks of the construction. But with each stroke, his mind raced over the significance of his find.

He must of course report the find to Bob Hopkins. That was his clear duty. It was hugely important in the scheme of the investigation that Tommy and possibly Gypsy were in possession of such an amount of cash. But the how and why nagged at him. He knew that they had sold everything they had previously owned and buried almost every hard-earned dollar into the resort. He knew from Gypsy's worried phone calls over the past months that they were in the deepest financial trouble. The resort simply did not trade well enough for them to escape the fiscal black hole that beckoned. Bill knew this; she had told him, totally open as always. She had been prepared to walk away with nothing, even sacrifice their home in Broome to the voracious bank rather than watch Tommy worry himself to an early grave. There was no way out, she had said. No white knight, no rich uncle, no chance of a windfall, she had told him, as she resigned herself to the failure of their eco venture. But now somehow, suddenly all was good?

'Things have come right, Billy,' she had told him when they were alone on the balcony after the resort had quietened for the day. But from his gentle inquiry it was obvious that she didn't know how things had corrected themselves to the point where Tommy had even bought a new troop carrier. Gypsy simply didn't know, Bill concluded.

He made an agent-on-the-ground decision that day as he painted through the warmth of the early afternoon. He would not immediately set the forensic hounds on the trail. He would not tell Bob Hopkins of the find—yet. First, he would simply ask Tommy why some $180,000 of used banknotes was hidden in his study. Easy really.

By late afternoon, with no one having disturbed his labour, the rooms inside and out to the balcony gleamed. In the tropic heat, the water-based paint had virtually dried within minutes of his careful applications, so there was no smell of paint. And finally, as he brushed his last strokes, he heard the soft sandal slap of someone coming up the cool slate stairs. As Gypsy squeezed past the clumsy barricade, Bill turned with brush in hand and spread his arms.

'Well?'

'Ooh, it's beautiful, Billy!' Gypsy walked into his embrace with a grin. He stood in her hug, awkwardly aware of his paint splattered man-sweat. But in the affection of her hug he felt an overpowering guilt. She was surprised at the sudden strength of his squeeze as he held her in an unutterable surge of apology.

Weary from a long day of healing the aches of others, she detached herself from him gently but stood back and held his arms. As was her way, she looked deep into his eyes, seeking an explanation that he could not provide. She let him go when he would not hold her gaze, and Gypsy crumpled down onto her bed with a sigh. She watched lazily as Bill collected and stowed his gear onto the trolley. As she shuffled back onto her pillows Gypsy sighed again in response to the aches and strains her massage work had taken on her very pregnant body. Bill smiled.

'Permission, please, to place my healing hands upon your gorgeous body, ma'am?'

She chuckled. 'Permission granted. You may board.' Now she rolled to lay side on, with her back to him and hugging a pillow. Bill knelt beside the bed with a dark blue glass vial of sandalwood oil taken from her dresser. She untied the strap of her bikini top and slipped off the tiny strip of cloth, leaving her lower body covered in a bright yellow sarong that contrasted marvellously with her light golden tan. Gypsy sighed in appreciation as his strong hands eased into the work that he most enjoyed.

As he massaged the tiredness and soreness out of her finely muscled neck, shoulders and lower back, he found that it was as if he were trying to force a silent energy of apology for his deception through his fingers. As she reacted sensuously, enjoying his healing touch and moaning softly below him, he reached a moment where he knew that he needed to tell her now. He would admit to her the real reason that he was here, what he had found, ask her about it. He took a deep breath: 'Damn the consequences,' he thought, but immediately the moment was demolished as a salt-encrusted, sunburnt Tommy Lawson burst through the bedroom doorway. Gypsy's man stopped then in over-exaggerated horror at the sight before him. His half-naked, moaning wife pinned to the bed by the hands of a scoundrel.

With a broad smile and a shake of his tight dreadlocks, Tommy adopted a terribly accented Inspector Clouseau manner and declared to the room, 'Allo allo allo! What have we got eer!'

43
DON'T TALK
TO STRANGERS

Bill made the call to Bob Hopkins that Monday night, alone again in his small teak-scented haven. Having decided that he would not reveal at this time the result of his search, he found himself going somewhat overboard to impress Bob that his search had in fact been impartial in attitude and immaculate in aptitude. 'Bob, I searched everything in every room, read every bit of paper, analysed all the legal and accounting and business documents, ledgers, everything.'

'Good, good, Bill,' said Bob.

'First, of course, there was no sign of any drugs, nothing suspicious at all. And there's nowhere else in the building where I would think they would keep anything. If there is anything at the resort, I reckon it would have been in their quarters. It's a bedroom with ensuite bathroom, and a study, soon to be baby room. I went through them all.'

'Good man, Bill. It's a great start, son,' Bob enthused over the sat-phone.

Bill assured Bob that he meant to work his analytical way through the staff, one by one. Bob asked myriad questions as Bill had anticipated he would. Bob was naturally determined to collect and collate for expert forensic analysis every scrap of potential evidence that Bill may have found in his search. Bob took notes of the couple's financial and legal advisers; the accountant, the bank details, the lawyer involved in the purchase of the business, all gleaned from the documents held in the small pile of binder folders Bill had found. But most of all, Bob felt now that his man was focused.

Finally, the agent was on the job.

44

WALK LIKE AN EGYPTIAN

On Tuesday morning Bill awoke worried and tired from a dream-disturbed sleep. The incomplete and therefore dishonest report to Bob Hopkins had troubled him. But he reasoned again that his acts, and more so his omission, should give him time. Knowing Tommy, he thought as he rose from the bed, he could only hope that when he did corner him, talk to him alone, that the explanation would confirm what he surely knew. Tommy Lawson was not a man to buy, sell or otherwise deal in illicit drugs. So accepting that as a fact, the money must surely have come from a rich uncle passing away, a lotto win, or perhaps from the forced sale of a valued investment unknown to his wife?

Bill decided to put the cash cache figuratively aside and to complete his master plan to search the digs of the staff and report back to Bob. With a sense of dread that would not dissipate, Bill knew that he needed to get his next target in his sights.

He showered and dressed in shorts and T-shirt and left his bure to enjoy the usual early team breakfast. He took the time then to check in casually with each of the targets, except for Bella, as to when the best time would be to paint in their quarters. Even with Gypsy's glowing references to the group over toast as to the effect of his work the day before, there appeared to be varying degrees of disinterest in Bill painting their digs. Salty, the laid-back dude, just grunted in relaxed agreement or possibly disagreement when Bill booked him in for that very afternoon.

Chip wanted to be last. Sally was appy to ave you anytime, big boy.'

He didn't check with the angry Spanish cook. First because she was busy in the kitchen, second because she clearly didn't like him. But the main reason was because he knew that Sally and Bella shared lodgings in a small suite of rooms located behind the kitchen. And talking to Sally was a much more enjoyable experience then trying to converse with the surly wee Spaniard. He tentatively pencilled Sally and Bella in for the next day, Wednesday.

Chip insisted that he could do his room Friday and Friday only as he would be out again in the fishing tender with Tommy and some guests all day. Bill was more than happy to agree, knowing that he would have the place to himself. That left him Thursday free, and Namu's tent sprang to mind. His week was planned. By close of business Friday he would know if he had anything to report back about the resort staff. On Saturday he would sit down with Tommy Lawson and ask the direct question.

But now he had some time to kill. Salty told him he could visit after four and wandered off to his day of pruning and mulching. Bill had overheard him singing soft verses of lyrically violent rock and roll songs that included the word fuck a lot to the uncomplaining palms, trees and shrubs that he tended so lovingly about the place.

With the sun starting to heat the world, Bill decided that he would take a walk around to camel land. Since his arrival on the barge he had not again sighted either Namu or the camels. Tommy had told him that unless a guest booked a sunset ride then Namu basically kept to his solitary self, out of sight, out of mind, around the small headland in the company of his breeding herd. Bill stripped off his T-shirt and tucked it into the back of his shorts and made the short journey on the soft strip of beach above the tidemark. As he crunched quietly through the morning-cool crystals of silica, he knew that he must take full advantage of this daytime recce of Namu's territory. He would have to return in darkness at some opportune moment to properly search the tent. Therefore, he maintained a strong focus on the lay of the land to assist him in that inevitable nocturnal challenge.

'Morning, Slim,' he greeted the big racehorse lizard that lay on the flat ochre surface of a rock up off the beach, desperate to warm its reptilian blood from the anti-freeze slow-down of the cold night. The lizard flicked out a dark blue snake of a tongue.

Bill's thoughts were mixed as he approached the small headland of the bay within a bay. Fleeting images: the cash in the briefcase; Gypsy, Tommy, Doc, Bob Hopkins; the drug deaths in Sydney; sadly memorable faces he had seen on Bob's CD. He thought about the tainted drugs. He considered and tried to imagine the terrible sensations that the victims must have felt as they died. The certainty that must have come to them from the muscle convulsions and the agony, that they would die, that they were damned. And surely each must have experienced dreadful emotions of fear, and of panic and of loss at the reality that they were leaving partners, kids, friends behind in those last few excruciating minutes. He grimaced and shook his head at the horrible ugliness of it all.

But this day was perfect, and nothing was going to spoil it, he decided as he rounded the bend and spotted Namu seated beside the ember-glow of small steel brazier outside his sturdy canvas nomad tent. Namu saw him immediately and waved. He beckoned his visitor across to the tent and Bill made his way across the beach and the strip of scrubby coastal bush. In a grassy clearing on the far side of the big tent he could see the small herd of camels. The big new bull towered possessively above the young cows, which mooched coyly around him as he surveyed the approach of the human with regal, nose-high contempt.

'Greetings, cobber!' Namu called as Bill closed the distance. 'Come join me for a brew.'

Bill thought to himself, 'Does anyone actually still say cobber?' and grinned at the broad Aussie accent clashing with Namu's appearance, all old-man-of-the-desert-Arab in his flowing gown and turban.

'Glad to, Namu. Hope you don't mind me arriving unannounced,' Bill said.

But the other stood and shook his hand and indicated a canvas camp chair opposite his own, with a 'No worries, mate.'

And so Bill sat and learned a little of the cameleer as they chatted over superficial issues as male strangers do. Namu poured for him a sticky, strong black coffee, the type of which Bill had never tried before but noisily enjoyed.

'Young Tommy,' the old man said with a cackle, 'he kills this brew with bloody milk and sugar! That's not right, Bill. Great bloke, Tommy, but that's just not dinkum.' Bill grinned at his genuine despair and his use of iconic Aussie slang.

'How's the big fella going?' Bill inquired, as the big bull, hobbled by a long braided leather rope, strode in awkward giant steps towards a pile of hay in a feed box set up at height.

'He's corker, Bill. Been bonking himself silly all week, the sheilas just love him,' the old Afghan muttered as if a wee bit jealous, but then laughed at himself and Bill joined in.

As Namu fussed about finding some caster sugar-dusted biscuits inside the tent for his guest, Bill intently surveyed its layout, murkily apparent through the heavy cloth flap that Namu had tied back for the day. He saw inside a simple cot, some wooden chests and a collection of cooking implements and stores around a circular Persian carpet that sat on a hessian base. A search even at night should not take that long, Bill mused, but a torch would be required. Finally with coffee and refill drunk and the shallow conversation slowing, Bill invited Namu to join him for a casual brew at his bure anytime he was in the neighbourhood. Bill stood to go and Namu thanked him for his company and waved farewell as the younger man wandered slowly back around the headland under the critical territorial gaze of the bull camel.

Now out of sight of Namu, but not yet in sight of the resort buildings tucked into the bay, Bill was suddenly alone in the breathtaking physical beauty and solitude of the place. He stopped and, as if by an ancient instinct, with arms raised to the heaven, spoke out loud a greeting to 'Mother Sea! Mother Sky! Mother Earth!' and felt a primal connection to this place. And he prayed that his covert purpose would fail.

45

POCKETFUL OF DREAMS

Salty travelled light, apparently—just a comb and a toothbrush and nothing to hide, or so it seemed. In the late afternoon Bill was there with his painting trolley rattling up the dirt track. He met his target lying near-naked, a grubby off-white G-string his only covering, as Salty John splayed casually in his sweat-stained hammock outside his quarters.

Bill knew that Salty's digs were within the equipment shed. This squat steel shed, built low and extra strong to the local cyclone standards, was also where Salty stored his gardening and general resort maintenance gear. Even as he arrived and took a seat on a red plastic milk crate, Bill could see past Salty's suspended bed through the open roller door into the shed. A dusty quad bike sat in the gloom, the twin of the one used up at reception to lug the guests and their baggage from the car park. Further back in the murk was the old open top four-wheel drive used to run keen fisherman down to the tidal creek where they fished on the changing tides for the mighty barramundi. He could see that inside the main body of the shed in apparent orderly disorder, stood the mix of slashers, cutters, diggers and a haphazard collection of other handy-man type stuff.

Gypsy and Tommy had told Bill of Salty's choice of lodgings in the shed. She explained that they had offered Salty better accommodation two years back when they had arrived at the resort and found him in residence. But the man had declined, content with his basic lot, camping in the shed.

Bill lifted the tall schooner glass prepared for him by his silent host, filled with ice and an opaque liquid that Bill was certain was not H_2O. There were several minutes of companionable silence as Bill gagged at the slightly metallic after-taste of his drink while his host refilled his own from the heavy glass jug perched on the half-log bench without moving from his hammock.

Immediate thirst apparently sated, Salty finally spoke.

'Welcome, digger, to me humble abode, though fuck knows what you can paint here, mate.'

Bill looked about and Salty laughed. 'Nothing here for ya, mate, it's all fucken steel.' He exploded in mirth. 'But hey! Let's just sit a while and enjoy a cold brew and a chinwag.'

'Sounds good to me, mate. By the way, what is this?' Bill asked with a curious nod at his virtually untouched drink.

'That, me boy, is Chateau de Beauty Bay. Your man Salty's own vintage, my friend. Distilled in me humble abode from nature's fruits,' and he laughed, and drank, then laughed and drank, and laughed, with Bill joining in both cyclical activities with cynical intent to bond and then to listen and learn as much as he could from this unusual man.

Bill finally came to a vague consciousness late the next morning, somehow in his own bed. He had no clear memory of how he must have staggered from Salty's dangerous alcoholic company. In the sweat-wet, limb-thrashed bed, Bill held his booming head, moaning in raw, dry-throated agony. He felt as if all of the blood within him was attempting a total flush-out of his dehydrated being. As if by searching the top of his cranium for a fault line that would give way under the immense pressure of his tortured cardiovascular system and erupt from the top of his head like a viscous red Krakatoa. At this moment he almost welcomed such a quick death. But finally, slowly, he calmed and with several litres of flushing water glugged into his being over the hours some semblance of isotonic balance eventually returned. He lay then and tried hard to recall the previous night.

The booze, yes! Lots of it; vague recollections. Yeah, Salty had tipped himself out of the hammock after the first jug was emptied. Totally unconcerned and uninhibited as to the effect of his wiry, curly-grey near nakedness in the sweaty G-string, his withered arse led the way as he took his curious, and at that early time, still sort-of-sober guest inside the shed to admire the still. And Bill recalled now the clear ingenuity of it.

'Got the design from a library book,' his proud host advised, as Bill saw the raw liquor drip and collect from the polished stainless-steel cylinders and piping as a heated gelatinous, toxic mix of canned and bush-tucker sweet fruits, honey and wild yeasts percolated and bubbled. Salty showed him several full brown bottles lined up in his old generator-powered camp fridge.

That was Bill's last clear memory. The rest would take several painful hours through the day to collect and re-join from a jigsaw of flashbacks. He even thought about trying a refreshing swim. Maybe staggering outside and getting under a long cooling shower. He thought about risking a light lunch in the bure but didn't have the energy or physical ability to do anything except lay on the bed as the confusion of his fragmented memories led him to an approximate recollection of what had happened.

First recalled fact—the nickname, 'Salty'.

'Yeah, mate,' both of them slurring then as the red sun began its descent toward the horizon. 'Yeah, see, I was a fucken rock legend! Chicks, mate, you wouldn't fucken believe it, beautiful young groupies. Yeah.' Wistful now in his own recollections. 'Yeah, the nickname, mate. It was a gig in Bunbury; thousands of kids, man! In our prime, pumping it, mate, great show. After it, a bunch of young chicks brought to our room by the roadies. Booze, drugs, naked girls and rooting every which way, man, all the boys hitting gold. I got this young spunk, probably too fucken young, truth be told, digger,' a sage nod now looking back. 'Yeah, a real looker, she hadn't been round much. Ya know what I mean?'

Bill's unsteady perch on the plastic crate, a nod, another gulp of the fatal brew. 'Yeah, digger, she gives me her first ever blow-job. Near blew her fucken head off. "Shit!" she screams, spitting the stuff everywhere, "shit, you're fucken salty!" she shouts. So all the boys heard it and from then on, mate, I'm fucking Salty!'

Drugs, they talked about drugs. Salty started it, he recalled. Spoke about how the band had dabbled. How Salty had tried what was going around the music scene, dope, speed, uppers, downers, LSD. How he had tried heroin but had a bad trip first up and never went back to it. How it fucked the others while he succumbed to 'hard licker' instead. Talked about how addictions ruined and finally finished the group. Spoke of friends still in prison now, years later; some dead, gone. How he hated and still hates the shit. And with the companionable authority of their alcoholic togetherness, mates now, Bill casually asked about the others here at Beauty Bay and any connection to drugs. Salty commented on each.

Gypsy and Tommy: 'Nah, special people, good people. I see you got the hots for her? Eh? Come on, Billy, it's fucken obvious.'

'Namu? 'Don't think so. Too old, mate. Just that fucken horrible coffee. The girls? Maybe. Hey, that fucken Sally's hot for it, eh? Don't be tempted, me boy, the angry-ant senora will have ya nuts.'

'Say what, Salt?'

'Yeah, mate, something's going on there, mate! Can't be certain but she watches young Sal like a fucken carpet-munching hawk.'

'Gay, you reckon?'

'Not young luscious Sal, mate, maybe both ways. But watch the Spaniard, son. But drugs? Well, maybe Sally. Seen her off her fucken head a few times.'

'What's she on, ya reckon?'

'Well, if she is it will be something like eccies, mate. That would be her thing. The love drug, mate. She's hanging for a root, mate. See her at the beach most nights, swims nuddie, mate! Great fucken body, great tits! Had a hand shandy a few times hiding in the bush,' he laughed.

Bill forced another chortle, slightly disgusted that so far Salty had confessed to the crimes of paedophilia and to being a voyeuristic pervert.

'Chip? Reckon he bats for the other side, mate, queer as a concrete parachute in my pinion. No proof but never seen him with a lady and he gets fucken tons of offers from the tourist tarts in the bar. Good lookin young man. Helps me in the garden. He's not normal like you an me, mate. Never talks about chicks. If I do he asks me not to "taawk thaaat waay" in his girlie Yankee accent. Hey, speak of the fucken devil,' and Salty pointed in the gloom of the early evening down towards the beach through the fringe of bush.

Bill recalled turning and nearly falling from his crate with the unbalancing effects of the Chateau de Salty, to see young Chip in flowing white cotton shirt and harem pants gliding purposefully along the beach towards the camel bay.

'Every second or so night, mate. He goes to Namu's tent. Don't know what the fuck for. I suspect that maybe the old Arab's giving him one, maybe Chip's a Saudi submarine, eh? Ya know, full of Arab semen!'

Salty near wet himself laughing at his carefully crafted and oft-used joke. Finally he settled down and commented, 'But to be honest, it's fucken hard to imagine, though. I followed him one time but the fucken camels chased me away. He goes into the tent. He's always there for hours, mate. Strange but true, Bill.'

And Bill recalled with dry horror that another jug went south.

46

EVERYBODY HAVE
FUN TONIGHT

In the end he lost an entire day—Wednesday gone! Precious hours spent comatose on the sweat stench of the bed. Unable to rouse the energy to even move as the poisons from the tainted alcohol slowly leached out of him. Oozed out in his sweat, pissed out in diluted solution from the gallons of water he forced down a raw throat. During that forgettable day only Gypsy came looking for him, saw that he was suffering and brought him cool flannels and sweet liquid concoctions of mulled native flora for his ills. He slept mainly, with his friend checking occasionally and assuring him gently that she believed that he might survive, and warning him off Salty's home brew with soft admonishments.

It wasn't until Thursday morning that Bill was ready to re-enter the world.

'No time to waste,' he groaned as the final toxic effects of Salty's curse faded from his cells. A swim in the cool morning waters and a long refreshing shower helped restore his equilibrium. Despite the collateral damage, Bill felt relatively satisfied with his efforts of the Tuesday night. He felt that Salty was in the clear drug-wise, although the man had a lot to answer for in respect of his chemical concoction that masqueraded as a drink. Maybe Bob Hopkins could charge him under the Trades Practices Act for false advertising, Bill chuckled to himself.

Feeling increasingly human again, he trundled his painting rig up the walkway towards the rear of the main building. He waved a friendly salute to Salty as his new friend chugged along the beachfront on the quad bike. Salty raised his eyebrows from fifty paces and made a phantom glass-in-hand-to-mouth invitation, at which Bill changed the salute to one raised middle finger and saw Salty roar with laughter as he departed, stage right.

It was time to do the girls; well, their room at least. Sally was one such girl, at least, and then there was the Spanish pocket battleship Bella, who glared nastily at him from the kitchen as he passed into the corridor and down to the back of the building to their digs. Bill could see that Sally and Chip were being kept busy as the guests enjoyed a prolonged lunch and early afternoon drinks session. He knew that with Bella in the kitchen and Sally serving food and drinks he had a window of at least a few hours to search their rooms.

He set his claymore mine barricade of trolley, paint pots and assorted tools, and bits and pieces that would warn the arrival of any visitors. Again he spent some early minutes with the quick spread of the whitewash along the timbers, and then arranged his spreadsheets handy to throw over furniture or places that he was searching should he hear someone coming. Bill was anxious again. The noise of the guests, the gregarious laughing and talking from the al fresco and restaurant only forty metres away, was confusing and echoed down the stone hallway into the room. He would have problems hearing a soft approach on the leather sandals that the staff wore as their casual uniform. He would have to be careful, have to make many quick visits to the door to look and listen as he searched. This was a lot harder and more dangerous than his efforts in Gypsy and Tommy's rooms.

First, an analysis and a plan of attack. This main bedroom was big. Two beds in set apart one along each wall with wardrobe and drawers in between. Off the bedroom, a shared bathroom.

'Shouldn't take that long,' he muttered and made the first of his quick trips back to the door. Lots of talk and laughter from the guests distorted by the distance. 'Right, no more fucking around, get into it.'

To the first bed: Sally's, he reckoned. A sweet scent of perfume and feminine musk as he stripped the sheets, lifted the mattress, searched the pillows.

Tucked down the far end of the pillow, his fingers found a small leather pouch.

'Fuck! OK, what's going on here?'

Inside, wrapped in tissue paper, four tablets, pale yellow, with an imprint of a flower, a tulip. 'Suspicious, no sign of purple camels, but a find nonetheless!

He replaced the pouch—one to report to Bob. Bill went through the same search of the second bed, with slight distaste at the stale olive-oily scent, at thick black short-and-curlies abundant on the sheet. Nothing.

Just the drawers and wardrobe left, then the bathroom. Obviously Sally had claimed the top drawer, a younger woman's clothes, sarongs, T-shirts, panties, all tiny G-wangers, he noted. Industrial strength bras to hold, lift and separate her perfectly heavy breasts, which, as far as he had seen, she never trapped in such constructions anyway. Nothing out of order. Drawer two held granny pants and wired brassieres to hold tiny angry-tits; he ruffled reluctantly through. Nothing of note in Bella's gear...wait on! Nothing except for a heavy cylindrical torch tucked away under her clothes. As he withdrew the weapon he heard footsteps, and in that moment he understood that he in fact held in his hands an impressive purple double-ended vibrator. He also knew that someone was almost upon him! In blind panic, he dropped the twelve-inch, rubber-studded machine with a thump of at least eight DD batteries back into the drawer and slammed it closed.

He threw his drop sheets over Bella's messed up bed and set of drawers even as he heard the first soft curse as the visitor found the barrier. By the time Sally was past the obstacles and in the door with a bright 'Allo, my love' Bill Peters was on the ladder above the bathroom door, oh-so-casually spreading white paint onto a timber beam.

'Hi, Sal. You are supposed to stay clear, my dear,' he cautioned.

But she just blew him a raspberry.

'Sorry, love, made a mess of meself. Got to quickly change. Won't get in your way.' From his ladder, brush in one hand, pot in the other, he saw that indeed there had been a spill of something reddish onto her white T-shirt as she made to squeeze past the ladder and into the bathroom. He suddenly realised that he was both defenceless and vulnerable at the same moment, for as she moved between the ladder and the door jamb she cheekily slipped both her hands up the legs of his shorts to grip and squeeze his naked buttocks. He instinctively gripped his glutes together to her appreciative, 'My, my, what a tight arse you ave, grand-muvver'.

'Sally, no!' he ordered, stuck with stuff in both hands and balancing precariously on the ladder as his tormentor smiled prettily up at him.

'Okay, love, just teasing,' she said, and removed her hands after one last squeeze.

Foolishly, he stayed where he was while Sally went into the bathroom. As he watched, she stripped. Not only was the stained shirt removed to reveal her heavy sway of braless pink-tipped voluptuousness, but her shorts and G-string came sexily down with an obscenely erotic bend away from him and the presentation of all her worldly treasures. Having adopted the position, her cheeky smile appeared again from knee level as she twisted to look up at him, fully aware of the effect on his maleness of her open invitation.

'Sally, noo,' he admonished, unexpectedly throaty now, remembering the smooth coolness of her hands on his butt, and she heard that tension and turned to him. 'Sally no! I have a girl...Bonnie...we...'

But still stuck up high he realised that damned Poindexter had stirred. Worse, he saw that she, with her eyes now at his groin level, had spotted the sly activity. Those magic hands again entered the leg of his shorts but from the front this time. She roughly pulled free the traitorous little bastard and rewarded the blushing swine with a fiercely applied soft suction to another pathetic 'Sally, noooooo!'

What to do? Drop the paint on her bobbing head? Fall backward off the ladder? She had him, had him good, as she chortled into her work. His ethics, his morality, his undying loyalty and love of his woman Bonnie became diverted by the overwhelming surge of lust and the effect that the powerful physical sensations of this woman's expert ministrations had on his other tiny fickle brain.

But then all the possibilities and consequences were avoided when he heard 'Sallee, nooooooo!'

Not from him this time! Confused! It was the Spanish armada! Bella charged through the door right at him like a tiny angry Spanish pocket battleship! Her shoulder smashed into the ladder to push her woman away from the rigid ugliness of the man on the ladder. There was a *pop!* of a powerful suction disconnected, but even as he fell with paint splashing backward in a sticky white arc, he had the wherewithal to ensure that he collapsed in the direction of Bella's bed. From under the ladder he struggled clumsily to disguise the mess of his earlier search while tucking a rapidly retreating whitewashed tumescence back under cover as his furious assailant bullied him out of the room with Spanish curses and raised fists.

47

DEAD MAN'S PARTY

The task force's agent had been in place for close on two weeks. Finally snippets of interesting information were dribbling out of Beauty Bay with Bill's nightly progress call to Bob Hopkins. But so far nothing forensically significant had happened. Even Sally's yellow tabs, although a possible in as a basis for a search warrant, were really not enough. Fred Hall was a worried man. It was not that his team was not still busy: it was. Surveillance stayed 24/7 on the Spiders, of course, but without a clear lead for the investigative and forensic squads to pursue Fred had used the opportunity to cover every possible angle involving the circumstance of each death.

In every homicide investigation there was the evidential need to ensure that every tiny bit of evidence available from that most precious of forensic exhibits, the deceased person, was collected, analysed and collated. In the early stage of the terrible circumstance it was the forensic freezing and minute examination of the immediate death site or scene that was vital. That early examination of the place where he or she had died, lay and was found, allowed collection and protection of any real evidence before and after the body was moved. Then there was the body itself. A detective was usually appointed the incongruously titled OC body. That officer had the unenviable task of staying at all times with the corpse during the initial activity at the scene. He or she was there when the body was finally released from that place and lifted into the body bag and sat beside the body as it was transported to the morgue, staying in immediate proximity as it was lifted from the bag onto the cold stainless steel of the mortuary examination table.

The OC body consistently records hand-written notes into the police-issue notebook about every single thing that happens to and therefore could possibly influence the evidential value of the dead person en route from death scene to autopsy location. The police officer is then perhaps an unwilling but typically professionally fascinated witness to the body's clinical dissection by the white-frocked forensic pathologist.

The officer stands or sits necessarily close to the gruesome activity, recording each comment by the expert in the act of forensic dissection as each organ is rudely sliced from its bodily connections and weighed in the stainless steel dish on the scales, and the data carefully recorded for the coroner's report as to cause of death.

But all that had been done, finished seven weeks ago. The collection of tens of thousands of other evidential exhibits had also been completed. The entire crime scenes, at Concord, at the nightclub and at Van's flat, could now be reproduced in 3D on video screens. Each body could now be digitally recreated back in its death location. The computer technicians had put mountains of data from the surveyors into the recreative technology, from the GPS logging and from the kilometres of digital images collected. All that work was ready for presentation to judge and jury at the court case when, or if, an accused ever stood in the dock.

Now Fred brought his team together again to impress upon them the importance of what he wanted them to do. In the main operations room at the regular debrief on Friday afternoon, four pm sharp, he addressed them as he always did before they left for what had quickly become an operational team ritual. They gathered at the favoured watering hole of the Globe Hotel where they enjoyed a much more relaxing and extended de-brief.

'People! If I could have your attention...thank you.'

Still united, still determined, vaguely aware that the senior command had other initiatives and secret investigations underway, they sat up and listened to Fred Hall. At each Friday meeting he gave the entire operation a new direction, an investigative tweak for the week coming. This tactic was a deliberate management tool to maintain their motivation in completing this thing.

'Now next week, starting Monday, I need you all here for briefing at 0700. Good news: none of you will be required this weekend!'

A Bronx cheer erupted. In this seventh week the operational soldiers were given two days off! Two whole days off to renew bonds with family and simply to relax. A brief window to recover from the debilitating effects of the tasks they had slaved over for the last forty-two days and nights straight.

Fred Hall smiled. 'I would ask you all to enjoy the time off. But I would also ask you to keep it confidential. I expect each of you *not* to discuss with those outside this team any functional issue...and I know that goes without saying. But I do say it, because it is important that the wrong message does not get out into the public arena.'

The gathering nodded as one, knowing that the rapacious media could twist the matter of the team being given a hard-earned weekend off as some sort of failure in the search for the killers.

'Folks, on Monday we start a phase of the operation that is of vital importance to our common goal. We look at each of our victims with the theory that the intent of the killer or killers was to kill that one person. You will be briefed and tasked. But the investigative philosophy of what I now need you to do is in your team's taking each single victim as if he or she was our *only* victim. Interview those around him or her. Research each life, their relationships, property owned, their bank records and telephone, computer, email, and diary records. Establish their entire history. Dig up all their dirty secrets. I need you to collect and collate that entirety of fact and–or fiction in minute detail.

'Your evidence then will be entered into a computer database and scanned by a program that our friends at ASIO have provided us. It's basically the software twin of ASIO's international terrorist predictive and tracking database. This program automatically searches that entire international database of information. It seeks out the key words, the names, numbers and dates. It finds the connections. It cross-indexes and alerts us by a detailed and extensive forensically digital analysis to any trends, connections and, need I say it, clues that may then lead us on.'

Fred stopped, aware of the intensity of renewed interest, the focus on him and his words from the gathered forces.

'Ladies and gents, enjoy your break.'

48

UPTOWN GIRL

It was Friday. Lily Phat had been in Broome for five days. Over that time, one by one, the gang within a gang had made its arrival, apparently smoothly and so far undetected by opposing forces. From different Asian airports the four young Vietnamese men had landed in Broome and were hidden immediately among the crowds of tourists arriving at the tropical destination for the sun, the beach and the pearling and nature tours.

Lily had patiently waited in the separate little world that the resort provided. Each morning, before the skin-tanning heat of the tropical sun beat down, she would dress in her white bikini and a tie-dyed sarong and join other early rising guests in the blood-warmth of the freshwater swimming pool. She would then enjoy a smorgasbord of tropical fruits on her sunlounge, under the protection of the wide beach umbrella that kept the damaging rays from her porcelain skin.

At the pool, many a middle-aged Caucasian businessman far from home tried to initiate a conversation, attracted and entranced by the possibilities of her tiny perfection and exotic looks, just as so many young servicemen had been similarly attracted to her kind on the streets of Saigon decades earlier. Lily, however, was a modern Australian woman, an intelligent, forceful big-city lawyer, and she swiftly cut down the clumsy approaches, as she often had in her other life on the beaches and in the bars of greater Sydney.

Lily, as the commander and forward scout, simply needed to wait as her troops gathered in the enemy territory. No communication was entered into, either with her father or grandfather in Sydney or with the men arriving to join her team. Two of them were her blood cousins, but each of them on arrival went to a different motel or hotel previously booked by the Happy Dragon Travel Agency of Serangoon Gardens, Singapore. In accordance with the plan, each man laid low, quietly within each mini-world, although within a ten kilometres radius of each other.

Finally on the fifth day, Lily booked out late from the resort, just before midnight. Her only baggage was her wheeled black suitcase. Waiting outside the grand entrance was an air-conditioned Toyota four-wheel drive rental van, one of dozens of identical or similar vans available from hire car franchises based in the township. At her approach and introduction, the hire company's pimply-faced young driver handed her the keys. He stowed her bag in the boot and left before she drove the van away. She travelled in the darkness along Cable Beach and then back into the tiny township for her immaculately planned sequence of four verge-side pick-ups from four motels.

49
DON'T COME AROUND HERE NO MORE

Earlier on that Friday night, while Bill sat comfortably in the usual gentle end-of-day conversation with Gypsy and Tommy on their balcony, Doc Patrick was busy getting predicably drunk in his smelly single room flat behind the Broome police station. Doc had basically been going increasingly crazy for the entire two weeks since he had watched as the Beauty Bay's supply barge, and *his* undercover agent Bill Peters, had chugged slowly away in the dark to the south. So far he had resisted the almost overwhelming urge to disobey his old mentor Bob Hopkins and make just a quick call to Bill on the satellite phone. Just a surreptitious connection to ensure all was well and to find out what the fuck was going on.

With Bob gone back to Sydney, and as the days ticked by, Doc was feeling more and more disappointed. His feelings had been hurt by the coldly delivered commands. Bob's directives, both on the night of Bill's recruitment and the next morning when he drove Bob from the Mangrove to the airport.

'George, I give you the thanks and appreciation of the Concord Task Force for what you have done,' Bob announced as they shook hands at the departure door.

The squat Qantas jet waited on the tarmac only a few metres away through sound-deadening heavy glass doors. Doc had glowed with rare professional pride, basking in the carefully targeted praise and the immediate company of the man he so admired.

But Bob had then continued: 'Now remember, George, you are *not* to make any contact with young Peters unless I give that direct order. Okay?'

And Doc, although somewhat taken aback, had agreed.

'Not unless you give the order, sir. Just like the old days, eh?'

Bob Hopkins had seemed satisfied with that.

But Bob was gone now and had been for fourteen fucken days. Doc was both pissed-off and increasingly more pissed on his faithful old friend 'whisky-whisky'. The thing was, he didn't really trust Peters! He was fucken certain that he needed to be in contact with him to have that steady, guiding, mature influence on his agent. Bob Hoskins didn't, couldn't understand this. Bob didn't know Peters like he did, Doc reasoned. The more he thought about it the more he couldn't understand why Bob had insisted that he make no contact. None! Not unless Bob gave him a direct fucken *order* to do so.

'It's just fucken wrong, boss,' he slurred to no one.

Doc was naked; the room's ceiling fan and the wheezing air-con cooled his hairy obesity as he lay, legs akimbo, sweating on the stained sheets of the single bed. The crumpled khaki of his discarded uniform sat in a moist pile near the door as a reminder to drop it to the local Chinese laundry the next day.

The tiny TV crackled on its rickety shelf on the wall opposite.

'Fuck it!' he would occasionally grunt as his Irish rose, but his sad penis refused to, as he pulled distractedly at it while watching the energetic faux passion of the girl-on-girl porno tape. This was one of dozens of his well-used DVD porn library stacked under his bed. The dirty discs were ordered and received in plain envelope anonymity from the mail order supplier based in the nation's capital. 'Nah, fuck this shit,' he grunted and with his left hand never leaving its sweaty reticent little *maaate* he took the satellite phone in the other and proceeded to blow *his* agent's cover.

One hundred and fifty kilometres to the south, Bill had himself made a mistake this evening. Having reported in as usual to Bob, he had forgetfully slipped the small black phone into the pocket of the faded khaki dungarees that he used for his casual night-time-visiting-Gypsy-gear. As they sat, late now, enjoying a last drink of the creamy cocoa she made so wonderfully well, Bill's phone rang. The three of them jumped at the unexpected blast. Especially Bill, not only because he had never heard it ring before, but because he had forgotten that he had it. But mostly because it immediately reminded him what he was doing here. Spying on his friends.

'Jesus!' he mumbled, confused.

'But why would Jesus call you here?' Gypsy laughed. 'Perhaps a lonely Broome girl, eh?'

Bill had a little time to think quickly as to how to handle this as he struggled to free the damn thing from his pocket.

What he did know immediately was that this could only be Bob Hopkins, and obviously Bob needed to talk urgently. That had to be the case if he had broken cover like this. So Bill stood and excused himself. By the time he was at the steps he had the phone in hand blaring out its electronic call to the quiet night.

When he finally pushed the receive button he was down the wide limestone stairs and onto the boardwalk back to his bure.

'*Maaaate!*'

'Doc, is that you?' Bill queried, now further confused.

'Yeah, course, maaate, how the fuck are ya?'

Bill was still thinking that something very urgent must be up. Bob must have asked Doc to call him.

'What's up, Doc? Why have you called?'

'Hey listen, Mr Cunt! You don't fucken aks me why I've called!' Doc exploded, and Bill immediately knew now what was up: the silly old prick was pissed.

'What's happening, Doc?' he queried, his own anger rising now.

'Doan fuck with me, Peters!' Doc barked back, feeling the fury of the snub from Bob Hopkins rise in him and realising, somewhat surprised, that his left hand now held a relatively proud erection. 'Report the progress, Peters. What the fuck is going on there? Look, don't you dare fuck with Bob Hopkins, maaate! Ya hear!'

Bill wasn't going to play this silly game. 'Doc, talk to Bob! You are not supposed to call me here,' Bill hissed.

'Na, mate, this call has Bob's okay,' Doc lied. 'So now what the fuck are you up to? What's happening, Bill? Look doan forget the dugong, maaate! Still got that in the fridge here, ya know!'

At that Bill lost it.

'Listen, Doc, sober up! I know that fucking dugong was never in your custody. I helped eat the thing, so don't bullshit me! Nothing's happened here so far. Now talk to Bob and for fuck's sake don't call me here again, you silly old cunt!' Bill spat and cut the connection.

In his small room in Broome, Doc's juices oozed pathetically out of his rapidly deflating tumescence to add yet another stain to the filthy kaleidoscope of the grey bed sheets as he fell into an alcoholic slumber.

50

ALIVE AND KICKING

'Fucken stupid old prick!' Bill announced with a quiet rage to the star splashed night sky, the majesty of the Milky Way and the iconic Southern Cross vibrant this close to the equator.

'Fuck!' he grunted, shaking his head not only at the thought of the obnoxious Doc, but with disgust at himself. By being here he was somehow tainting Gypsy's paradise through his connection to Doc's ugliness. He stood on the boardwalk, looking out to the dark sea as a slight zephyr puffed from the southwest bringing the aroma of the faraway bush fire.

He felt a need to be clean and cool, so he stripped and flipped the shower on, immediately glad of the relief of the water. It was then that he saw his man in the moonlight. Young Chip was down on the dark beach, striding to the north again on the short journey toward Namu.

'No time like the present,' Bill muttered. He quickly dressed and found the small torch that he had borrowed from Salty for this very purpose.

Chip's flowing white cotton clothes made the pursuit easy. Bill saw that the ghost-like moonlit figure skipped and danced with extravagant but surprisingly expert flourishes and twirls that spoke to Bill of dancing classes, at least, and probably serious ballet training in the young's man past. By the time Chip turned around the rocky headland and onto camel beach, Bill was only fifty metres behind. By using the fringe of the bush to hide himself, he also ensured that there was no possibility of leaving footprints in the softer beach sand.

Chip's entry to Namu's tent, even at this midnight hour, was unannounced as the slim young man simply lifted the flap and disappeared into the soft yellow gleam of the interior. Bill would have to get close, slink, skulk and crawl right to the tent and find a way to look and listen. He remembered that typically Chip would stay some hours in Namu's tent. Bill would need that time to creep close.

He began his careful approach in a half crouch from the darker side of the big tent until he began to hear audible proof of the humanity inside. With senses sharp, he was close now, only five metres away. He lowered himself for the final commando crawl to the rear of the tent and edged carefully between the guy-ropes. He was three metres away from the canvas now and could hear the strange muffled noises. The young man's rhythmic moaning spoke to Bill of a scene he was not sure he wanted to witness, and he reluctantly imagined what the old man was imposing on the younger. But, damn it, he had to know. So he crawled further between two of the guy-ropes until his face was against the fabric flap that was held down by a series of curved steel pins. Stealthily, and with the aid of the moonlight, Bill pulled one, then two of the pins silently loose and found that he could now lift the fabric from the sand, giving him a ground level view into the tent.

As his eyes adjusted from black to lamp-lit, Chip's moans increased in clarity and intensity and were now accentuated with little yelps of what had to be intense bursts of physical pleasure. There they were! Bill cringed into the cool sand. Chip was naked, face down on the cot with his head towards Bill, the wiry, hairy blackness of the older man obscenely straddling his pinned victim from behind. Shit! Not a memory Bill wanted burned into his brain cells. But then, as the night sky suddenly blackened above him, surely a cloud over the moon, Bill saw that this was not in fact a love scene—thankfully not a meeting of nations. With oily hands and loincloth modestly in place, Namu climbed off Chip and moved around to the side of the low cot. Bill saw then that Chip's modesty was also intact, covered by a pair of white Speedos.

Bill suddenly realised with almost audible relief that Namu was merely vigorously committing the act of massage.

'Phew,' Bill breathed. Not that he considered himself to be

homophobic. Each to his own, was his philosophy. It was just that he didn't want to watch.

Okay. Time to go. But as he put his limbs into reverse crawl, a horribly sticky snotty glob splattered mysteriously from above onto the back of his head. With his initial shock replaced by disgust as the slime slid viscously down the side of his face, Bill twisted around to see what giant bird or stinking bat had picked him out to fertilise.

'Oh, shit!' Bill gave a gasp of visceral terror as he realised that the cloud that had so completely blocked the moonlight was not a cloud. The barrier between him and the sky was the threatening testosterone-musty bulk of the bull camel. Clearly, the massive beast had silently padded up behind this intruder, perhaps recognising a threat to his beloved master. Now, on the enormous soft sandshoe pads that were his feet, he stood either side of the snake in the grass and ruminated on how to kill him.

'Fuck, got to go,' Bill muttered uselessly as the bull chose the knee-crush option and began the lowering himself to mush the life out of his frail opponent.

Bill's instincts and tae kwon do training arced up and he kicked out with a hefty side double axe strike to the camel's left knee, just as the beast began to lower his front down, sticky strings of the greenish saliva swinging gloriously from his gob. The bull roared as the blow shifted him sideways. He fell onto his side, kicking furiously away from his intended victim, taking out several of the guy ropes and starting a spectacular collapse of the tent.

Bill was up as the beast was down but he was blocked by the dromedary's immense bulk, still barred from any escape into the uncertain safety of the dark. The camel struggled to rise and Bill took the only route on offer. He jumped the beast's chisel sharp teeth as the camel attacked the break-dancing human with snapping ungulate jaws. Bill cleared the snaking head and landed awkwardly on the bull's right shoulder. With two clumsy steps across the fatty cushion of the hump and the furiously kicking hindquarters, Bill was up and almost away. Almost, because the damn thing tripped him! Well, the leather leg hobble did anyway.

Bill hissed a desperate curse as the big beast finally folded itself up straight and vertical, bloody murder in its reddened eyes. Bill knew that he would not outrun this thing; he would have to fight it. A fragile black belt seventh dan against a one-humped fucking monster! Roaring in its rage, the beast made a direct approach to end this tiny human life. Its head led, teeth snapping, determined to grab or simply smash the man down and then take some time and some camelus dromedarius pleasure in mushing and chewing and stomping its pathetic humanity into the soaking sands.

But Bill was waiting. With the advantage of high intelligence against brute force and size he met the lowered head of the beast with a kick. This tae kwon do special was a rotated uppercut that connected with the camel's jaw and snapped shut the imperfect bite, and the kinetic energy of the blow snapped the head upward against the mechanical restriction of the vertebrae of its neck. The camel's lights of consciousness switched off. A king-hit! A KO! The fancied but furry super-heavyweight falling to the smooth-skinned featherweight. But even as the camel crumpled, Bill was running. He had gained a quick ten metres across the small clearing towards the camouflage of the scraggly bush as the camel came to and rolled madly against the tent in his effort to get back up and chase the man down.

Meanwhile, the massage session had turned to shit as the heavy tent folded down on the men inside with the added effects of a one-tonne maddened beast rolling and kicking against it. By the time Chip and Namu appeared, bedraggled, from the safe side of the smashed structure, Bill was fifty metres away in the dark, running furiously towards the headland.

Namu screamed Arabic curses and commands at the big humped animal but the bull ignored him, eyes rolling in a crazed hormonal rage as he had picked up the running man against the moonlight and began his pursuit, dismemberment on his tiny mind. But he was hobbled so his chase was a comical stumbling, tripping affair that had his master to him before he could raise even a half gallop. With a length of polished slender hardwood the old man thrashed against the bull's rump until the creature's limited sanity eventually prevailed and the beast cowered to his alpha male master. But as Namu and Chip surveyed the disaster of the tent and wondered at the insanity of the bull, the huge beast stood rigid, watching the man running round the headland. A man that he would surely kill.

51

FOREVER YOUNG

Daybreak in paradise. A kookaburra, that avian Australian hunter of insect, lizard and fish, cackled his raucously merry greeting to the early Saturday morning from a tree branch right next to Bill's tiny haven, and brought him yawning and stretching awake. He laughed at the events of the night before and 'Ka-ka-ka'd!' back at the bird. He reached from the bed to pull the wood-slatted blind opens and watched the bird as it cocked its handsome strong-beaked head from side to side in apparent and comical disbelief that an unknown stranger would dare to enter his territory, let alone attempt his language.

Bill heard first the barefoot patter on boards of an approach to his hut and was delighted when Gypsy tapped a short warning knock on the door before poking her lovely head inside.

'Coming for a dip, my friend?'

'Love to,' he responded and covered his nakedness with a pair of shorts while she waited outside. The pair then walked the ten paces through the bush fringe to the high tide. She laid her towel down above the high-water mark and slipped the knot of her sarong and spread that on the towel, revealing a tiny lime green thong bikini to Bill's ever admiring but brief gaze. Gypsy told him that Tommy had 'shot away' by road earlier for the hour and a half road trip to Broome.

'His fishing boat's engine has blown something called a fufu valve,' she said.

Bill laughed at Gypsy not realising that Tommy had been teasing her with his description of the alleged mechanical problem.

'He will be back late afternoon. He said to make sure I reminded you that it's Saturday and you are not to work; you deserve the weekend off,' she insisted, all businesslike. 'Tommy said if I find you working he won't take you fishing with him tomorrow.' They both grinned at the soft threat.

As they approached the lap of the water against the white sand Bill knew that with Tommy away he must wait until the evening to talk to him. That was when he would make his stand, test Tommy's friendship. Ask the question.

Gypsy slipped gracefully under the warm, perfectly clear waters but gently cursed at the tsunami effects of Bill's Tarzan yell and dramatically executed bombie into the shallows. The resultant wave rolled back at her and, with her higher centre of gravity from the bulbous tummy, rolled her over. This had her laughing and splashing furiously back at him as she righted the good ship Gypsy and sat regally with the clear salted waters just over the tanned symmetrical swell of her bikinied breasts.

Feeling all macho-athletic and just plain healthy in this beautiful environment, Bill went for a showy fifty-metre power sprint demo of the Australian crawl along the shallows before returning and sliding under the water to gnaw on her pretty toes like an oversized lobster. Finally, after much giggling and attempts to kick her tormentor away, she lost patience and with a strong grip on his hair, dragged his suddenly limp body up and beside her in the shallows.

'Tarzan's still an idiot,' she giggled.

He laughed with her in the beauty of the tiny bay with the sun just starting its journey from the east. The slight onshore breeze brought the perfume of the tropical seas and blew away the floral scented wood-smoke that they had sometimes been immersed in recently from the bush fire to the south. He moved behind her and sat with his legs either side of her shoulders and arms. She hooked her arms with comfortable familiarity back and across his knees and laid her head back, her face to the sky. Her long, lush hair, shiny with good health, swept across his belly, and with the memories of past times he began then a soft massage of her shoulders and upper back, his thumbs pressed either side of the gentle curve of her spine.

She sighed in appreciation and asked, 'Does Bonnie have you massage her, Bill?'

'Not really, Gypsy girl. I would never get to finish a massage with that ratbag.'

Gypsy laughed, suspecting that her young neighbour would have sought a much more energetic connection with Bill.

'You've still got that touch, mister,' she said. 'If you are free late this afternoon, I would very much appreciate a massage in my healing studio. This little bundle places some strains on my body that need some attention from strong hands.'

'Well, it's a dirty stinking job but I suppose someone's got to do it,' he replied.

As they sat now in silence he thought that he might try to sound her out her about the cash in the suitcase if the opportunity arose during the afternoon massage. Aware that his attention had wandered she twisted her head around to him.

'Show me your ballet again,' she asked, and he laughed at her description of his martial art. She had liked to watch him in times past on early morning workouts at Cable Beach as he practised the focused routines of his tae kwon do, enjoying the precise physical beauty of the defensive and offensive patterns.

Bill stood and dramatically bowed before her as if to some Korean master judge of his craft. Wading slightly deeper, the black belt engaged in the flow and snap of the immaculately choreographed dance of his art form, complete with perfectly timed grunts and barked Korean commands. He danced the routines in the white-froth splash of the Indian Ocean and completed his seriously showy performance to Gypsy's applause. He concluded comically, as was his way, with another deep bow that had his head go underwater and barking nonsensical Korean commands as if drowning for his art. Finally rising, Bill helped his giggling friend to her feet and accepted her soft peck of affectionate thanks onto his cheek.

He felt her soft hand reach down and touch the old scarring on his right thigh where the cruel talon of the spearhead from a gas-powered spear-gun had gouged through his living flesh so long ago. She stood so close to him her radius of tummy bulge just touched and her eyes looked directly up and into his. Her gaze was through him, deep into his soul, as was her way, and she smiled as his gut churned at his deception of her. Gypsy turned then and he watched as she walked lithely into the curtain of vegetation that soon hid her as she made her way back toward the main block and the needs of her guests.

52

BROKEN WING

Bill may have decided to ignore Doc's alcohol fuelled act of blatant stupidity the evening before, but a livid AFP Commander Bob Hopkins, who sat on this Saturday morning in Fred Hall's office at the CTF headquarters, was thinking thoughts far removed from Bill's sentiment of mere disgust.

They had given the troops the weekend off, but never the command team. On their arrival for the usual short and sharp briefing of the command team leaders, Bob and Fred were alerted to a recorded sat-phone conversation. Doc had been clearly told by Bob, but had obviously forgotten, no doubt in the fog of his daily consumption of Scotch, that every time any one of the three linked phones was activated—be that in Beauty Bay, Broome, or wherever in the world that Bob Hopkins was at any given time—the magic of the digital technology simultaneously started an internet-linked computer-based recorder at the CTF office.

Now at 0600 Australian Eastern Standard Time, three hours ahead of Western Australian time, Bob Hopkins and Fred Hall listened in the sober light of a Sydney morning to the drunken ramblings of Senior Sergeant George Patrick. They heard him in one short conversation break his agent's cover, directly disobey an order from his operational commander, and abuse and lie to the operations delicately placed and carefully managed undercover agent.

For the first time in the years that Fred Hall had known and worked with Bob Hopkins, he witnessed the compact man explode.

'You bloody imbecile!' The dreadful curse was delivered in cultured private-school English from the correct little commander. The curse was short and sharp but its delivery as impressive as the flushed bloom of anger in his face.

'Ah…I know it's stating the obvious, Bob,' Fred offered, more in sympathy for his friend, 'but he's out of control.'

Bob nodded with gritted teeth. 'Leave it to me, Fred.'

53

BEDS ARE BURNING

Broome nine-fifteen am. 'Whaa the...?' croaked from Doc Patrick's phlegm-crusted upper orifice as somewhere beneath his naked, ammonia-scented carcass an electronic signal screeched

Doc struggled into murky consciousness as he scrabbled to grab the sat-phone. Finding it, he threw it across the small room with a violence that he immediately regretted as the accompanying rise in blood pressure pushed against his temples, threatening embolism. 'Fuuuuuuuuck!' he growled, grasping a sopping pillow from the floor and wrapping it around his aching cranium.

'Nuthin that can't wait till later,' he assured himself. 'Fuck! It's me fucken day off,' he whimpered and reached down under the bed, where, nestled against the stack of porno tapes, he always kept an emergency bottle of his Scots mate Johnny Walker. Eyes still closed, he twisted free the top and sighed as the liquor coursed into him. Doc lay, eyes closed, quaffing again and again from the bottle until half of the medicinal cure of old Scotland was gone from the slender inanimate container into the obese, barely animate, one.

The alcohol's effects slowly soothed Doc's searing pain. Now he could once again slow his racing mind and think. But as he forced himself to consider action and activity he was suddenly jolted bolt upright as the flashback of the previous night's phone call kicked him awake.

'Oh no! Fuck no!' Doc grunted to the fetid room. At that moment he also realised that the phone that he had just so rudely discarded was the sat-phone, and he was off the bed, all belly-and-arse wobble and varicose veins, as he stumbled over the clothes on the floor and found the phone by the door. A quick inspection in the half-light revealed that the phone had apparently survived its short but dramatic flight. But Doc could see from the red flashing light on the face that a message was awaiting him.

'You stupid fucking cunt!' he admonished himself as he anxiously returned with the phone to his bed, and sat heavily on the side, bulbous gut hanging low, forcing his thighs apart, as he activated the message bank on the phone and listened.

'George!' Bob Hopkins's recorded voice barked angrily from the speaker. 'You must call me immediately, George. Use the sat-phone. I am going to call you at your office now on the landline. As soon as you get this message you must call me.'

As surely as he urgently needed another drink, Doc knew that he was so far deep in the shit he may never be able to crawl out. He was, however, certain of one thing. He needed time. Time to think. He needed a plan, needed to wait until he had an explanation. Until he had manufactured a credible reason for what he now more clearly remembered he had done last night.

'I called Bill Peters!' Doc announced with a surprised and disgusted tone. But then he realised, stunned! 'Peters! That cunt's shafted me! Fuck, he's shafted me to Bob!'

An incredible fury rose in him. His career had just flashed past his eyes, and in that moment he knew that he owed Bill Peters big time! And he reached to crack open the bottle of JW.

54

THE FUTURE'S SO BRIGHT
I GOT TO WEAR SHADES

In Sydney at nine am, Bui Xua Han, revered head of the Spider Gang, Cabramatta chapter, sat in the small shop in Sydney's picturesque Chinatown. He slurped the dusty tang of the gunpowder green tea that he so enjoyed from the ancient bowl of a finely crackle-glazed porcelain cup.

The shop was magically, exotically scented with a multitude of plants and herbs and spices, some hanging upside-down in drying bouquets, others ground or whole and stored in batteries of solid green, brown and clear glass jars. A high rise of dark-wood drawers took up an entire wall from polished floorboards to pressed-tin ceiling in the perfumed gloom of the tiny Chinese medicine shop.

Bui's old friend Xing Xao, the shop owner and medicine man, was mainland Chinese. Many decades ago he had come on a ship to Sydney as a small child with his parents. His father, a coolie labourer, slaved for the *gwaello* contractors on half the wage of the white employees on the major road and bridge works that had transformed the transport networks of early Sydney town. He had found his lifelong profession in the mysteries of the herbal medicines taught to him by his father's friend, the Chinese chemist. He had also learnt the skills and magic of the fortune-teller, translating the meanings and messages held in the intricately–hand-painted cards revealed when a client shuffled, cut and picked from the heavy pack.

Bui had come to Xing's shop twice a year for the last forty years. And for those prosperous years he had acted on the mystic's guidance in the path forward, to his and his extended family's contented enrichment. With the stress of recent events and the immediate and future fate of his precious granddaughter Li Li foremost in the old man's thoughts, he sought once again guidance and reassurance from the readings of his soothsayer friend.

They had talked first, as always, inquiring about the health and happiness of wives and sons, about business and about self, as both had grown old now and both knew that their mortal end was in sight. Eventually the reading began in the darkened rear office. They would not be disturbed, as Xing's middle-aged son now ran the shop where Chinese and increasingly Anglo Australian customers sought ancient oriental potions and cures.

Xing took the old cards from the sturdy red and gold painted wooden box and passed them to his Vietnamese friend. Bui shuffled, and at Xing's soft command selected thirteen cards one by one with his left hand and passed each in turn to the mystic. But as Xing laid the other's future bare before them, he suddenly blanched at the import of the progressive completion of that destiny. He sat motionless and stared again at what the Bui's future so certainly held.

Bui saw his companion's reaction, but he had also read the cards and his heart sank.

'Say nothing, old friend,' Bui spoke. 'Say nothing.' He rose and, with now bent shoulders, left the shop. He would never return.

55

COMING UP CLOSE

A red-dusted Toyota van slowed to a stop on the bitumen highway that runs north to Broome 150 kilometres away and another 280 kilometres south to the busy oil and gas offshore-onshore service industry hub of Karratha.

Opposite the signpost that read *Beauty Bay 5 k's this-a-way*, the van turned right towards the unseen sea. The vehicle bumped down off the lip of the seal and along the gentle corrugations of the red dirt road leading to the resort. Lily Phat eased off the accelerator of the unfamiliar vehicle.

Beside her in the front passenger seat sat her cousin, her father's brother's eldest son: the Market Gardener. Thirty-one years old, he was a hard-working entrepreneurial son of Cabramatta. He had worked energetically to achieve a home in the suburbs, a shop, and later a wife. She was the daughter of a lower tier lieutenant, he marrying down, she up. And now he was repaying the debt he had owed the gang since he was funded at twenty-one years of age into his first acreage, and onto his first tractor. Back in Sydney, his young wife, heavy with baby number four, waited resignedly for his return from *the business.*

In the seat immediately behind Lily, lounging arrogantly, sat the Soldier. His grandfather was only number five in the high command pecking order of the gang. This twenty-five year old man was impatient. He was also determined that once he had fully learnt the deadly array of skills that his Australian Army paratrooper battalion was happily teaching him, he would transfer those skills to the business of the gang that one day he intended to lead. The Soldier was also angry; angry that a bloody woman led this operation, and what a smart-arsed bitch Lily had grown to be. But, he counselled himself, be patient. This job is simple, and she is the senior man's granddaughter, and the daughter of the man he would at some time in the near future unseat.

Seated behind the soldier was the Teacher. Twenty-nine years old, he taught primary school kids at Cabramatta Primary and he loved his job. He had chosen to maintain a single status. This choice was to the great displeasure of his parents, and of his grandfather, ranked fourth in the command structure of the Spider Gang. At this time in his life he enjoyed the various fleeting pleasures available in the nightclubs and party scene in Sydney. He was busy enjoying the energetic physicality that the busty blond beach Amazons of the Bondi female *skip* population had on offer to a smooth talking, good looking, muscular Asian dude with a ready supply of the latest party drugs. At some stage he knew that he must succumb to the pressure of his family and find a shy Vietnamese virgin bride to bear his children. Otherwise, as had been pointed out to him by his father, he could kiss the inheritance goodbye.

Next to the Teacher, and chatting amiably to him, was Lily Phat's other direct line cousin, this time from her mother's side. The Chemist was the oldest at thirty-eight and was happily married with a brood of five growing kids back in Sydney. He had moved away from Cabramatta when the gang had financed him into his first twenty-four-hour chemist shop when he had finished uni. He had then gained a year's experience under the close tutelage of a friend of the gang in his shop in Redfern. He now owned a chain of shops and employed the sons and daughters of other gang members. Many gang parents often held up the Chemist as an example of what their own miscreant modern kids should be striving to achieve. Normally he might not have been called to repay his debt to the organisation, but his special skills were needed. He carried in his suitcase certain tools of his trade to sample, to test, and to analyse.

Lily slowed the van to a halt as they reached the dead-end semicircle of a gravel car park off the dirt access road. Before them they could not see the resort, only heavy bush. But a painted sign invited new arrivals to push a large buzzer. This alerted the reception staff 500 metres away over the disguising bush-covered rise of an ancient dune. Off the dune was the boardwalk that led to the main building, its limestone block base and teak-and-tin bulk rearing up out of the seaward aspect.

A tinny electronic voice answered the buzzer via a small speaker as the men got out of the van and stretched limbs stiff from the trip. They had left Broome in the black of midnight and had then parked off the road for several hours and tried to sleep. The plan was that they would arrive into the resort at midday. With Lily talking into the intercom and confirming the booking made from Singapore weeks before, soon they heard the *ring-dinging* of a four-stroke motorcycle approaching.

Chip soon appeared driving a quad bike, which towed an elongated trailer with eight seats. With a cheery greeting, he loaded the group's suitcases onto a cage on the back of the motorbike and invited the guests to take a seat on the trailer. Within five minutes of putting gently along the wooden boardwalk they were deposited at a small grouping of three bures. These were past the main block, down the slope towards the bay. There was only one such bure closer to the bay and that was the temporary home of a Mr Peters of Broome.

Bill did not witness the arrival of his new neighbours. He was resting on his bed catching up on the latest adventures of Les Norton in the well-thumbed Robert G Barrett paperback that he had found in Gypsy's small library in the resort bar.

Tommy was still in Broome, impatiently awaiting the arrival of his *fufu* valve off the two pm. Virgin flight from Perth. Gypsy was enjoying a welcome siesta-for-two under the slow rotations of the overhead fan in the main bedroom of the top floor. The resort was quiet. Except for the small group of new arrivals from the Singapore booking, all the guests had left that morning in the resort bus back to Broome, and the next group would not be arriving until Monday.

Down at camel land, Namu pulled up the sleeve of his cloak and checked his Rolex Oyster Perpetual. Midday.

It was time to prepare for tomorrow.

56

GREAT SOUTHERN LAND

As Namu checked the time at Beauty Bay a huge high-pressure weather system developing to the south of the nation swept over the coast of the Great Australian Bight and swung the winds around until a strong easterly began to freshen from the heart of the island continent. The massive airflow picked up the heat from the desert to dry again the drought-parched lands of Western Australia.

One hundred kilometres south of Beauty Bay and 80 kilometres inland, the arrival of the convoluted forces of the winds brought the embers of a long, narrow finger of the bushfire back into glowing, sparking life. This renegade child of the mother blaze was close to exhaustion, having consumed the strata of vegetable fuel along a gully. The previous night's mild zephyrs had at first pushed and encouraged the breakaway, but as that breeze faded the fire was forced to sit and wait like a sulking toddler. But now the means of its ability to leap and grow and consume had come back, and come back with vengence, to run towards the coast and the promise of a bigger meal on better-vegetated coastal plains.

57

ON A WING
AND A PRAYER

At 1500 hours Western Australian time, Bob Hopkins and a team of five were two hours into their five-hour flight across the continent. They had left Mascot at 1000 hours AEST, the only passengers on the chartered executive jet.

Fred Hall had signed off on the expense. To fly to Broome from Sydney by commercial airliner would have had them into Broome late that night, but they would have had to fly west to Perth and then wait in the terminal for a transfer for the 2250 kilometre flight to the north. Bob had argued, and Fred had immediately agreed that they couldn't afford to waste that time.

Efforts throughout the morning had failed to locate Senior Sergeant George Patrick. The young day shift constable at Broome Police Station had taken Bob's calls, had personally and conscientiously looked for his senior sergeant. He had nervously checked Doc's dank room, driven through the town, popped in at the local pubs to no effect. He had reported his failure back to the increasingly frustrated AFP commander. The constable told Bob that the police Land Cruiser was missing and that the station's double-barrelled shotgun had also gone from the armoury.

58

WAITING FOR
A GIRL LIKE YOU

The Virgin flight into Broome was late. It and all other commercial airliners flying to the northwest from the capital city of Perth had ventured far out to sea in a wide detour around the ash and dust clouds that had risen from the massive wildfire below on the parched land.

Tommy waited patiently in the small fan-cooled bar inside the Broome terminal, icy beer in hand and whiling away the afternoon in conversation with other locals.

Finally, at four o'clock Tommy took possession of the freight envelope that held the vital part he needed to get the fishing tender working again at the bay. Soon he and the paying guests could enjoy once more the great reef fishing off the coast. Back in his vehicle, Tommy started his ninety minute journey back to Beauty Bay. The recently purchased troop carrier was crammed with provisions and supplies for the resort, and a gift of sweet French perfume for his Gypsy woman.

As he left the township and headed south, Tommy saw again the far distant but vaguely threatening dark horizon. For weeks now the wildfire had bellowed up and out and created an airborne wave of ash that sat as if waiting to plunge forward and down towards the tiny resort perched precariously on the edge of the continent. Still, Tommy knew it was over a hundred distant klicks away, and, barring a disastrous change in the winds, would never track north.

60
ETERNAL FLAME

Thirty minutes ahead of Tommy's troop carrier, one hour from the resort, Bonnie Anu chugged incrementally south in Bill's old jeep. Bonnie had not lasted the scheduled full two weeks at the tribal get-together up the coast. What was happening with young Randy was secret men's business really, she reasoned. The women, although welcome in supporting roles, had little to do except gossip, gather and cook bush tucker for the feasts, feed the men and gossip some more. Bonnie was all gossiped out after ten days and almost to her own mild surprise was really missing her man.

'My una! My love! Me want Bill,' she shouted to the sky as the warm smoke-scented air flowed over the short windscreen of the convertible jeep She sang along to the home-grown melodies of the Waifs blasting out of the jeep's old cassette deck. She was quickly closing on the resort, away from the ceremony where a boy was turning into a man. Towards the man who *means stuff to me*, she warbled. She had plans for young Bill. And she was looking forward to seeing her friends Gypsy and Tommy. Anyway, she reasoned, Gypsy had secretly invited her to join Bill at the place during that funny phone call from the family home the night before Bill had left.

But even as she drew nearer to Bill and the bay, at ninety kilometres an hour, Bonnie looked up at the southern horizon and at the black roiling smoke cliff that rose to several hundred metres above the horizon. A sense of unease stirred at the weird threat of driving towards, instead of fleeing, something so hugely dark and dangerous.

***

Far to the south, the freshening easterly wind had pushed the single finger of fire to the west coast fringe of vegetation, where it now gorged on the heavy load of fuels untouched by flame for decades. As if reinforcements had been called to the front by a bugle call, the red and white surges of heat and flame appeared to resupply and bolster the forward scouts of the charging conflagration and the fire quested south and north as it consolidated and then rested, as if waiting.

60
BACK ON THE CHAIN GANG

It was late afternoon on a gorgeous tropical day in the most beautiful of physical locations, and Bill was eagerly en route to a much-anticipated date with another beautiful physical location, planet Gypsy. They had set the time and place earlier that day over a succulent tropical salad lunch at the main block. 'Five pm at the healing dome,' she had ordered.

Gypsy's massage and healing studio was tucked away from the main body of the resort in a small valley. The healing dome was a high-beamed, teak and stained glass pyramid. Inside was all soft candle lighting and soothing mystical music from Gypsy's collection of such minority taste masterpieces. This was Gypsy's haven where she performed her magic and occasional miracles of spiritual and physical healing on the damaged bodies and psyches of the resort's guests. Now with the sun gliding from an azure sky towards the western horizon, Bill and Gypsy met at the dome as they arrived from different directions.

'Greetings, Master,' she teased, and bowed to him; he bowed to her, dressed as he was in his sarong and the skin-coloured Speedos that she called his budgie smugglers.

'Greetings, glorious victim,' he responded.

She led him into her studio and pointed him towards the collection of massage oils. She switched on a soothing CD track of ocean sounds, the occasional whale calling through the soft rhythms and stringed accompaniment adding to the atmosphere of tranquillity in the bure.

She fussed about setting up the massage table with towels and cushions to cater for her advanced pregnancy, so that she could lie comfortably, almost side on, to allow the bulge of her baby to rest easy.

Bill selected Gypsy's favourite oil and presented it to her as if it were a bottle of fine wine.

'I recommend the eighty-three sandalwood today, Madam,' he said, all plummy maître d' accent, as she adjusted herself on the table.

'Silly boy,' she said, and sighed the moment his oily hands started to smooth the natural salve onto her tiny, perfect toes and feet.

And so began the *dirty work* he liked the most: servicing by gentle massage the wonderful body of his friend. A process of careful symmetrical attention, alerted by sighs or movement toward or away from the treating fingers and hands, responding to force of touch, continuation or cessation of rotation or probe. At times unspoken obedience when she gestured, eyes closed to a place, a spot, a muscle, a joint that needed just that little bit extra attention. And to her delight, as was his silly way, he introduced himself verbally as well as by touch to each part of her body with a 'hello little toe' and a 'bonjour derriere'. Soon, she the receiver and he the giver entered into a trance of enjoyment as he eased up onto her back and shoulders in a combination of deep tissue and gentle caress on that wondrous bodyscape.

But as Gypsy sighed and floated on her own clouds of warm sensual relaxation and as the orange sun set on the western horizon, the distant gods of wind and weather had fought, and from the cold of the Southern Ocean just above Antarctica thousands of kilometres to the south, a huge and brutal cold front had been born. The convolutions had risen hours before up the lines of latitude, as if on a ladder blasting towards the continent. Now, after a journey above a cold sea, the massive wind shift smashed the easterly winds contemptuously away and blew a southerly buster at fifty kilometres an hour straight up the west coast of Australia. It was six pm as the first dry storm-front hit the waiting wildfire, now ninety kilometres from the resort. In ecstatic celebration of its destructive potential, the blaze exploded to the north.

61

BURNING HEART

At dusk, before the southerly wind change reached Beauty Bay, Bonnie manoeuvred the jeep off the main highway and down onto the sandy corrugations of the entry road.

Bonnie had been here months before helping out Gypsy and Tommy for a few blissful days, preparing food and serving guests when her friends had just taken over from the previous owners.

Now, as the jeep crunched onto the small gravel oval of the car park, she braked and killed the motor. She grabbed her overnight bag and almost skipped along the solar-lit walkway through the bush. Bonnie was thirsty and hungry. Thirsty for refreshment, hungry for her man. 'Maybe man first, eh?' she laughed to herself, really eager to just see him again, let alone hold him, let alone bonk him!

At reception, Sally greeted her. Bonnie didn't know Sally and didn't like the way the young English girl looked at her when she asked where *my man Billy Peters* was.

But the English girl told Bonnie where to find Bill and she discarded the tinge of suspicion. Bonnie near trotted down the walkway towards the massage bure, anticipating the surprised look on Bill's face when he saw her.

But she saw him first. She had decided that she would ambush him, find him, stalk him, leap on him like a ravenous dingo hunting a fat joey! So her final approach was covert and silent. On bare feet she entered the candlelit bure and there he was, standing with his back to her. Naked! Or so she thought. Leaning over a massage table over an apparently naked moaning woman! And his mouth was at her crotch and his head was moving about in what had to be his erotic worship of the unseen woman's feminine core.

'Fucken bastard!' Bonnie declared. Bill was still bent over, legs apart, the calls of orgasming sperm whales loud in his ears.

It was as if things happened then in slow frame-by-frame motion. He did hear the noise of words muttered from behind but sadly the meaning and intent was muffled by his antics at Gypsy's belly. He registered the anger but had no recognition of the source of the profanity. But as he began to turn his head, a hard-footed kick from behind met his relaxed and comfortable testicles. As the bone-hard arch of Ms Anu's foot cruelly squashed the Peters' twins up against the bone-hard structure of his lower pelvis, his immediate world exploded in a star-burst of primal agony. With a high-pitched squeal that he prayed was not a portent of his future timbre, Bill Peters crumpled slowly to the polished floorboards.

Bonnie exited immediately, stage left. Job done, she stalked determinedly back towards the car park, tears of anger and disappointment streaming from her eyes.

Gypsy half-rose off the massage table in confusion. One minute her silly friend, close to the end of a wonderful relaxing therapeutic massage, was teasing her baby. He was muttering sweet num-nums to the pregnant swell of her belly. The two of them had delighted in the clear ripple of movement from the baby in the womb translating to gentle fluctuations on her stretched, tanned tummy. The next minute there was an angry curse, a double *splat!* and no sign of her masseur.

'What's going on?' she wondered out loud, still fuzzy from the massage. Then Gypsy heard the moans from the floor and awkwardly rose and leant down to Bill as he lay in his pink budgie smugglers in a genital-cupping foetal curl, moaning 'hurties, hurties' as slowly the intensity of that very special male pain faded.

'Bill, what happened?' she asked, but as he responded with, 'I was hoping you could tell me' they both heard it. Tommy shouting for them. Urgent, panicky shouting!

Bill started the relatively slow process of standing upright while

Gypsy ran out through the doorway. Still bent over, cupping the bruised and battered hangers-on, he followed her out towards Tommy's call. As they left the dome and jogged the hundred metres up out of the healing valley they could smell the smoke. Up the rise they suddenly felt the heat and then saw the light coming from the dark to the south.

'Fire! Quick! It's coming.' Tommy met them and protectively held Gypsy. 'The wind's changed! It's coming up the coast direct at us, it's only a few k's south and coming fast!' he yelled.

Now they heard it, a terrifying rushing of crackling, popping, whooshing. Now from the height of the main block they could clearly see the flame. The heat was beginning to build and surge on the front of the wind that was now smashing the resort from the south.

'We have to get out of here and really fucken quick!' Tommy uncharacteristically swore. 'We can't go by road, too late, too risky. Bill, I'll get the staff onto the barge. Mate, can you get down there and set her up to go? Take Gypsy with you. We got no guests, right?'

'Yes we have, Tommy, we have! Number thirteen, fourteen and fifteen, five Singaporeans,' Gypsy replied.

'Shit!' Tommy cursed.

Bill spoke, thinking clearly now: 'Tommy, you get Gypsy down to the barge, and get the staff down there on the way. I will get the guests...and Namu! I will get him last.'

'Done,' Tommy responded.

They could see sparks and embers flying into the bush at the southern boundary. The fire was still kilometres away, but the wind carried tiny hot igniters forward.

'Let's go! Go! Go!' Bill insisted, and Tommy and Gypsy turned to run into the main building. Even as they ran, Tommy turned as if in afterthought.

'What was up with Bonnie?' he yelled.

'Bonnie?' Bill shouted back, puzzled.

'Yeah, she came past me in the jeep at a million miles an hour toward the road,' Tommy called.

Like a light bulb popping on in his head, Bill suddenly realised what had led to his immediate past personal injury. Bonnie had come to him! Found him and in the gloom, she must have thought he was up to no good with Gypsy! A cunning-linguist!

'Shiiiit!' he shouted. 'Will she be okay on the road?' Tommy just shrugged.

'Mate, she's got a head start. That's all I can say. She wouldn't stop for me, just kept going—fast—almost out of control'.

And then he and Gypsy were away.

Bill was in a quandary. The woman he loved was in danger! Or had she made a clean getaway? The jeep was old. What if it had stalled? He had to at least check the approach road. He needed transport. The motorbike! He ran to it and found the keys in it, as was the norm.

Looking down through the smoky bush he saw the posse of escaping resort staff led by Tommy and Gypsy reach the jetty and board the barge. He could see from this height that the southerly was whipping the sea outside the bay into a storm, but the barge was heavy, solid, safe. It would be uncomfortable out there, but they would be okay.

Bill kicked the quad bike into life and zapped down to the small grouping of bures. The occupants were apparently oblivious to the danger as the fire accelerated towards the resort through the bushy coastal strip. He skidded up to the door of number thirteen and pulled it open to the surprise of an attractive young Asian woman lying on the cotton softness of the doona.

'Sorry! Quick!' he called as she rose. 'Quick! A bushfire is coming—very close, very dangerous. You understand?'

'Yes, of course,' Lily replied, in her faultless private school English.

'Oh sorry. Right. Please get your group down to the jetty, onto the barge, right?' he shouted, urgently, desperately needing to get away to check on Bonnie.

By this time the four men were outside, and at his urging, scurried into the bures for bags, then the group ran off towards the beach.

Bill turned and gunned the bike back up the hill towards the road. He saw in the darkness of the coming night that the fire front was now two kilometres to the south but closing at the speed of the wind as it swallowed up all of the oxygen in its direct path.

He pulled his T-shirt over his nose and mouth as the bike swerved into a cloud of thickened grey pungency and skidded up off the boardwalk and into the car park. Tommy's troop carrier sat where a desperate handbrake slide had swung it, driver's door still ajar. Bill sprayed it with gravel as the bike roared towards the highway bouncing on the ripples of red sand and rocky subsoil. Within a minute he was on the slight rise that gave a view along the highway north and south. He skidded to a clumsy halt and stood on up on the foot rests to scan the smoky confusion of the landscape. A mini front of fire tore up the far side of the highway along a long, grassed verge.

And then he saw it! His jeep; consumed by the flames! A tyre exploded, and he called out helplessly, 'Bonnie! No! Fuck no! Bonnie!'

The jeep, his jeep, the jeep that Tommy had just seen her in, was upside down, eighty metres north of the turn-off. In her anger, in her sadness, she had lost control, as Tommy had predicted.

She had rolled it and now she was in the fire. The reality hit him like a punch in the solar plexus. 'Bonnie! No! No! Not again! Not fire!'

But he knew that he could not go to the jeep, could not go to her. He had failed her...lost her! As the petrol tank of the jeep boomed and mushroomed, he knew that he would carry this guilt for as long as he lived.

62

KING OF PAIN

Five kilometres northwest of Beauty Bay, out on a tumultuous sea of wind-smashed white horses and deepening swells and troughs, the bulky grey aluminium-plated ten-metre Broome police launch, the *John-Damn*, punched her way into that wind.

'Fuuck me, it's a freakin storm,' shouted Doc Patrick, but he was not overly concerned about the conditions.

This boat had been built for tough northwest conditions by experienced local boat-builders in. Doc Patrick was a different story. Fuelled all day only by whisky, it was now evening, and he was seasick.

When Doc had faced the gut-wrenching import of Bob's phone call and the realisation that Peters had betrayed him—after all he'd done for the cunt—his first instinct had been to run. Through the fogging consequences of his continual intake of the whisky, he had analysed and reanalysed and of course over-analysed what had happened. He listened and re-listened to the tone and timbre of Bob Hopkins's recorded commands. Doc reaffirmed his earlier conclusion. He was in trouble. He was scared. So he ran. He didn't want to admit it, especially to himself, but he was confused; frightened by the situation that he now suddenly had found himself in. He found himself tipping away from reality, from logic.

Doc's demons now manifested and were real to him. Only the whisky seemed to dull their suggestive attacks on his overheated psyche, mute the voices. So Doc had taken the police issue double-barrelled shotgun from the armoury. The weapon now sat in blue-steel intimidation beside him in the small cabin of the lurching boat, like a comforting toy for an insecure toddler.

Doc had chosen to run, but he knew that the police-liveried four-wheel drive was not the way. He had hidden it from his pursuers, tucked it away in the silo that sat bulky on the shore above the port. Then he had just sat for hours in the *John-Damn,* moored securely against the wharf. At first, Doc had kept the boat marine two-way radio on, but after repeated calls that he respond urgently from his troops at the station, he turned that off, unwilling to break cover before he had a plan.

Late in the afternoon, another bottle splashed empty over the side, he finally had a plan. And it was 'fucken genius', he decided. The only way Doc could retrieve the situation with Bob Hopkins, save the operation, save himself, was to make the breakthrough in the case. Simple really, his addled mind reasoned. Obviously, Bob's idea to insert Bill Peters undercover had failed. Peters was too close to Gypsy and Tommy. 'Probly rooting her—dirty fucken bitch!'

But it was obvious that the Vietnamese bloke must have got the drugs at Beauty Bay. So fuck it! He would do what he had done as a young enthusiastic detective in the long gone past to break a case. Get the cough from the two fucken hippies! How fucken hard could that be? Get a signed confession, with a little gentle persuasion, and he patted the shotgun and laughed. After all, this is the wild west!

Three hours later and nearly off the coast at Beauty Bay, Doc vomited once more over the rubber-clad gunnels. He wiped away the bile with the back of his hand and raised his whisky bottle to the lashing hot winds that even this far off the coast carried the tiny glow of the devil embers.

63
BURNING DOWN THE HOUSE

Physical action displaced emotional reaction. Bill knew that others now relied on him. To simply stay and stare at the place where Bonnie had died was not an option. If he stayed he would die—simple equation. Incredibly angry with himself, angry at the huge consequences of the series of small, related events that he had just witnessed, Bill furiously twisted the accelerator and spun the bike wildly away from the approaching fire and back towards the bay. With the broad bubble-tread of the rear tyres kicking and spitting sand and gravel, he gunned the powerful machine in a swerve along the red soil road and then into the car park, desperate to get down along the boardwalks to the beach. He needed to find Namu.

As the bike veered down the planks of the boardwalk, Bill looked left and saw that the closing of the superheated oxygen-sucking fire front was within 500 metres of the southern edge of the bay. That was where the jetty was, and where the barge had been. He breathed a sigh of relief through his T-shirt filter as he saw through the surging luminescence of the fire the navigation lights of the squat barge slowly chugging out of the tiny bay to round the headland. 'Thank God,' he celebrated grimly as he saw Gypsy and a group of other people on the deck: surely the staff and the Singaporeans.

As the barge moved away from him Gypsy waved frantically at him and pointed north as if to reconfirm their rendezvous once he had Namu safe with him.

He was down then, bumping madly onto the beach and revving the four-stroke down through the gears to gain better purchase in the soft silica that hugged the gentle half-moon of the shore. With the tide right up to the high-water mark there was only a metre or so of beach in front of the curtain of the bush. A waist-high stratum of smoke surged into the basin as Bill sped away from its threat. He raced along the beach toward the tiny red rock headland that separated the main resort bay from camel land.

The bike's weak headlight reflected back from the smoke and bounced back off the water. He found increasingly that the light only dimly penetrated forward. Reaching the rocks at forty kilometres an hour, he slowed rapidly. He smashed down on the main rear brake pedal and twisted the handlebars to deliberately manoeuvre the machine to the left and into the first few inches of sea in order to avoid the slanted rocks of the headland and make the sharp right turn into Namu's bay. He was necessarily close to the dark shadow of the sudden rise of red ferrous rock that reared up ten metres off the sandy base.

Suddenly his momentum altered. He didn't see it coming: a solid, sun- and sea-cured tea-tree limb swung as a deadly pendulum by the Soldier hidden in the shadow of the headland. The wooden club hit Bill across his chest, smashing all breath from his lungs, fracturing the bony spring of rib. He catapulted backward off the seat of the bike and splashed heavily onto his back in the shallows.

The bike ran on riderless, and that was what stopped the intended coup de grace from the grandson of Spider Number Five. For as the Soldier went towards the fallen man, commando knife drawn and ready, his commander, Lily Phat, pulled him back.

'No time,' she called. 'He's not moving.' The Soldier hesitated but saw that the man was lying dead still. Satisfied, he turned and joined her, the Chemist, the Market Gardener and the Teacher in a game of chase-the-motorcycle as the machine meandered up the beach of the small bay toward the tree line.

64
UNDER PRESSURE

Bob Hopkins was in the air again. The small executive jet had finally arrived into Broome airport just on the fall of a tropical darkness. They were on the ground as the huge orange globe of the Broome sun set, exiting stage west below the smoke smudged horizon. En route Bob Hopkins had been busy with in-flight phone calls and focussed planning and organising with Fred Hall and the senior command at the CTF headquarters. An urgently commandeered off-shore oilrig helicopter was warming its turbo engines. The Lear jet eased to a stop near it and well away from the small town's airport terminal. With the huge floppy rotors lazily rotating in neutral lift, Bob and his team exited one avionic muscle machine to trot across the warm tarmac and into another.

Bob took the co-pilot's seat and they clicked on harnesses before the bright orange behemoth rose smoothly up and, with a dip of its Perspex nose, slid gracefully sideways and up and away across the coast.

As Bob adjusted his headphones and responded to the pilot's queries that crackled through the internal systems, he was deeply troubled. Bob knew now that Doc was somewhere on the police boat. He had no doubt that his old agent was headed toward his new agent. Bob knew Doc too well.

Through that day at 30,000 feet he had spoken periodically and impatiently to the eager young police officer who had fruitlessly tried to cooperate with his many requests and requirements.

During one of those conversations only an hour before, and while still seated in the executive jet 200 kilometres to the east of the tiny township, the young copper had told Bob what he had just learnt from the town's emergency services. Beauty Bay resort was under immediate threat of destruction from a big wildfire and attempts at communication with the resort had failed.

'We have some local fishing vessels and the customs patrol boat headed down there at best speed,' he was told. Bob thanked the young officer for his continued assistance from that first angry call when he was seeking to track down Doc Patrick earlier that same morning.

The big chopper arrived at flight altitude above the sparkling fluoro patchwork of the night lights of the tiny town, then banked and tracked south at maximum flight speed. Bob tried again to ring his agent on the sat-phone. Again, as had happened all day, the phone rang and rang but was not answered by Bill Peters. With an increasing sensation of dread and frustration Bob again tried Doc— again no answer.

66

DAMNED DON'T CRY

As the big Sikorsky had lifted heavily off the black tarmac of Broome airport, a much more basic vehicle had smashed out of the calmer waters of Beauty Bay and met on its starboard side the increasing swell of the Indian Ocean. The white-horses immediately crested the two-metre-high bulwark of the barge's rusted steel plate sides to flood across the checker-steel and wood-planked decking. This barge would survive much tougher conditions than Mother Nature was throwing at her on this black night, however. Tommy steered her away from the calamity of the fire as his five passengers huddled together near the tiny cabin set aft and centre. As one, all heads turned and looked back towards land now that their immediate personal danger was diminished. As they watched they saw the resort's main block explode into flame. The massive fire front was in the bay. As they instinctively cowered low on the barge and looked back in disbelief and shock, the fire seemed now to settle. It sat awhile while its conflagrate forces leapt up upon the main buildings, their home, their paradise, like a pride of fiery lions in for the kill. In fact, it was a quirk of the geography of the bay that had temporarily slowed the inevitable northern advance of the voracious wildfire. It had leapt gleefully over the crest and crashed down into the heavily vegetated bay, but once down there it found the shelter that its owners had so enjoyed. This protection afforded by the land stymied for a moment the beast's mad dash forward.

Tommy steered the barge north and the following sea surged under her, lifting her heavily as she rode the swell. The passengers relaxed a little as they realised now that they would survive this. Gypsy, though, was frantic. She had seen from the barge when it was still abutted against the small jetty that Bill had got to the guests. The five quiet Asian people who had not made an appearance outside their bures in the short time they had been there. Gypsy had watched as that small group had picked their way down to the beach through the initial mini surges of confusing wood smoke and flying embers as the thunderous surge of fire had approached. Then, with total amazement and much fog-horn blasting, shouting and frantic waving from the barge, they had all watched that small group inexplicably turn north on the beach, instead of south. They watched as the group of five trotted out of sight into the dark night. Tommy's first instinct was to go after them. Dash off the barge, run along the beach to bring them back to safety; back to their only possible means of escape. But wisely Gypsy had stopped him.

'No, Tom, they saw us. You know that they saw us. They were told by Bill. If you go, you won't make it back...we won't make it out.'

Tommy knew that to be true. So he cast the barge off, backed her around, and headed out to escape the trap of the bay and to bash down to his hopeful rendezvous with Bill and Namu.

'Bill will get them off with him?' Tommy called hopefully across to Gypsy. He saw then that she was waving furiously now toward the shore, anxious still but happier when the headlights of the motorbike had appeared like a mad glow worm zigzagging down the boardwalk to the beach. Gypsy had breathed a sigh of relief as she saw Bill wave back at her and then turn the bike and disappear at speed into the smoke, north toward Namu and the camels.

67

EVERY BREATH YOU TAKE

His pocket was ringing. He realised with a fuzzy and very painful awakening that there was a clanging sound from his pocket. It hurt to breathe.

'What the fuck!?'

Bill was sore, confused, looking up at a smoky ceiling a few metres above him, laying prone in the wet and warmth of a few inches of soothing sea.

'What happened?' he asked the clear breathable air that lay under the heavy layer of wood smoke, as the southerly pushed that strata north and also out to sea. He coughed, and then wished he hadn't. His chest felt as if a camel had kicked him. He felt with his hands up under the T-shirt and on the right side the gentle touch of self-examination caused a gasp of pain and consternation.

'Fuck, broken rib,' he deduced. His quick diagnosis left him relatively happy under the circumstances that he had felt only one uneven fracture. 'What happened?' he repeated, unwilling to move just yet. But his known-known was that he didn't know what had hurt him. One minute he had been cruising along on the bike, then, bang! Here he was, a broken rib and ears full of sea water.

He raised himself to a hurtful sitting position, feeling the urgent necessity for action as the fire in the cup of the bay was creeping forward again inevitably toward his heating back. He looked back, wincing at the reaction from the damage in his chest. The fire wall was still 300 metres back, temporarily sheltered from the unfettered southerly, but due to meet again its partner in rapid forward movement in short order. That connection would again immediately accelerate the destructive fire forward at forty knots. Had to move, go north, had to find the bike, find Namu; find the barge off the coast.

He stood, hunched and gasping from the pain of his rib and from the necessity of keeping his head low and in the clear air under the pungent poison of the smoke layer. The white-red glow of the fire behind him lit his immediate world, and then he saw that his fall from the bike was not inexplicable. He saw the footprints, shoe prints in the sand, several sets, some big, one set tiny. He made a quick inspection, saw the pattern of the group of imprints in the soft telling cushion of the beach that told him the owners had gathered beside the rock. And there near where the heavy cudgel of the branch lay, he saw the tyre tracks of the bike. He followed the trail and saw where the shoe prints ran to join the tyre prints in the sand. Footprints met tyre prints but only the tyre tracks led away.

'They are all on the bike, whoever the fuck they are!' he spoke out loud but softly under his ragged breath. Then he realised they had gone north—toward Namu.

The phone stopped, he hadn't even thought to answer it. Too busy trying to live. He began a trot, keeping just inside the darkness of the bush where it met the beach, following the tracks of the bike. What else could he do? He needed to go that way, futilely probably, but at least away from the fire. He ran barefoot softly in the sand and he heard the windborne rush-roar of the fire behind as once again wind and flame met and joined as one force and surged forward, gulping oxygen.

Bill came around the small scimitar shape of the camel bay, and there, 200 metres forward and right on the water at the high tide mark he saw them. A strange grouping. The big camel automatically took his immediate attention, and there, he was sure, was Namu. The cloaked man stood next to his agitated bull, and it appeared that he was gesturing it down, as if perhaps to mount it and to ride away to safety into the distance. But also there, and clearer now in the flashes of intense light as the fire front reared behind, he saw the motorbike parked. And next to it, almost beyond his comprehension, he saw the group of five guests; the Singaporeans.

68

ALL OUT OF LOVE

'Any sign?' Tommy called to Gypsy, as Sally, Bella, Salty and Chip spread at her command along the port side of the barge, all scanning back toward the beach as the barge rode the swell in the slightly calmer waters closer to the camel bay. But then as the big fire ate its way north again, out from the coast and from behind them, a complete fog of suffocating and blinding smoke surged from the burning land and enveloped them. Coughing and with eyes streaming, finally Tommy was forced to steer away from the suffocating danger of the coast out to clear air, 1000 metres off the beach.

'Tommy what can we do?' Gypsy demanded, desperate to know where Bill was. 'Is he safe?'

Tommy went to her.

'Gypsy girl,' he soothed, and he put his arm around her. He was also worried, but helpless under nature's attack. 'He's a resourceful bugger. He's got the bike. He's probably got Namu and gone north to cut back to the road, or just headed north up the beaches.'

Tommy tried to hide his own real fears from her. But there was nothing they could do but sit out there and wait for the fire to pass.

And then Tommy spotted the police boat, cutting awkwardly across the prevailing wind and swell, rocking and rolling towards them as they sat heavy, chugging in neutral. Tommy had dropped the anchor off the square bow to hold the barge into the swell off the invisible camel beach. As the other vessel closed, Tommy laughed with relief as he saw the skipper and only occupant. He had never been so happy to see Doc Patrick!

As the *John-Damn* rounded the barge on its approach, Doc eased the police boat into the calmer lee of the bigger vessel against the port side truck tyre buffers. Tommy caught Doc's thrown stern rope and tied the boat off against the side of the much heavier barge.

'Come aboard, you two!' Doc shouted over the noise of the wind and the cacophony of destructive sound from the land. He reached a helpful arm across and first Gypsy and then Tommy took his arm in a sailor grip, and clambered over the yawing surfaces and safely onto the rear deck of the police boat.

'Just pop down into the cabin!' Doc shouted to Gypsy. Their heads were close and she smelt the sickly stench of stale whisky and vomit. Still, she thought, having known Doc for years now, both scents were familiar; the whisky smells almost part of him.

Assuming that her staff was to follow her and Tommy from barge to boat, Gypsy carefully manoeuvred herself down into the forward cabin by the small stairwell toward the bow. Behind her, unseen by the five staff still on the barge, Tommy followed her from the back deck and then down into the lower cabin. But Tommy was unconscious as he collapsed face first down the stairwell onto the floor of the cabin, assisted by Doc's sudden forceful application of the stock of the shotgun against the back of his bent head. As her man crumpled dramatically into the cabin, Gypsy shouted out in furious protest. Doc locked the door.

On the barge deck, Salty, Chip and the two girls, sea-sickening now from the plunging of the steel deck, were incredulous as the policeman cast off the rescue craft without explanation. Doc waved a casual farewell and a far from reassuring thumbs up to their shocked and pale faces as they were abandoned to a surely uncomfortable and possibly uncertain fate.

69

ANOTHER ONE
BITES THE DUST

'What the fuck is going on?' Bill asked himself from the camouflage of the darkness of the tree line, even as he moved forward and toward the grouping of camel and humanity on the camel beach. He needed to get closer. But the fire behind him reminded that he also need to get away—with his life, if at all possible.

His instinct was to run to those people. Namu he knew; the others were obviously the Asian tourists. But a very recent painful experience confirmed again by the grating of his damaged rib reminded him that it could have only been them that had inflicted his world of hurt. 'But why? And what the fuck were they up to?' he wondered.

He watched the apparently casual grouping around the huge bull. He saw it collapse down awkwardly as only camels do in the comical origami-fold-down to a seated position at the command from the cameleer. Whatever they were doing they had no time to do it! Bill was sure of that. The fire was maybe ten minutes from rushing around the corner, cresting another insignificant bushy ridge while the southerly prevailed.

'They must be all going to ride the fucken camel to safety,' he muttered under his breath. He was now only eighty metres off them and closing easily and invisibly along the sand at the high-water mark. But as he closed the distance at a silent trot, he could not believe what he saw. Namu took an object from under his cloak, a short black stick.

He placed that on the back of his bull's massive rounded crown of head and he pulled the trigger. Bill stopped dead in his tracks, stunned.

The *boom!* of the sawn-off shotgun barked back at him against the wind, arriving a split-second after the act. The camel's head exploded in an arcing spray of flesh, bone, brain and the poor creature's lifeblood. The huge beast stiffened and convulsed, his legs trapped beneath him, and Namu pulled at the wiry coils on the soft hump to roll the dying creature over, its legs now kicking free towards the sea as it died.

Against every instinct, Bill started towards the activity again. Having rounded the curve of camel bay he was now in a more or less direct line with them on the beach, and only fifty metres to the south of where they all gathered at the back of the dead bull. Bill went slightly inland behind the first few lines of the fringing bush. He began a commando creep–dash–creep from cover to cover until he was as close as he felt he could be. The camel's long outstretched legs still feebly twitched, splayed akimbo toward the smoky horizon, and just within the waters of the bay. The bull's keeper and executioner now stood on the beach side of the animal. The Singaporeans stood behind him only a few metres down from the high-water mark.

Bill watched with a voyeur's morbid fascination as Namu, apparently comfortable in the presence of the quiet audience of tourists, began a weird dissection of the camel's hump. With the light surging from the fire just cresting the ridge 200 metres south, Bill could only wonder if some strange satanic Afghan–Asian sacrificial ceremony to the fire-gods was taking place before his confused gaze.

But then the forensic penny dropped with a fucking clunk!

Namu slit the fatty hump open with the razor-sharp scimitar of his ancestral homeland. He cut the hump from the beast and it plopped down, held only by bloody hide, onto the sand. Bill saw that within the fatty tissue was a foreign implant. Namu busily sliced and snipped and half-metre-long plastic-wrapped sausages dropped messily out onto the sand. The audience of the four men and the young woman busied themselves at the autopsy tableau. All five of them picked up and quickly washed the gunk off the five parcels retrieved from the dead animal in the shallows. But then as the woman and three of the men were still busy, the most muscular male of the group quietly placed a small pistol onto the back of Namu's turban and pulled the trigger. The innocuous crack that reverberated as Bill crouched in the darkness belied the fatal effect. The .32 calibre round easily entered and messily exited Namu's skull and he fell across the neck of his camel in a final sad embrace.

'Fuck me!' Bill groaned. 'I've just seen a murder!'

The death of a man that he had met! A man he had spoken to. It was a weird sensation; a numb sickening shock deep in his gut. He hated watching animals die, let alone see a man die by a violent act only a few feet away. He saw then that his emotion was mirrored to varying degrees in the reactions of three of the other four of the gang of five. The woman screamed and cursed at the shooter. A mass debate broke out in a language Bill did not understand, with more finger waving and some pushing and pulling.

Unknown to Bill, the Soldier had based his impulsive act on the debating point that Namu was not 'one of them', and that 'dead men tell no tales', while Lily correctly, but a few minutes too late, argued Namu's potential to help them escape with the benefit of his local knowledge. This discussion, heated and passionate as it was, simply highlighted the Soldier's egotistical intent to be seen by the others to lead, rather than to blindly follow 'the woman'.

But as their dispute faded and as Bill began to move past them towards the north, the fire was making itself very obvious again behind them. He saw the group start to gather their packages and mount the motorbike together, no doubt to escape north. And in that second Bill knew that he could not let that happen.

70

TRUE COLOURS

At 200 kph the big orange chopper was soon above Beauty Bay. The resort was invisible, however, some 2000 metres down under the convoluted blanket of smoke, let alone the contributing mantle of the dark night.

Bob Hopkins and his men were witnesses only to the apparent terrible effects of the fire. Yellow and red flares of pyrotechnic destruction exploded periodically from the fire front that was clearly advancing in a ragged line below them. The pilot confirmed to Bob that they were directly above the resort. Bob looked down and muttered a simple Catholic prayer to Mother Mary that his charge and any others below were safe. The pilot suggested a lower sweep out in the clear air of the ocean at the delineation of the smoke and Bob quickly nodded with a thumbs-up of agreement.

The pilot, long experienced at finding and landing on tiny steel pinpoints of oilrig platforms in vast seas, slewed the chopper down in a wide banking dive until the machine *whup-whupped* along the edge of the smoke cloud at 200 metres above the wind-scudded waves.

The chopper reached the coordinates off the small bay where the big camel lay inshore. Suddenly below them, Salty, Chip and the girls waved and screamed as the big machine's spotlight lit up their world and their sorry predicament. The pilot swooped to a shuddering hover against the force of the southerly. With a twist here, a pedal push there, he lowered the chopper carefully until she sat to the windward side of the upturned faces metres below. The pilot and the policemen counted heads and Bob saw immediately that there was no Bill Peters and no Gypsy or Tommy Lawson on board.

Communication between the barge and the chopper was impossible but the pilot radioed the GPS coordinates to the captain of Her Majesty's Australian Customs patrol vessel *The Broome*, closing now at thirty knots, and half an hour north. The pilot gave exaggerated thumbs-up of reassurance from through the small plexiglass window to the five castaways below, and they appeared to understand that help must be on its way. They waved in thanks and gave their return thumbs-up in clear relief. Then the chopper rose again and continued on its heading north, skirting along the smoky cloud bank and climbing up and away from the roiling disturbance of the ocean.

At flight altitude they began the track back to Broome and Bob Hopkins sat back in worried reflection as the what-ifs that coursed through his mind.

Suddenly his sat-phone rang and blasted him back into immediate optimism that his agent was at least alive. Bob grabbed at the phone tucked into his suit pocket, clicked open the receiver, and in his relief shouted 'Bill! Is that you, son?'

'No, boss... ahhh look, it's me, George.'

'George? Where are you? Where have you been?' Bob snapped back, forcing himself to keep his cool against all his instinct to shout at and berate the man.

'Look, maate, I will explain back at Broome. I am on the police boat, I am heading back now. Should be a coupla hours. What I will do is call you from the base. I will call you at Sydney there. But Bob, I just got to tell ya. I think Peters was caught in a bush fire. Pretty sure he's dead, Bob. Did what I could.'

'Go on, George,' Hopkins encouraged, curious.

'But Bob, what's happened is I have the two suspects on board with me. I have a signed confession from Tom Lawson, Bob.'

'A what? A confession?' Bob stuttered.

'A signed confession, boss!' Doc said proudly. 'He admits that he smuggled the drugs in through boat parts. In a valve for his boat from Japan. The drugs that killed those people, Bob. He's signed a written confession and I am taking them both back to lock-up,' Doc crowed. 'You may want to head back across, boss?' Doc suggested all self-important suddenly. 'I've got em for ya! She said nothing, but he's taken it.'

'Good man, George' Bob answered. 'Get them back there. But treat them with all due care and courtesy. I will have men there to meet you at the wharf. Right, George?'

Bob thought quickly. In the absence of evidence to the contrary, Bob was entirely willing to believe that Doc had broken the case.

'George, this is sounding good, but you must treat these people with due respect and care. Do you understand? This is of vital importance. George, do you understand? It's for the good of the case.'

The happy voice of his old agent responded with a suspiciously merry, 'Aye-aye, sir, care and courtesy.'

71

TWO TRIBES

The only way a quad bike could escape the camel beach to the north was up a steep, well-worn sandy track at the northern curve of the tiny bay. Here, a corridor through the coastal bush had been carved from the heavy pads and bulky bodies of the camel herd over the last year. That track cut across the rise of the ancient coastal sand dunes and through to the scrubby plains behind it: an escape route that ultimately would lead to the highway.

Bill gambled that Namu would have told the gang of five the way out of the bay before his bloody demise on the beach. By the time the struggling bike and its clumsy overload of five humans and their mystery packages arrived at the entrance to the track off the beach, Bill Peters, tae kwon do black belt, seventh dan, was secreted in the dark bush halfway up the first rise.

Bill waited, puffing painfully from the effects that the mad dash through the scrubby bush had had on his rib injury. But as his breath calmed and he readied himself, a cold, deliberate resolve settled over him. These strangers had murdered Namu, but they had also attacked him—had left him lying unconscious in the sea; they had damaged his body, broken his rib. His life had been placed in danger by these dangerous criminals. He was still in danger as a consequence of whatever the hell they were up to. So, as he waited he focused through the regimes and mind control techniques of his martial art. He analysed the events as if to qualify the violent acts that he proposed to visit upon them. Bill concluded that it was a time for a little revenge. He would poke a stick in the spokes of their planned escape. What did he have to lose anyway, his life? The fire was closing in. He couldn't run from it; the bike was the only possibility of an escape on land. He had already decided that once the fire front caught him, before its inferno could scorch and burn him, he would take his chances in the sea. He knew the barge would be out there somewhere. He knew that Gypsy and Tommy would be worrying and wondering where he was. But even if they were not there, even if he couldn't find them in the maelstrom, he had instinctively decided that he would choose the uncertainty of the water over the certainty of the fire.

But there was a complication, a consideration. Since the smoke in front of the fire had first appeared, Bill had seen the mass migration of crawling, scuttling and flying insects. He had noted the excited slithering from certain death on the land of the small, medium and larger, longer reptiles. He had watched and heard the cacophony of the birds in the air; the mad dash of the tiny, secretive native mammals and larger iconic marsupials breaking frantically from the bush to converge on the beach until the heat and smoke forced them into the alien medium of the ocean. He also knew that the voracious creatures of the sea would welcome the panicked arrival of the rare treats. Schools of shallow-water, cold-blooded carnivores ate the insects in massed attacks that splashed and rippled the surface waters. Bigger creatures, such as wallabies and a variety of snakes and lizards, swam into deeper waters where they faced the dangers of the bigger piscatorial predators.

Bill suspected that the sudden abundance of land dwellers in the warm seas would be attracting the hungry and curious Spanish mackerels, the aggressive blue fin tuna and barracuda, and the ultimate predator of the region's seas, the sharks.

But now his immediate danger was revving noisily towards him up the sandy track, the machine struggling with its near 350-kilogram load. Bill saw the headlight jerkily illuminating the approach and he stood up from his crouch in readiness, careful to stay hidden behind a bushy acacia tree. The bike came parallel with his position. The driver was Namu's murderer His target! In the fluid beauty of the ancient Korean martial art, Bill pivoted off his left leg. His focused mind, now in the zone of combat, dulled the pain and restriction of his fractured rib. The swinging rotation off the pivot allowed his straightened right leg to swing his foot in a pendulum arc, and that flexed weapon of bone and flesh met the Soldier's face in a sickening crunch. As his nose cracked and crunched flat, the Soldier was flung backward into his four precariously-seated passengers. The force of the Soldier's sudden backward momentum did two things: It changed the entire centre of gravity and the balance of the bike. The machine reared up and dumped its overload of humanity onto the track. The second reaction saw the three hundred kilograms of the machine add to the carnage by flipping completely over and smashing onto the bodies of the fallen.

The Soldier was out cold. Lily Phat lay on her back in a sudden burst of white-hot agony as she took the weight of the handlebars of the bike. Her right femur and her pelvis shattered and grated. The Market Gardener, although uninjured, screamed in primal fear. He crawled frantically away in a blind panic then up and ran. Towards the fire. The Chemist and father of four lay where he fell. His neck had broken when the flipped bike and his cousins crashed on top of him. The Teacher had rolled down into the bush off the sea side of the bike and he rose now in the cover of the scrubby vegetation in a half crouch, desperately scared but desperate to act. To his surprise, the Teacher had found that he had, until this unexpected development, rather enjoyed the raw adrenalin thrill of playing the Spider heavy. The shooting of the old Arab had excited him, fascinated him. He was discovering a side of himself that he could not have previously imagined. The Soldier had seen it in his cousin and had appreciated the finding of an esoteric companion amongst this disappointingly timid little sample of the extended family. Now the Teacher held the gun. The Soldier had entrusted him with it while he drove the bike, choosing him over Lily Phat. Lily, the great commander, who now lay moaning and crying like a girl up on the track.

'Who attacked us?' the Teacher wondered. 'Where is he?' He forced himself to be still, although his instinct was to go to Lily. Go to the others; check his friend the Soldier, who only now appeared to be groggily stirring beside the heavy upside-down bike. All was quiet now. The bike's engine had finally ground to a halt, although the headlight still shone out, dimming as the battery drained. So the Teacher waited.

Finally the Soldier came to, blood streaming viscously from his shattered nose. Rising, he wiped it tentatively as he crouched, dazed and confused, and called out to his companions. The Soldier checked the Chemist, saw death. Checked Lily, saw the broken leg. He called to the Market Gardener: no answer, now long gone. He called to his friend the Teacher. A more experienced warrior than the Teacher may have not responded to the call, but he wanted the Soldier to lead him now. He rose and went to him. Then they heard the Market Gardener screaming from the south! A raw plaintive scream of agony, of fear. They knew then that the mystery attacker had got him, and confirmation came in the sudden strangled halt to the screaming.

'Quick, the bike!' the Soldier called, and the Teacher was with him and they rolled the machine back onto its four tyres. The Soldier jumped wide-legged onto the black seat and kicked and kicked again at the starter pedal. Now they could hear the rapid approach of the wildfire and could feel the increasing heat and even see sky-bursts of treetop flames from the approaching inferno as it raced down the camel bay's southern slope.

Bill also heard and felt the fire. He had backed quietly away from the consequences of his attack. He waited and watched, knowing that his skills against a gun were an uneven contest, and not one he was willing to risk, certain that he had done enough anyway.

While he watched the frantic activity through the vegetation he soon knew that the bike was mechanically deceased. The final mechanical grinding of its upside-down death throes had convinced him that the sudden lack of lubricating oils in a madly revving engine had super-heated and seized her steely vitals beyond immediate repair. With his transport gone, Bill could afford time to assess, analyse his enemies' position and tactics. It was not Bill who had attacked the Market Gardener. He had met his fiery fate when he had realised that his panicked dash away from the attacker had led him too close to the fire front. As he had frozen in an almost parody of indecision, the fire had leapt forward on a zephyr and hungrily engulfed him. With his clothes and hair aflame and his skin and subcutaneous fat igniting, and eyeballs poaching, he had finally run. He ran screaming noiselessly and blind in desperate circles and back into the flames.

Realising finally that the bike was not going to take them anywhere, the Soldier barked orders at the Teacher and both set about gathering up the plastic wrapped packages that had delayed their chance of escape from the wildfire.

Bill watched with interest. He wondered what was so valuable to these people in those packages. Then he gasped at his own stupidity! It was one of those Eu-fucking-reka flashes of insight. He knew immediately that it had been Namu and not Gypsy or Tommy that had been the conduit of drugs into Beauty Bay. The packages must surely contain drugs! And if these were drugs and the camel had carried them to the bay in his body, then that was how the other drugs, the purple fucking camels, had come in through Beauty Bay as well. Bill suddenly recalled the dead camel bull that the sharks had been feasting on that day of the fishing.

'Fuck yes! That was just before the deaths in Sydney!' Despite the clear and present danger, he felt immediately relived. 'Fuck, it was Namu, not Gypsy or Tommy,' he thought, careful to stay silent.

It didn't explain the cash in Tommy's case but Bill was the only one that knew about that. His friends were in the clear, but only if Bill could live. He knew now that he had to tell them what he had seen Namu do. Somehow, he must get this information about the drugs in the camel's hump to the authorities, to Bob Hopkins.

In the swirling smoke that preceded the fire front, Bill saw the Soldier and the Teacher gather up the strewn packages and head off at a trot. They had looked across but ignored the helpless cries of the broken Lily on the ground, and they disappeared away north and into the darkness of the camel track. Bill watched them scanning furiously about with the pistol ready for their unknown attacker. Bill let them go. They had chosen death anyway. Through ignorance of how wildfires worked in out-of-control scenarios, they had decided to run away from it, in front of it. The problem was that it was now approaching at full speed as the 50 kilometre per hour winds swept down over the bay's geography.

Bill knew that he would surely be engulfed within a few short minutes unless he made immediately for the sea. The two men running away at eight kilometres an hour had no chance.

But Bill had his own problem. When satisfied that the two men were not returning, he broke cover to move back down the track to the sea. Moaning and twisting in her own private world of agony, Lily lay bloody and dirty on the track where her men had left her. Bill's problem was there was no way known that he could leave her there to a certain fiery fate.

And so, always the fucking gentleman, Bill Peters emerged from the shadows knowing that he must help the maiden in distress. She saw him and knew immediately that he had come to finish her off. Lily Phat, big-city Sydney lawyer and failed Spider commander screamed hysterical tears of pain and fear as the apparition from the night approached. Bill knelt and soothed her, but quickly.

'Listen to me, listen to me!' He was forced to shout over the express train rushing howl of the fire front. 'Listen, I need to lift you. I know you hurt, but I need to get us away from here to the water...to the sea!'

She sobbed and nodded helplessly at him. Urgently, he humped her up and onto his shoulder. Mercifully, she screamed herself into the oblivion of unconsciousness as fractured femur grated against fractured femur, and smashed pelvic bones cut into hyper-activated nerves. She was tiny and light, maybe 50 kilos, so he could actually run with her. As he ran, his own fractured rib shot white sparks of agony across his own consciousness.

Running down the track towards the sea, he nearly tripped over the only plastic wrapped package that the two men had missed in their hurry to run away.

'Might need that,' he muttered, and crouched clumsily down on the trot to scoop up the contraband as evidence. But it was evidence only if he made it out alive, he reminded himself.

With Lily Phat flopping and grunting involuntary sighs from the rough ride on his shoulder, he was gasping now for clean air. He dropped down in the heat and stratums of smoke onto the soft sand; only eighty metres away the terrifying fire front approached. He hit the sea and splashed into the cooler tide, knees high, with huge, awkward steps until he was waist deep. He pulled Lily into the cradle of his arms and dipped down, desperate to avoid the blistering flames. But as he looked out to sea he saw the patrolling fins, only one hundred metres offshore in the deeper, cooler waters that afforded his only chance of survival. He knew that Lily was bleeding; the jagged femur had punched through her fine inner thigh muscle, a ragged tear evident in her porcelain skin. He saw the massive bruising from the haematoma visible through her tattered clothes, a consequence of the internal damage to soft tissue from sharp bone. He knew then that he was not going to swim out deeper. He would not tempt the local aquatic predators with a fine Asian entree to be followed by a meaty Caucasian main. No fucking way thank you, Noah! He had to think out of the square and fucking quickly. His head only just above the water, Bill looked around all three hundred and sixty degrees. Then he saw it but shook his head. Thought again and recalled an old Star Wars movie, and thought, 'Fuck! Why not?'

72

SOMETHING SO STRONG

Bob Hopkins sat impatiently in Doc's office at the Broome Police Station. He was tired but a wee bit excited by the news that had come so unexpectedly from George Patrick. A signed confession, no less! And from the main suspect, Thomas Lawson. By his reckoning and through confirmation from the man of the hour, George Patrick himself on the station's marine UHF radio, the *John-Damn* and her eagerly awaited cargo was due in one hour—sixty minutes. Although still desperately worried about the fate of Bill Peters, Bob had to admit, a little uncomfortably perhaps, that he was professionally intrigued about this confession to the biggest serial murder that the nation had suffered.

Bob had seriously considered calling Sydney to advise Fred Hall of the possible immense breakthrough in the Operation Concorde investigation but customary Hopkins caution nagged at him. And so he decided that a one hour wait to meet George at the dock, read the confession, talk to George, perhaps interview Lawson himself on video to confirm the confession, wouldn't hurt.

73
SOME LIKE IT HOT

Bill couldn't quite believe what he was about to do. He towed Lily over to where the big bull camel's body still lay on its side, its legs and lower belly just in the lapping sea. He propped the unconscious girl against the heavy hindquarters, tucking her in safe against the underbelly and huge scrotal bag that cradled her head. Quickly, he was out of the water and around the huge beast that was starting to steam from the approaching heat, as his own wet hair and clothes also began to do.

He found Namu's scimitar in the sand and grabbed it. Namu's unrolled turban began to smoulder, then caught like a wick that would take the fire up to his damaged head. Bill ducked back around to the beast's belly, appreciating the shelter that the bull's meaty bulk afforded. He placed the razor-sharp blade's tip into the camel's chest, in the triangle just below where the two rib cages met. With a strong and smooth sweep, he sliced the scimitar down, clicking through the breastbone and then easily along the two metres of belly skin. The huge gut split wide, releasing an immediate methane stench as coils of silvery-white gleaming intestine spilt down into the tide. Bill stayed low and, gagging, reached deep into the carcass. He pushed his head and shoulders into the dark bloody cavern until he was in past his waist. Bill retched again and again, spitting bile as he grasped blindly into the soft kaleidoscope of warm organs and slimy tissues and pulled. Heart, lungs, liver, ungulate bellies and bowels all spilt from the beast into the shallows as he furiously slashed with the sword. Finally, the camel was gutted. Bill reached down then into the bloody pile of innards and threw the glutinous mess as far as possible behind him and out to sea, to the immediate appreciation of the myriad of fishes that raced to the scene. With one last quick look, Bill saw that even the sinister dorsal fins had now turned from their patrol deeper out and were headed into far shallower waters than they would normally risk. But he had no time to be a spectator to a feeding frenzy because the fire was on them. He grabbed Lily Phat, unknowing whether she was dead or out cold, plucked the contraband package floating beside the beast almost as an afterthought, and bent, pushed, splashed and crawled inside the curtain flaps of the massive belly. Bill gasped desperate breaths of fetid death-stench as he clambered awkwardly inside of the dead beast. Once ensconced, it was as if he had found dreadful refuge in a mammalian womb once again. He prayed this would be safe haven from a certain death by fire.

74

CARELESS WHISPERS

They saw her coming from the south. The *John-Damn*, her navigation lights flickering through the gloom of the late night, aimed her bow at Broome port as Doc Patrick returned with his two prize catches.

Bob Hopkins, his four specialist AFP detectives from the task force, and the young and very weary Broome police constable waited on the high wooden platform of the dog-leg jetty.

Doc slid the launch close and busied himself securing her forward and aft. She was fitted with a self-adjusting mooring system typical of these waters where tidal flows raise and lower the sea level and any vessels on its surface by several metres twice each day.

Bob Hopkins was the first man down the steel mesh steps. He stepped aboard the launch and shook the startled skipper's hand.

'Oh...sir...you are here already?' Doc slurred, obviously surprised if not confused that Bob was in Broome, when he thought that he was in Sydney.

Bob saw, smelt and heard the evidence that this man was drunk.

Of course, Doc had not known that Bob was already in Broome, let alone in a chopper in the air somewhere roughly above him when they had spoken two hours earlier. Doc had thought that he would arrive back at Broome, tuck the baddies away, and, after a refreshing celebratory drink and sleep, he would be proudly welcoming the AFP commander and his entourage to Broome the next day, shaved showered and sparkling clean in a new uniform. So he had continued his day long pre-celebrations courtesy of a Scottish distillery on the two-hour trip back to Broome. Doc had to think quick. Although very surprised to see Bob Hopkins and his men in the official flesh, the alcohol now cruelly fooled Doc into believing that he could hide its effects from the other man.

'Where are the suspects, George?' Bob asked.

'My prisnas are secured below decks, boss' Doc responded smugly. 'I have him in handcuffs. He had a go at me and we had a bit of a scrap. But I got him in the cuffs okay.'

Doc smiled and breathed his sour foulness across the small rear deck as Bob became increasingly uncomfortable.

'Righto...' Bob reflected. He was assessing what must be done to ensure that at least from here on in strict and correct procedural fairness was afforded to the two suspects. This was vital so that, when transferred by testimony and under cross-examination into the formal legal propriety of the High Court of Australia in Sydney, NSW, months or years later, the events in the tiny town of Broome would translate as just and reasonable in the circumstances.

'Okay, George. Well done. Now let's get you back to the base.' Bob looked up at one of the Task Force officers. 'DI Lopez here will take you back and take a statement immediately from you. Okay?'

Doc nodded. Doc understood the need but was somewhat miffed that he was basically being removed from the action, so to speak.

'And, George, the DI will take possession of the signed confession that you obtained to ensure the chain of evidence,' Bob said without response from Doc.

Doc was desperate for another drink. His mouth was dry, and his body and brain weary from a long day of rare action, not to mention seasickness. But the day was obviously going to be a lot longer in the chill professional hands of the unsmiling Detective Inspector Lopez, who was waiting for him up on the wharf.

'By the way, George,' Bob called up, as Doc was escorted by the steadying arm of the task force officers onto the jetty platform. Doc turned to look back down at the AFP commander on the police boat. 'We will need your handcuff keys.'

Doc took them from his belt and handed them to one of Bob's men.

'And, George, where is the signed confession?' Bob added.

Doc grinned like a ginger dingo and reached into his grimy shirt pocket. He pulled out and dramatically flourished a crumpled and stained document that Bob Hopkins saw with dread was a single page torn from an A4 pad. DI Lopez accepted the paper from Doc as the local copper tripped and nearly fell up the last step of the wharf as the little group of three exited.

Bob Hopkins was seriously worried. It was not that the confession to a major crime from the prime suspect was apparently scrawled in biro onto a single dirty page of A4. That was not necessarily a fatal flaw. Such a document could still be legally acceptable in that a confession was freely made and could stand the various evidential tests in a court. No, that didn't particularly worry him. What did worry him was everything about how Senior Sergeant George Patrick had just presented. Little bricks of concern were forming as to whether what George said he had, was what he had. Suddenly Bob was glad that he had not heralded the news of the breakthrough back to Fred Hall at CTF headquarters just yet.

With DI Lopez and his passenger headed back to the station, Bob Hopkins looked at the two remaining task force detectives, one of whom was using a compact digital video camera to record every second and each unfolding event of this moment.

'Rod, you come down with me, I need you to capture everything on the camera. Yeah?'

Bob unlatched the door that led down into the cabin. He looked cautiously down and saw two people. One obviously very angry, very upset, and very pregnant young woman was cradling a battered man. The man lay uncomfortably back on the narrow bench seat, wrists handcuffed behind him. Not a good look, Bob thought as the camera captured the view. Bob's heart sank as he walked down the steep steps into the main cabin.

'Hello, my name is Bob Hopkins. I am a commander in the Australian Federal Police.'

Bob took a seat opposite the couple as the second officer entered and stood filming the events.

'This is Detective Drake. I understand that you are Tommy and Gypsy Lawson?' Bob asked.

The woman answered. 'What is going on, Commander? We have been abducted and assaulted by Doc Patrick. He is drunk. He left our staff in danger on the barge. He threatened us with a shotgun. He beat Tommy. What is going on here?'

She spoke in a strong and angry voice and Bob officially cringed but tried not to show it.

'Please let me get those handcuffs off you,' he offered, and leant across the few metres as Tommy twisted his body. 'Please can I ask you to bear with me,' Bob said, as Tommy sat upright and rubbed the red circles that the over-tightened steel cuffs had left. 'I need at this time to formally caution you both, that you do not have to say anything to me, and that anything you do say will be recorded by the digital camera being used by AFP Detective Rodney Drake and will be used as evidence against you. Do you understand the caution? Bob asked.

Gypsy spoke again, eyes flashing in righteous anger, 'Commander Hopkins, I do not understand a thing that has happened since that drunken old fool tricked us on board the police boat. We thought that he had come to rescue us from the bushfire! He has left our staff helpless on the barge in the storm! Now what the hell is going on?'

Bob Hopkins squirmed but soldiered on. 'May I call you Gypsy?' She nodded. 'Gypsy, can you tell me what happened today with Senior Sergeant Patrick?'

So they told him about the wild fire, the escape on the barge, the fear that people had died on the beach, some guests, the cameleer, and their friend Bill Peters.

'So you think Mr Peters is dead?' Bob asked.

She sat then and looked at him, suddenly contemplative. Then she surprised him. 'I want you to tell me the truth about something.'

Bob nodded, aware that the conversation that had just moved away from his control was still being videoed. 'Yes, of course. Well, if I can,' he stumbled.

Gypsy pounced. 'It was something that Doc told us. Yes or no! Was Bill Peters acting as your undercover agent at Beauty Bay?'

Bob Hopkins was stuck.

'Yes or no!' she demanded.

He was so shocked that he could only answer, 'Well, I can't really... umm yes.'

75

ASHES TO ASHES

Detective Inspector Alonso Lopez sat across the graffiti-scratched wooden desk in the cramped interview room of the Broome Police Station. Opposite him were the bleary features of the usual king-of-this-castle.

Doc Patrick was no longer enjoying the moment. His triumphant return had soured. He was tired and emotional from the events of the day but, worse, he was sobering up and in desperate need of another calming drink. He was also increasingly frustrated that this 'fucken plastic cunt!' was cold and unrelenting in his manner and in the execution of his duty.

Doc had wanted the interview to be conducted over the broad, messy expanse of his own desk in his station OC's office. There, he could sit in state and hold the dominant interview position. But more importantly, his desk was where he had secreted several stashes of the amber fluid for emergencies. But no, this prick Lopez was determined to impose his 'high-fucken-faluting' procedures and 'boring rules of evidential conduct' upon the local hero. Even when Doc had attempted a diversion of taking a leak, Lopez had his junior feddy detective follow him in to the shitter! Doc had had no chance to take a surreptitious gulp to carry him through this 'fucken bullshit'. No, Doc's humour had definitely faded and now he just wanted to get this over and done with, sign the brief and escape to his flat for his own celebratory drink or three.

'So, Senior Sergeant Patrick, again for the recording, at approximately

2020 hours this evening you rescued the suspects from the barge off the coast at Beauty Bay?'

'Yeah,' Doc sighed.

'Right, now, you have told me that the two are known to you as Gypsy and Tommy Lawson?'

'Yes, yes, correct.'

'Okay.' The federal man paused, allowing his junior to catch up as he paraphrased Doc's spoken word into a typed statement on his laptop in his well-practiced ten-finger typing.

'And you have known both these persons for several years as they are or were Broome locals?'

'Yep, correct,' Doc barked.

'Okay, Senior Sergeant, now please take me through what happened after you had both these persons on board the police launch.'

'Right, okay... right, what happened was that the male...'

'Tommy Lawson?' Lopez asked.

'Yeah yeah, Tommy, anyway he sent the woman Gypsy down below the deck and then he had a go at me'.

'What do you mean by "he had a go at you"?'

'Well, when I was helping her down the stairs, cause she is pregnant as you would've seen, he king-hit me on the back of the neck with something. I almost blacked out. But then I fought back, and I managed to get the better of him.'

Lopez nodded, forcing any appearance of doubt, or any emotion at all from his demeanour.

'Yeah, so I got him down. But he struggled, and he more or less pulled me down those stairs with him. Don't forget the boat was yippin and yawing. It was basically a storm out there, ya see?'

'Go on.'

'Right, yeah, right, so we fell down together and that's when he knocked himself out. He hit his head on the floor. So cause he had attacked me, I put the cuffs on him. See? She had a go, too. But I just told her to resume her seat. Anyway, she is very pregnant so she could do fuck all, oops sorry, I mean she couldn't do much.'

Lopez nodded sympathetically. 'I understand that you have just come through a very stressful time, Senior Sergeant, but please watch your language.'

Doc continued. 'Anyway I took all due respect and care of the two.'

Lopez almost winced at the transparent falsity of the phrase when uttered by this man. But urged Doc to continue.

'Yeah so, with all due respect to them both, when Tommy come round I asked him why he had attacked me. That's when he told me that he wanted to come clean on the drugs.'

Again the professional investigator opposite cringed a little but kept an outer facade of polite interest in this increasingly problematic tale.

'Now, is that exactly what Mr Lawson said to you?' he asked, glancing at his counterpart.

'Yeah, he just come out and told me that he had brought the drugs in to the country and that he hid them in boat parts.'

'Did he say where the drugs had come from?' Lopez asked.

'Yeah, he said Japan,' Doc responded and then continued unprompted. 'He said that he had brought the stuff in that killed all those people in Sydney.'

'He said that to you?' the Detective Inspector asked in his flat, formal monotone.

'He not only said it to me,' Doc gloated, 'he wrote it down on the statement.'

'Sorry, did you say *he* wrote it down?'

'Yeah, I didn't have me reading specs with me, so he wrote his own confession out. See, I put the questions to him, and then he read it back to me and then we both signed it.' Doc hesitated, enjoying the effect that his brilliant outback detective work was apparently having on these eastern states city-slickers who were now all focused attention.

'Okay...' Lopez almost stuttered, thinking quickly. 'Now, do you have your glasses handy?'

'Yeah, I do, in my office. I will go and get...'

Lopez quickly intervened, and asked the younger junior find the reading glasses on Doc's desk. He returned with them in a sweat-soiled kangaroo scrotum leather case usually sold as hilarious gift shop items in tacky tourist Australiana stores.

Lopez addressed the digital cameras lens. 'As we continue this interview, I will ask you now, Senior Sergeant, to read for the purpose of the tape the handwritten statement you have referred to as have been written by Tommy Lawson under your direct view.'

He nodded at his junior who removed from a manila envelope the 'confession'.

Proud once again, Doc pulled the grimy A4 sheet from the official envelope. He smoothed it on the desk and layered another smear of grime and smudged biro across the document. He carefully took his John Lennon glasses from the soft case and slowly and deliberately began to read Exhibit A.

'My full name is Thomas De Tank Engine...What the fuck?'

Doc stopped reading, looked up at the other man, slack-jawed. Doc's flushed face went an unhealthy sallow white. He looked back down at the statement and then reality bit.

'Fuck! Fuck! Fuck!'

76

HOLD ON TO
THE NIGHT

It was hot, fucking hot, and fragrantly steamy in the casserole of the camel's gut. Bill had taken the rear position, his own backbone up against the massive knobbed spinal column, but lying relatively cosy, supported by the curve of the lower rib cage like a bony hammock. This allowed him to prop with his feet and push back from the flaps of the fleshy opening. He had pulled the tiny limp form of Lily up against him, her back spooned into his front, with his arms around her in a tight hug of desperation.

Bill soon felt the fire front come onto them. He was scared, shit scared! He was not convinced by any stretch of his usually active imagination that his chosen hidey-hole would protect him and his little damaged companion from a dirty, stinking, horrible, hot, smoky death. He didn't want to die. He desperately needed to get away from this one. He had unfinished business.

And then for the first time since he had witnessed her death, even as the roar and rush and heat from outside tried to force its fatal way inside his protein envelope, he thought of Bonnie. With all the intense distraction of the events since the stark visual shock of her death on the highway he had not thought of her. Now he had the time, *damn it!* Her image and that of the burning upturned jeep returned in his mind's eye. He saw it all again in the living colour of his imagination and the shock forced a guttural sob.

'No!' he called out to nobody. Lily Phat moaned and he guiltily realised that he had tightened his grip around her. 'No,' quieter now but denying it didn't change it. He was responsible. There was no other conclusion to draw. Bonnie was his girl, she had come to see him. She had misunderstood what she saw in the massage dome, innocent though that had been, and now she was dead. He knew that if he made it out of this he must, he would, stand in front of her family. He would tell them what he had done to the woman he loved, the girl that they loved. He would tell them, but he would not ask for their forgiveness. He would take whatever they needed to do to him to avenge her death. Others might argue that fault was not his, that it was tragi-comedy of errors, her misunderstanding; how could he be blamed? But all that mattered was how he felt.

And then the fire was on them. The camel's excised fatty hump ignited. The coarse wire of the hair on its back and side scorched away. Then the heat burnt the hide and down into the subcutaneous fat. With the fat rapidly burnt away, even the fibrous muscles ignited under the superheated flame. The heat cooked through the meat and Bill felt it on his back and then all round him, like a juicy oyster in a carpetbag steak. It was almost impossible to breath in the hot smog of the steaming remnants in the gut. As the temperature within their fleshy oven rose, Bill and Lily began a slow broil, and he started to contemplate his chances with the sharks. But slowly, as the coastal strip of bush exploded into ember and ash and the bigger tree trunks off the beach began a long slow burn, the super intensity passed at fifty kilometres per hour to the north. Luckily, the camel lay several inches deep in the cooling surge of the ocean. The immediate atmosphere cooled as the fire front moved away in tag with the winds. With the hyper destructive front past them, the slow burn would still make life untenable in the bay for several hours yet as a life destroying heat remained with the suffocating fog of black–grey smoke that sat heavy along the coast.

Bill had been raised a Catholic. He had been baptised and then confirmed in the fascinating ancient Romanic-religious ceremony when he was a young teenager. But Bill had revolted early at the strict regime of that faith and had wandered from the flock. Now, just as terrified soldiers sometimes do, he discovered a sudden renewed interest in his past religion. A selfish, even desperate interest perhaps in the slightest possibility of protection from any listening or watching spiritual entities. So he tried to remember the prayer to Mary. Slowly, almost imperceptibly through the dreadful night, the fire and the heat went. The terrible shelter that they were in was cooled again. Bill realised that the waters lapping into the flap of the belly were repeatedly puffing inside a breath of the sweet ocean breeze.

Outside, this narrow stratum of life-giving clear air sat below the toxic smoke of the fire that had rolled off the ravaged land and out onto the sea. With the interaction of the hot and cold air layers, there was a rolling fluctuation out from and back toward the heated land. Eventually, their living space once again became bearable, life supporting, liveable.

As they lay inside the camel carcass, both now glazed with its stinking juices, Li Li woke to what must have been a dreadful vision of a hell. Li Li lay in absolute blackness, held from behind by an unseen thing. She was in agony from her fractures and wounds to bone, tissue and organ. Unbeknown to her, her life blood was seeping internally from a laceration to her liver from the pelvic smashing of the heavy bike.

Awake, Lily screamed, and screamed again. He held her, soothed her, told her that she was safe. He said that he was looking after her. They were all right now. But she screamed until she could scream no more in her fearful raspy dehydrated exhaustion. Only then could she force her mind to listen to him. She remembered then, from the beach, from the track, and she realised that he was that man. It was not some monster, some devil, who restrained her and held her against his horrible hard stinking masculinity in the unbelievable stench of the black hell that they lay in.

Finally, she sobbed, weakening, terrified and helpless, and spoke back to this man.

'Help me. Help me, please, I need a doctor. I am dying.'

Bill knew that she would soon go into shock, and that may prove fatal, so he needed to help her understand that they were alive and there was hope. He comforted her and made soft assurances and promises that he knew he couldn't keep. She calmed then and listened to his voice.

'What is your name?' he asked. 'Mine is Bill. I worked at the resort. I saw you. I tried to get you and your friends onto the barge...do you remember?'

'Yes, I remember,' she whispered and was quiet then, contemplative, until finally in that claustrophobic envelope she spoke. 'My name is Li Li Phat. You can call me Lily.' She cried out as a surge of pain from her pelvis and thigh punished her.

'Lily, look, I think we are going to be okay. We have survived the fire. We are inside that big camel.' He paused. 'Lily I...I saw Namu kill the camel. I saw your friend kill Namu...the camel man.'

He her stiffen in his arms.

'I did not know that he would do that that. I did not authorise that,' she whispered.

'Were you in charge, Lily?'

'Yes, I was in charge'.

And they talked, and he encouraged her to relax as much as was able. She understood that this man, against his own interests, had saved her life, helped her where her own team, her own family, her cousins, had run! They had abandoned her to a certain and horrible death! Weakening from the pain and the blood loss, and terrified of her own approaching death, Lily Phat decided to die with a clear conscience.

'Bill, I want to tell you why I did as I did. Why my cousins did what they did, I need you to understand, as my witness before my God.'

77
DON'T LOSE MY NUMBER

Bob Hopkins was with Tommy and Gypsy in the clinical white-tiled confines of an examination room at the Broome Regional Hospital. Tommy was laid out on the gurney being attended to by a young doctor, and two nurses. A detailed medical report was being compiled at Bob's request as to Tom's exact injuries and photographs taken. Gypsy sat in a heavy rattan chair being comforted and fussed over by a large white-smocked Aboriginal nurse. The nurse clucked and cooed at Gypsy's distress and her precarious pregnant condition in between glowering at the compact federal policeman who appeared to be the cause of at least one of those conditions.

Bob's sat-nav phone blared in his suit pocket and he started. Across the room, Gypsy recognised that electronic clanging heard not so long ago from her friend's pocket on the balcony at Beauty Bay.

In retrospect, it may have been more judicious for the sake of privacy and operational confidentiality to have taken that phone call away from the small group in the clinic, but he was increasingly concerned that rather than cracking the case, Senior Sergeant George Patrick may have had an even more dramatic effect on the reputation and integrity of the investigation.

So he answered the call. Later he might agree that he had assumed. Assuming was something he counselled his junior detectives that they must never do. But he had assumed that the only possible caller on the exclusive network must be Concord Task Force HQ, Sydney, NSW. He assumed the caller was a curious and concerned Fred Hall and so he answered the call.

'Hopkins here!'

And everyone turned towards him to hear him splutter, 'Bill…Bill! Son! You're alive!'

78
ALL CRIED OUT

Fred Hall received his early morning phone call from Bob Hopkins on the exclusive operational line a short time later. Their quick discussion had Fred speeding on his rapid blue-lit way to Task Force HQ in the CBD. With hands-free mobile activated, he barked urgent instructions to senior officers as he drove. By the time he trotted from the lift into his office his command team were wide awake and on their way, issuing their own instructions to subordinate officers. Fred sat at his desk anxious for the connection. Meanwhile the entire task force, given this second weekend off, was in a variety of ways being shaken from rare deep sleep and gruffly ordered to attend at HQ ASAP!

At 0200 Sydney time, Bill Peters once again pushed the transmit button on his phone. In Broome, Bob Hopkins pushed his receive button.

'Bill, this is Bob.'

'Hi, Bob, are you ready?'

'Yes, son. I have you loud and clear. Now push the red button and it will go to the speaker phone.'

'Okay, done. Right, so as you know I survived the fire. I am in a camel. A dead camel that I gutted. We hid inside its body to escape the fire. We are on the small camel beach north of Beauty Bay. Copy? '

'Copy loud and clear, son. Go on,' Bob responded.

Inside the stinking camel, Lily heard the conversation from deep within her clammy fog of pain. The onset of critical shock attacked her consciousness as her blood pressure dipped in concert with her inability to circulate the reduced blood volume in her damaged body. Lily didn't know it as she struggled to live, but her overwhelming emotions of foreboding and dreadful anxiety were in fact symptoms of the state that her body had entered. Now she stirred and spoke with a determination.

'My name is Li Li Phat. I am the daughter of Gao and the granddaughter of Bui Xua Han of the Cabramatta Spider Gang,' she said and then paused.

Bob interjected, 'Ms Phat, I understand from Mr Peters that you wish to tell us, tell the police, information that may or will incriminate you and others?'

'Yes, Mr Hopkins, that is so,' she announced.

Bill held her carefully and wished he could comfort her a little more.

'Ms Phat,' Bob began again, 'I need to formally caution you....' but she cut him off.

'Mr Hopkins, I am a lawyer. I am fully aware of my rights and I make this statement to you on this phone of my own free will and on the understanding that you are recording the statement'.

In Sydney, Fred Hall and his senior officers sat transfixed, all ears and eyes aimed at the black speaker from which the drama of the intercontinental conversations emanated.

'May I just say, Ms Phat...' Bob's voice simultaneously crackled into CTF HQ, Sydney, NSW and at the same moment into a much smaller space in the camel's gut on the beach. 'We have medical help urgently on the way to you'.

'Yes, I understand that...thank you,' she responded. 'But I am dying.'

The comment sent an unexpected shiver down most of the listeners' spines.

'Okay, what do you wish to tell us, Ms Phat?' Bob asked.

He held his breath as did all of the audience, in Broome and in Sydney, as they waited, always fearful that the formality of the caution may silence the witness.

'Mr Hopkins,' said Li Li, 'bring my grandfather to the radio. Tell him that I wish to speak to him.'

79
ROCK THE CASBAH

As Bob Hopkins listened, fascinated, to Bill's first précis of the incidents that had started with the fire, and then through the events that had taken him and Li Li Phat into the camel's gut, DI Lopez had coincidentally arrived at the hospital. He found Bob and the rest of the team in the privacy of the nurse manager's commandeered office.

As Bill ended the transmission from the burning beach, Bob's mind was racing. He still felt the immense relief that Bill was alive, but his head was full with a tick-list of crucial tasks to do within the hour. Bob turned to DI Lopez and requested his sit-rep.

'We've got nothing, sir,' Lopez responded.

Bob was distracted. 'What do you mean, Alonso, nothing? Where's George?'

The AFP detective inspector sat his boss down and read him the confession of *Thomas De Tank Engine*.

Bob heard a brief but wonderfully crafted tale of fiction and some important fact. Lopez read from the scruffy note paper the story as written by Tommy Lawson. No one questioned that, at the time of the creative writing, Tommy was under Doc's threat of the shotgun and even further assault. Bizarrely, the tale had been signed and witnessed as a 'True and correct account' by the man himself. Doc had signed under the name 'Snr Sgt George Patrick' and had included the date and time of the completion of the comedic script. As Doc had threatened and beaten a dazed Tommy into writing his own confession in the cabin of the boat, Tommy had quickly realised that the older man was so short-sighted he had no idea what was actually scrawled on the A4 sheet. Although angry and sore, Tommy indulged his sense of cynical humour as the events unfolded on the good ship *John-Damn*. In his messy writing Tommy had further disguised the actual content of the confession from the short-sighted half-pissed older man.

Perhaps many years later Bob might appreciate the comedy of the situation, but now at the hospital he winced as DI Lopez read excerpts such as, 'My wife Gypsy and I bought ecstasy, joy and love to Beauty Bay.'

Doc, if asked, would say that was fucking certain Tommy had written, 'My wife Gypsy and I imported the ecstasy drugs in through Beauty Bay'. There was, however, a subtle but telling difference of meaning between the two versions a sober High Court judge might have found. Where Doc had told him to write, 'I hid the drugs in boat parts from Japan', Tommy had written. 'I did not do what Doc has told me to write'. Where Doc had dictated, 'I have been afforded every courtesy by Senior Sergeant Patrick and made this statement of my own free will', Tommy had written, 'I have been beaten and threatened by the drunken Senior Sergeant George Patrick and did not make any confession to him'.

Bob made rapid command decisions. He sent his inspector to immediately arrest George Patrick.

'Charge him with one initial holding count for the assault of Tommy Lawson. Place him quickly into the cells and get back here'.

The follow up interview and further charges would have to wait. Bob needed all hands on deck, there was much to do. He then made the phone call to Fred Hall in NSW. Necessary if embarrassing call made, Bob returned to the examination room and sat across the gurney from a bandaged Tommy and a still smouldering Gypsy Lawson. The assorted medical professionals only reluctantly agreed to leave the three of them alone and had to be shooed from the room.

Bob cut to the chase.

'Gypsy and Tommy. Please allow me to personally, and on behalf of the Australian Federal and the NSW Police, sincerely apologise to you both. It is with immense regret and embarrassment that I say I am sorry for what George Patrick has done to you. That his actions were his own and in no way authorised or even known by myself or my men, I am sure is of no comfort to you.'

The two bedraggled and now very weary people opposite just nodded back at the officer, relieved that at least this aspect of the nightmare was seemingly resolved.

'You heard the call a few minutes ago from Bill?' Bob asked then spoke to Gypsy. 'Gypsy, I need to tell you why Bill Peters did what he did. Why he agreed to go undercover at your resort for me,' he began, and with that blunt but incomplete delivery Gypsy began to cry silent tears.

'Please, Gypsy, I need to tell you that the only reason that Bill did what he did was at my official request to him. He did it because he saw this as a way to protect you.' He paused and then completed the sentence, 'And of course to protect Tommy.'

Bob stopped as the couple took that in without comment or obvious reaction. 'Now please let me have you taken to the Mangrove Hotel. We need very urgently to try and get Bill off the beach. I can't tell you what is going on there at the moment. But I can say that Bill may have helped us to solve the matter of the drug deaths at the Concord Oval in Sydney,' he paused as if to emphasise the momentous news. 'Please, Ms Lawson, and Tommy, would you be so very kind as to stay there until I have a chance to return to you later today. I need to take formal statements from you so that George Patrick can be properly dealt with.'

But they had had enough. Gypsy spoke for both.

'Commander we will be at our house in Chinatown. You know the address. When you are ready come to us,' and she rose and Tommy followed. Before she left she turned and walked back towards Bob Hopkins. She stood and looked him in the eye. 'I do accept your personal apology, Bob,' she said. 'I know that Doc Patrick was drunk, is a hopeless drunk. I know that of course he acted on his own. We will make those statements to you when you are ready.'

She turned to leave but stopped again. 'Please,' she asked quietly, 'please do get Bill Peters off the beach. But when you talk to him, tell him that I do not wish to see him ever again.'

Bob winced. Regally pregnant and escorted by the bandaged Tommy, Gypsy walked with a graceful dignity out of police custody.

80

UNION OF THE SNAKE

The unmarked police sedan pulled up at the electric gate of the imposing mansion on Panorama Avenue, Cabramatta. Before the driver had a chance to get out and push the bell, the gate slid smoothly open. Detective Superintendent Fred Hall in the passenger's seat was bemused. Who would be up at this hour? He checked his watch: 0307. As the Commodore crunched onto the gravel drive, he spoke calmly into the vehicle's two-way, instructing the two CIB escort sedans to wait outside the gate to make it obvious they were his backup.

A few minutes earlier at headquarters, Fred had made a command decision that he would be the one to go and talk with the top Spider. He would simply tell the sinister old man only that his granddaughter needed him; that she wanted to speak to him.

All they had from a forensic investigative perspective was an interesting development. Lily Phat had told them nothing—yet. They knew that Bill Peters had the woman and what appeared to be part of a drug importation, but they were still stranded on camel beach. Bill Peters had told them via Bob Hopkins that he had witnessed criminal acts. Peters had heard certain admissions by the young woman. But to all evidential effects and forensic purposes, they had no real evidence. It was all mostly hearsay; evidence of another conveyed by a third party, the weakest of the evidential classes. They certainly had nothing yet on this evil old man who Fred had come to collect and no way to force his cooperation. Nothing really, other than to politely ask him to accompany them to an electronic date with his treasured granddaughter.

The vehicle eased smoothly up to the imposing front door and Fred got out of the car and climbed the steps between snarling stone lions up towards the high oak doors. The door opened and the old man stood in the portal under the soft entrance lights.

'Good morning,' Fred said politely.

The old man pulled shut the door behind him and walked forward, a small overnight case in his hand.

'Good morning to you. I have been awaiting you. I am prepared. Let us go.'

81

SHOCK THE MONKEY

DI Lopez and his colleague, the young local copper, had found Doc. Under pressure to quickly charge him and secure him in one of his own cells to await Bob Hopkins's closer attention, the officers found that they couldn't follow that precise command issued to them at the hospital.

They tracked Doc to his quarters, knocked but received no answer. They pushed the door open and sort of wished that they hadn't. Doc was sprawled flat on his back, snoring like a concussed warthog, all slobber and snot. A whisky bottle sat empty in his moist, hairy crotch, the glass magnifying its wrinkly prop. Try as they might with gentle and then not so gentle prods and finally shouted commands, Doc simply would not wake up. A quick call to Bob Hopkins and the inevitable was accepted. Don't waste time, he can wait, he's obviously going nowhere fast. They left him a note: 'On AFP Commander Bob Hopkins's command: Stay in your quarters'.

***

Doc finally woke in the early hours, mouth and throat snore-sore and desiccated. Rising to pee, he saw the note. He read it with a sense of impending doom but accepted the command. As coherent thought became more possible as each hour passed, however, he recalled the events of the day before. The reason that he was confined to barracks.

Doc moaned in self-disgust, holding his sweaty head in his hands. Ah well! At least he had another chance to recharge the cells with his personal battery fluid, thanks again to Mr JW, late of bonny Scotland. In fact, after the long hard day before and his little sleep, half of another 750ml bottle barely touched the fucken sides. And yes, the booze sort of helped. Apart from quenching his thirst, it helped him see things better, clearer. Yeah, there was no doubt about it, Doc surmised to the dark of the morning after, he had been had. 'Fucken tricked like a fucken rookie by a freakin hippy and his fat-gutted hippy bitch'. Conned! The victim 'once a-fucken-gen. Stick it up good old fucken Doc, eh!' he complained loudly to the room. He tried to stay put. He knew that he was in so much shit already that he simply had to wait there. Anyway, he needed to talk to Bob. Bob knew him. Bob would look after him. Bob would know that the ferals would be lying, or at least exaggerating. Shit, it was Bob that told him in the first fucken place that they were the fucken suspects for the drugs coming in! Yeah Bob would help him. Wouldn't he?

So Doc reached under the bed, knocked over one tower of the porno DVD stack. He reached back further, found the carton, and pulled another whisky bottle awkwardly out. Lying back naked on the damp bed, he perched the vessel against the foothills of his hairy beer gut. Doc twisted the top off for a sip-sigh of appreciation and the one-line ceremonial ritual of his signature tune, sadder this time: 'Whisky, whisky my old friend, I've come to talk with you again'.

And he did wait. Doc waited for fucken hours! But they showed him no respect, left him stewing like a fucken common crim! He got angrier by the hour and by the volume of whisky consumed. It's gotta be deliberate! Never thought fucken Hopkins would treat me this way after all I have done for that little cunt back in Melbourne.

'Fuck it!' he shouted at the moaning girls on the screen. 'Nah, just fuck it all!'

Doc Patrick would wait for no man! So he packed his camping gear, canned and dried food, water, survival rations. Packed his .227 roo rifle, and his own Winchester double barrel shotgun. Packed a tent, a sleeping bag, his fishing gear. Packed cartons of ammo and the half carton of whisky into his vehicle. He went to his personal Toyota Land Cruiser parked safe in the lock up garage at the back of the block and stashed his gear. With the back gate opened he fired her well-maintained diesel into life. Doc sat a minute or two to let her warm, and then slunk her away, lights off, the personalised rego plate 'MAAATE' reflecting back softly in the darkness of the early tropical morning.

82

PAPA DON'T PREACH

On the smoky camel beach near Beauty Bay, Bill Peters could only wait for events to unfold. He was powerless, but he was impatient. Impatient for the fire's deadly toxins to disperse and impatient while waiting for cool oxygen-bearing breezes to move in to replace the suffocating smog that still hung heavy outside. Earlier he had clumsily moved his leg across Lily to lift the fold of singed hide that hung as a curtain with his foot. Above the few centimetres of clear air above the sea sat choking death; a thick, deep stratum of wood smoke. So he waited and wondered at the miracle of their survival while Lily moaned and writhed in her agony, and he felt so dreadfully impotent.

***

'Granddaughter,' the old man announced to the black microphone on the desk of Superintendent Fred Hall in NSW.

In the grisly grotto some five thousand diagonal kilometres to the northwest, Lily heard a familiar voice and stirred in Bill's arms. He held the sat-nav phone close to her face in the dark.

'Grandfather?' she pleaded. Lily was weak from the bacterial soup that had entered her body via the puncture wound of her shattered femur. She was a living host to the toxic breeding cycle of deadly microbes.

'I am here, Li Li,' he replied in his own language.

Fred had made his own contingency plan earlier with Detective Sergeant Joey Van Nao who was seated at the table with fresh A4 sized journal in hand.

'Grandfather, I am so frightened,' Li Li Phat cried, and the old man's heart broke as her distress crossed the cold night deserts of the vast land via the electronic airways.

'Li Li, I am here,' he said again, impotent and unable to do a single thing to help the precious granddaughter. She, who he had sent into battle as his commander in the criminal war games that he had played now for decades. 'I am here, Li Li, and I am told that medical help is on its way to you. Please granddaughter, please be strong for me.'

'Grandfather, my love for you is strong. But I am dying.'

Joey scribbled notes in his *he-said-she-said* chronology.

'Li Li, I love you also,' said the old man. Then, bound by the destiny foretold by the soothsayer's cards, he invited the destruction of his own and of his extended families' immediate future with an invitation to her. 'Tell me, Li Li, tell me what has happened'.

So she did. With the certain knowledge that she was dying, the Spider commander reported in damning detail, each sentence paraphrased messily in the hand of Joey Van Dao. But more significantly, Lily's report was captured by the digital electronics including CCTV that recorded her quiet testimony, and the stony countenance of her grandfather as he visibly shrank and aged in his seat.

The names and the dates and the terrible circumstances were spoken by the young woman and were not challenged by the old man. Finally the line fell quiet and Li Li Phat spoke no more, despite increasingly despairing encouragement from her grandfather.

From the camel beach, Bill Peters sober voice confirmed their dreadful suspicion: 'She has gone'.

As the notoriously ruthless Spider leader collapsed into himself, Fred Hall nodded a silent command to his senior command officers present. They stood and left Fred and Joey Van Dao alone with the bereft old man.

The Concord Task Force men and women galvanised, speeding teams of four, armed with search warrants and a fearsome official resolve, into the suburbs.

Meanwhile, Fred Hall with Joey Van Tao's assistance began the formal recording of the full interview and detailed confessions of

Bo Xuan Han under the all-seeing eye of the camera lens. But before the CCTV camera was turned on Joey made the old man a cup of green tea. As he sipped, Fred Hall asked him how he had known that he was coming to him. Why he had said that he was ready. This question had been nagging at Fred since he had picked up the old man, and the elder's reply was suitably enigmatic.

'It was shown in the cards,' was all he said.

Fred left it at that. Then followed the formal to and fro of the evidential interview with questions carefully crafted to elicit incriminating responses. When it came to the matter of the tainted drugs, the old man took from his bag a small GPS unit and handed it to Fred Hall.

'Superintendent, have your men follow the coordinates of this machine to French's Forest—have them take a shovel. They will find the purple camel waiting'.

83

I THINK I'M ALONE NOW

Bill Peters had seriously had enough of being in the stinking hulk of the three-quarter cooked camel bull. Lily was dead, still in his arms. He felt no triumph that Bob Hopkins's case had been solved by her revelations.

Although she had spoken in the tongue of her grandfather, he knew what she had told them at Concord Task Force HQ. It was what she had told him earlier. But now she was gone. He still held her only because in the tight confines of the beast he had no choice.

Now he had time to think, and his first thought was of water. A terrible dryness had cut deep fissures into his lips and his throat felt red raw from the smoke. But then he heard it. At first the change in the sounds from the world outside made no sense. A lifetime ago it seemed, the hurricane rush of the fire front had been terrifying but that had passed quickly, and hours earlier. What had followed then had been a gentler noise; a smoke-muffled crackling and occasional crashing *thud* as fire-hollowed trees crashed damaged limbs to the ashen ground. This was the time that the body of the fire, left behind by the madly rushing head, had settled and busied itself in a more patient and almost complete destruction of the remaining fuel load. Over those interminable hours, Bill's perception of the world outside the beast had been distracted and muffled, but now he began to listen again. A soft pattering slippery noise sounded to him incongruously like rain. Surely not. But if not, what?.

So he waited and finally the day appeared to lighten beyond the ragged flap of camel hide.

Inexplicably, he had a sudden shock of emotion. A cold sober realisation that Lily was in fact dead! Very fucking dead! He immediately urgently instinctively had to get away from her!

'Ahhh!' he screamed , panicked. 'Fuuuuuuuuck!'

He had to get out of this tiny enclosed horrible prison of dead stinking rotting flesh. Despite his tae kwon do training, despite his proven proudly held ability to control his emotions, he had just had e-fucking-nough!

It was clumsy, and it was awful, and it was crazy. He pushed Lily down away from him, and he struggled horribly over her, crushing her tiny form face-down into the pond of stinking, crawling muck that they had lain in all night. As his weight on her tiny back forced the final air out of her she sighed a bubbling whoosh into that pond, he screamed in fear and self-disgust. Finally, mercifully, he rolled sobbing out through the fleshy lips of the camel's belly and splashed into the pure warm waters of the Indian Ocean.

It was the dawn of a new day and in the gentle grip of the sea a mad man rolled over and over in the shallows. He rolled away from the roasted camel, away from the grotesquely burnt and twisted effigy of a man that had been Namu still crouched behind it. Bill screamed, grunting in primal fury and fear. It was as if his soul, his spirit, his being was outside of his own body. His view was from above looking down, watching as his own body splashed furiously and yelled out nonsensical obscenities. Finally he tired and sat chest-deep in the ocean and sobbed. Then, wonderfully, the warm tropical rain splattered in huge translucent drops onto those waters from roiling black clouds that had drifted from the northwest, the southerly buster gone. As the rain grew in intensity its cleansing liquid fell through the smoky particles in the strata layers above the land. The rains took those ash particles into their fluid form, cleansing the air and finally soothing a burnt land.

Bill, calmer now, submersed himself again and again into the sensual hug of the seas. He took handfuls of the pure white sands and scoured pink every inch of his skin to remove the dreadful muck from the camel, but also as if to scrub away the memories of his terrible night.

Naked except for his shorts, the man stood in waist-deep waters and howled like a gut-shot dingo at the lightening sky.

84

HEAT OF THE NIGHT

The cavalry arrived: A huge orange dragonfly buzzed in from the sea, tracking down its coordinates like a merciful cruise missile. As the Sikorsky lit the early morning landscape beneath it with its million candle -power lights, Bob Hopkins looked down from the co-pilot's seat and spotted his man.

'There! There he is!' he shouted through the sensitive intercom.

The pilot flinched at the aural assault, but understood the emotion.

'Roger that. I think I can put us down in that clearing,' the pilot said, and then issued short commands to his helmeted crewman by the open sliding door.

With his booted feet on the top of the skid and an uninterrupted view of the descent to blackened terra-firma, the crewman guided the pilot down. At last the big machine set gently onto the burnt panorama where fat camels had mooched and cud-chewed only twenty-four hours before.

Bob was the first man out. The compact little commander, incongruously dressed still in his Pierre Cardin suit and patent leather shoes, sprinted from the machine down the sandy slope toward his agent. They met as Bill staggered from the waters and unsteadily up the beach, stopping briefly to pick something up near the corpse of the camel.

Bob's relief and emotion surprised even himself as he reached Bill, now close to collapse. Bob took Bill into his arms, held him in a mismatched tango, as he spoke in comforting and congratulatory tones to his limp dance partner.

Ritually, Bill presented to his commander the plastic wrapped contraband that the camel had carried across sovereign borders.

The others arrived then and helped him walk towards the chopper.

Bill turned his head to Bob and croaked, 'See, sir. Not Gypsy.'

'It's all good, son, Gypsy's in the clear.'

Blackness closed down Bill's consciousness until all he saw was a tunnel of light diminishing to a pinprick, and heard faint, faraway voices of concern, then he fell unconscious.

A paramedic brought the stretcher to where he lay crumpled on the moist, blackened ash. and they lifted him onto the stretcher, covered in the protective comfort of a soft wool blanket. The paramedic busied himself with an intravenous line to start the rehydration.

Meanwhile, Bob and his officers quickly peered inside the camel's diminished body, careful not to contaminate the scene.

Finally once they were all safely inside, the chopper's massive rotors accelerated from neutral into an ash-churned whirlwind and they rose to return to Broome.

As the Sikorsky gained height and curved in a gentle power arc out to sea to bank north, below and anchoring off the devastated bay, Her Majesty's Australian Customs patrol craft *The Broome* sat sleek and gunmetal grey. She was to sit as an imposing guard to await the arrival of a joint Federal and WA Police team of forensic investigators, accompanied by the regional coroner. These experts in death were on the way from Broome by fast commandeered tourist boat. They were armed with cameras, sophisticated surveyor's equipment, GPS plotters, and exhibit and body bags.

Their task was to plot and freeze forever in evidential accuracy the terrible scene of death and destruction at the desecrated Beauty Bay.

85

DON'T PAY THE FERRYMAN

Concord Task Force officers brought their surly but unusually cooperative targets from quiet suburban family havens into the intimidating reality of police interview rooms. With so many search warrants executed, and many sleepy-eyed Spider soldiers arriving for formal interviews, they had been assigned to different police stations all over the big city of Sydney.

Almost immediately, it all became clear to Fred Hall and to his massive task force team. They had their kill, but their result, even in their moment of investigative triumph, was orchestrated—planned and perfectly organised by their quarry.

Full confessions were obtained and admissions secured on tape and in writing to the conspiracy to purchase and import the drugs, and to their distribution and sale. Confessions included everything up to and including the terrible, but according to each witness, the 'accidental' consequences were made. But they were made only by five very old men. Each of the five spoke to the cameras and confirmed by signature the words recorded on the tape and transcribed into statements. In choreographed accuracy, each old man took personal and group-of-five responsibility for the events that had followed the fatal tracks of the purple camel. Each of these old men's grandchildren, now lying dead a continent away on the beach at Beauty Bay, had been ordered to their task and therefore to their deaths by their paternal relatives. But the middle rung, the sons of the old men, the fathers of the five fallen, denied any knowledge at all. And their denials were supported by the old men, who collectively fell on the sword in a carefully planned sacrifice to assuage society's forces of good and society itself.

86
ALWAYS SOMETHING THERE TO REMIND ME

'Urrgh!' Yeah! He was fucking her! Deep inside her from behind! Pumping his hard, cruel, swollen masculinity viciously into her between soft buttocks. His mean hands gripped like talons, holding still her tiny hips, the better to smash his painfully erect cock again and again into her soft, bruised heat. And as he inevitably approached that moment, that excruciating confirmation of his manhood—his power, his rage— he took her head in his hands to brutally twist her face around so that he could claim her lips as he came. But in the darkness as her head turned he saw that she had no face! His lips met a wriggling mess of maggots!

'Uhhhh!' He grunted in repulsion but could not withdraw. Lily had him! She clamped his rapidly fading rigidity into her dead cunt and he couldn't move! Then the curtain of flesh opened in front of him and a terrible vision filled that space. A face peering in! But burnt! Burnt away! And even in its horrible destruction he knew Bonnie had come for him! She reached for him and he tried to back away, screaming now. But there was a mushy wall of bone and rotted flesh behind him! And Lily wouldn't let him go, so he screamed! Then mercifully he awoke into reality.

Bill sat up, sweat-wet frozen but released from the incredible terror of his nightmare in a dishevelled bed in Broome Hospital.

87

ONE THING LEADS TO ANOTHER

The forensic scene examination of Beauty Bay and the camel beach took five full days from sunrise to sunset to complete—five days before the exhausted team of detectives, photographers, scientists, surveyors, pathologists and the coroner left the sad bay behind them on board HMCS *The Broome*.

The first day was of careful videotaping and photographing including overhead from a chopper. They measured, and 3D-plotted the entire geography of the scene to freeze it forever in evidential time, before there was any deliberate or accidental movement. It was a crime scene that included many mini-scenes of violent human death spread over several hectares of burnt land. By late afternoon on day one they removed from the degenerative influences of heat and humidity—not even to mention the frantic egg laying attention of the great Australian bush fly—the bodies of Lily Phat and Namu the cameleer. Two black plastic body bags lifted off the sand of the bay and into the chopper. The pilot, retching from the all-pervading stench, ordered both side sliding-doors open. Finally, the chopper rose and made its rapid way back to Broome with the diminished remains for immediate refrigeration in the tiny hospital morgue.

It was not until the second day that they found the burnt-out vehicle where Bonnie Anu had perished.

On the morning of day two they located and dealt with the fallen

Spider soldiers. A careful low altitude hovering flight in the chopper had assisted the forensic teams to find them. All were within a one kilometre radius of the burnt quad bike. Four charred lumps were examined. The Chemist, the Market Gardener, the Teacher and, fifty metres on from where he lay, the Soldier.

The subsequent post mortem autopsy back at Broome Hospital morgue a week later, would reveal that the Soldier had died before the fire had burnt him: a self-inflicted gunshot to the head from the same weapon that had caused Namu's death. The pathologist's findings as to the Soldier's cause of death had been relatively easy. A fire-blackened pistol was still inside the charred skeletal jaw with a corresponding exit hole in the cracked skull, proving the accuracy of his final selfish violent act.

And so, by the late afternoon it was time to find and bring home Bonnie Anu, back to her grieving family waiting for her in Broome. Those who had loved her impatiently camped on a casual duty roster each day at the airport in sad anticipation.

Bob Hopkins knew well that he needed to bring her back for her family as much as for a shattered agent who lay lonely and distraught in the hospital. As hard as it would be for Bill, both he and the Anu mob needed at least that imperfect closure. They needed their princess back.

88

OBSESSION

Bill Peters had arrived at several decisions. Lying in the freshly laundered linen of his bed, he had decided that his collapse at the beach had been simply a physical response to dehydration. In fact, with the intravenous flush of liquid salts and vitamins back into him, by day two he was feeling okay.

His psyche, although emotionally bruised by the horror of the deaths of Bonnie, Namu and little Lily, had taken full advantage of the neutralising effects of the cocktail of drugs prescribed for him by the concerned medicos. He had slept a deep dreamless sleep for twelve hours. The nightmare had not recurred, although he still shuddered at its memory. Strangely, he almost felt refreshed. He was guiltily embarrassed to discover in himself the triumphant reality of his own selfish survival. He suddenly realised that despite all the bad shit he had just gone through, he was at least still alive! What's more, he thought he had a life to live.

The decisions that he arrived while picking at a lunch of tropical fruits were all of the clichéd things he had to do—loose ends to tie up, unfinished business to take care of, and so on.

Loose end number one: first he had to go to Mozzie and Millie Anu and the boys. He had to sit with them. Had to tell them what had happened; tell them that he loved their treasured relative. He needed to show them how devastated he was at her death. He knew that he would tell them that it was his fault— because it was. Bonnie would not have run into the face of the fire if she hadn't thought he was up to something with Gypsy. Simple. He would tell them he had her blood on his hands, and he would stand there and he would take whatever the Anu family threw at him.

Loose end number two: he needed desperately to talk to Gypsy. Bob Hopkins earlier that morning had sat with him and debriefed him formally on camera. Bob had told him that he must be available for some weeks, maybe for months, as events in criminal and coroner's courts on the other side of Australia unfolded.

But then with the tape off, Bob had passed on the message from Gypsy. 'She said, Bill... she said that she doesn't want you to see her again...I'm so sorry, mate.'

Loose end number three: Bob Hopkins had told him that it was Doc Patrick who had gloatingly revealed to Gypsy and to Tommy on the *John-Damn* that Bill had been working undercover at Beauty Bay. He needed to find Doc Patrick. And quietly beat the living shit out of him.

89
STRAIGHT FROM THE HEART

Bill found the male representatives of the immediate Anu family at about five pm on that second day. Having arrived at his loose-end decisions in the hospital, he booked himself out with the cautious blessing of the doctors and walked the short distance into the shopping precinct of the tiny town CBD.

He borrowed a convertible jeep from a fishing mate and told Bob that he needed to go to the *Freedom* in the grain silo to pick up his gear, his money and his effects. But first he went to the Anu house and found only Millie and a noisy mass of female relatives, who clucked and wailed and hugged him and sympathised. They were unaware of the events that had resulted in their princess's death, but they knew that this wadjela was staunch. They knew that he had loved their girl as they did.

Bill took Millie into the quiet of the small office in the house, and he laid it out to her. Bill told her what Bonnie must have thought she had seen, why she had run, why she had died. He was surprised as Millie simply admonished him.

'Silly bugger, Bill, that's not your fault! What you talking bout? It was Gypsy! If my girl thought Gypsy would shame her, then that's her fault. But, Billy, I know you loved my girl. She was your una, and you were hers.'

Millie cried again through tear-red eyes, sobbing and rocking on the wooden seat. Bill sat opposite her, notable to force words past the lump of emotion that gripped his throat.

'No! Don't you take no blame, Bill. I thank you for telling me, son, but don't you take no blame, Billy' Millie wept, and he reached over awkwardly and held her, but he could not talk again.

The men had gone out to the feedlot along the highway. 'Seventeen k out towards the Derby turn-off. You'll see the sign,' Millie had said as he left her.

As he trundled, fat-tyred, on a red dust track down the long driveway, he saw them gathered. Mozzie, Uncle Rock, and the twins Elvis and Snowflake. They stood around the high gated pens that held mooing fat-necked cattle. This herd of brahman cross steers was due for transport down to the Broome port soon.

The men turned to watch him arrive in the fading light of the tropical day as he parked the jeep. He alighted and forced himself to walk toward their solemn faces.

'Mozzie...boys,' he spoke, and despite his steely intentions noted a slight quaver in his voice.

'Billy, you okay, son?' Mozzie asked.

So he just told them.

'Mozzie, boys, I am here to say sorry. Sorry Bonnie died.' He saw Mozzie flinch at the saying of her name. 'I need to tell you all, tell you what I just told Millie back in town. Tell you that she died because it was my fault.'

The three younger Anu men shuffled in a trinity of increased attention.

'What do ya mean, boy?' Mozzie asked confused. This was not what the police had told him. 'Coppers told me she rolled ya jeep, Bill?'

'That's what happened, Mozzie. But she was running away from Beauty Bay. See she saw me with Gypsy, and...and she must have thought I had shamed her.'

Mozzie shook his head as if to clear it. Bill stuttered on, his voice breaking from the stress of recollection and of the telling.

'Must have thought that Gypsy and I were up to no good—you know, humbug—so she took off. And the fire was coming, and she must have rolled the jeep because she was scared. You see?

Mozzie shook his head again.

'That's why it's my fault...that's why...' He stopped then, clumsy confession made and out in the open. He waited for judgment, and if necessary—and in a weird way he hoped it was—for physical punishment, retribution.

The small familial tribal council met, semi-circling away from the defendant. A discussion went on in their own tongue, the words mysterious to the crestfallen young white man who stood stock still.

Snowflake quietly diagnosed the problem to his kinsmen.

'You know what? I reckon he's urtin so bad he needs to feel something to take is mind off it. Ya know? Some pain. He needs to feel that he can settle his wadjela guilt thing. Needs us to punish him now so he can move on! Whaddya reckon?'

Elvis, contemplative and silent up to that point joined in.

'Reckon Snow's right, dad. He's a wadjela but he's pretty staunch, eh. He sorta understands. Remember what she said about him, he almost feels the song lines.'

Mozzie nodded, knowing the love that his daughter had for this young man and feeling saddened that it had been cut short with all its potential, and for his lost mocha-coloured grandkids.

'Yeah. Okay, boys, let's help im out. Spear his leg, Snow, a special favour just this once,' he ordered.

Bill faced the tribunal of Mozzie, Rock and Elvis as Snowflake snuck around behind him and did the wadjela the big favour he was after. A controlled bunting of the end of a branding iron smacked against the big muscle of Bill's previously damaged right thigh.

Thunk was the onomatopoeic confirmation of the cruel collision of pig-iron against muscle fibre via skin.

'Aww, fuck!' exclaimed Bill as he collapsed with the mightiest dead-leg ever experienced. But as he writhed in the red-dusted agony of the blow, Bill did feel a strange release as emotion and attention was forced away from the immediate past events to his immediate pain. As he realised that effect and an acceptance of his punishment, the four Anu men simply squatted and offered tokens of sympathy.

'You okay, mate? Pain will go soon. Just rub it, Bill,' and the like. Sure enough the dull pain started to ebb. But then all eyes, including Bill's watering ones turned to the driveway as a massive Kenworth prime mover chugged down toward them with a red dust tail swirling behind.

Snowflake Anu helped Bill to his unsteady feet then the entire group gasped! A discordant chorus of masculine amazement erupted as the prime mover crunched to a halt next to their small gathering. From the passenger's seat a very much alive Bonnie Anu lithely jumped down from height and barefoot onto the ground in a little welcoming spurt of dust!

'What you fellas doin?' she asked.

Her gorgeous face was curious at the sight of Bill Peters falling again helplessly to the ground. His leg would not yet take any weight and Snowflake had unconsciously withdrawn his support to join his father, uncle and brother in a hysterically joyous meeting with Bonnie. There were kisses, there were hugs and there was lifting of their cherished kin in a dervish spinning of delight from one to the other as she screamed and laughed at their craziness. Finally, dizzy, she was able to go to Bill.

'What ya doing on the ground?' she said, as she helped him stand and leaned him against a post. 'Bonnie girl, I thought... we thought you were dead...on the road...The jeep was rolled over and burnt.'

'Nah, ya silly bugger. Bloody old thing just stopped going. Then the fire come, and I did think I was in trouble. But this deadly bloke in the truck there come along running from it too. He stopped, and I went with him. Hey, sorry bout the jeep, Billy—this fella had to push it into the ditch with his truck to clear the highway.'

'But, daughter, why didn't ya call someone on the truck radio to let us know what appen?' Mozzie asked, quite properly, Bill thought.

But she was casually dismissive in her response.

'Nah, couldn't Dad. Bloke's two-way was stuffed. So I just went on his run through to Fitzroy with him. We did that trip and we just come back now.'

She smiled her wide toothy grin at them. Bill started to laugh, and Mozzie, always up for a giggle, joined in both the laughing and the sudden realisation of the ridiculousness of the situation. Then the boys joined in, and Bonnie joined in and so did the stocky handsome young part-Aboriginal prime mover driver, who had now joined the grouping and had moved beside Bonnie. They all just about pissed themselves.

Bill was first to stop, his leg hurt too much to ignore. A huge and visibly sub-surface haematoma was colouring his entire thigh and sending small tributaries of bruising down towards his knee. Plus, he had suddenly seen his future, a small promising glimpse. His mad, exciting, vivacious sensual lover–friend was suddenly back!

He would ask her to marry him! Now! He would bend down on one sore knee and propose to her with her family as witness. So he sank to that knee, just as she turned away to make a simple introduction.

'Bill, Dad, boys, this here's me new man! Troy Mosquito from Kununurra!'

90

ORIGINAL SIN

Loose end number two: he had to find Gypsy. When loose end one had so dramatically turned to shit in the red pindan dust, Bill was left floating like a blind mullet in the turbulent wake of the joyous family. The clan, whooping with the high spirits of the reunion, had left him behind, inadvertently on their part but deliberately on his.

He watched as the Anu mob, and Bonnie's new man Troy-*fucking*-Mosquito headed off back toward the family home to tell Mum! They invited him, of course they did. But really it had been as a sympathetic afterthought as he knelt, clearly forlorn and heartbroken at the news she had so happily and rather cruelly, he thought, announced to the world. Her new man! 'Fuck me!' That was quick! Still, Bill thought much later, that was her. Bonnie Anu was an innocent of spirit, a wild indigenous child, a gorgeous, natural, untamed woman. And just when he had wanted her most he had lost her. So although he forced a smile and pretended that he would follow them, he couldn't. How the fuck could he? Two's company and all that 'Shiiiiiiiiit!' he shouted at the huge half globe of the moon rising above him from the eastern horizon. In his absolute helplessness at his loss and with a resigned sigh, he just banged his head softly against the massive ancient hardwood trunk of the deep-dug corner strainer post that held him up.

He watched Mozzie's old Land Rover lead the flashy prime mover and Troy-*fucking*-Mosquito away up the drive. The raucous gaggle was still audible from a hundred metres as they exited the farm road and turned left on the main highway to set off toward Broome and what would be, he had no doubt in the world, a wonderfully explosive happy reunion of the favourite girl with her mum and extended family.

'Damn!' He missed her and the mob already.

But now that his immediate world of future opportunity had been significantly remodelled, he needed to see Gypsy. He had to make that good again at least. She had to know, just had to listen to him. He had to convince her so that Gypsy would accept that he had done what he had done for her. He had only agreed to do it protect her, her future with Tommy, and to protect their little bundle of soon-to-be-born-joy.

He staggered across in an old man's limp to the jeep and clambered in wincing from the pain of his stiffening thigh muscle. His leg threatened to cramp, but he fired up the vehicle and by degrees and with immense discomfort, kangaroo-hopped the manual away from the feedlot and towards Broome. Hopefully towards a meeting with a justly disappointed Ms Gypsy Lawson.

91

GOODBYE
IS FOREVER

The night was black and raincloud scudded by the time Bill turned the flash borrowed jeep into Herbert Street. Gypsy and Tommy's house in the old Chinese section of the town was up the road from that of a very recent ex-girlfriend of his. Bonnie Anu.

'Sob!' he mocked himself. He was acting on a dangerous assumption that Gypsy would be here, because he didn't know of any other place that she would be in Broome. He was cautious as there was no way known he intended to shame himself by being seen by the Anu mob. He didn't think his fragile ego could stand being laughed at, or worse, someone feeling sorry for him. So he parked the jeep back along the road and then limped cautiously in the darkness into the front yard of Gypsy's house.

With night vision improving as he reached his destination, he listened to the sounds of the party nearby as Millie's raucous cackling laughter emphasised her joy at the miraculous reappearance of her precious daughter. The party was pumping as the previously saddened extended family and hangers-on rejoiced and no doubt met and no-freaken-doubt much approved of Troy-*fucking*-Mosquito! 'No hard feelings,' Bill muttered ironically.

He was distracted by his dark thoughts in the dark night as he manoeuvred through the tropical flora in the yard. Pushing through the broad greenness of banana leaf with one eye up the road toward the

Anu's, his night vision failed him and he walked into the back of a big black object.

'Ouch! Fuck,' he grunted, as forehead met warm metal, and he realised that there was a bus parked in the driveway.

'Wait on. It's Mavis's bus,' Bill realised. Mavis, his favourite grey nomad. With more care now, he felt along the dusty side of the beast and saw the front door to the house, dimly lit from a soft light inside the dwelling.

'Right time to face her,' he breathed, and knocked on Gypsy's door. He heard a shuffle from inside the old Broome bungalow. But as the door opened he saw only Mavis, her wiry old frame wrapped in a colourful sarong as she smiled in greeting.

'Billy! She said that you would come, come on in, dear.' The old woman stood back as he dragged his increasingly swollen right leg behind him in a hunchback-of-Notre Dame shuffle up the stairs and into the teak-scented coolness of the home.

Mavis helped him onto a chair in the kitchen and fussed over the impressive contusion and bruising to his leg. Bill's thigh muscle cramped with the pressure of the internal bleeding from the fibre tearing and crushing. She found ice and applied a massive towel-wrapped icepack to his leg. Mavis then raised his leg up onto another kitchen chair and stacked it with pillows until he was at last comfortable. She turned to start the kettle brewing for soothing green tea and she answered his unasked questions.

'Gypsy said that you would come, Billy'

'Where is she? Where are they, Mavis?' Bill pleaded, but she stilled him as she went to the side table and took from it an envelope.

'This is for you, son.' She spoke sympathetically as she handed him the message.

The envelope was scented with Gypsy's most familiar scent of sandalwood oil. He slit opened the envelope and took a fragile sheaf of rice paper from it. Mavis brought to him a mug of the musky green tea and then left him alone as she went to run a bath for him.

'Bill Peters,' the note started, somewhat formally and abruptly, he analysed. No sign of the usual dear; no love-hearts.

'I need to tell you how I am feeling. I am very disappointed with you.'

Well there it was. Surely it could only get worse. He took a break, and took a sip and then went back to Gypsy's words, so beautifully crafted in her graceful hand.

I thought that you were my friend, Bill. Special! Tommy's friend too. But you betrayed me, hurt me, and through a consequence of your actions you hurt Tommy.

I do not forgive you.

Your friend Mr Hopkins has tried stoutly to defend you, and to defend your actions. But, Bill, they are not defendable. You do not 'protect' a friend by lies and deception. I thought that I knew you. But clearly, I don't.

Anyway, we are going away, and it will be up to destiny alone if I ever see you again. I am going away so that Tommy and I can enjoy the arrival of our little man Saxon. There! I have shared another part of my life with you, the name that we will call our son.

I write this letter of goodbye to you, Bill Peters.

Goodbye friend (?).

92
RADIO GA-GA

The Pigeon was preening. He was in his element, a political triumph in front of the world's media as he took vicarious responsibility for the investigative smashing of an organised criminal organisation by his hand-picked man: Superintendent Fred Hall OC of the Concord Task Force.

Standing beside but deliberately behind the premier on the rostrum of the formal press boardroom at Parliament House, Fred was well aware of what the silver-maned politician was up to. But he didn't care. The job that he had been tasked to do by his boss the commissioner, who stood on Pigeon's left, was done. The dreadful crime, the agonising deaths of so many of the innocent citizens of his patch, Sydney city, had been solved.

Yet even in the bright glare of an enthusiastic and congratulatory media, Fred Hall was angry. He was angry that the crafty old men of the Spider Triad had, even in the moment of their own destruction, been able to engineer the final act. It had been an effective ploy. The five old men had collectively taken the bullet for the benefit and continued existence of the evil organism of the gang.

Now at their relayed command, the rest of the gang hunkered down, lay low. The Spiders would lay quiet until the glare of publicity and the focus of the city's law enforcement faded. They would simply wait, as they had learnt to do in other places and in this new world over time.

They would wait until an aggrieved society's angry scrutiny wavered and was distracted as more immediate and pressing matters took over and they were safe to wake up the organisation again. Then, slowly, cautiously, the Spiders' nest would stir again. The sons of the old men newly empowered, bruised but educated by the errors in planning, execution and in contingency, would return again to the old tried and true ways of making nefarious gain for the benefit of the whole.

But for the now, the premier took his man's hand and to the accompaniment of the speed drives clicking in machine-gun staccato, the proud Pigeon brought the victory-lap to a close.

93

THINGS CAN ONLY GET BETTER

'Right, son, we have released the crime scene at Beauty Bay.' Bob Hopkins spoke to his downcast companion who sat with him at the Zoo Café near Cable Beach.

After she had sent her sad and sorry young friend to bed in the same sleep-out that Bill had inhabited in happier days, Mavis had rung that 'Nice police man from Sydney' as she had promised when Bill inevitably had turned up at the house.

Bob had arrived there at a respectable eight am to find Bill and say his goodbyes over a brew in the town.

'We are off this morning, mate. Back home to New South Wales. Bill, look, thanks very much for your work,' Bob said. 'From a cold, hard forensic investigative perspective the job is done and done well.'

But Bob could see from the look on Bill's face as he lifted the over-sized china bowl of pungent coffee to his mouth that he had the sad human consequences heavy on his mind.

'Just so you know, mate,' Bob offered, 'the drugs that were tainted with the synthetic strychnine came by the same method as the lot you grabbed. We know now that Namu was the syndicate's man here on the ground in Broome. The drugs came from Holland. Amsterdam. Through Interpol, we now know of an incident at a nightclub there some months before the events in Sydney. Twenty people died after taking purple camel ecstasy tabs. From the exact same batch as Concord.'

Bill paid attention, interested now as Bob told the tale.

'God knows why we weren't made aware of that, you know. There should have been an Interpol alert, but somehow this one didn't get out internationally,' Bob said. 'But anyway, the old men of the Spider gang based in Cabramatta have admitted a conspiracy that includes the purchase and transport of those drugs down to Indonesia by merchant ship. In a fairly complex operation, the Indo organisation based in Bali was a suspected fundraiser for a fundamentalist terror group. Anyway, it had involved itself as a legitimate-looking endeavour to breed up racing camels for one of the mega-rich Saudi princes. They were experimenting with breeding race-proven Saudi bulls with the big Australian cows to see what they could get. The staging post from Saudi Arabia to Australia for quarantine purposes is the Cocos Islands off the northwest of the West Australian coast. From Bali, the drugs were put ashore at Cocos by Indo fishing dhow. There are hundreds of such tiny wooden vessels in those waters. With the help of a corrupt veterinarian, who is currently in a holding cell in Sydney Central, it was actually in our Australian Commonwealth Quarantine facility that the bulls had their hump enhancements. It was simply a larger adaptation of the breast implant plastic surgery.'

Bill drained the final pitch-black swirl of the juice of the bean and signalled across to the waitress for a refill.

'It worked with the tainted drugs, so they did it again for this replacement batch.' Bob completed that chapter of the agent's debrief.

'Anyway, son, the indications are that the old men will plead guilty on a plea bargain to all the charges. If they do there will be no need for you to give evidence, of course. They will never walk from prison. However, having said that, I suspect that the director of public prosecutions may accept a plea of guilty to the mass manslaughter at Concord Oval and the Fish Nightclub.'

'Manslaughter?' Bill asked surprised.

'Yes, strange isn't it? You see, although they clearly committed the criminal acts, they are what is known in legalese and in the Latin as the *actus reas*. The acts of the crime. But in every crime there also needs to be established the intent. This intent is known as the *mens rea*, and both together complete the criminal recipe of the physical act plus the intention, if you like. So, their legal argument is that they had a clear intent to bring the drugs in and to sell them to their client base. But the fact that the purple camels were tainted with poison was not known to them. In other words, they did not intend to kill anyone.

'Therefore, the deaths caused by poisoning were an unknown and could not have been intentional.

Bill was now listening intently as Bob continued.

'It is argued that although their actions did cause the deaths, they lacked the intent to kill, and the consequential deaths fall within the manslaughter provisions of the legislation and not within the murder provisions.'

Bill contemplated that as Bob continued.

'The Spiders have told us that Namu was their connection, the conduit at Beauty Bay. He was apparently employed by the Indo group. The Spiders didn't even know who owned the resort when we interviewed them. But, mate, the old men did tell us that their courier Van Nguyen paid nearly a quarter of a million dollars at the resort for what they called comfort money. We don't know why that was paid or to whom. In the scheme of things, it was play money. Their imports via the camels would have made them many millions. We can only suspect that money went to Namu. Your evidence, the search of Gypsy and Tommy's quarters and of the staff, and the total destruction of the resort by the fire means we may never know.'

Bill nodded. He decided that there was no obvious need to mention the orange fabric suitcase that Bob had nearly tripped over earlier as he had arrived to visit Bill. Bill had seen the familiar case as they left the home. He saw that it lay with other rubbish on the verge of Gypsy and Tommy's home, apparently discarded before they left for parts unknown.

'Hey anyway, mate, listen, thanks very much on a personal basis. I know you are not happy at the moment with what went on, with Gypsy's reaction, and with what happened with Bonnie.'

Bill nodded again, but then despite himself laughed quietly at his embarrassed recollection of Bonnie's grand arrival at the tribal punishment scene that he had engineered.

'I hope that Gypsy comes around with time.'

Bill's replied sadly, 'Oh well, Bob, I suppose that's life.'

'What are you going to do in the short-term, son?' Bob asked as he reached for his wallet in the pocket of his suit jacket.

'I think I need a break from Broome, Bob' Bill said. 'Suddenly there doesn't seem much here for me at the moment.'

'What about your boat?' Bob asked as he stood in concert with Bill, who grunted softly, still favouring his leg.

'I think I'll just keep her in storage in the old silo while I make up my mind where I want to be.'

Bob paid the waitress and waited for his change under the cooling swirl of the large rattan blades of the overhead fan. As they walked toward the two hire cars, Bob took his agent's hand for a last time.

'Oh, by the way, Bill. George Patrick has disappeared off the face of the earth. Just so you know, we believe that he has gone bush and will probably stay there until in his judgment the heat has died down.'

'Or his whisky runs out,' Bill offered, and they both laughed at the thought.

'Oh, and another thing, Bill—Gypsy and Tommy withdrew the assault charges against Doc. They just want to forget about what happened.'

Bill wasn't really surprised.

'So, all Doc has to face is an enforced retirement once they work out where the hell he is,' Bob added. 'Anyway, young man, again I want to thank you for what you have done. Don't forget to stay in touch. You have my mobile, work, and home number. Anytime, anywhere, call me if you need to.'

94
EVERY ROSE
HAS ITS THORN

Bill was reminded as he waved Bob away from the café how small a town Broome really was, particularly after the seasonal influx of tourists had left before the wet season began. With only the true locals left the population shrank back to a few thousand hardy residents mainly involved in pearling, prawning, fishing, mining, and the service businesses to those primary industries.

With Gypsy and Bonnie counting amongst the long-term locals, the Chinese whispers of rumour had begun. The half of the town's population that knew, or knew of Gypsy, and the other half that knew or knew of Bonnie, also now knew of Bill, and they were either angry with him or laughing at him. Those who had known both local lasses felt both emotions, so as he passed them in the streets he felt an uncommon focus on him that was troubling and unwelcome.

'Yep, time to move on,' he thought to himself as he drove away from the town and the scrutiny of the town people. He had decided. He was going to pack-up an old kit bag from his meagre possessions on the *Freedom*, and head to the airport and decide where to go from there. Perth first up, he thought, and then, who knows?

As he drove he ignored the occasional finger pointing and thankfully rare yelled curse or taunt from one of the Gypsy or Bonnie teams of supporters. He thought now about the cache of dollars that he had found in Tommy's study. Bob's clear statement was that the drug courier had taken that money to Beauty Bay. As a comfort payment; but a payment for what? Turning the eyes away maybe? or allowing the importation of drugs? Surely not. But if that payment was the same money that he had seen in the study, and it just had to be, what did that mean? Bill pondered as he drove toward the Broome Port. He could not fathom any circumstance where Tommy would deal in drugs no matter how hopeless his financial plight, no matter how dire his need. All of his own instincts and his knowledge of the man told him that Tommy would not take any amount of money if it involved drugs. So there had to be another reason that Tommy had that money. It was in their fucking study for God's sakes he thought. And then was the fact that he had quickly counted about one hundred thousand US dollars and maybe eighty Aussie. If the Spiders were to be believed, their man had paid a quarter of a million. Was this the luck that had saved his friends' business? It had to be. But he was resigned now to ask that question of Tommy at some future time, probably in some other place.

That decided, Bill was relieved as he approached the huge old grain silo where *Freedom* waited. As he drove up to the port he noted that off to seaward not far to the northwest horizon, the typical tropical black thunderheads were building as a midday storm threatened. He accelerated the jeep toward the haven of the huge corrugated steel barn. He pulled the vehicle in under the protective rusted eaves, glad to have just escaped a drenching as fat blood-warm droplets came smashing down in liquid battalions from the scudding cloud above.

'Phew! Perfect timing,' he congratulated himself as the incredible noise of the rain against the cavernous echoing structure confirmed that a wet season storm had indeed arrived. The noise of the rains almost masked the dry metal screech of the massive sliding door that he pulled open and then shut behind him.

'Where the fuck are the lights!' he cursed and tried to recall from previous visits exactly where the old switch-bank for the battery of overhead fluoro lights was. He groped blindly but carefully, not wanting to risk a bare finger search among the messy sticky webs of the big carnivorous spiders who sat and waited for a careless insect to enmesh themselves. He found the switch and flicked several of the old ceramic triggers down but only darkness remained, and he realised that the power was off. Not totally unexpected in the old building used now only to hide vessels like his from the dangers of the wet season weather.

'Okay, let's get my night vision happening,' he ordered himself. He waited with eyes deliberately forced wide open and looking out into the pitch blackness. Slowly, murky shapes began to emerge from the cave of the silo. And then there she was. One of about ten fragile fibreglass and steel vessels tucked away for the season, sitting on trailers or cradles around the interior of the shed. *Freedom* was farthest away from the door. As she was the biggest vessel, Bill had deliberately tucked her against that far wall of protective steel that rose twenty metres up to the roof.

'Hello, pretty girl,' he muttered and made his way the 150 metres across the dusty concrete floor towards her. He noticed the occasional criss-cross of tyres marks left in the carpet of dust from other owners' vehicles. He reached his prize—the swaddled body of his twin-hull Shark Cat. She was his home and his livelihood; the charter fishing vessel *Freedom*. Bill reached to pat her starboard hull as he accessed the inset steel ladder at her stern to climb up under the canvas covers and into the safe haven.

Bill reached the top step. He needed to unclip a small section of the covers immediately around the back deck to clamber aboard and stand cautiously erect in the absolute enclosed darkness. As his eyes slowly adapted, Bill tried to recall where he had left his big plastic torch for just such a blind entry. With arms outstretched, Bill shuffled forward like a blind man dancing a clumsy moon-walk. As he did, his nose wrinkled in disgust as the stink of something surely long deceased wafted from the cabin.

'Fuck, must have left some bait on board,' he muttered.

He was immediately transfixed as a human voice came out of the darkness with a gruff and horribly familiar, 'Gidday, maaate!'

95

MESSAGE IN A BOTTLE

They were at five thousand metres and climbing when Bob Hopkins suddenly jumped in his seat against the tight restraint of the seat belt as if stung!

'Bloody hell!' he swore to the surprise of his companions.

Up to that rude interruption his five officers were leaning back in the comfortable seats into the smooth acceleration of the executive jet. Each man was looking forward to touchdown in Mascot in five hours, back to families and familiar surroundings after their great and highly successful tropical adventure.

'Bloody hell!' Bob repeated, and then to their surprise and against the clear instruction of the aero-etiquette, their usually sober and respected commander unbelted himself and ran up the small carpeted cylinder toward the cockpit, yelling, 'The silo, the bloody silo!'

96
CHURCH OF THE POISONED MIND

'Fuck me dead! Doc! I near shit myself! What the fuck are you doing here?' Bill gasped.

Doc lit a kerosene camp lantern to illuminate the canvas grotto and Bill was equally stunned by the sight of the senior sergeant. The obese apparition was horribly naked except for a discoloured pair of pinkish budgie-smugglers that were transparent with sweat—or worse!

Doc lounged in one of the vinyl rear deck chairs, but Bill saw the oily twin threat of the double barrel shotgun laid casually across his lap and aimed right at his own suddenly very nervous guts.

'Maate, I've bin waiting for ya.' Doc smiled grimly up at him, his piggy eyes dark with panda-rings of stress, madness and fatigue circling them.

Bill forced his brain to register and interpret what he saw. From the evidence on the rear deck of empty whisky bottles, pyramids of crushed beer cans, moulding scraps of discarded foods, and a stench of stale shit from the inoperative heads beside the stairwell, Bill knew immediately that Doc had been here since he did the runner from Bob Hopkins and his team. But why? Doc must have seen that question on his face.

'You fucked me over, maaate! After all I done for ya,' Doc whined. Bill saw then that he was in his usual state of intoxication, a half empty whisky bottle tucked in between his fat thighs.

Outside the rain continued its noisy splattering symphony against the steel corrugations of the roof and the slab sides of the silo as Bill began a quick analysis of his situation.

'What do you mean I fucked you over, Doc?' Bill queried faux calmly, playing for time.

'Ya fucken fucked me over!' Doc shouted. 'You and that little cunt Hopkins!' His entire head reddened. Ropy blue neck veins pulsed; reddened eyes bulged with the pressure of his discontent. 'Sit down, ya cunt,' he ordered abruptly.

With an angry jerk of his chin he indicated an esky across the camp table that separated them. Bill shuffled anxiously to the sturdy plastic cool-bin. He watched as Doc parked his grime caked bare feet on the table like a huge ugly V rifle sight between which the deadly eyes of the shotgun glared.

'I gave you me friendship, Bill! You an me coulda been a team, boy, I coulda showed you about life, maate. Taught ya bout women! We coulda been good maaates! But na! You chose to fuck me over! Chose those feral hippy cunts over the friendship of a good an decent bloke, and that ain't right.'

Doc was rambling and Bill was increasingly worried that the man was seriously unhinged. Too much whisky and too much tropical heat had fried his brain. Doc slammed the whisky bottle down on the table next to the lantern. He began to wave the shottie while ranting at Bill, at Bob, and at the injustices of life. It was everybody else in the world versus Doc fucken Patrick! Bill decided if he didn't act soon he may not get a chance to act at all.

Doc laid himself a bit back, humping his fat arse down slightly on slushy sounding vinyl to heft the shotgun and lower it in the direction of Bill's rapidly retreating genitals.

From his low base on the esky, Bill took a calculated risk. He lay back, throwing both arms and palms down onto the deck behind his seat. This flattened his profile and confused Doc, who immediately began to adjust the weapon in response. Bill used the axis of his body as a lever over the solid esky to kick both feet up under the camp table. The lantern and the half empty whisky bottle catapulted back towards Doc who took both items awkwardly on the face and the chest. Doc's legs flicked upwards the cool kerosene from the lantern and the warm whisky from the bottle flooded out onto his bare chest and gut. Luckily, the upturned lantern did not ignite the kerosene, but the flame and the lantern light went out. In the dark confusion, Doc's panicked fingers found the shotgun's double triggers and he pulled them both.

In a split second of pitch-black mayhem punctuated by the flash the shotgun's eruption and the ear shattering double boom of the explosion, Doc did literally what he had managed to do figuratively all of his life. He shot himself in the foot!

Bill was down and crawling, unaware of Doc's injury. With arsehole-twitching intent, he crawled towards danger and past the thrashing maniac only a metre or so distant.

Doc's body rolled and crashed about through the rubbish on the deck, while he howled a blood-curdling shout of anger and pain. But even in his agony, his instinct of survival reigned and he was awkwardly reloading the shotgun. By the time Doc fired again into the darkness, Bill had passed him in his combat crawl and reached the starboard side rail. Bill followed the rail by touch along the entire port side of the big vessel up towards the bow, and raised to a half crouch he ran like a bow-legged escapee.

As Bill removed himself from the immediate terror of the aft deck, Doc continued to reload and fire the shotgun wildly, with the massive explosions of the buckshot echoing within the huge steel cavern. The super-heated lead shot tore through the canvas dust covers, pock-marked the white fibreglass, rattled against gunnels and ultimately sprayed against the various steel and concrete surfaces of the silo. The echoing noise merged with the cacophony of sound outside. The tropical storm intensified, with sheets of smashing rain battering the land and the expanse of the silo's steel hulk. In that insanity, Doc finally realised from the barrel flares that he was alone on the deck. That realisation terrified him even more as he backed up, fat arse sliding on the blood, whisky and kerosene slicked deck as his Speedos surrendered and became a tangled G-string. Doc shrieked as he expected his invisible enemy to suddenly strike from the blackness. Then it sank in through the adrenalin and alcohol-fuelled fog that he had shot himself but it didn't actually hurt until he saw it. Doc found the dolphin torch with a scrabbling search through the trash, flicked it on, and squealed like a jugular-stuck porker.

Bill was up at the bow, panting in combined fear and exertion. He wondered at the wetness on him. He brushed his chest and held the fingers close to his eyes, smelt the musky iron tainted confirmation. Blood! But he was certain that it wasn't his and that he was unmarked by the lead pellets of the shotgun. His fingers found his hair matted with the viscous red liquid. And then he found it, a warm fat stick trapped by his curls. He held its strange heavy softness and brought it close before his eyes in the gloom. Centimetres from his face was an extremely ugly corn-callused filthy big toe. Despite himself, he snorted repugnantly as he biffed it away.

Doc heard him. And knew now where Bill was. The fury rose again in Doc, an anger that he was hurt, and Bill was not. With the bellow of a wounded hippo, he stumbled around to the bow walkway and saw his man crouched twenty metres distant, low on the bow. He fired the shotgun just as Bill rose and leapt up and out, and abandoned ship.

Bill felt the rush of wind pass close by as a spray of white-hot pellets whooshed by him as he jumped. Just under the twin projections of the white fibreglass bows of the cat was the dark shape of Doc's four-wheel drive, secreted. Bill's fall from the high deck was not onto the unforgiving hard concrete floor of the silo but onto the forgiving thin steel roof of the Land Cruiser. With a *whump* the roof panel collapsed into itself in an everlasting impression of Bill's clenched buttocks and outstretched legs.

Doc lost sight of his target, his view obscured by the angle of the twin hulls between which his prey had jumped. Bill rolled lithely off the dented roof of the vehicle and down onto the hard floor without much sound, urgently retreating in a reverse duck-walk under the huge bulk of the *Freedom* as she sat regally on the steel cradle. A minute of silence passed.

'You okay, maaate?' Doc called, as if suddenly concerned as to Bill's fate.

Bill decided not to play Marco Polo with a madman today. But he realised that Doc had no idea where he was, or even if he still breathed. With no response from Bill, Doc stayed quiet and limped back to where he had stashed the heavy leather hunter's belt that held a baker's dozen of fresh red plastic shotgun shells. He strapped the bandolier around himself just above the heavy sag of his gut. Using the torch to find the boat's first-aid box he began to dress what remained of the top of his right foot. He whimpered in pain and self-pity as he saw the damage. All his toes except his pinkie had been sacrificed, leaving a ragged mess of black-ringed red flesh and snow-white fragments of the toe and foot bones. Doc clumsily wrapped dressings around the damaged foot to staunch the heavy flow of blood. As he finished, a harsh reality occurred to him. If he didn't seek medical help soon he was in deep shit. Doc began to feel the light headiness typical of such a gushing of the life force from the body. He felt dehydrated as much from the intense burst of aggressive and self-survival activity as from the still pulsing wound. So, typically, he reached for the last bottle of whisky from his much-diminished stock and drank with gulping desperation.

Bill was in a conundrum. He felt relatively safe for the moment, but at the same time vulnerable tucked under the *Freedom*. He sat on the dusty concrete, back up against the lead-red painted steel of the cradle strut. What if Doc climbed down the short stainless-steel ladder off the stern, shotgun in one hand, the big boat torch in the other? He would pin him under the boat like a spotlighted rabbit awaiting explosive death from the shotgun. The nearest object that he could conceivably hide behind was a seventy-five-metre zigzag sprint across extremely open terrain to where another vessel sat waiting out the cyclone season. Bill knew that Doc was injured but he could hear him moving heavily about and muttering angrily almost directly above his hidey-hole. He heard Doc unclipping and removing the rear canvas dust covers off the boat. The covers slipped down with a dusty crumpling either side of the boat. Bill knew now that Doc had the classic hunter's high ground—a raised panoramic view of the landscape around the boat. To run from the boat towards the sliding doors so far away would be certain suicide, an invitation to take a spray of shot through his back. The rains finally stopped and an incongruous peace enveloped the cavernous building. Now Bill had also lost the cover of noise. Then the sun emerged from the cloud cover and the interior of the building lightened with sunlight streaming in via the plastic skylights. The odds were massively shortening in Doc's favour. Bill did the only thing he could do. He lay doggo and quiet and waited to be forced into action.

Above him, Doc waited too. In the first aid kit he had found a box of a basic over-the-counter analgesic pain relief and he consumed twenty of the white tablets, washed down with whisky. Both medicines gradually soothed the razor-sharp edge of the pain. Doc pulled a folding chair over to the back rail and sat now with the shotgun at the ready and his bloody bandaged foot raised onto the gunwale. He was pretty sure that he had at least wounded Bill. He had heard a heavy body smash into the Land Cruiser, but despite his best efforts with the torch he could not spot a body, alive or dead. He decided that he would wait. Wait for the pain relief to truly make a difference. Wait for just a little more Dutch courage from the whisky. As he sipped he realised that with the blood loss the whisky was having more than the usual effect. He would wait because he was also too shit-scared to clamber down the stern ladder and search out Bill. For the time being, anyway.

So they both waited. From Doc's perspective he would either find Bill dead or alive. If he found him alive he must make him dead, as that was his intention all along. He must destroy the cunt who had hurt him. Doc meant to win this fight. He even had put a police issue body-bag in the four-wheel drive, ready to take a little off-road trip into the broad expanse of the Great Sandy Desert to dig a little anonymous hole. There, following a brief but sincere ceremony, he would say a last goodbye to a bloke who coulda been a maate. He would plant Bill six foot under; or maybe just a lazy foot or so. His vague plan after that was that he would wander around the outback for a while, hiding at day. Eventually, he might turn up at the police union lawyer's office in Perth and lodge a quick stress claim against the Western Australian Police. Just for enough of a compo payout to live a comfortable life of camping and fishing.

But as the day dragged on, Doc knew that he had to act. His head felt quite good now, floating a bit on waves of analgesic and alcoholic relief. Anyway, he held all the fucken aces. Even if Bill was alive, how was he going to face off to a shotgun? It was time to act. And, Doc reasoned, Bill was probably dead. Time to find out!

Doc groaned heavily to an approximately upright stance, supporting himself on the wide fibreglass gunwale. He tucked the shotgun under his left arm, clipped the torch to the bandolier, and checked that the shotgun was fully loaded. He limped across to the ladder, the white bandages blackening as the flow had stopped and the blood congealed in its own death. With no small degree of agony, Doc turned and stepped his good foot back to the top rung and started his backwards descent.

Bill heard it all. In those interminable minutes as each waited for the other to move, he had made decisions about loose end number three. He knew that Doc must eventually come after him and that he would see Doc's feet and legs, then gut, chest, face descend the boat's stern ladder. Bill had already decided that he was not going to run; he was not going to play a fatally unfair game of tag as Doc stalked him with the deadly advantage of the weapon. No. He was going to attack, take full advantage of a surprise ambush. He had looked about him during their stand-off and found a useful tactic. He hoped.

As Doc's damaged foot followed the good one down the ladder, Bill was as close to that ladder as he could manoeuvre in the three-foot crawl space between the hull at the stern and the concrete floor. When Doc's mangled right foot gingerly took his weight on the third last step, and with Doc's fetid groin only inches from his nose, Bill sprang. He had found his weapon under the *Freedom*: a large steel U-bolt; a wood worker's clamp. Bill had spit lubricated and quietly unwound the big nuts of the clamp turn-by-turn, until the clamp was open.

Now, as Doc shuffled his damaged foot on the steel step, Bill reached through under the hull and hooked the clamp around Doc's fat calf and the rail of the ladder and pulled swiftly backwards. The big man howled and roared as Bill urgently screwed the second nut back on tight until the bolt pinned the Doc to the boat ladder like a foot-snared orang-utan.

97

DON'T DREAM IT'S OVER

With Doc roaring and frantically twisting in the grip of the U-bolt, the door of the silo screeched open, flooding the bright light of fine day deep into the building.

Bill had scurried back from the stern of the boat once his trap was sprung and was hiding behind the steel cradle near the *Freedom's* bow. Doc still had the shotgun and was trying to angle it down past his legs into the space under the vessel to fire a ricochet of pellets into the void.

At the noise of the door opening, Bill peeked out from his crawl space. The figures of Bob Hopkins and a half dozen assorted task force and local police officers were silhouetted against the sun's glare.

'Bob, stay there! Stay there!' he shouted. 'He's got a shotgun!'

'Bill! Are you okay?' Hopkins called from the door.

'Yes, Bob, unharmed. But be careful— Doc's been firing the shotgun. I have clamped him to the ladder. He can't move, but he's still got the shotgun!'

'George! Throw down your weapon,' the cool commander announced to the now sobbing man stuck fast.

'George, it's Bob. Mate, throw the gun down, so I can help you.'

Doc finally knew it was over. The agony of his 140-kilogram body on his injured foot focused his thoughts. He realised that any further delay was simply foolish and he surrendered.

'Bob,' he cried out, 'Bob, if youse, just youse, come and help me.

If just youse come, maate. I will surrender to you. Keep those other cunts away! I will surrender to you, maate,' he begged.

'It's okay, George,' Bob called back, walking towards the boat, his empty hands held wide as if nailed to an invisible crucifix.

Doc's soft back and dimpled buttocks shook like a massive pink jelly to complete his absolute humiliation.

Bob Hopkins waved his men to the sides as they moved into the silo behind him.

'George, throw the shotgun down, mate,' Bob asked gently as he got closer. Doc obeyed and the weapon clanged onto the concrete, the sound echoing back off steel walls and the roof.

Bob broke into a trot towards the *Freedom* as Doc appeared to faint forward, half of his huge carcass folded over into the deck area.

'Bill, come on out,' Bob called.

Bill had crawled back under the stern, ready to unscrew the clamp and free the pinned captive when the troops arrived to help the limp Doc from his perch. Bill could see Bob coming, though Bob was not yet aware of his exact location in the dark under the boat.

Then Bill saw two things happen. As he began to undo the nuts, Doc's fat calf tightened and twisted around in its huge ankle cuff. Then he heard *crack, crack, crack*!

Pandemonium broke out with the advancing rear guard of federal and local coppers shouting and ducking and diving as they produced a variety of weapons and fired them in the general direction of the *Freedom* and the captive Doc stuck to the stern. Bill ducked back into cover and was shocked to see that Bob Hopkins had gone down. He lay deathly still on the dirty concrete floor.

'He's got a rifle!' one of the officers screamed as he dived for safety.

Doc did have a rifle; he had the roo-shooting .227 that he had clip-loaded and placed just beside the stairs on the deck. Twisting awkwardly, he fired again and again at the numerous moving targets and at the prone body of Bob Hopkins.

Bill did the only thing he could do. He set himself quickly onto his back just under and as close to the steps as he could. He then fired out from that solid base both his callus-hardened feet into the soft under gut of the unbalanced Doc, still fixed to the ladder. The effect was startling and awful as the behemoth took the force of the twin blow that disappeared initially into a soft layer of thick blubber. But then the kinetic energy of the strike resulted in an immediate loss of Doc's slippery one-handed grip on the boat's stern.

Doc's twisted body fell back and away from the boat and the big man's leg snapped clean through the tibia and fibula with a startling double crack! When the full weight of Doc's body found the absolute resistance of its steel cuff, Doc's lower leg ripped from below the knee with a dreadful tearing sound. Doc's final conscious moment was a slow-motion backward-somersaulting realisation of what had happened and a last upside-down view of his nemesis's face peering out from a black cave. Then his head hit the concrete the weight of his falling torso broke his neck.

98

DON'T LET THE SUN GO DOWN ON YOU

One week later, Bill was once again in a room in Broome Regional Hospital, but this time he was a visitor.

Surgery to plug a neat .227 bullet hole in the flesh of Bob Hopkins's shoulder and a week's recuperation had him almost right to board the jet that Premier Pigeon himself had made available to fly the national hero home.

Bill was there to say goodbye. He had tidied up all his affairs in the tropical paradise of Broome and was due to fly out in two hours to the state's capital Perth.

'Well, son, once again, thanks for everything, especially for saving my life,' said Bob.

'It was nothing, Bob,' Bill responded, embarrassed.

Bob held out his hand from the bed. 'Wherever you end up, Bill, you have a friend for life.'

Bill knew that to be true, and he reached out and shook the surprisingly firm hand of the immaculate little man, dressed in perfect silk pin-striped pyjamas.

One hour later, Bill sat in the relaxed confines of the departure lounge at the Broome airport. He drank from an ice cold Matso mango beer, enjoying the local Broome brewery's tangy concoction as the humid air wafted over him from the fans rotating above. He ticked again through the mental check-list. The *Freedom* was in the hands of a broker.

'Clean her and put her up for sale,' he had instructed. 'No hurry, get the price or just leave her in storage.'

He had no other farewells to make. Gypsy had disappeared; Bonnie was just as invisible, unattainable. There was nothing for him now in the small town that he loved. Nothing except the distrust and righteous anger of Gypsy and Tommy's friends, and the finger-pointing laughter of Bonnie's extended family.

'Time to go. May come back, who knows?' he announced to himself as the flight was called over the airports PA, and he rose to pick up his kit bag and his worldly possessions. Then he noticed the dartboard. It was set against the wall near the bar providing a game for bored travellers awaiting flights. Unusually, it was designed as a globe, the map of the world bold upon it. On an impulse, he decided to choose his next destination randomly.

Bill Peters took one of the darts, stood back, closed his eyes, and threw it at the world.

MORE FROM PETER G WILLIAMS

PUBLISHED TITLES IN THE TRACKS SERIES

Book One: Tracks to Exile
Book Two: Tracks of the Purple Camel

FORTHCOMING TITLES IN THE TRACKS SERIES

Book Three: Back Tracks
Book Four: Angel Tracks
Book Five: Tracks from Tamworth to the Taliban
Book Six: Tracks to the Prepper's Ark
Book Seven: Tracks of Her Tears

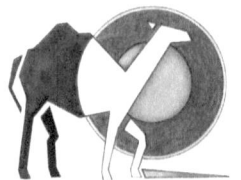